The
Riverdale
Diaries

Hello, Betty!

BuzzPop

For my dad—see, it **was** worth it
to buy me all those comics
—SK

To my nieces and nephews
—JB

BuzzPop

An imprint of Little Bee Books
251 Park Avenue South, New York, NY 10010
Copyright © 2020 by Archie Comic Publications, Inc.
All rights reserved, including the right of reproduction
in whole or in part in any form. BuzzPop and associated
colophon are trademarks of Little Bee Books.
Lettering by Hannah McGill

Library of Congress Cataloging-in-Publication Data
is available upon request.
Manufactured in China RRD 0520
First Edition
ISBN 978-1-4998-1055-4 (hc)
2 4 6 8 10 9 7 5 3 1
ISBN 978-1-4998-1054-7 (pb)
2 4 6 8 10 9 7 5 3 1

buzzpopbooks.com

For more information about special discounts on bulk purchases,
please contact Little Bee Books at sales@littlebeebooks.com.

THE CAST

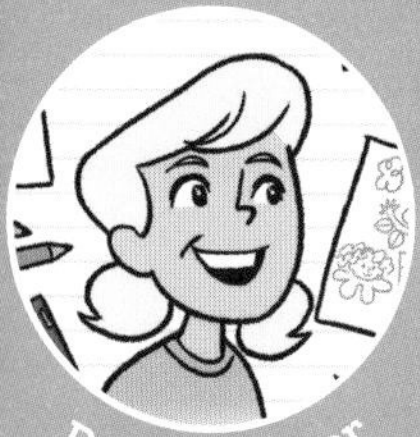
Betty Cooper
the writer

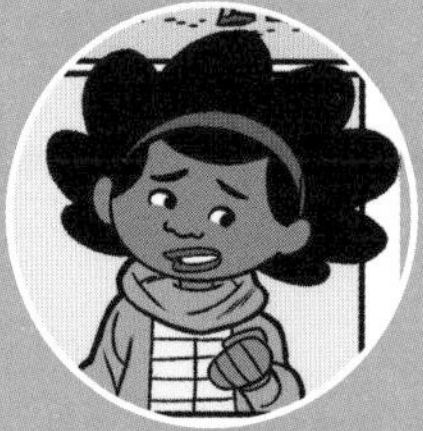
Val Smith
the rock star

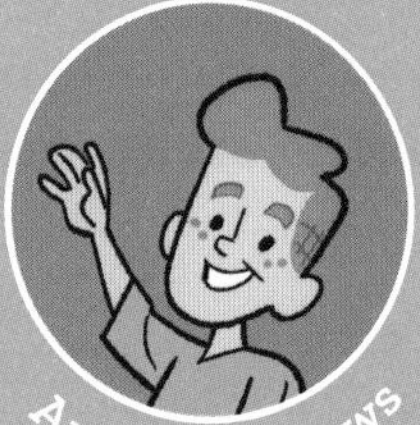
Archie Andrews
the clumsy kid

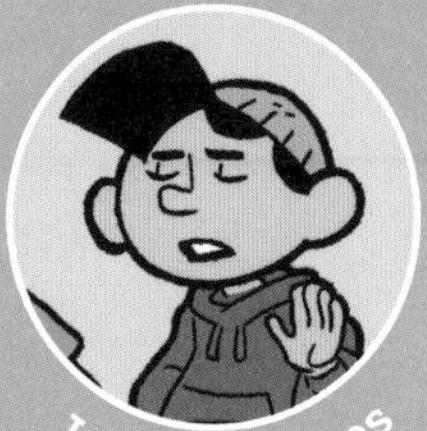
Jughead Jones
the mysterious kid

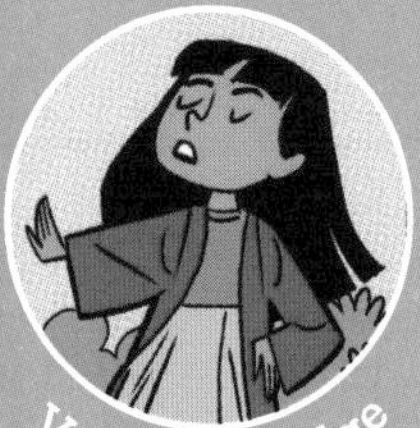
Veronica Lodge
the prima donna

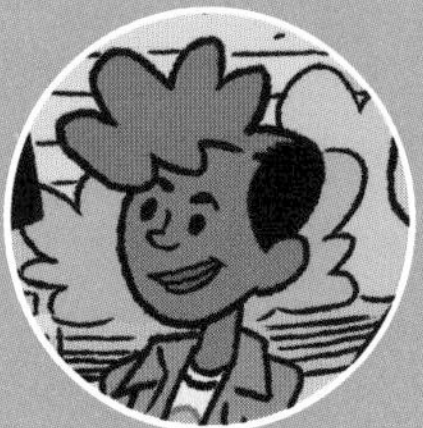
Toni Topaz
the coolest kid in town

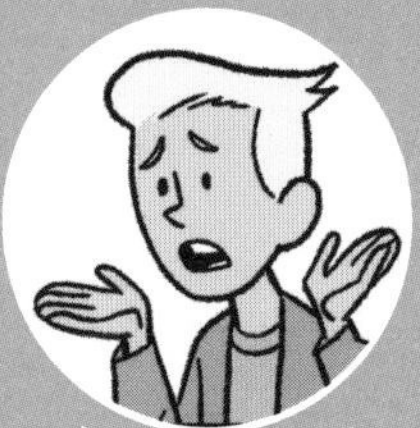
Kevin Keller
the nicest kid in town

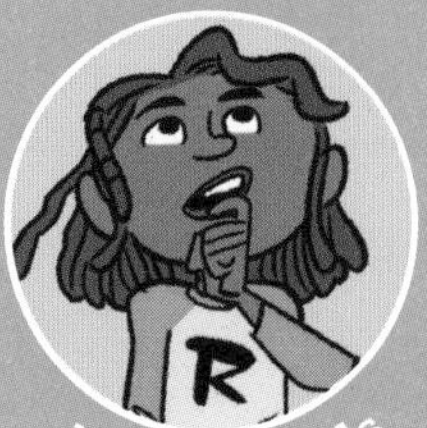
R
Nancy Woods
the jock

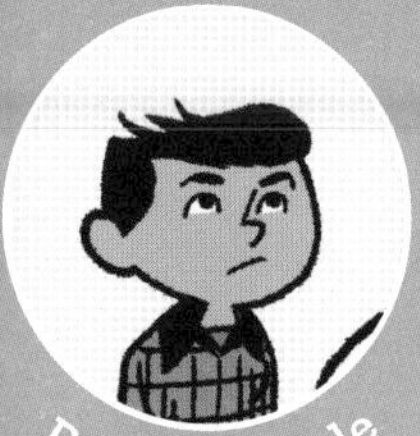
Reggie Mantle
the grumpy kid

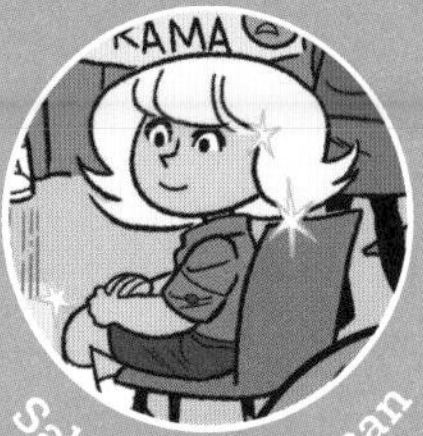
KAMA
Sabrina Spellman
the magical kid

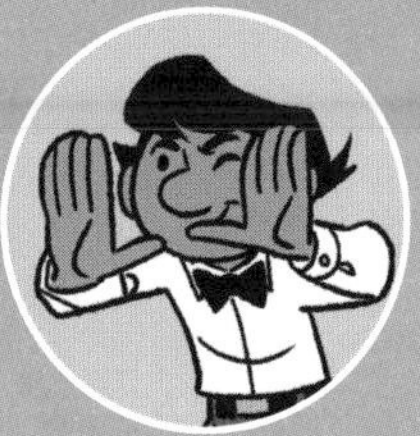
Raj Patel
the visionary

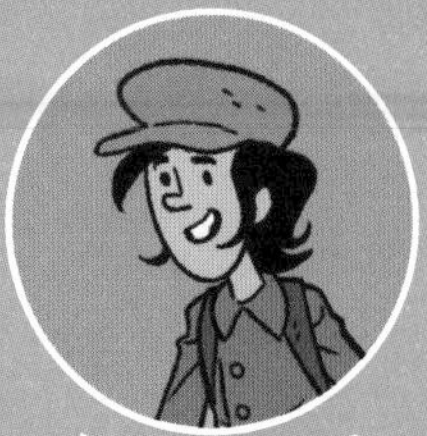
Ethel Muggs
the henchgirl

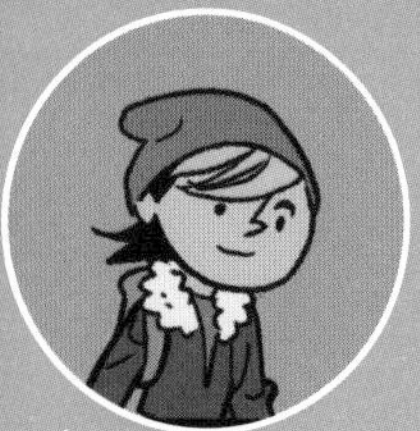
Midge Klump
the other henchgirl

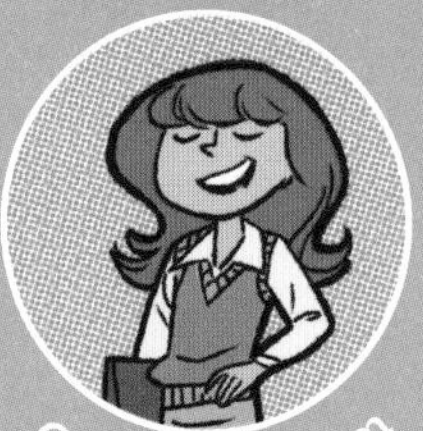
Cheryl Blossom
the older kid

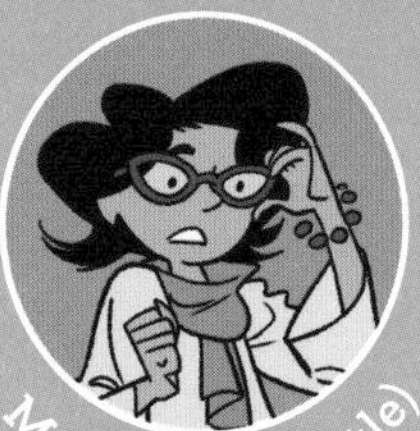
Ms. Vicky (Mantle)
the adult

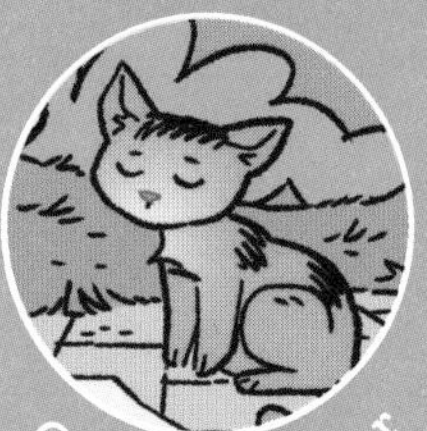
Caramel Cooper
the cat

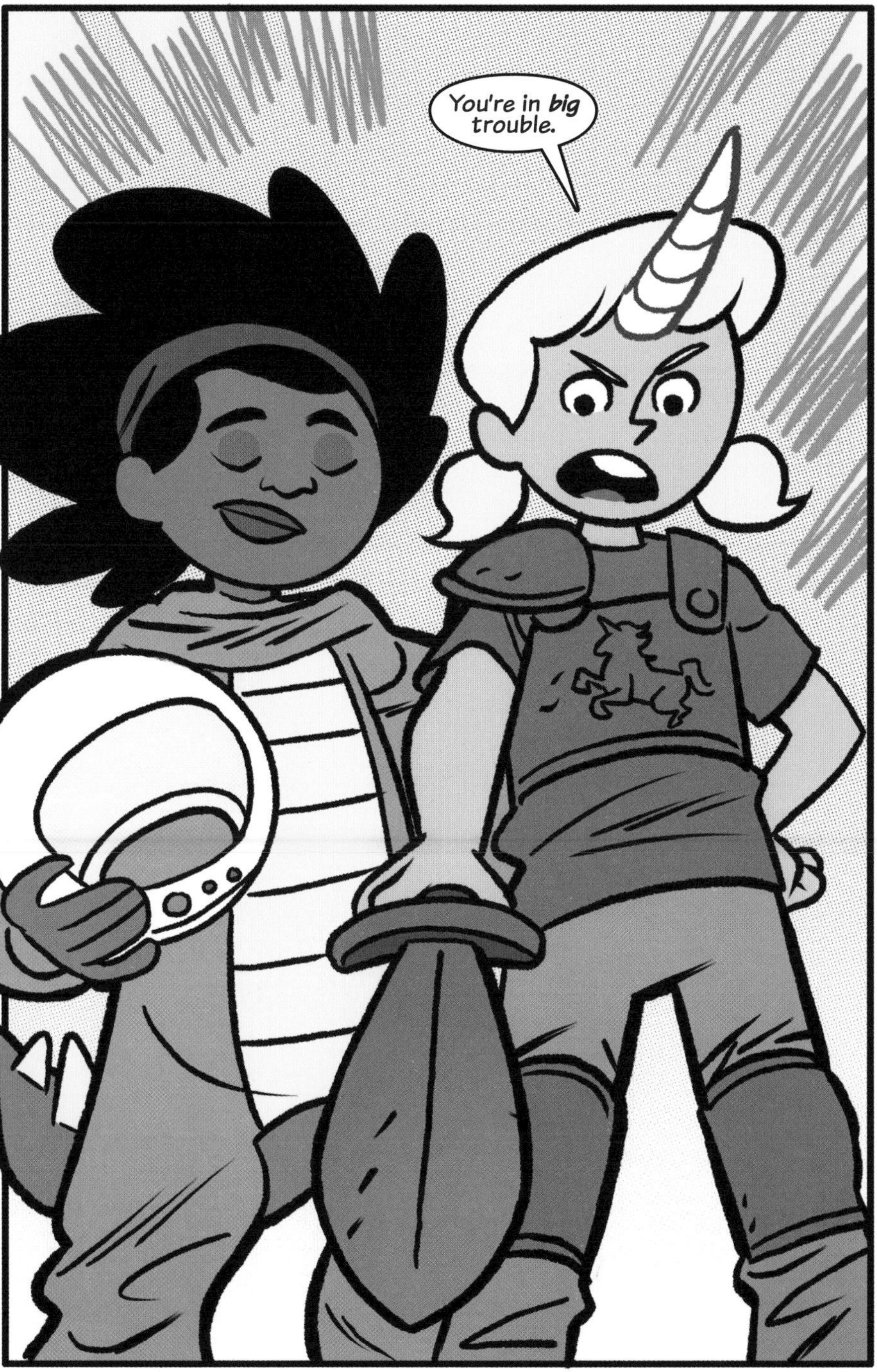
You're in *big* trouble.

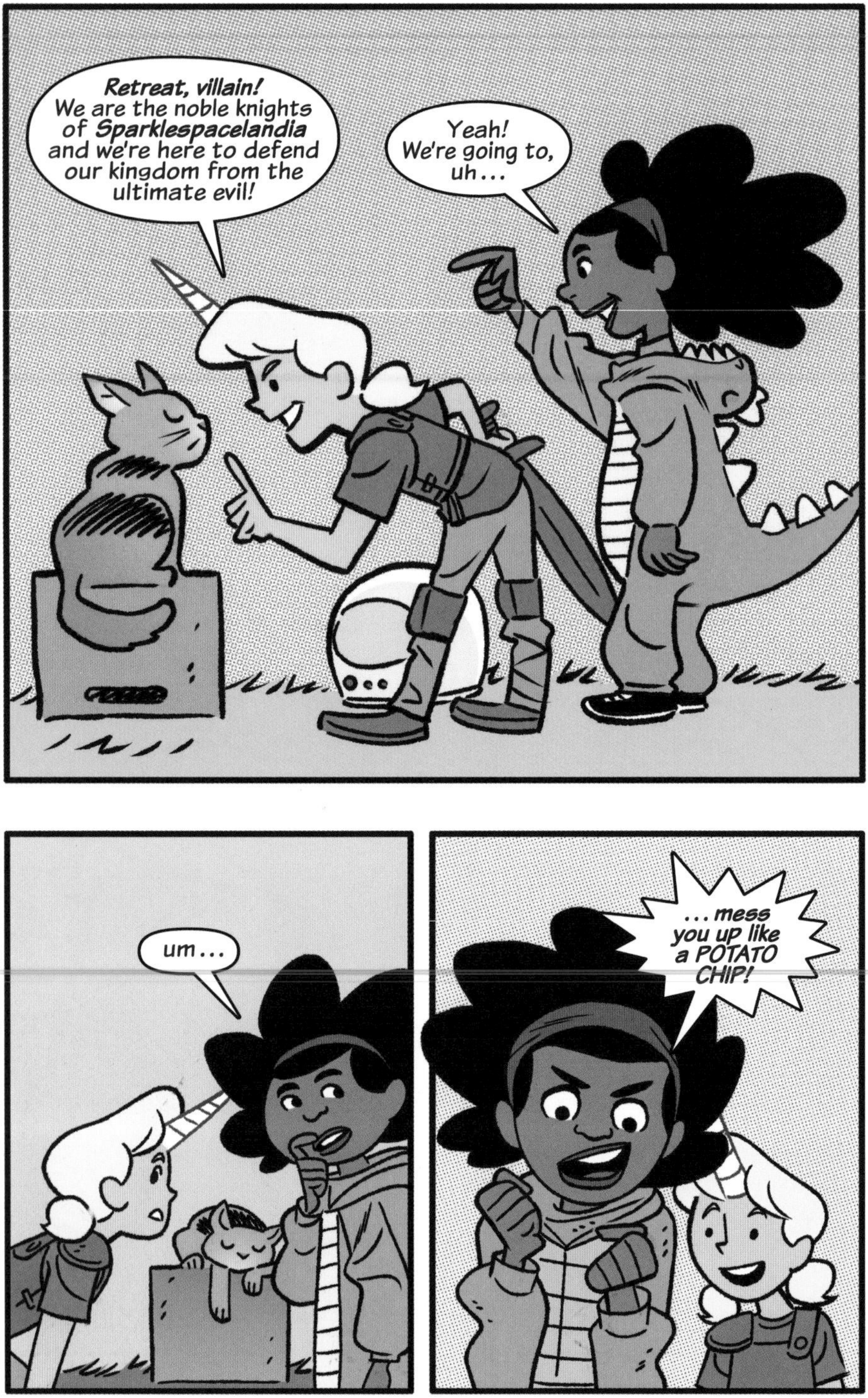
Retreat, villain!
We are the noble knights of ***Sparklespacelandia*** and we're here to defend our kingdom from the ultimate evil!
Yeah! We're going to, uh...
um...
...mess you up like a POTATO CHIP!

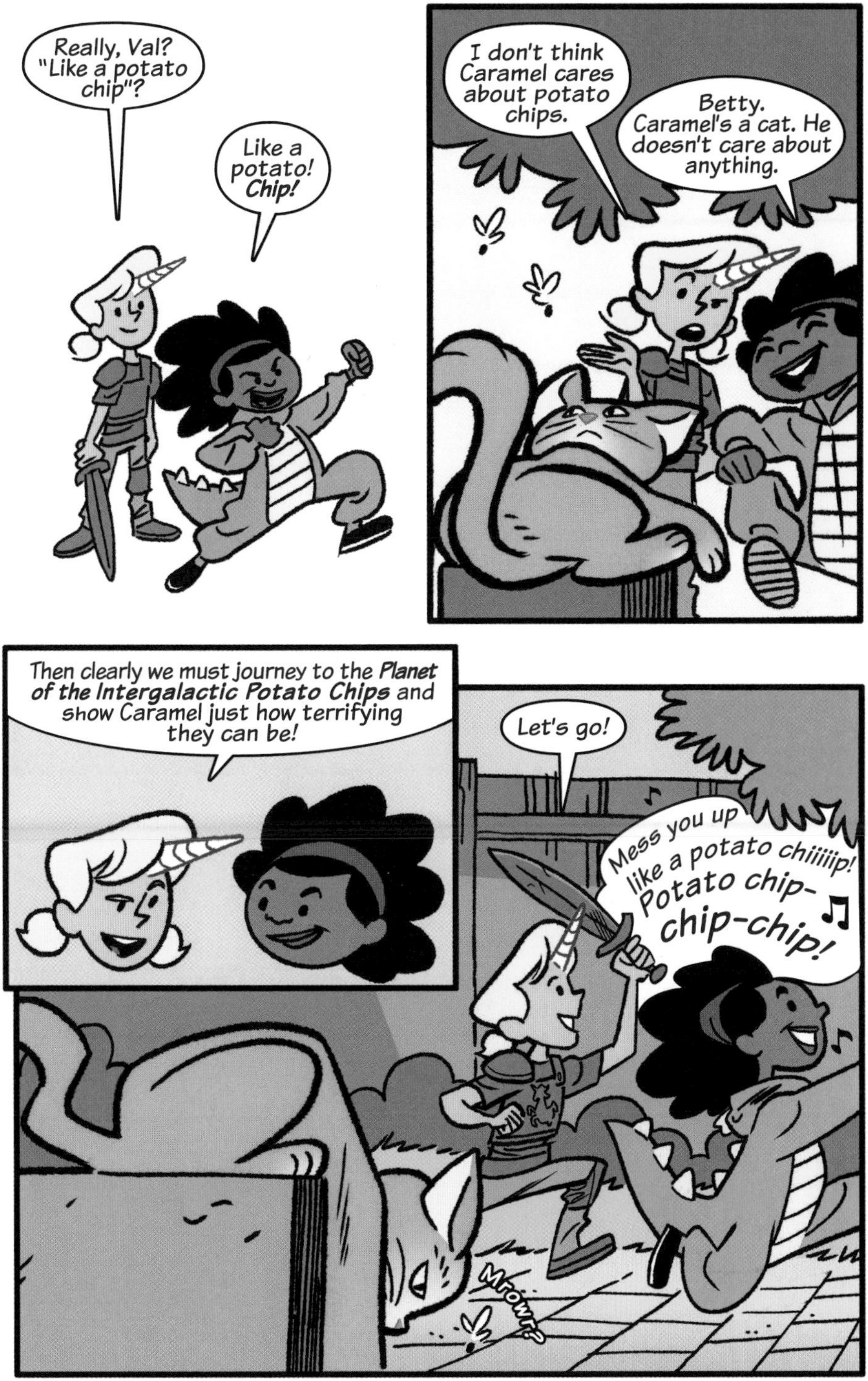
Really, Val? "Like a potato chip"?
Like a potato! Chip!
I don't think Caramel cares about potato chips.
Betty. Caramel's a cat. He doesn't care about anything.
Then clearly we must journey to the Planet of the Intergalactic Potato Chips and show Caramel just how terrifying they can be!
Let's go!
Mess you up like a potato chiiiiip! Potato chip-chip-chip!
Mrowr?

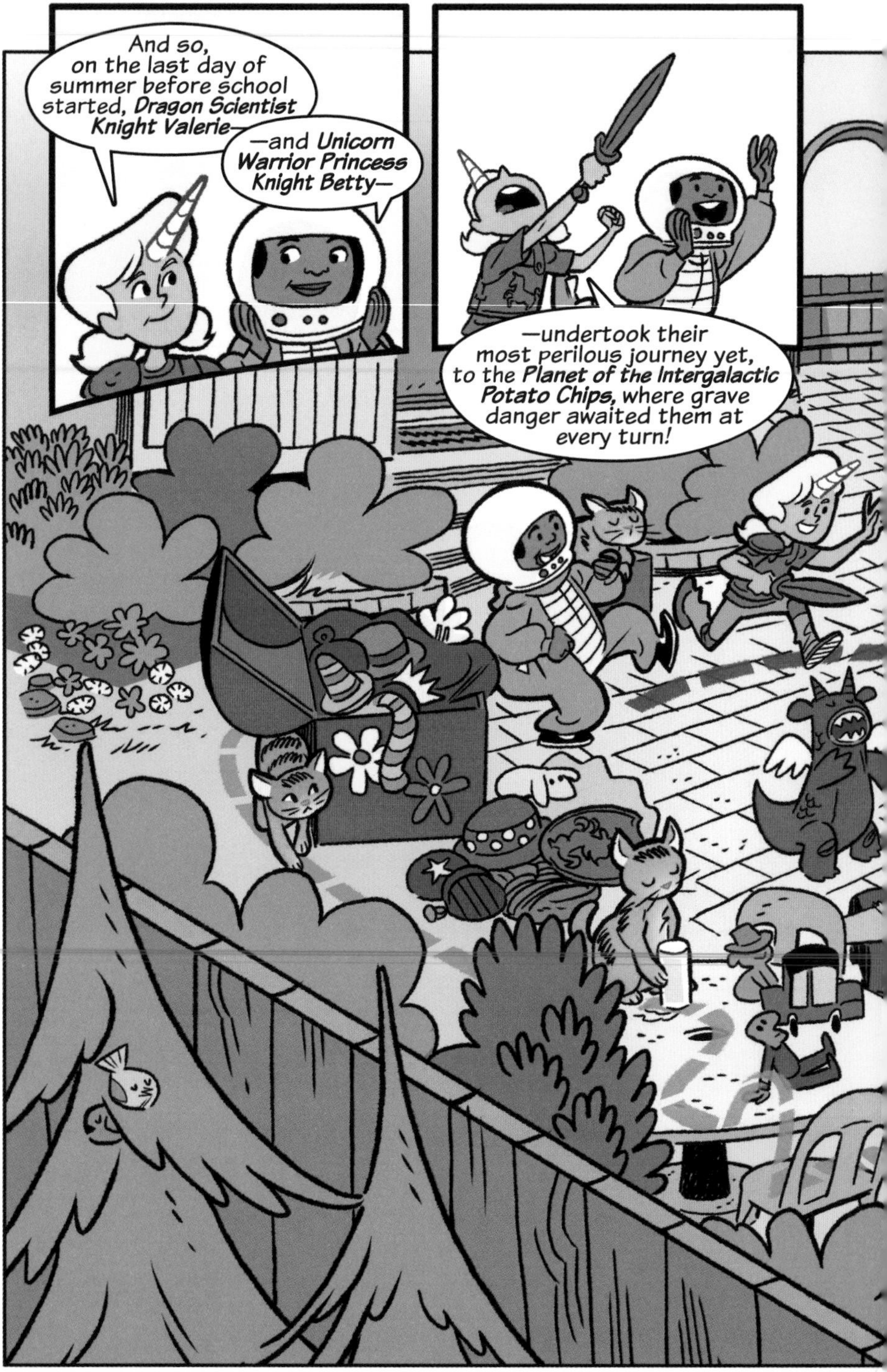
And so, on the last day of summer before school started, *Dragon Scientist Knight Valerie*—
—and *Unicorn Warrior Princess Knight Betty*—
—undertook their most perilous journey yet, to the *Planet of the Intergalactic Potato Chips,* where grave danger awaited them at every turn!

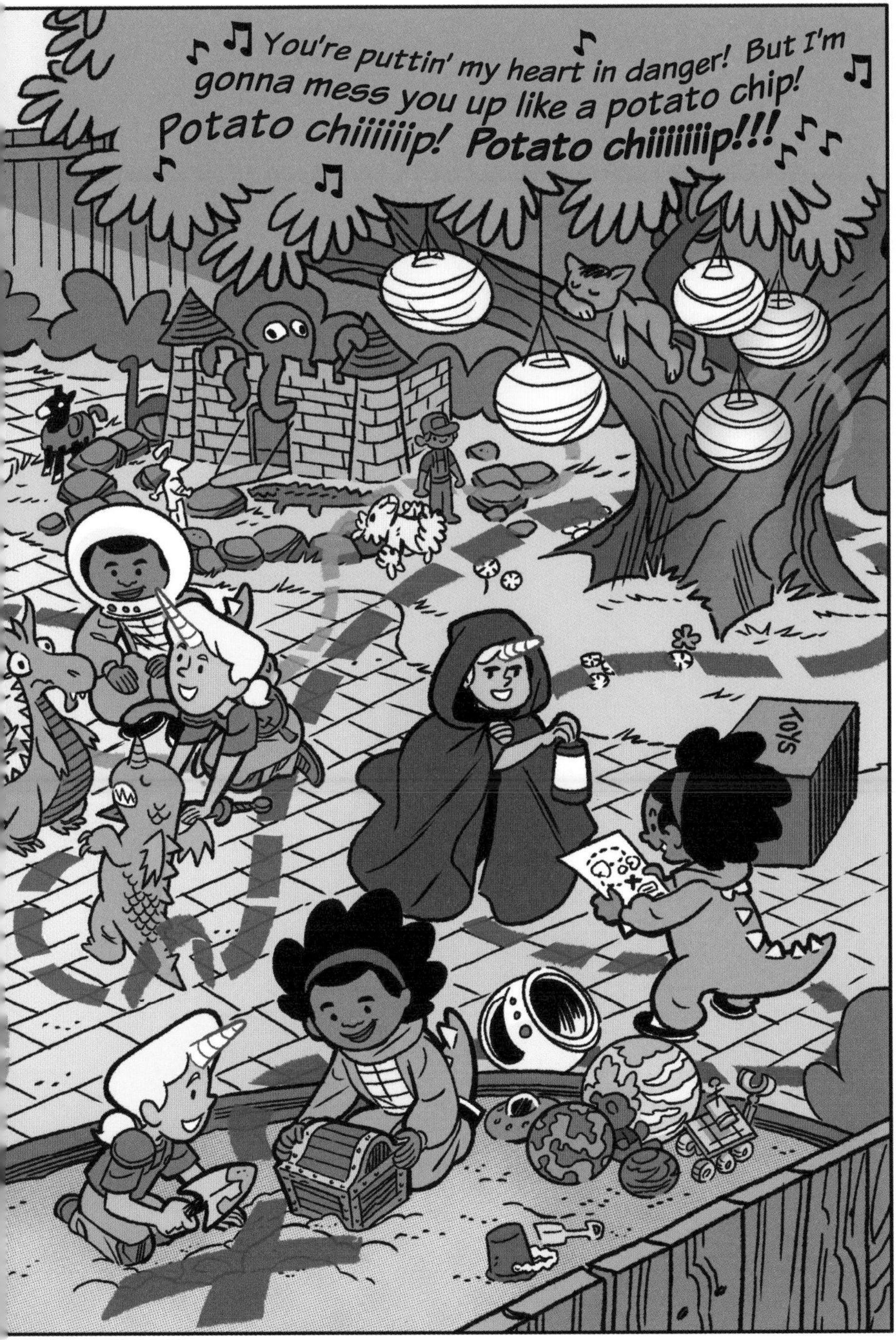
♪ ♫ You're puttin' my heart in danger! ♪ But I'm gonna mess you up like a potato chip! ♫
Potato chiiiiiip! ♪ ♫ Potato chiiiiiip!!! ♪ ♪ ♪
TOYS

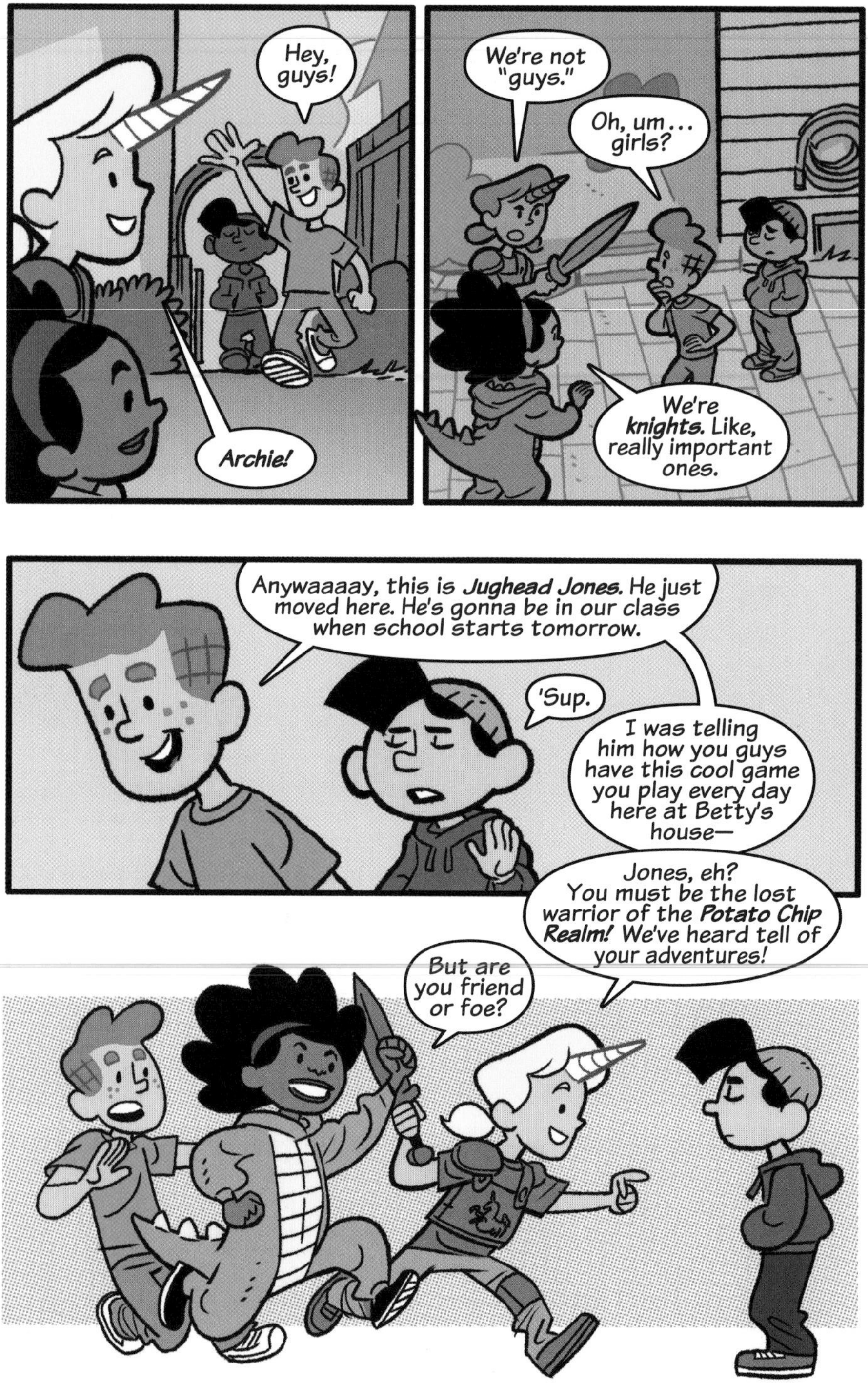
Hey, guys!
Archie!
We're not "guys."
Oh, um... girls?
We're **knights.** Like, really important ones.
Anywaaaay, this is **Jughead Jones.** He just moved here. He's gonna be in our class when school starts tomorrow.
'Sup.
I was telling him how you guys have this cool game you play every day here at Betty's house—
Jones, eh? You must be the lost warrior of the **Potato Chip Realm!** We've heard tell of your adventures!
But are you friend or foe?

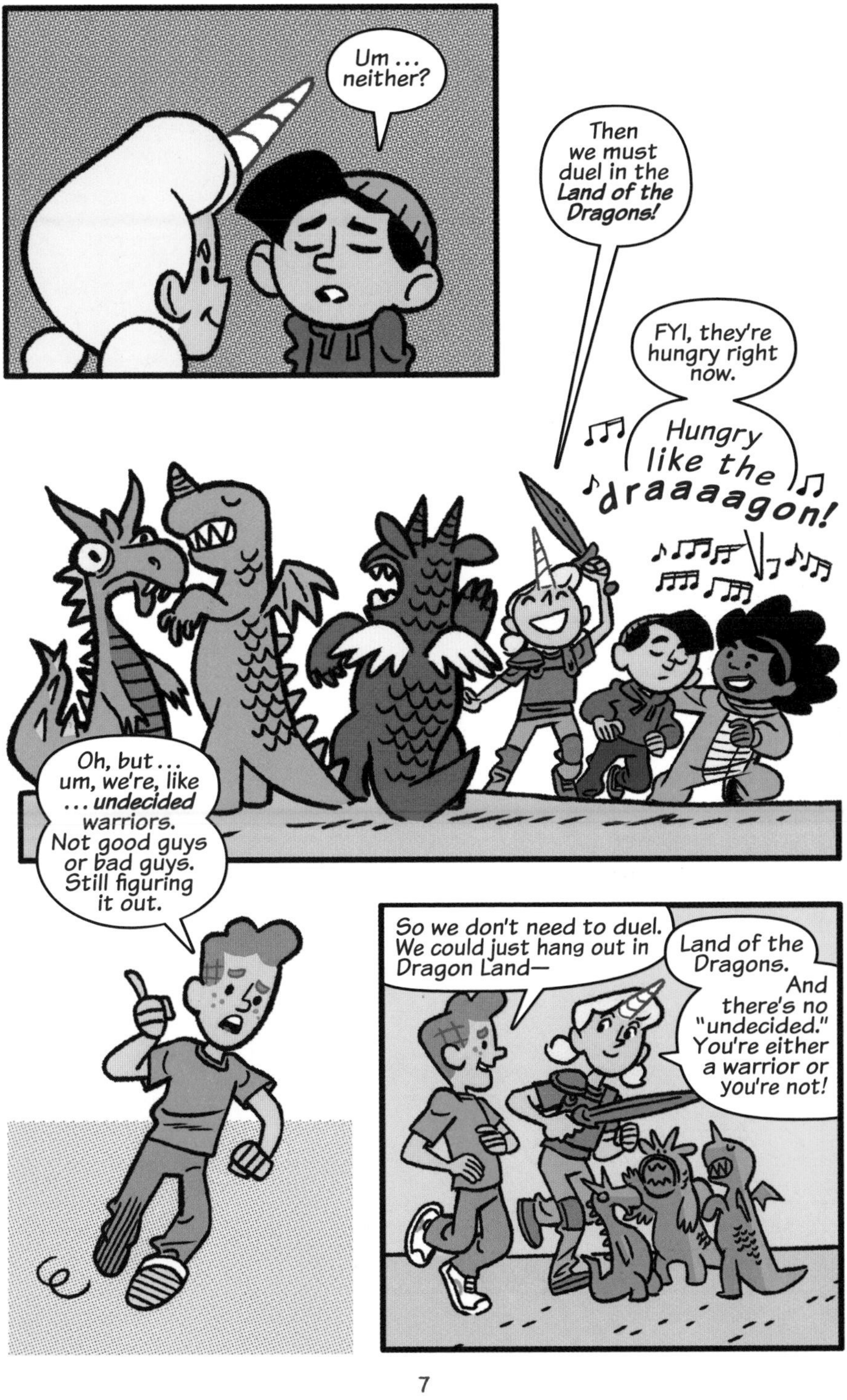
Um ... neither?
Then we must duel in the *Land of the Dragons!*
FYI, they're hungry right now.
Hungry like the draaaaagon!
Oh, but ... um, we're, like ... *undecided* warriors. Not good guys or bad guys. Still figuring it out.
So we don't need to duel. We could just hang out in Dragon Land—
Land of the Dragons.
And there's no "undecided." You're either a warrior or you're not!

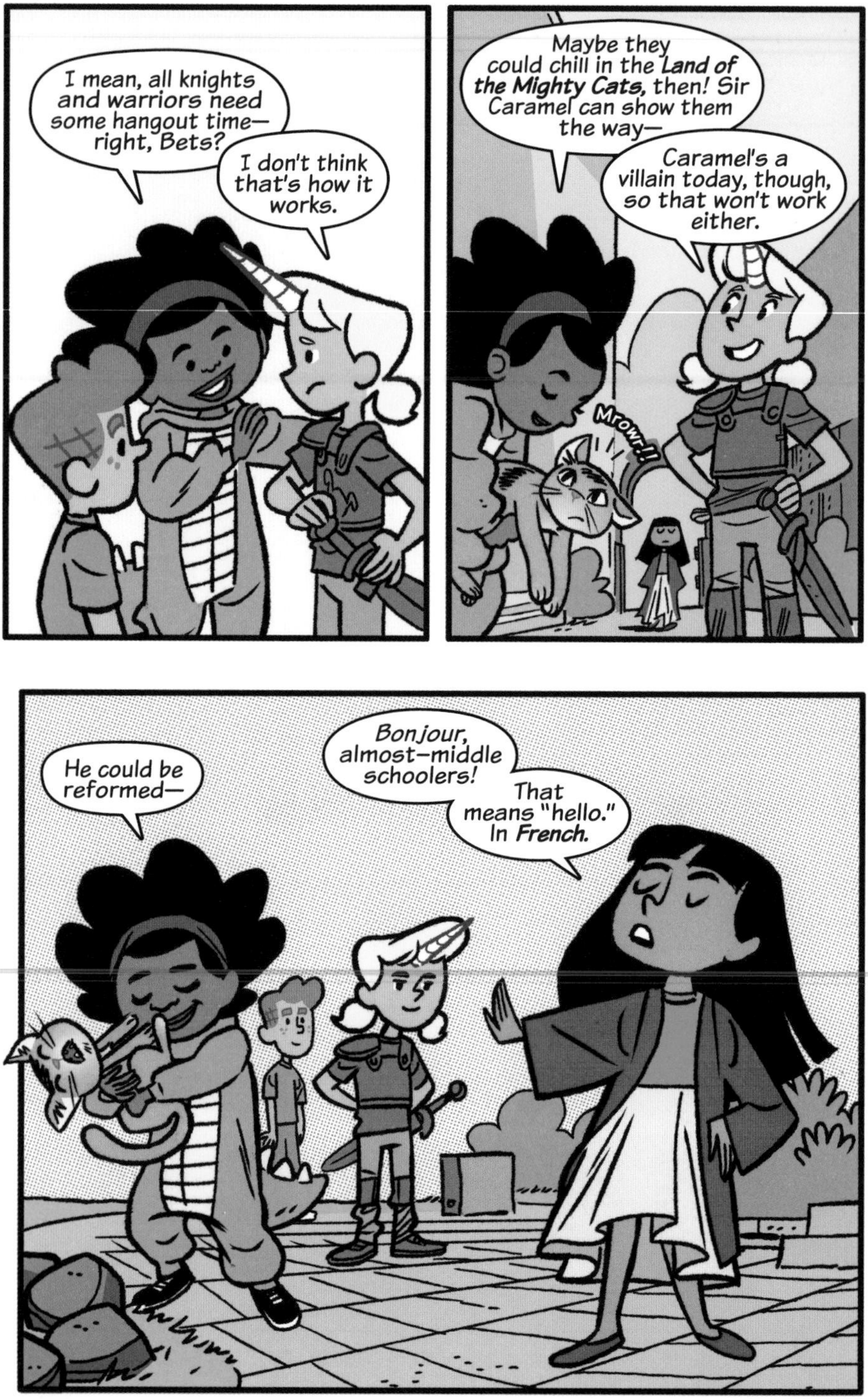
I mean, all knights and warriors need some hangout time—right, Bets?
I don't think that's how it works.
Maybe they could chill in the **Land of the Mighty Cats**, then! Sir Caramel can show them the way—
Caramel's a villain today, though, so that won't work either.
Mrowr!!
He could be reformed—
Bonjour, almost-middle schoolers!
That means "hello." In ***French***.

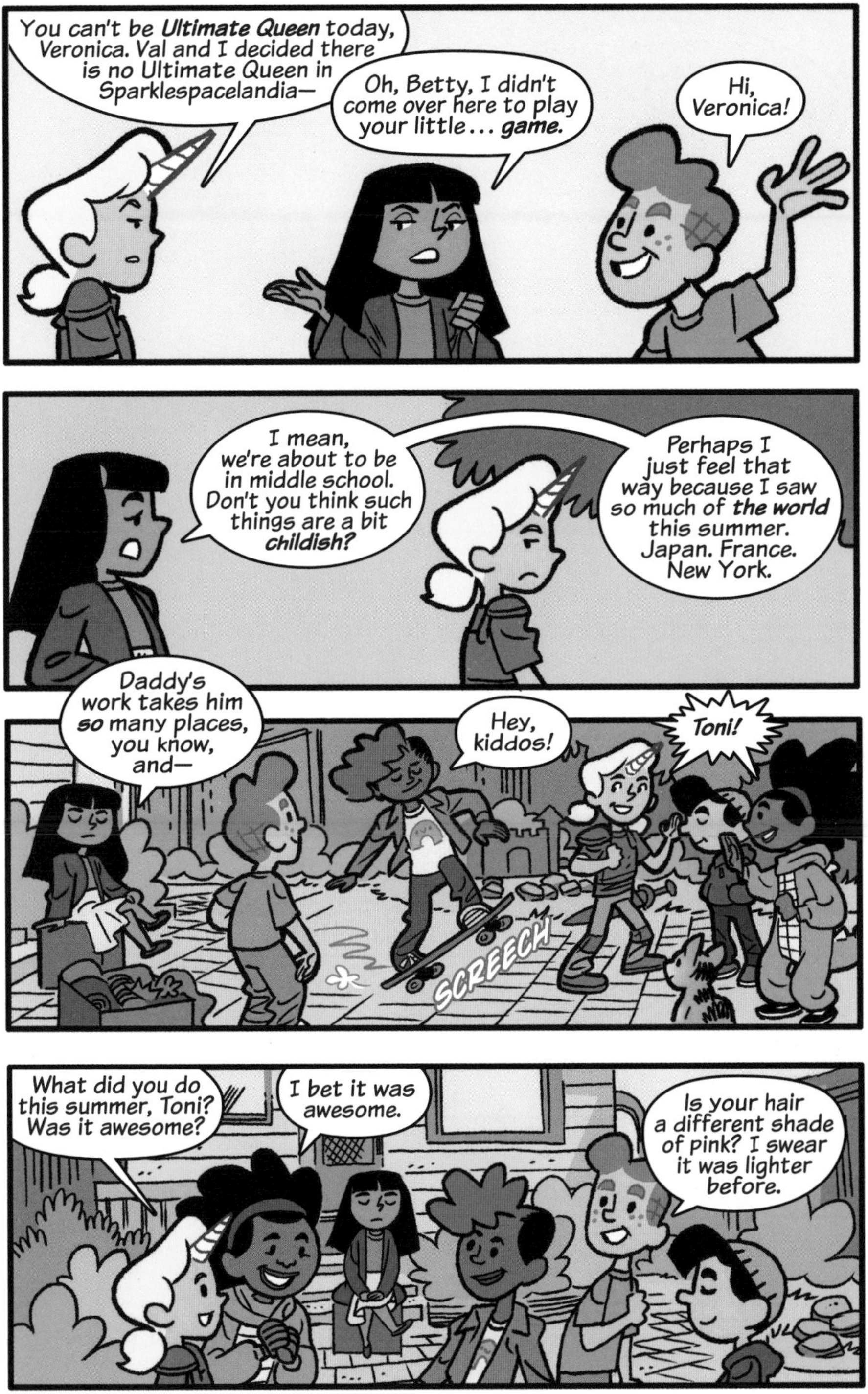
You can't be *Ultimate Queen* today, Veronica. Val and I decided there is no Ultimate Queen in Sparklespacelandia—
Oh, Betty, I didn't come over here to play your little... *game.*
Hi, Veronica!
I mean, we're about to be in middle school. Don't you think such things are a bit *childish?*
Perhaps I just feel that way because I saw so much of *the world* this summer. Japan. France. New York.
Daddy's work takes him *so* many places, you know, and—
Hey, kiddos!
Toni!
SCREECH
What did you do this summer, Toni? Was it awesome?
I bet it was awesome.
Is your hair a different shade of pink? I swear it was lighter before.

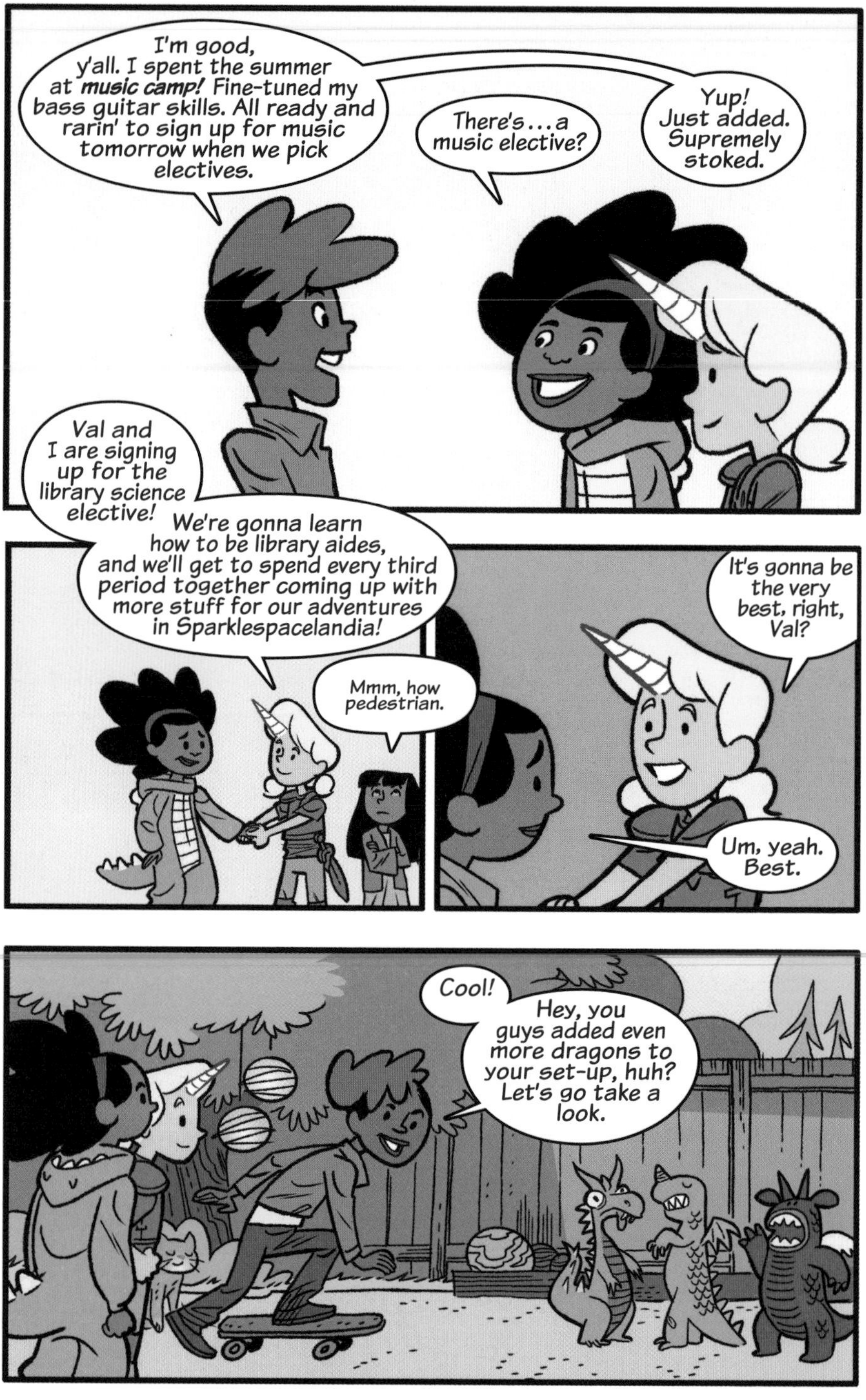
I'm good, y'all. I spent the summer at **music camp!** Fine-tuned my bass guitar skills. All ready and rarin' to sign up for music tomorrow when we pick electives.
There's...a music elective?
Yup! Just added. Supremely stoked.
Val and I are signing up for the library science elective!
We're gonna learn how to be library aides, and we'll get to spend every third period together coming up with more stuff for our adventures in Sparklespacelandia!
Mmm, how pedestrian.
It's gonna be the very best, right, Val?
Um, yeah. Best.
Cool!
Hey, you guys added even more dragons to your set-up, huh? Let's go take a look.

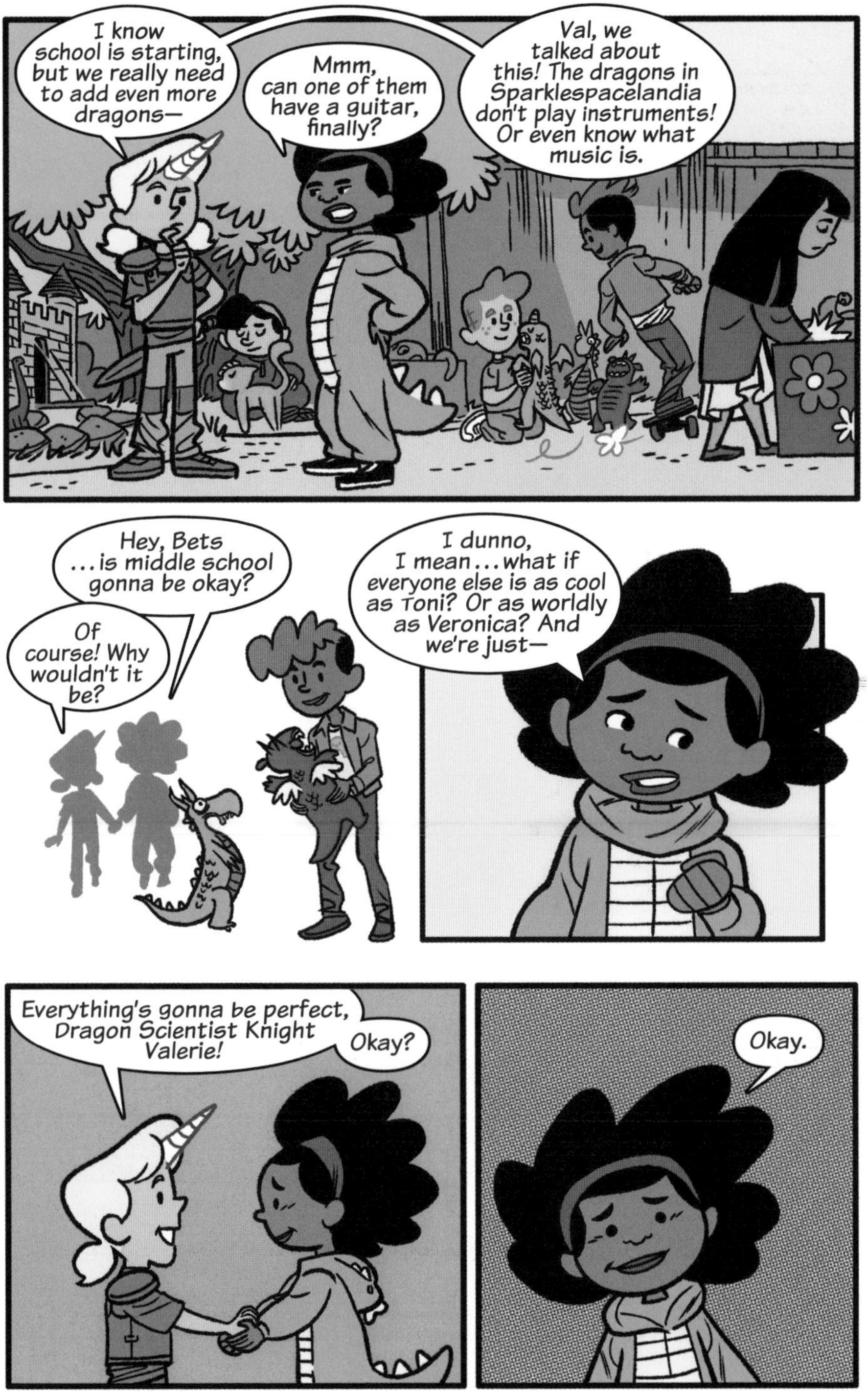
I know school is starting, but we really need to add even more dragons—
Mmm, can one of them have a guitar, finally?
Val, we talked about this! The dragons in Sparklespacelandia don't play instruments! Or even know what music is.
Hey, Bets ...is middle school gonna be okay?
Of course! Why wouldn't it be?
I dunno, I mean...what if everyone else is as cool as Toni? Or as worldly as Veronica? And we're just—
Everything's gonna be perfect, Dragon Scientist Knight Valerie!
Okay?
Okay.

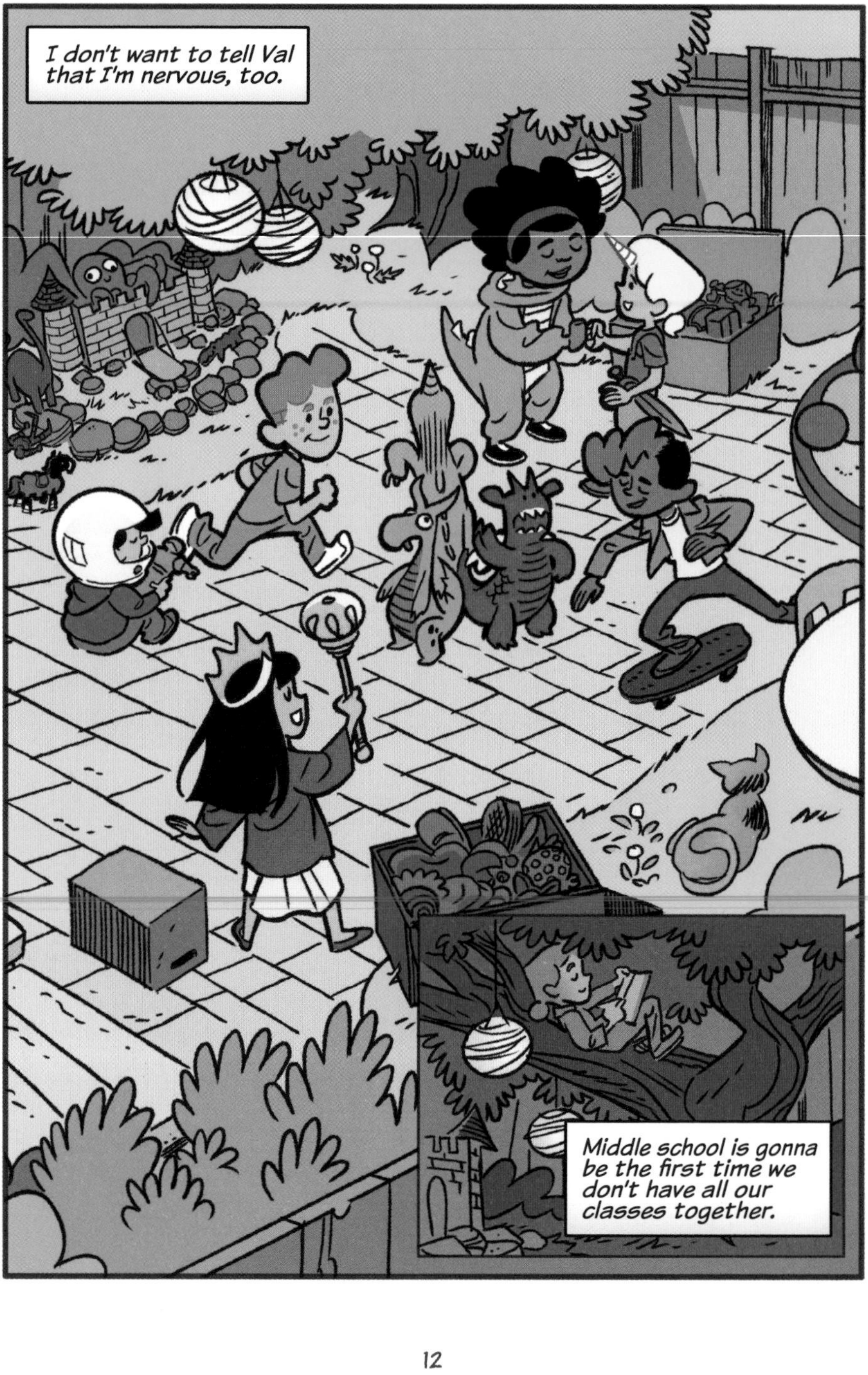
I don't want to tell Val that I'm nervous, too.
Middle school is gonna be the first time we don't have all our classes together.

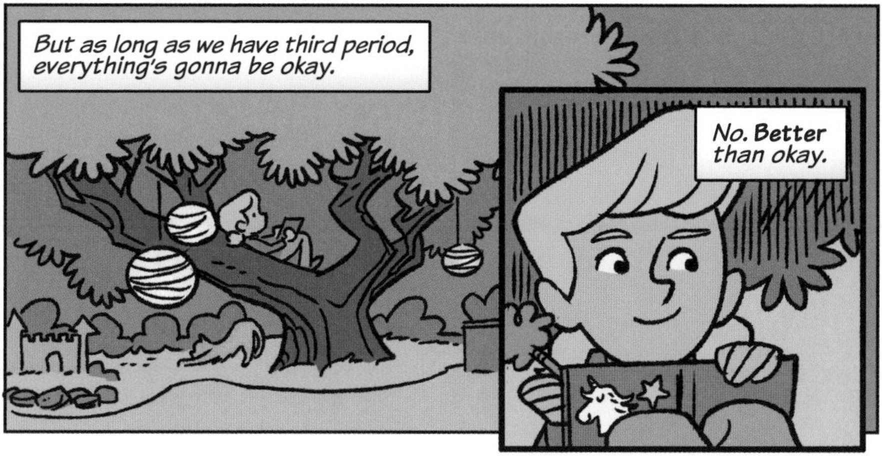
But as long as we have third period, everything's gonna be okay.
No. Better than okay.

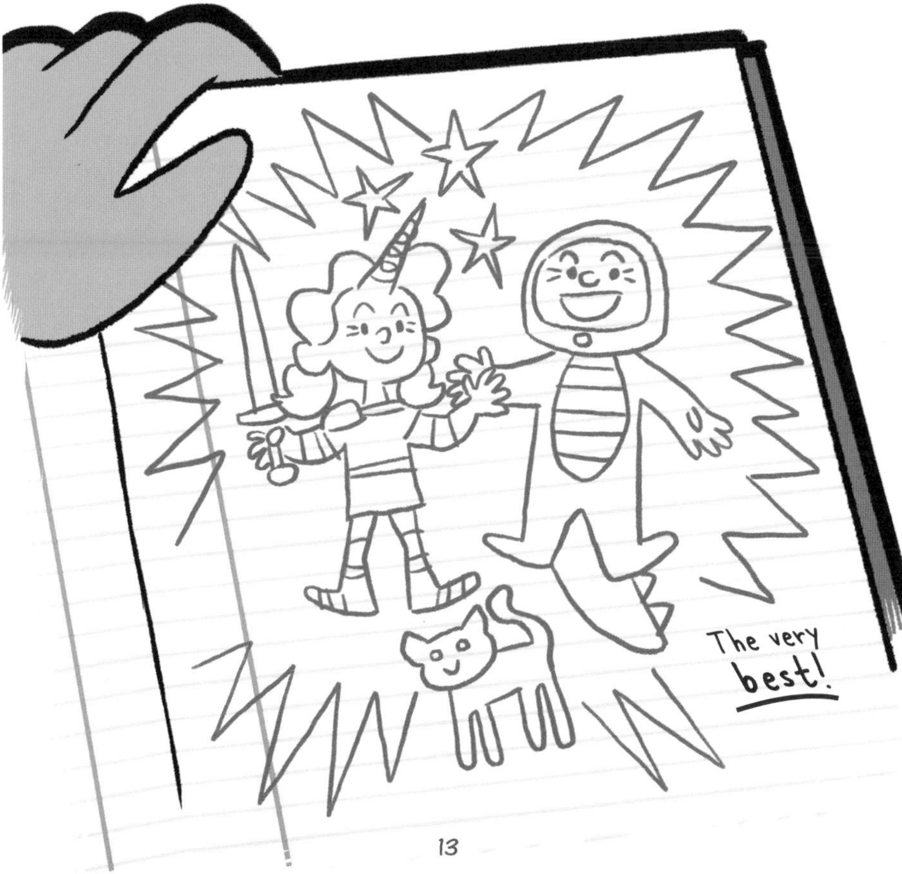
The very best!

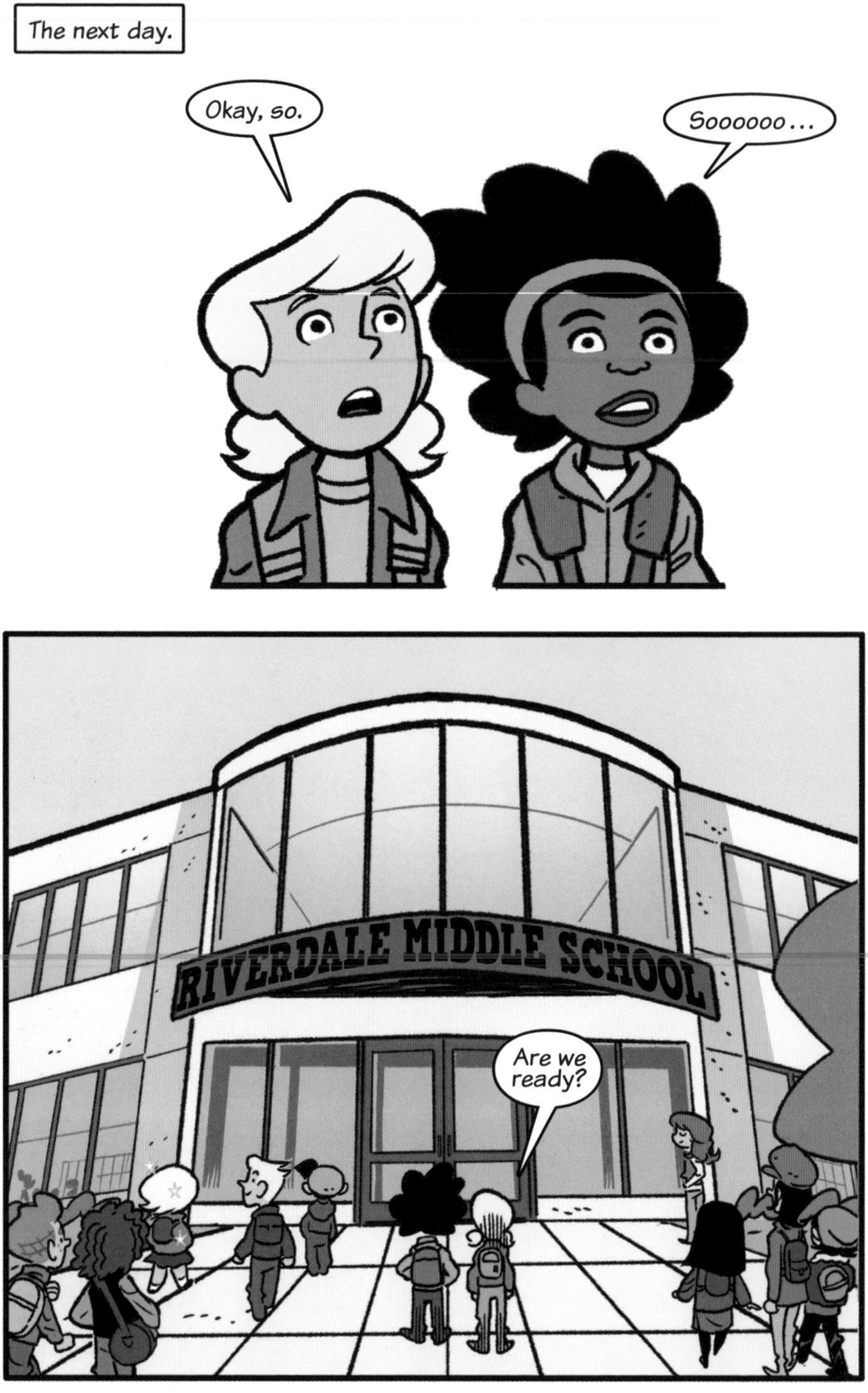
The next day.
Okay, so.
Soooooo...
RIVERDALE MIDDLE SCHOOL
Are we ready?

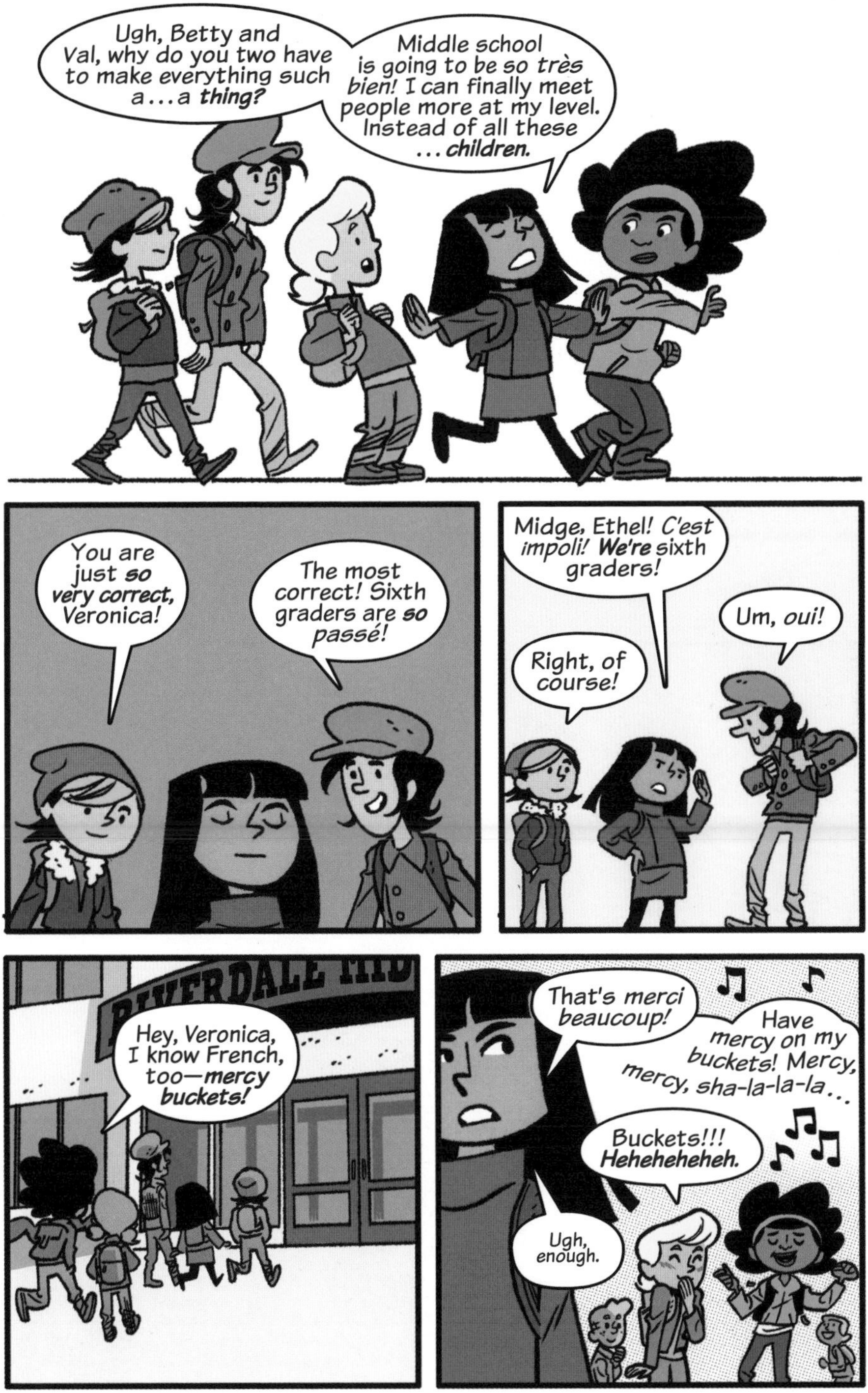
Ugh, Betty and Val, why do you two have to make everything such a... a **thing?**
Middle school is going to be so *très bien!* I can finally meet people more at my level. Instead of all these ...**children.**
You are just **so very correct,** Veronica!
The most correct! Sixth graders are **so** *passé!*
Midge, Ethel! *C'est impoli!* **We're** sixth graders!
Right, of course!
Um, *oui!*
Hey, Veronica, I know French, too—**mercy buckets!**
That's *merci beaucoup!*
Have *mercy* on my *buckets!* Mercy, mercy, sha-la-la-la...
Buckets!!! **Heheheheheh.**
Ugh, enough.

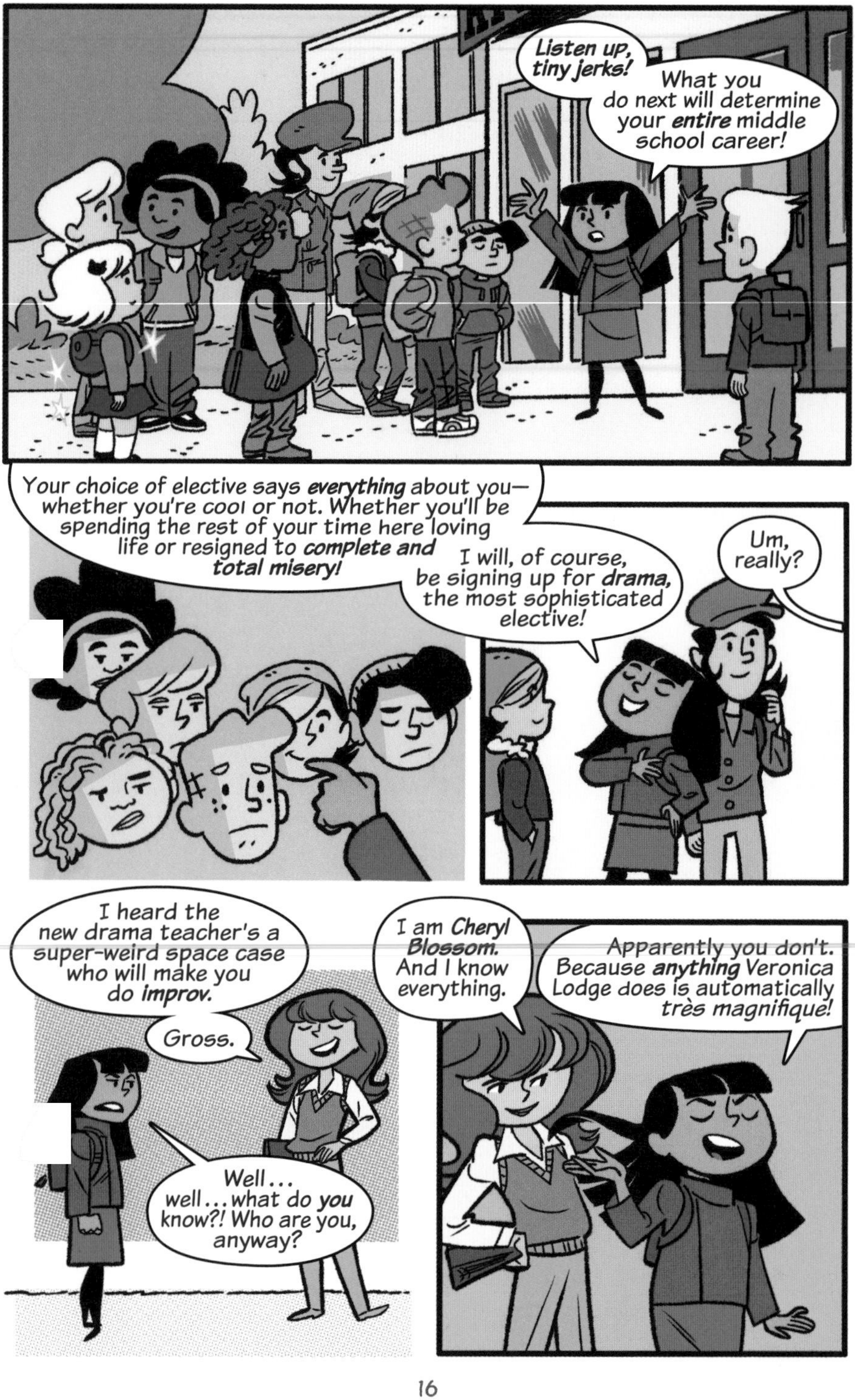

Listen up, tiny jerks!
What you do next will determine your *entire* middle school career!
Your choice of elective says *everything* about you—whether you're cool or not. Whether you'll be spending the rest of your time here loving life or resigned to *complete and total misery!*
I will, of course, be signing up for *drama,* the most sophisticated elective!
Um, really?
I heard the new drama teacher's a super-weird space case who will make you do *improv.*
Gross.
Well... well...what do *you* know?! Who are you, anyway?
I am *Cheryl Blossom.* And I know everything.
Apparently you don't. Because *anything* Veronica Lodge does is automatically *très magnifique!*

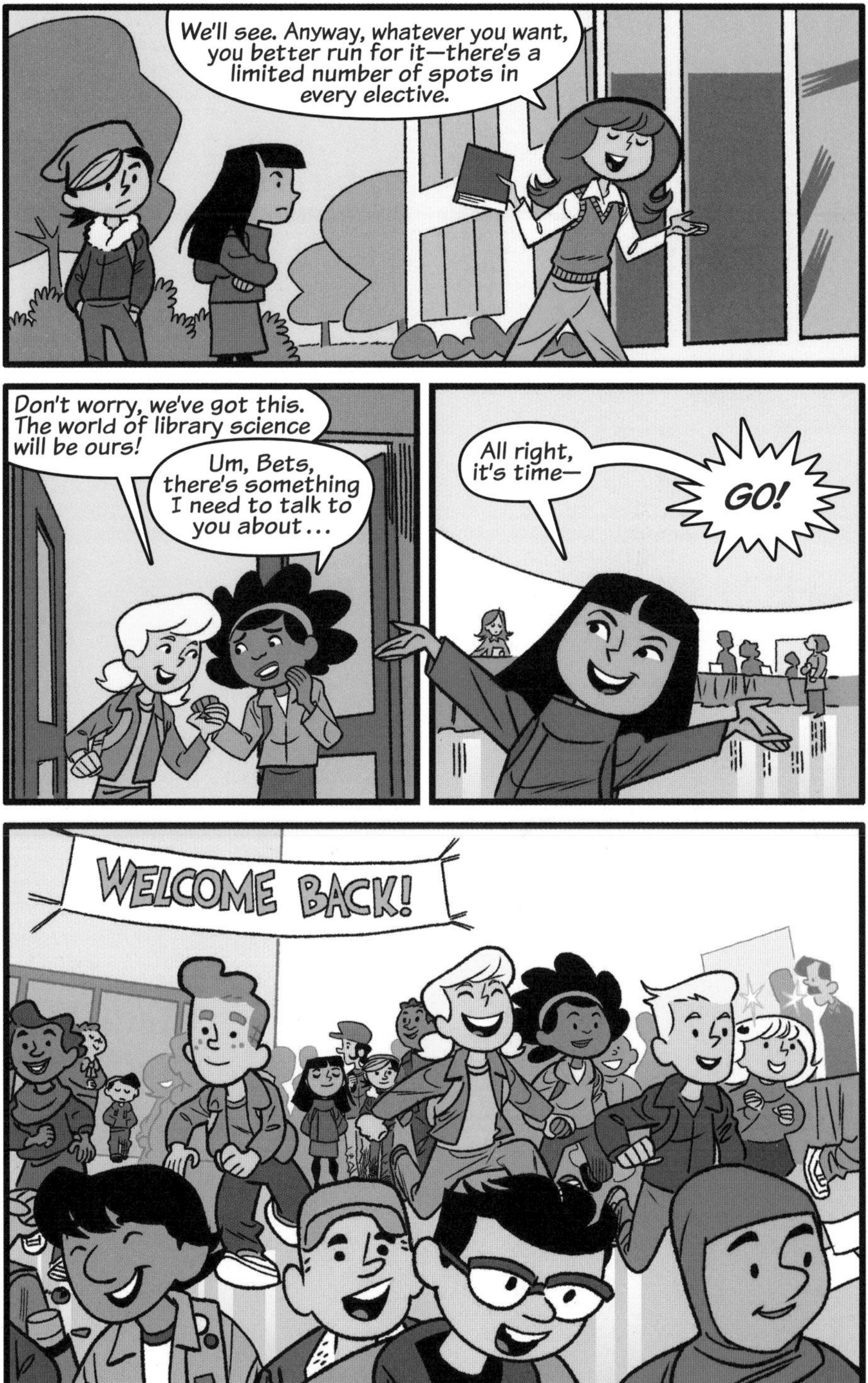

We'll see. Anyway, whatever you want, you better run for it—there's a limited number of spots in every elective.
Don't worry, we've got this. The world of library science will be ours!
Um, Bets, there's something I need to talk to you about...
All right, it's time—
GO!
WELCOME BACK!

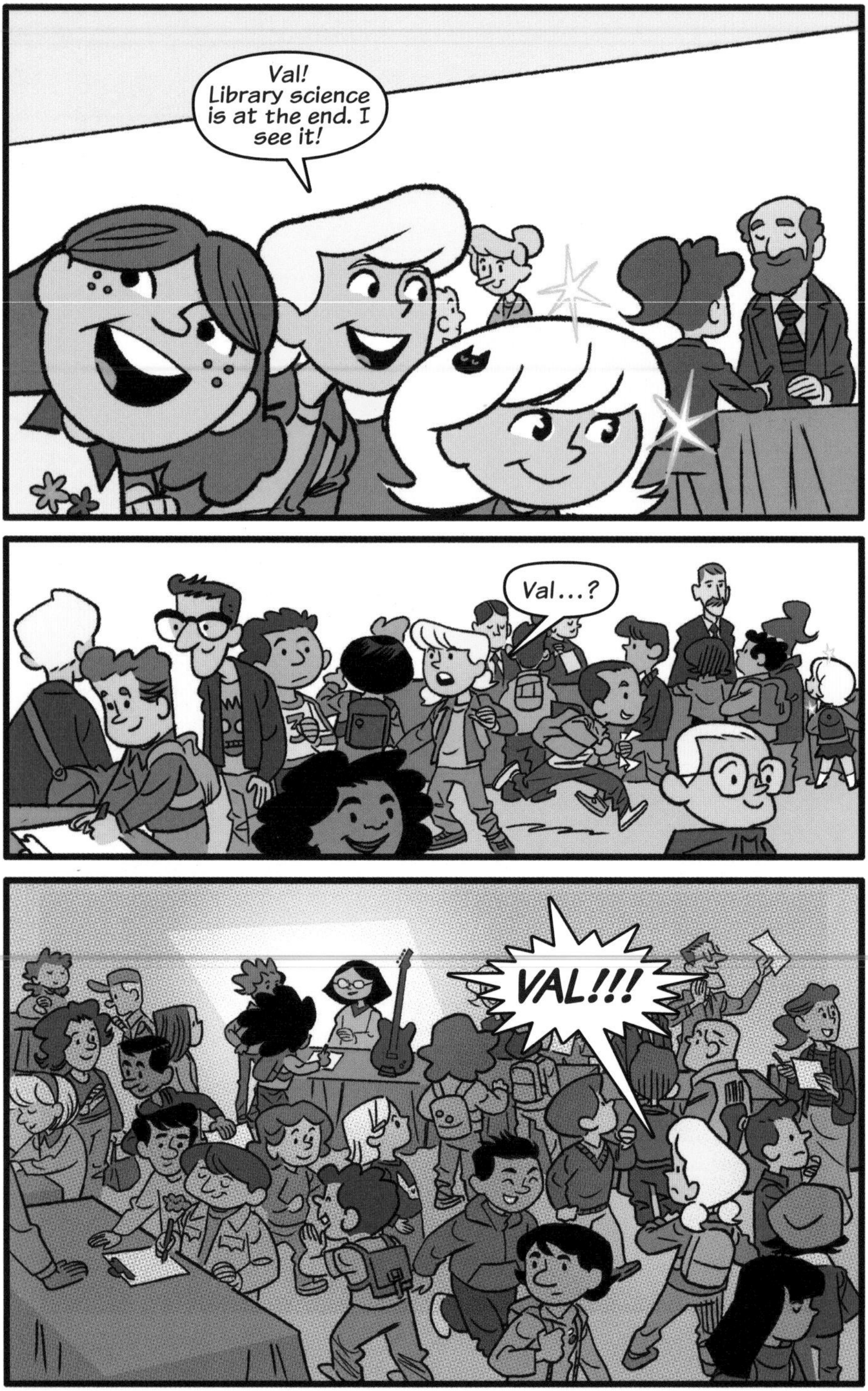
Val! Library science is at the end. I see it!
Val...?
VAL!!!

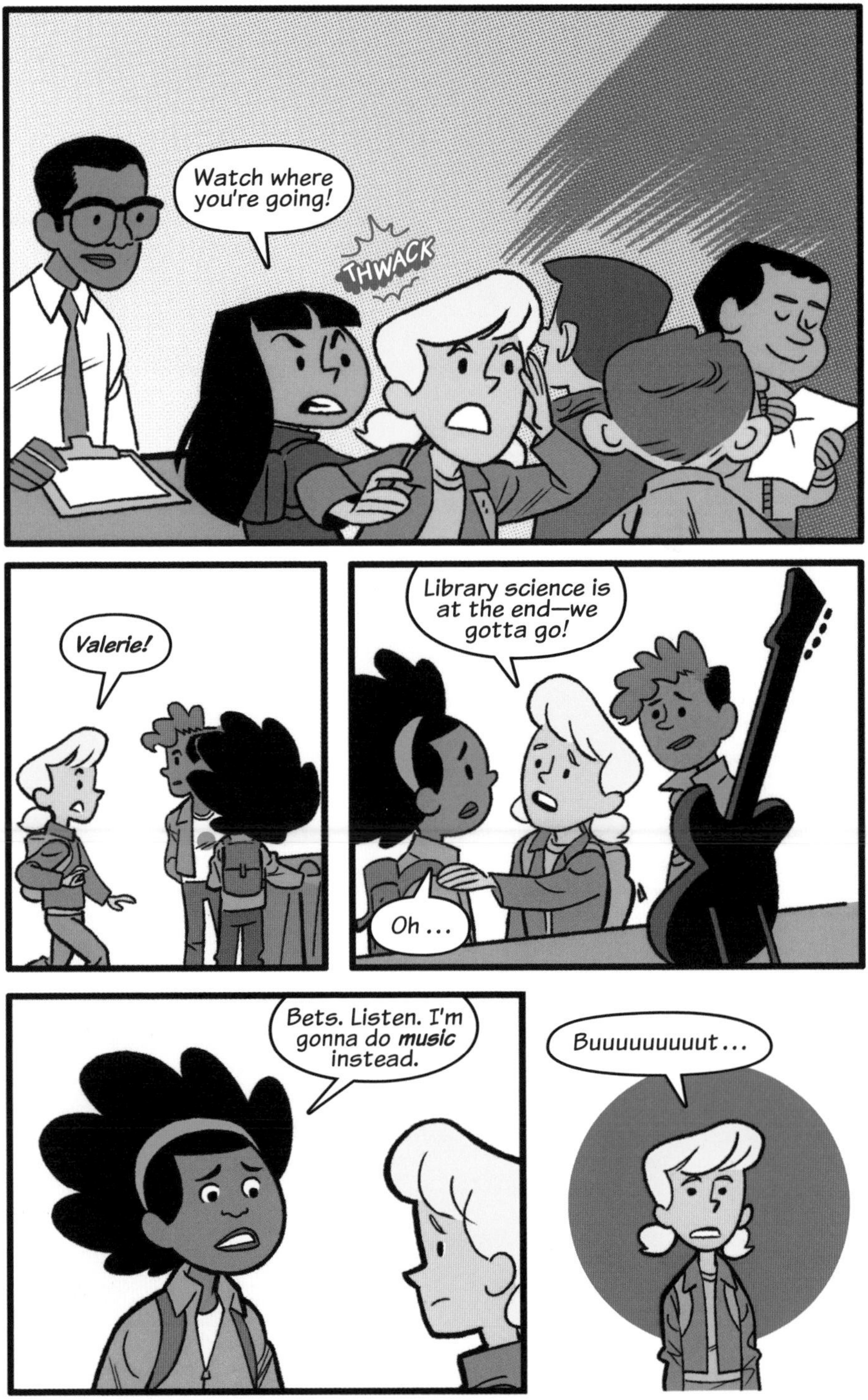
Watch where you're going!
THWACK
Valerie!
Library science is at the end—we gotta go!
Oh . . .
Bets. Listen. I'm gonna do *music* instead.
Buuuuuuuuut . . .

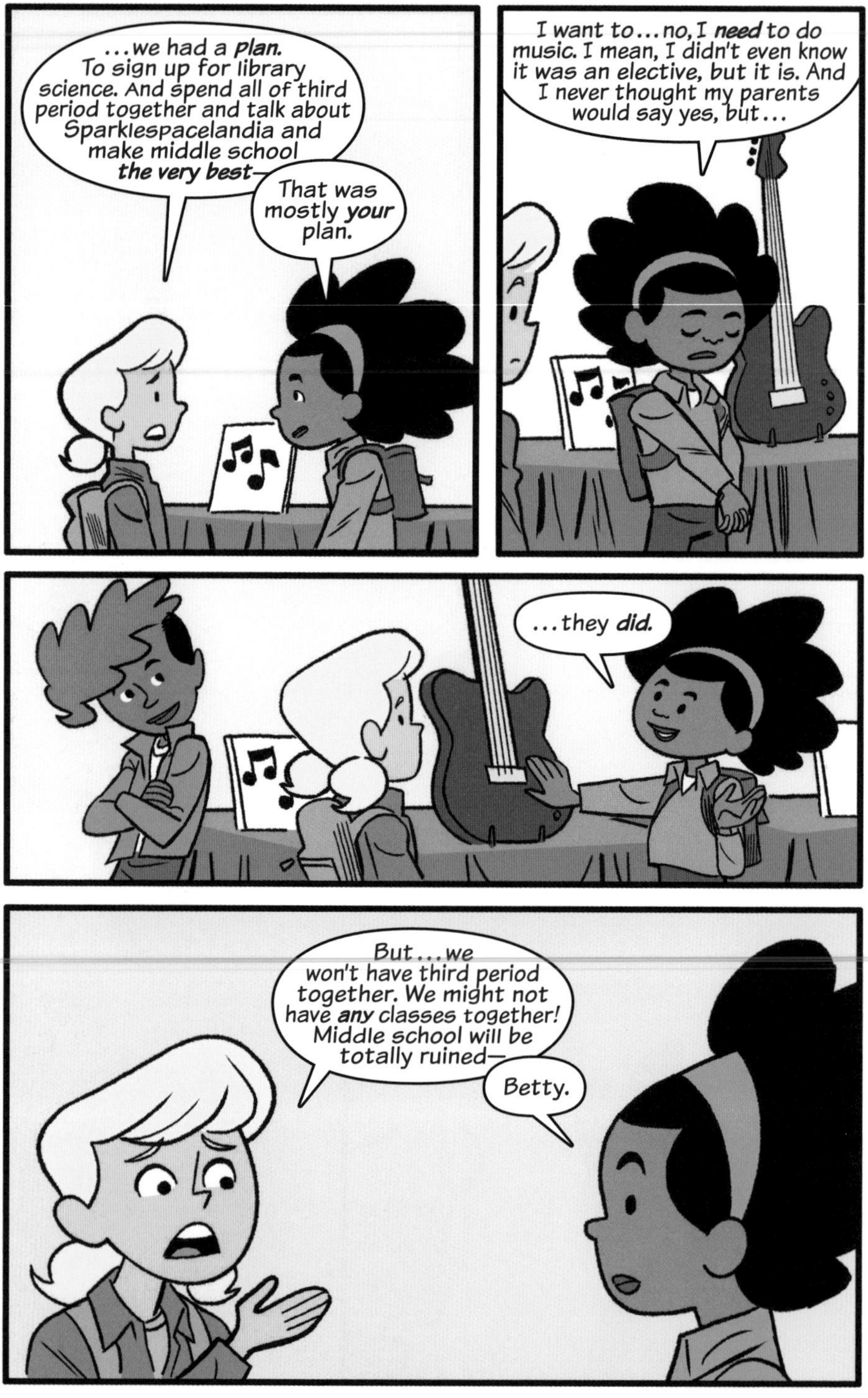
...we had a *plan.* To sign up for library science. And spend all of third period together and talk about Sparklespacelandia and make middle school *the very best*—
That was mostly *your* plan.
I want to... no, I *need* to do music. I mean, I didn't even know it was an elective, but it is. And I never thought my parents would say yes, but...
...they *did.*
But... we won't have third period together. We might not have *any* classes together! Middle school will be totally ruined—
Betty.

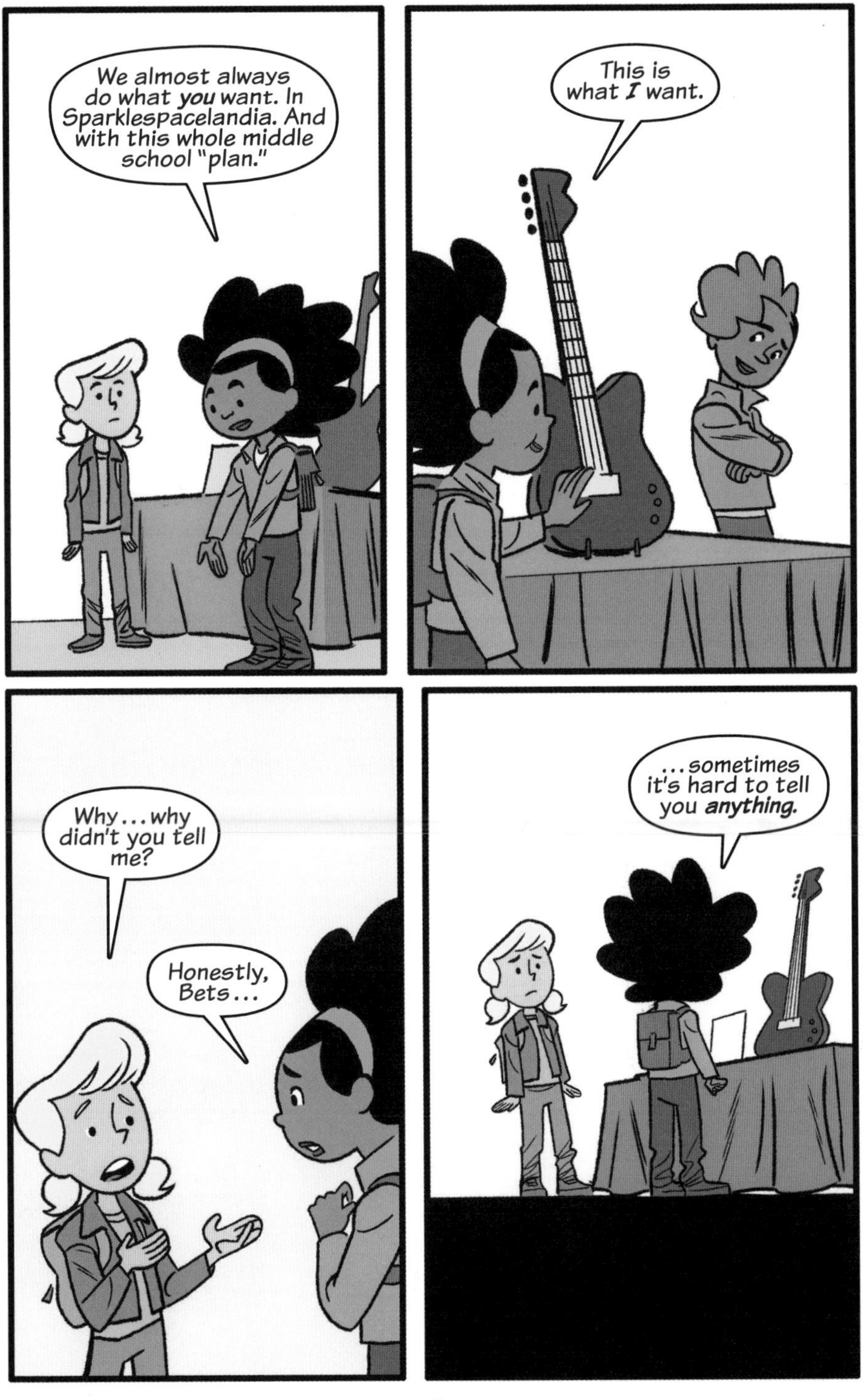
We almost always do what *you* want. In Sparklespacelandia. And with this whole middle school "plan."
This is what *I* want.
Why...why didn't you tell me?
Honestly, Bets...
...sometimes it's hard to tell you ***anything.***

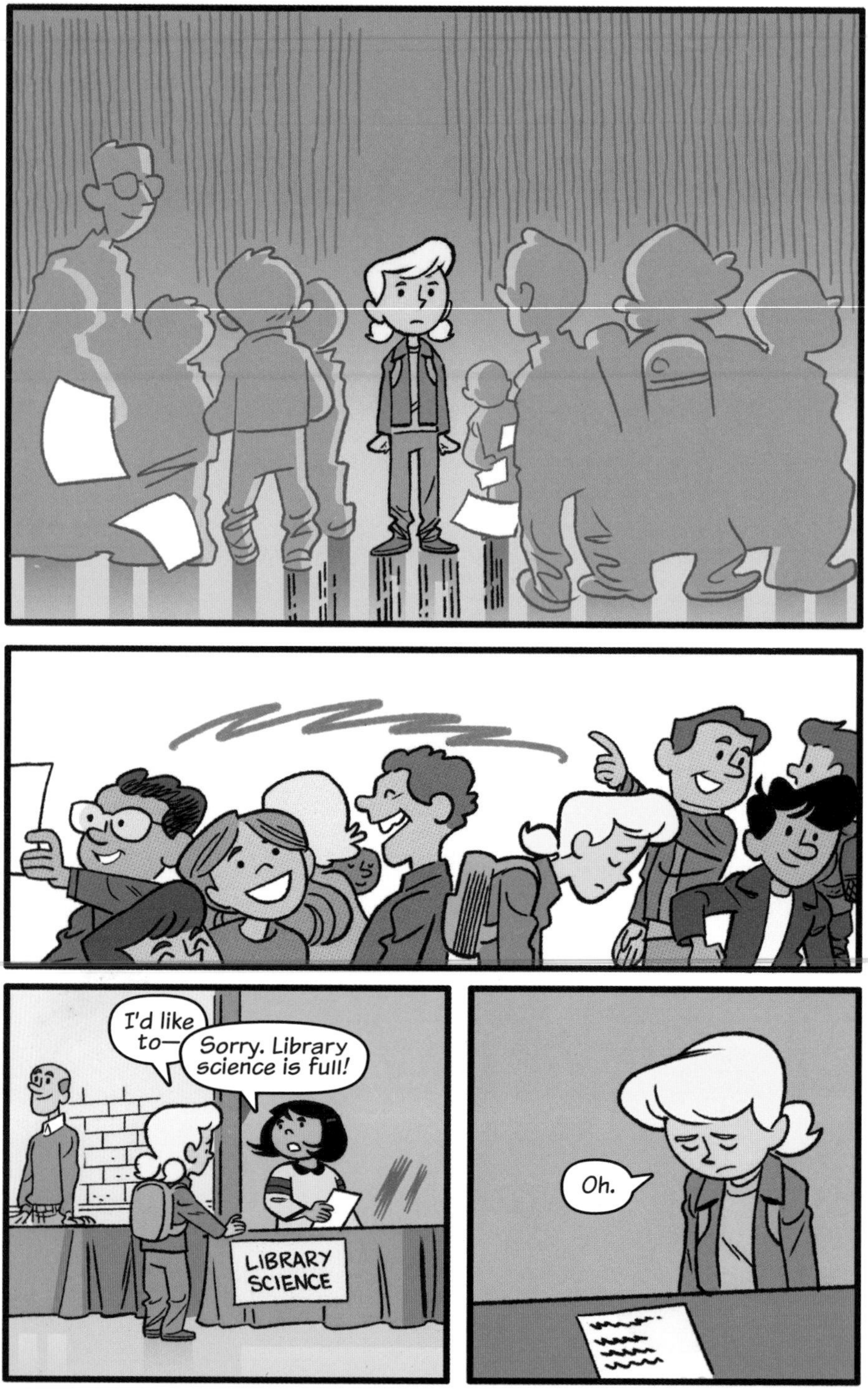
I'd like to—
Sorry. Library science is full!
LIBRARY SCIENCE
Oh.

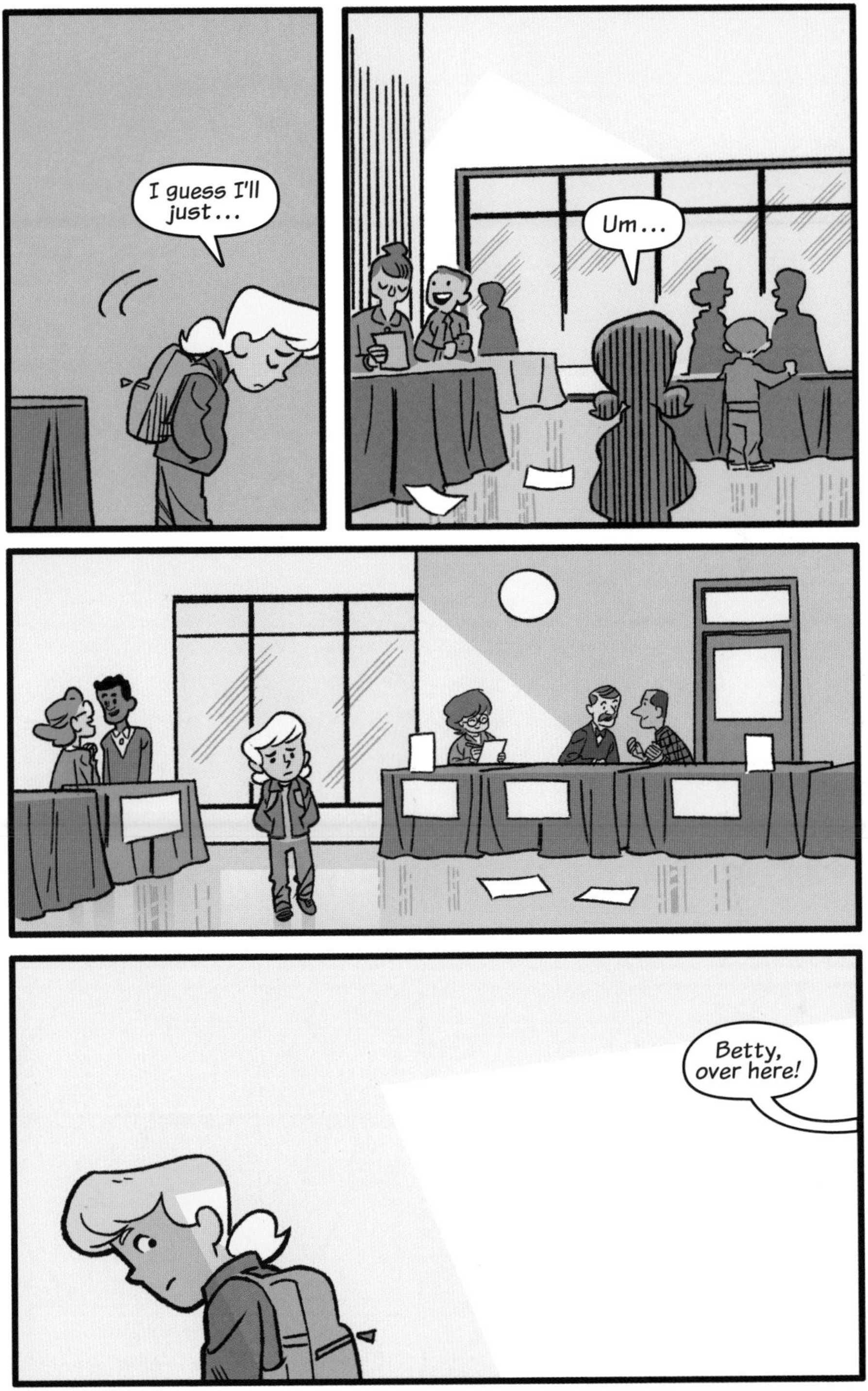
I guess I'll just...
Um...
Betty, over here!

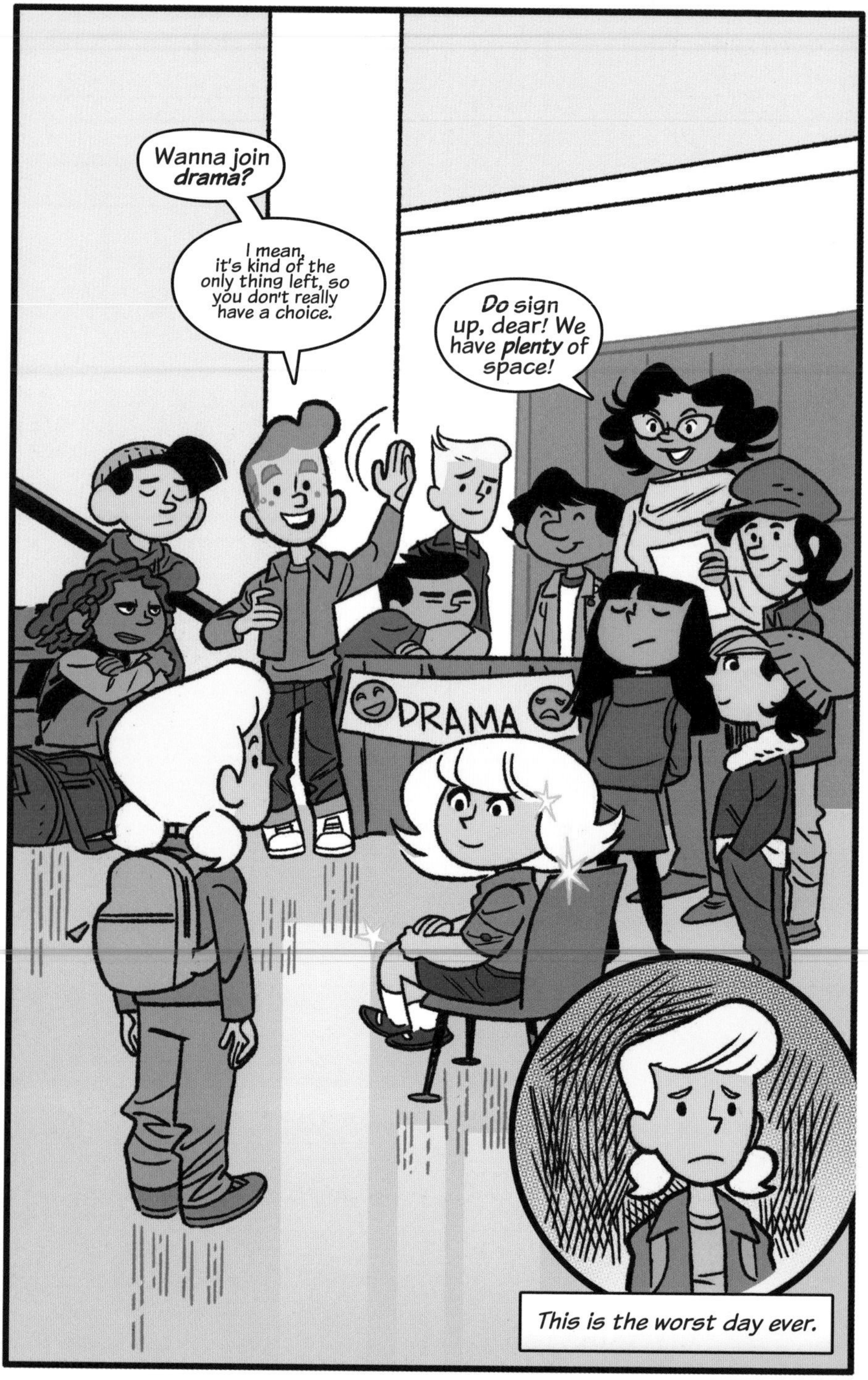

Wanna join drama?
I mean, it's kind of the only thing left, so you don't really have a choice.
Do sign up, dear! We have plenty of space!
DRAMA
This is the worst day ever.

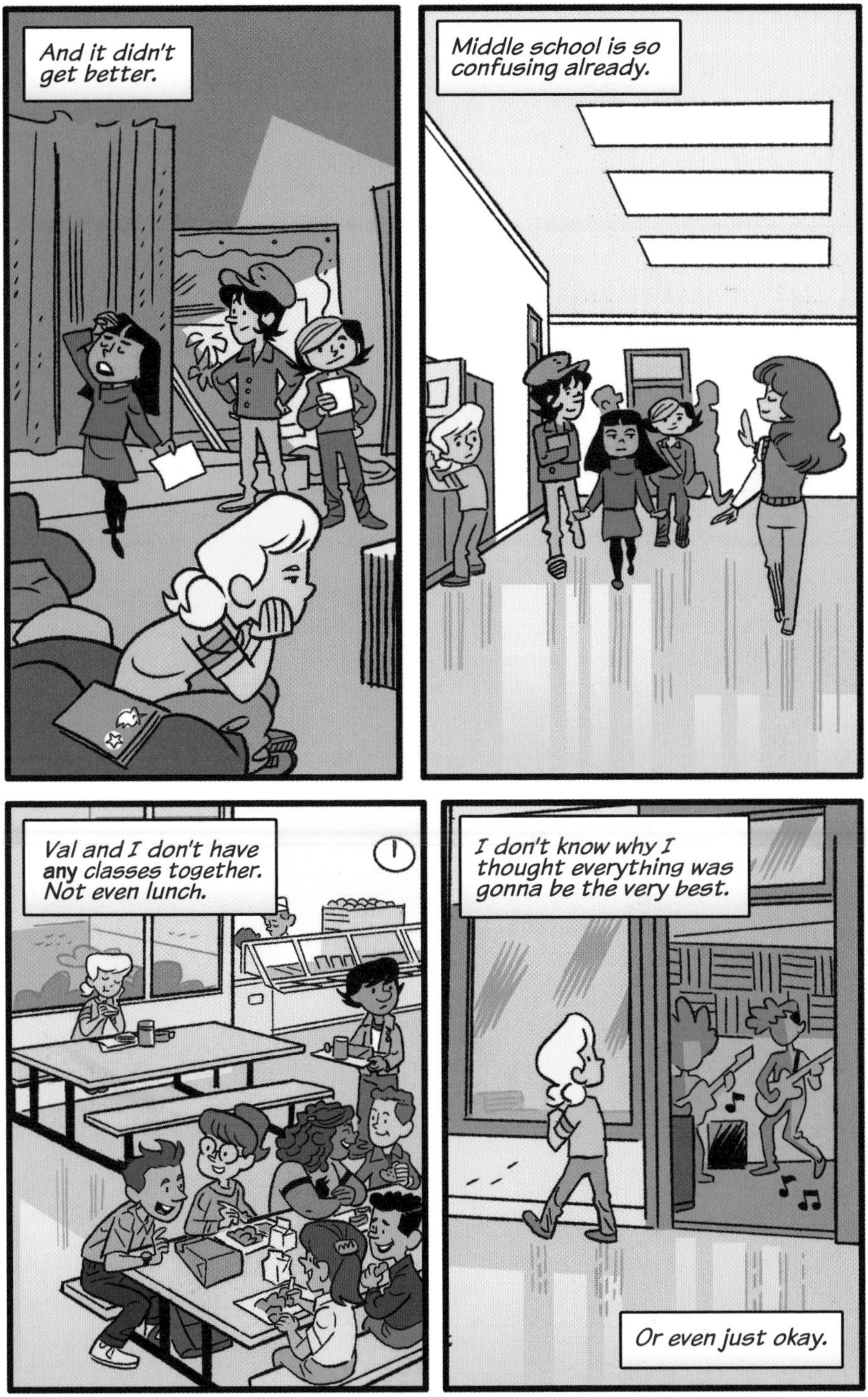
And it didn't get better.
Middle school is so confusing already.
Val and I don't have **any** classes together. Not even lunch.
I don't know why I thought everything was gonna be the very best.
Or even just okay.

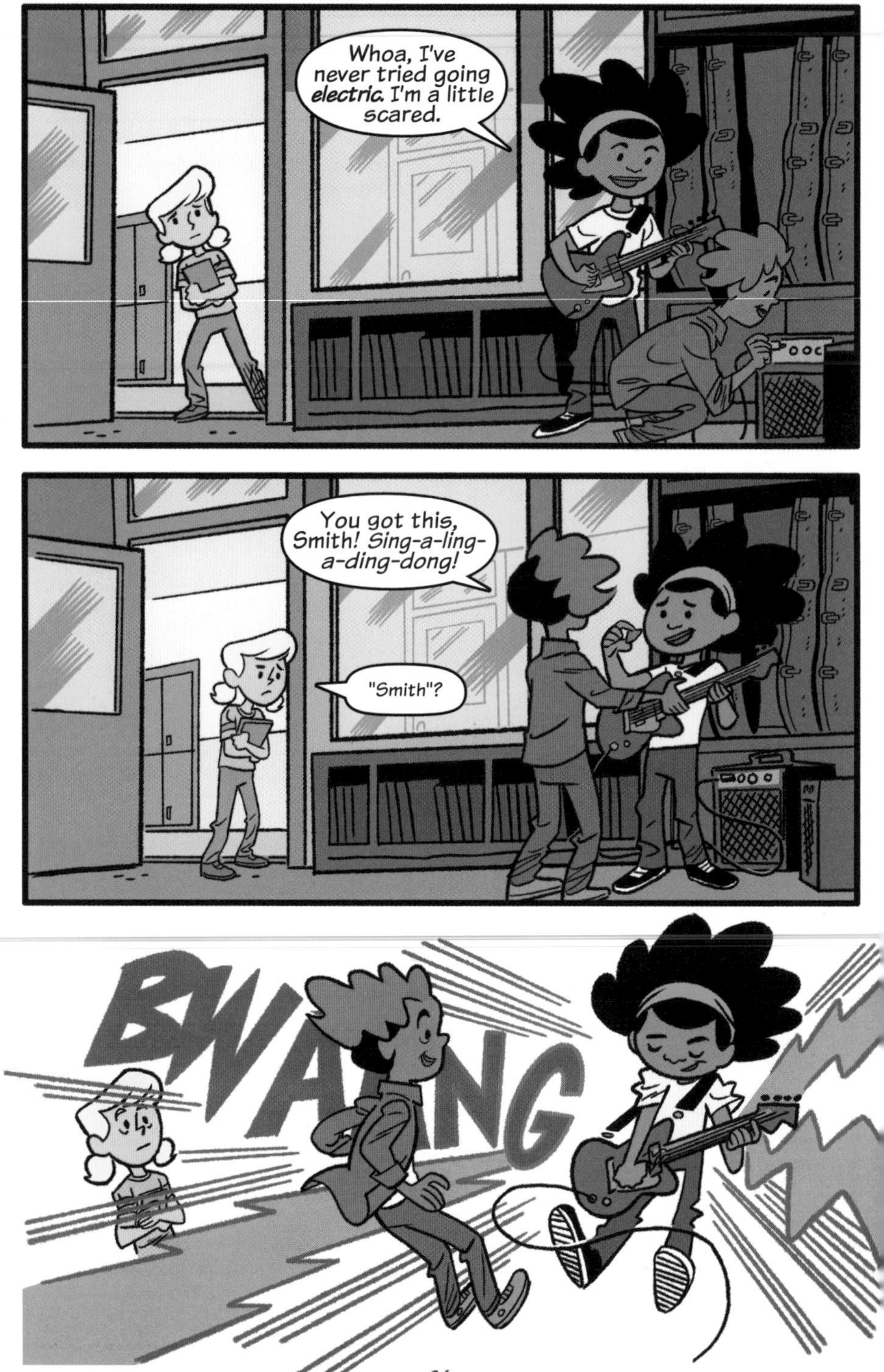
Whoa, I've never tried going *electric*. I'm a little scared.
You got this, Smith! *Sing-a-ling-a-ding-dong!*
"Smith"?
BWANG

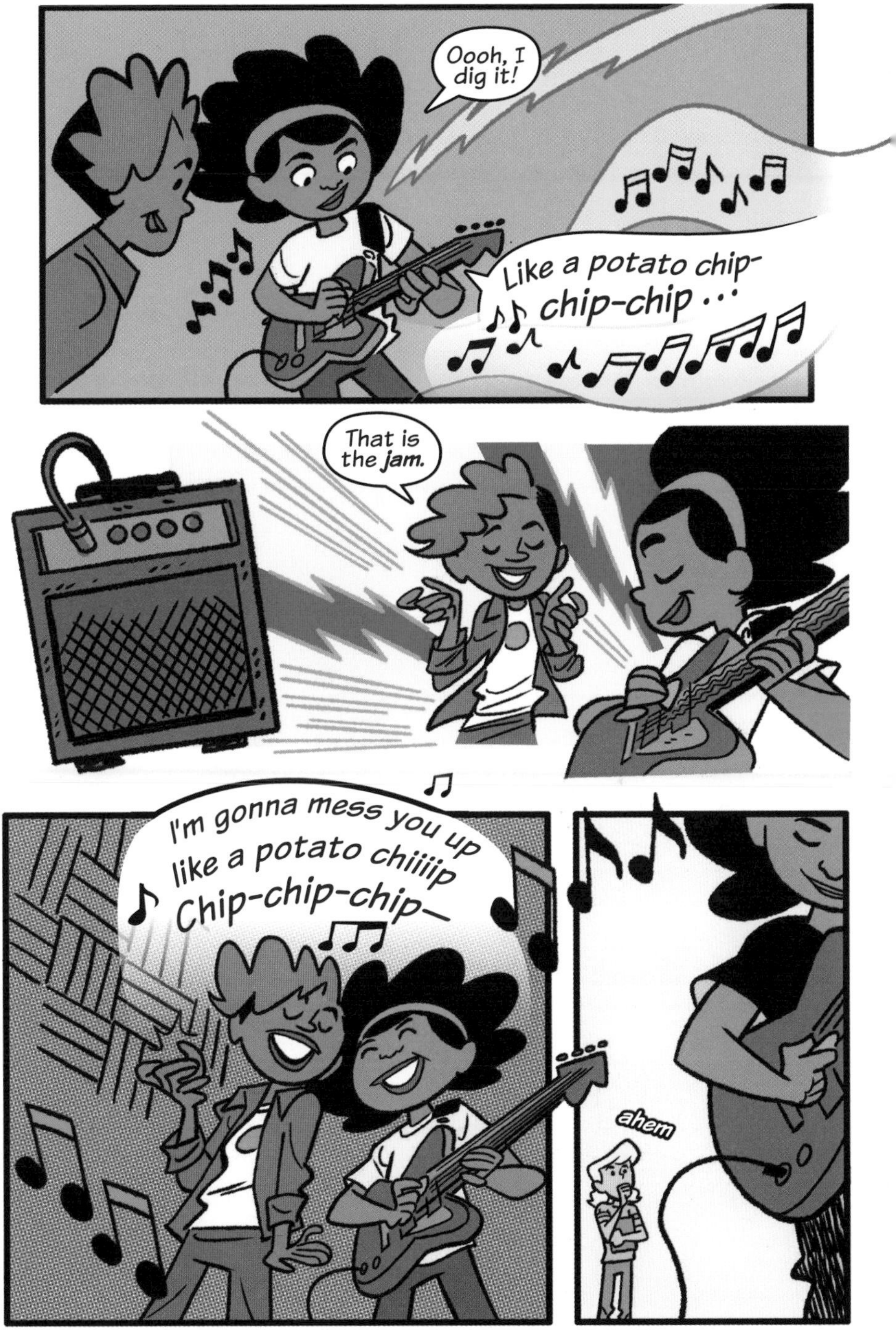
Oooh, I dig it!
Like a potato chip-chip-chip...
That is the *jam.*
I'm gonna mess you up like a potato chiiiip Chip-chip-chip–
ahem

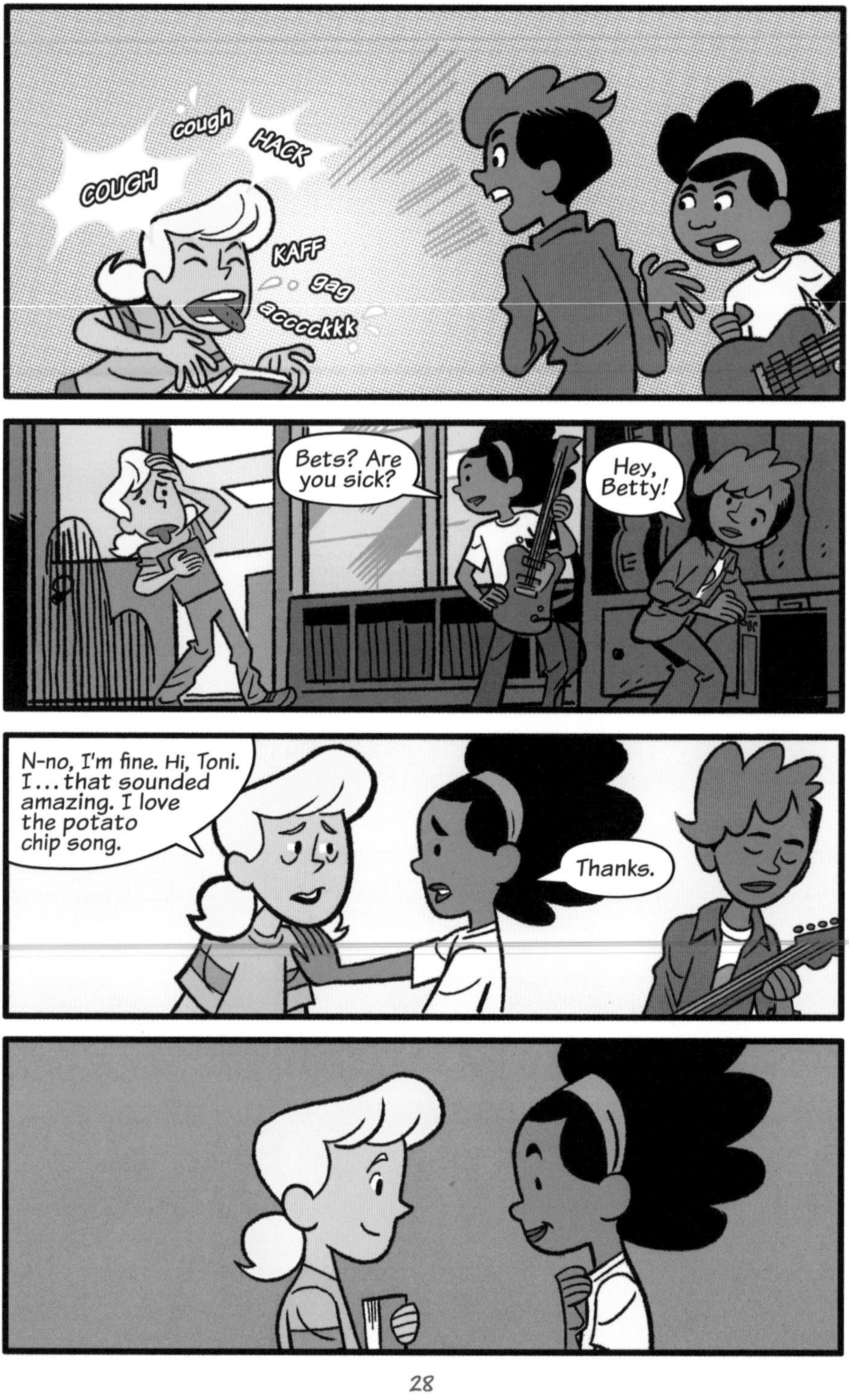
cough
HACK
COUGH
KAFF
gag
acccckkk
Bets? Are you sick?
Hey, Betty!
N-no, I'm fine. Hi, Toni. I... that sounded amazing. I love the potato chip song.
Thanks.

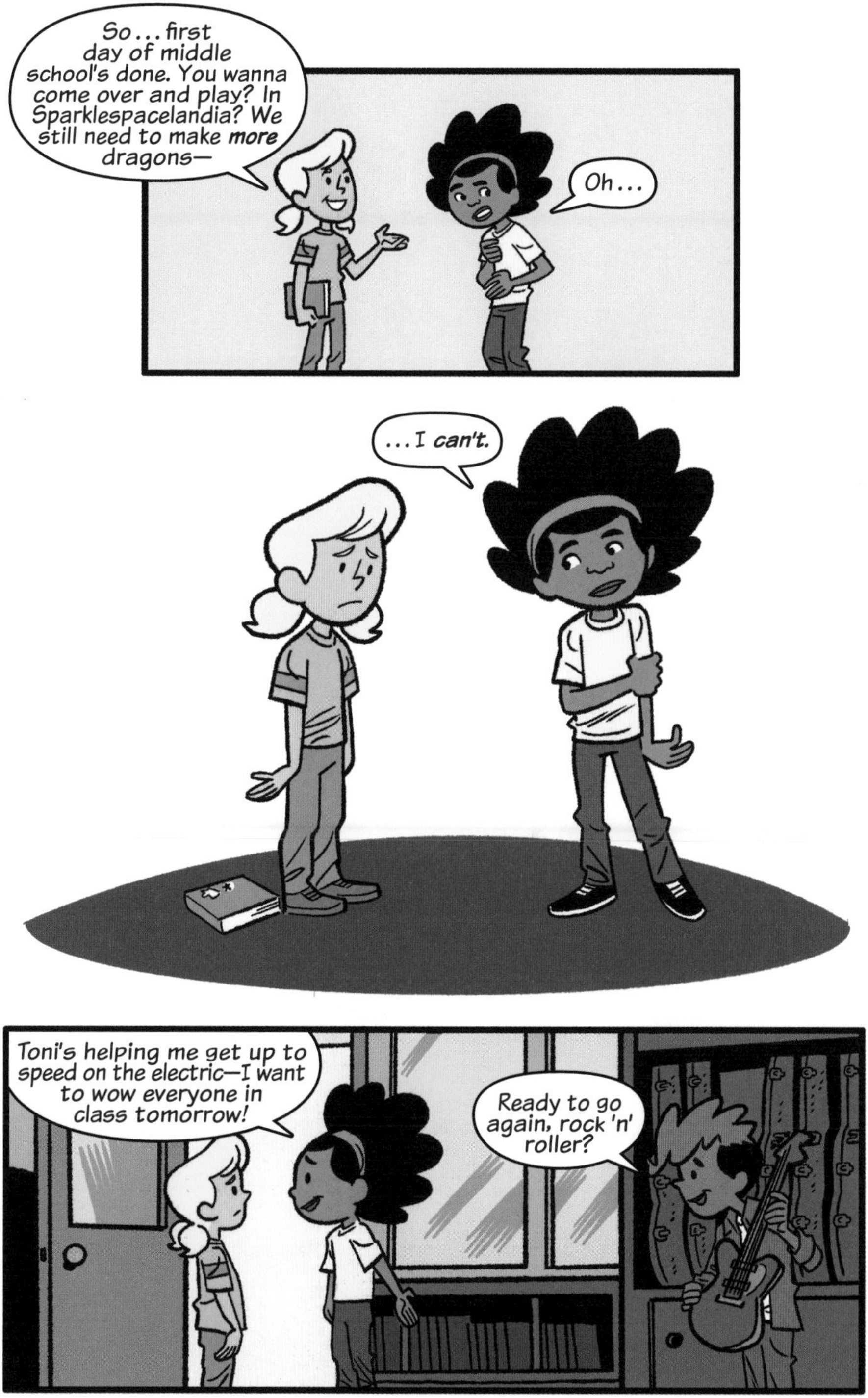
So... first day of middle school's done. You wanna come over and play? In Sparklespacelandia? We still need to make *more* dragons—
Oh...
...I *can't.*
Toni's helping me get up to speed on the electric—I want to wow everyone in class tomorrow!
Ready to go again, rock 'n' roller?

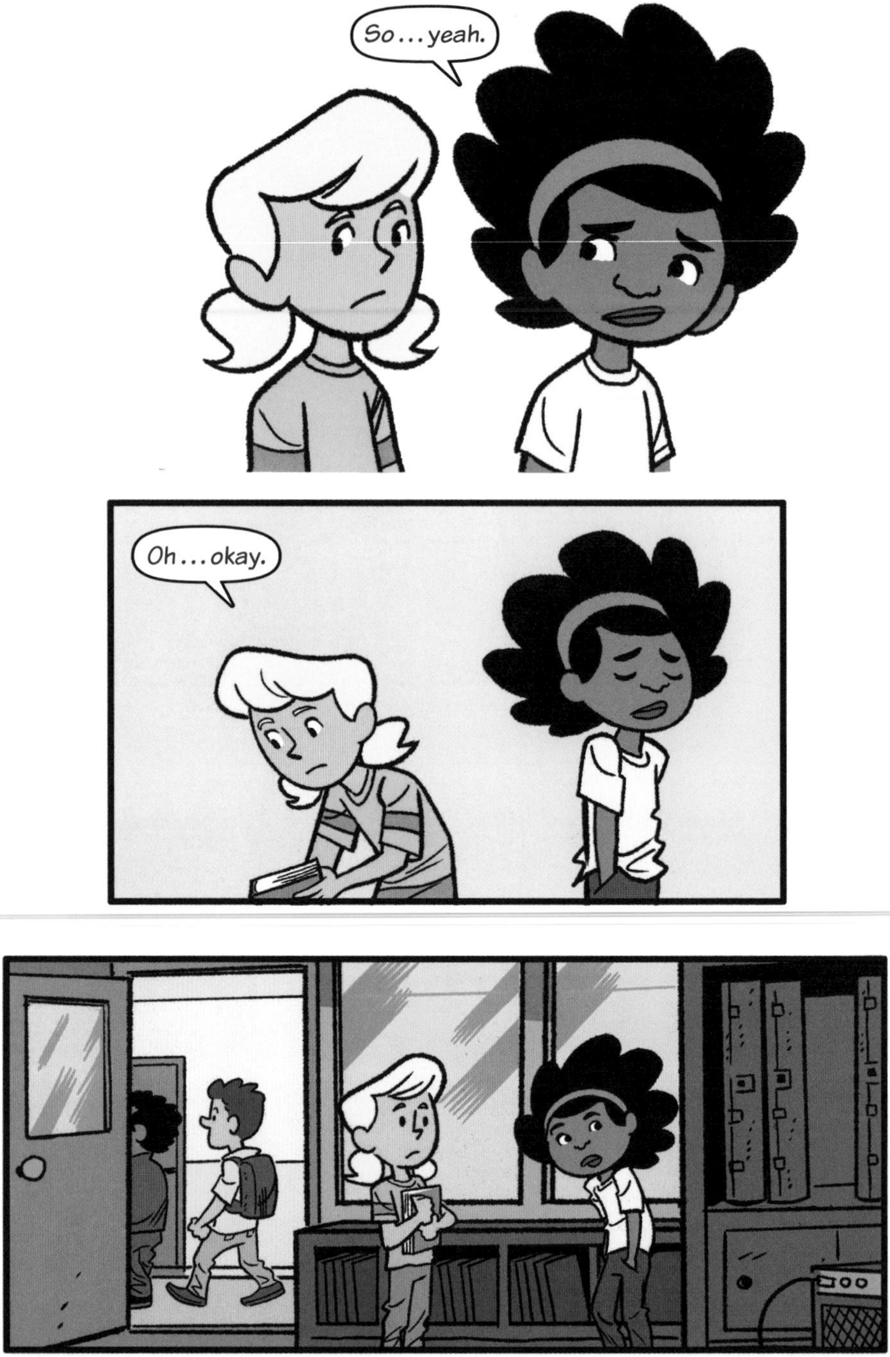
So... yeah.
Oh... okay.

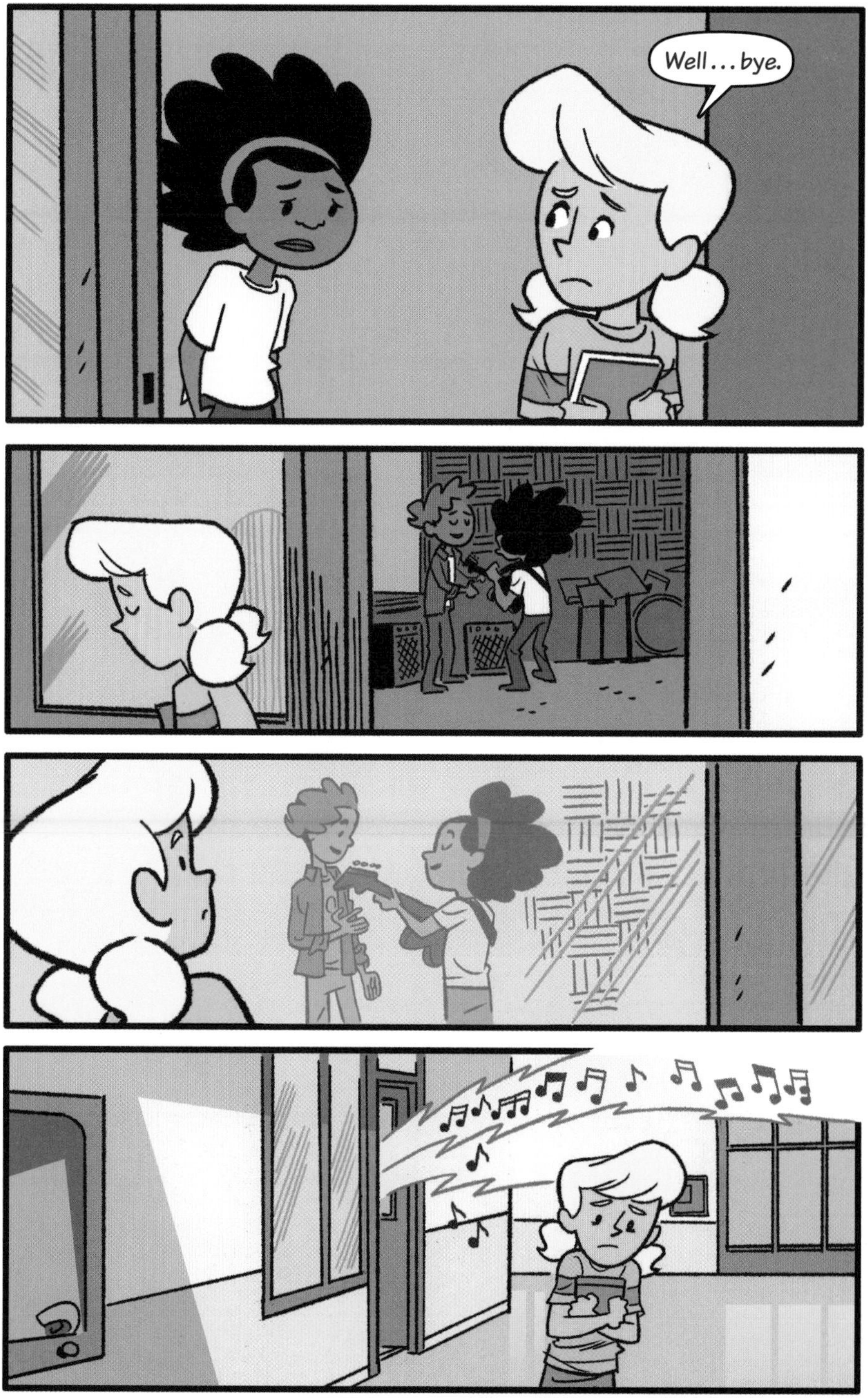
Well . . . bye.

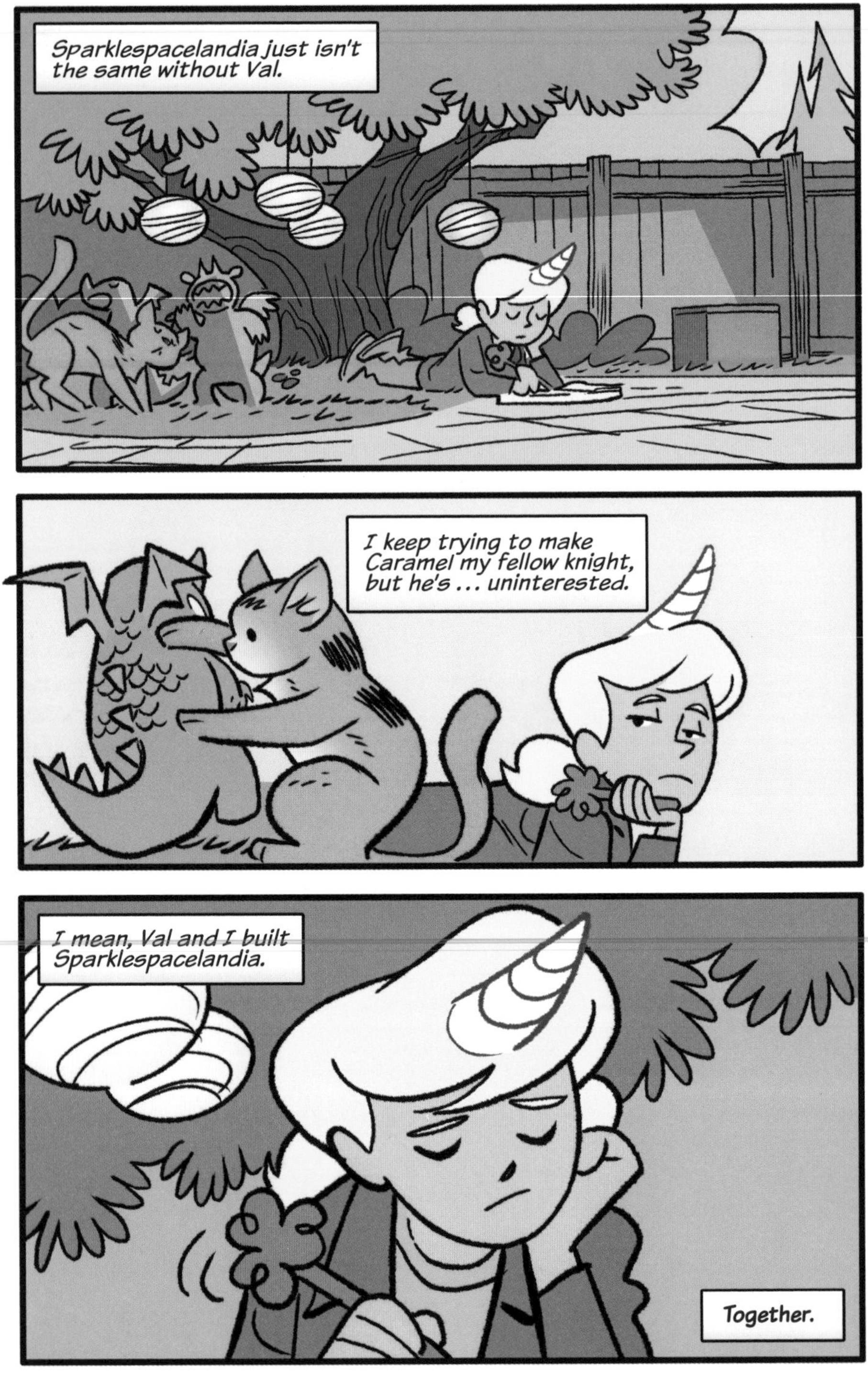
Sparklespacelandia just isn't the same without Val.
I keep trying to make Caramel my fellow knight, but he's . . . uninterested.
I mean, Val and I built Sparklespacelandia.
Together.

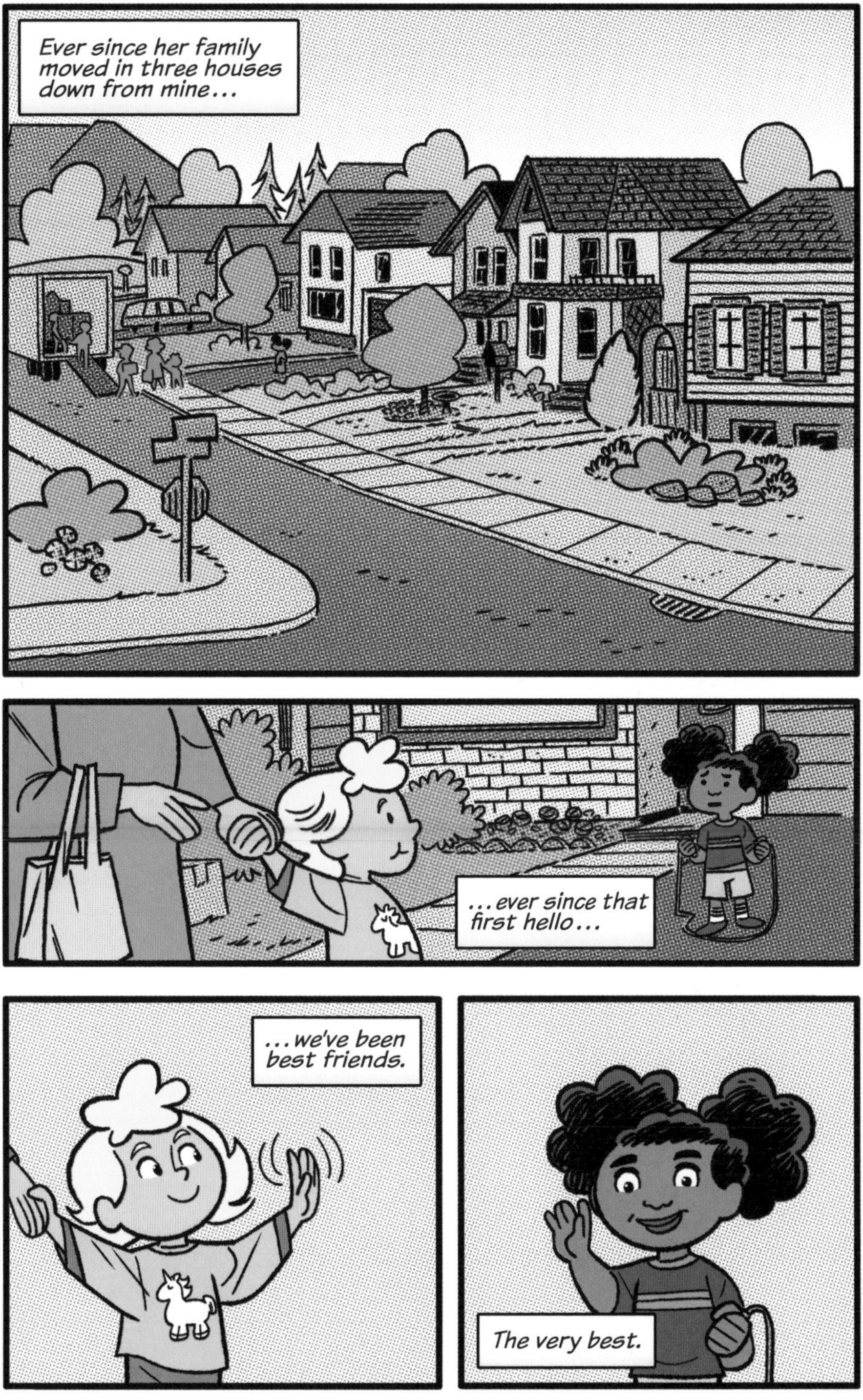
Ever since her family moved in three houses down from mine...
...ever since that first hello...
...we've been best friends.
The very best.

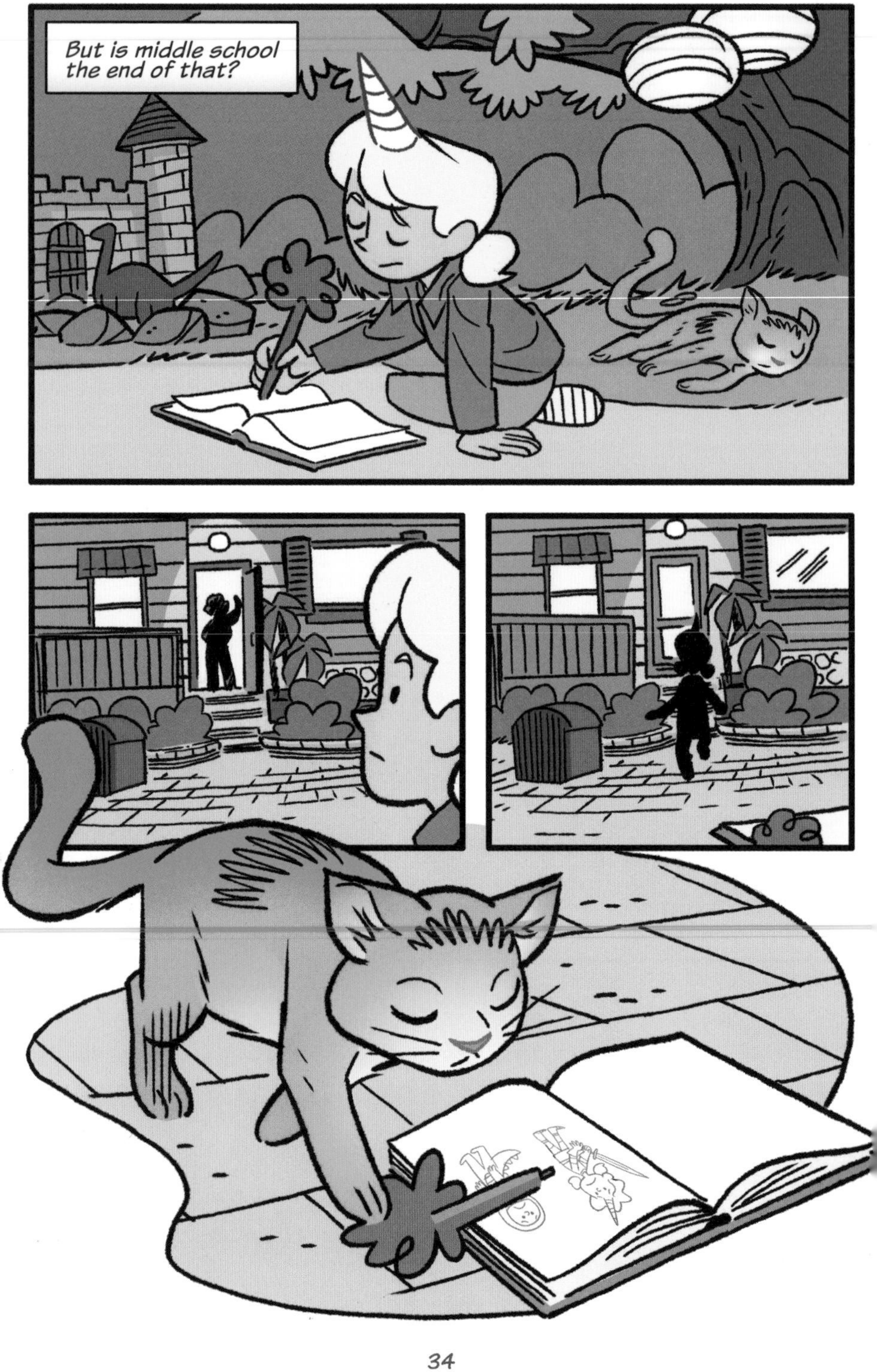
But is middle school the end of that?

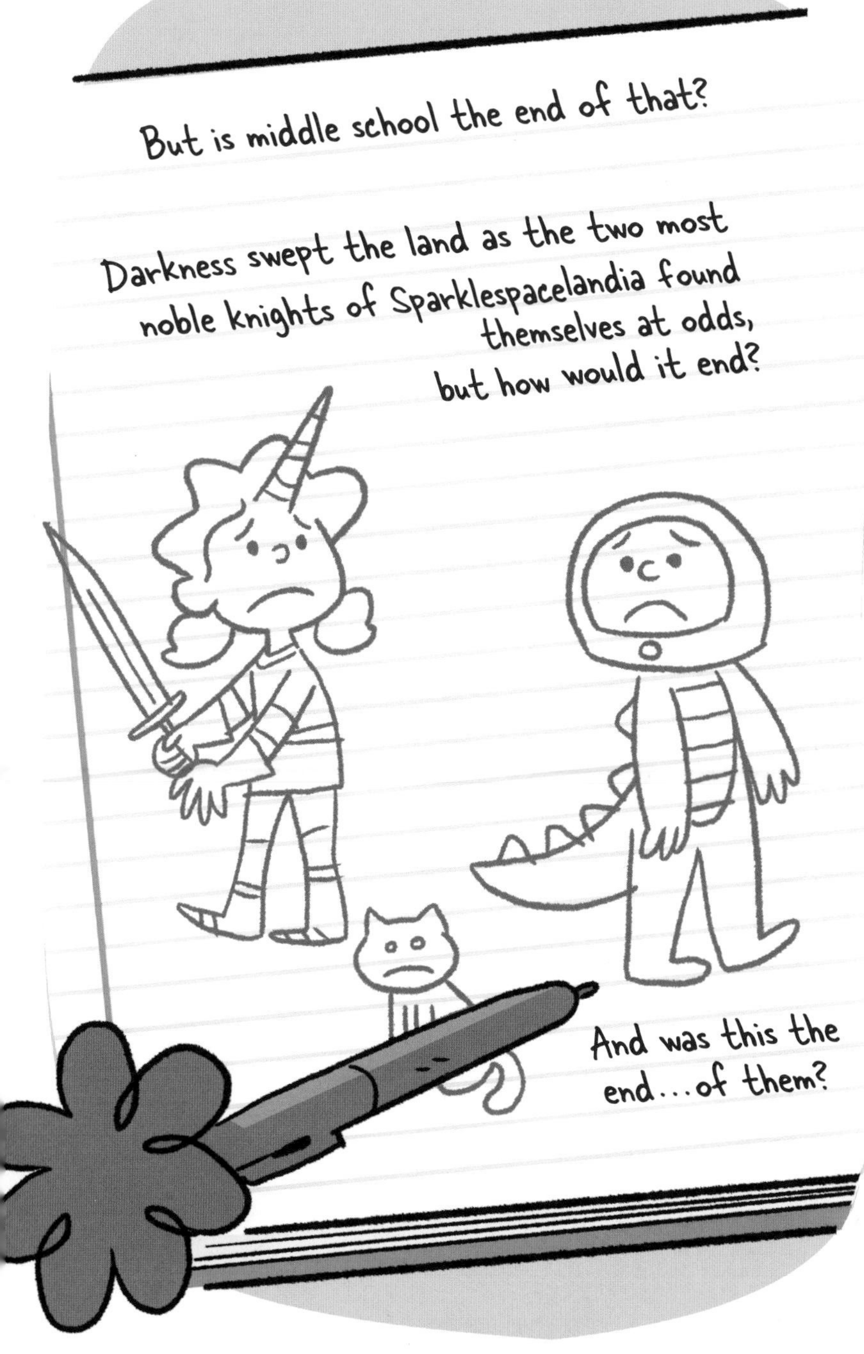
But is middle school the end of that?
Darkness swept the land as the two most noble knights of Sparklespacelandia found themselves at odds, but how would it end?
And was this the end...of them?

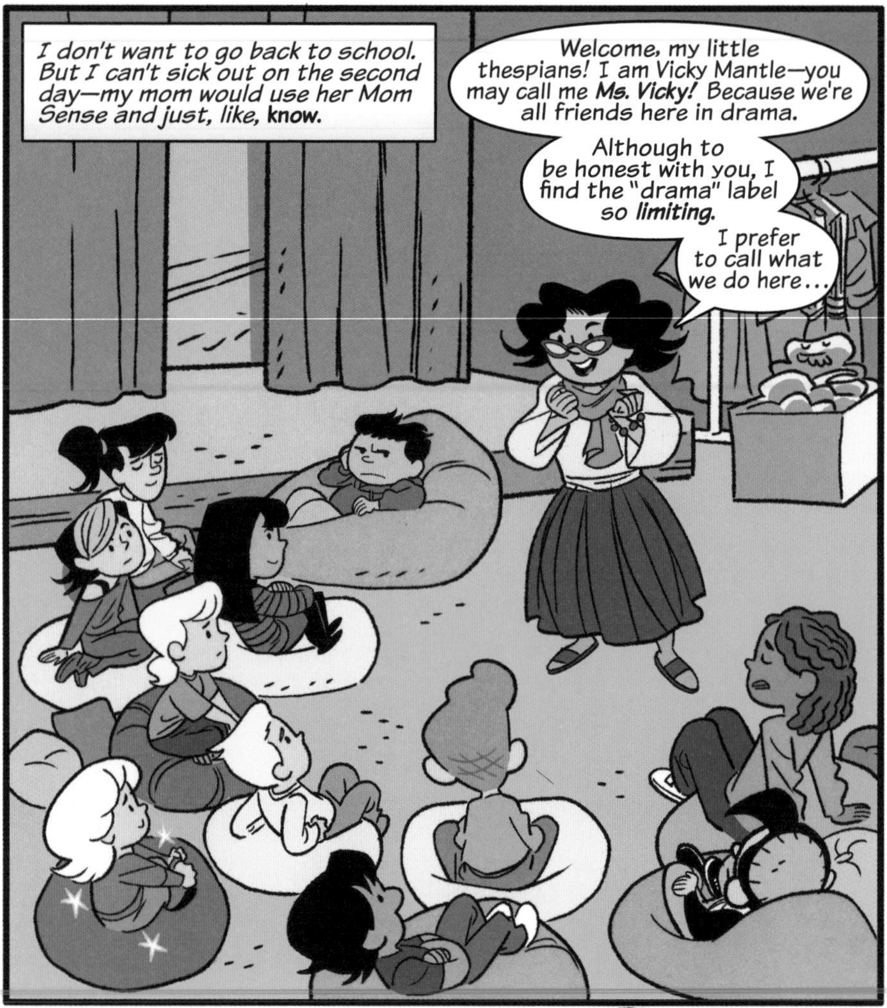
I don't want to go back to school. But I can't sick out on the second day—my mom would use her Mom Sense and just, like, **know.**
Welcome, my little thespians! I am Vicky Mantle—you may call me **Ms. Vicky!** Because we're all friends here in drama.
Although to be honest with you, I find the "drama" label so ***limiting.***
I prefer to call what we do here...

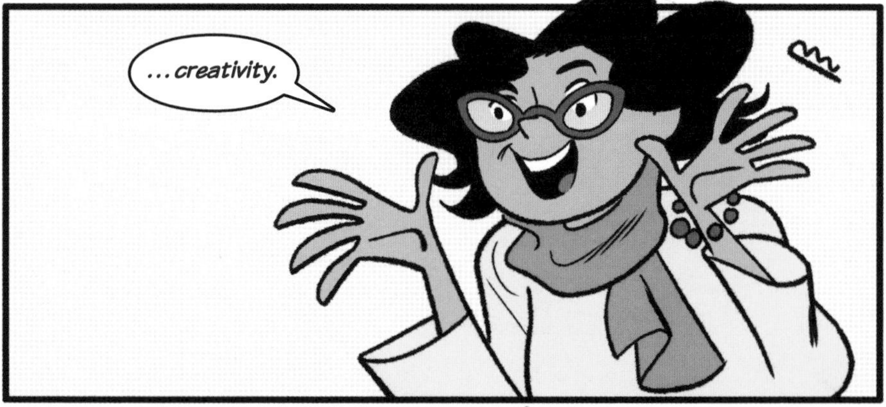
...***creativity.***

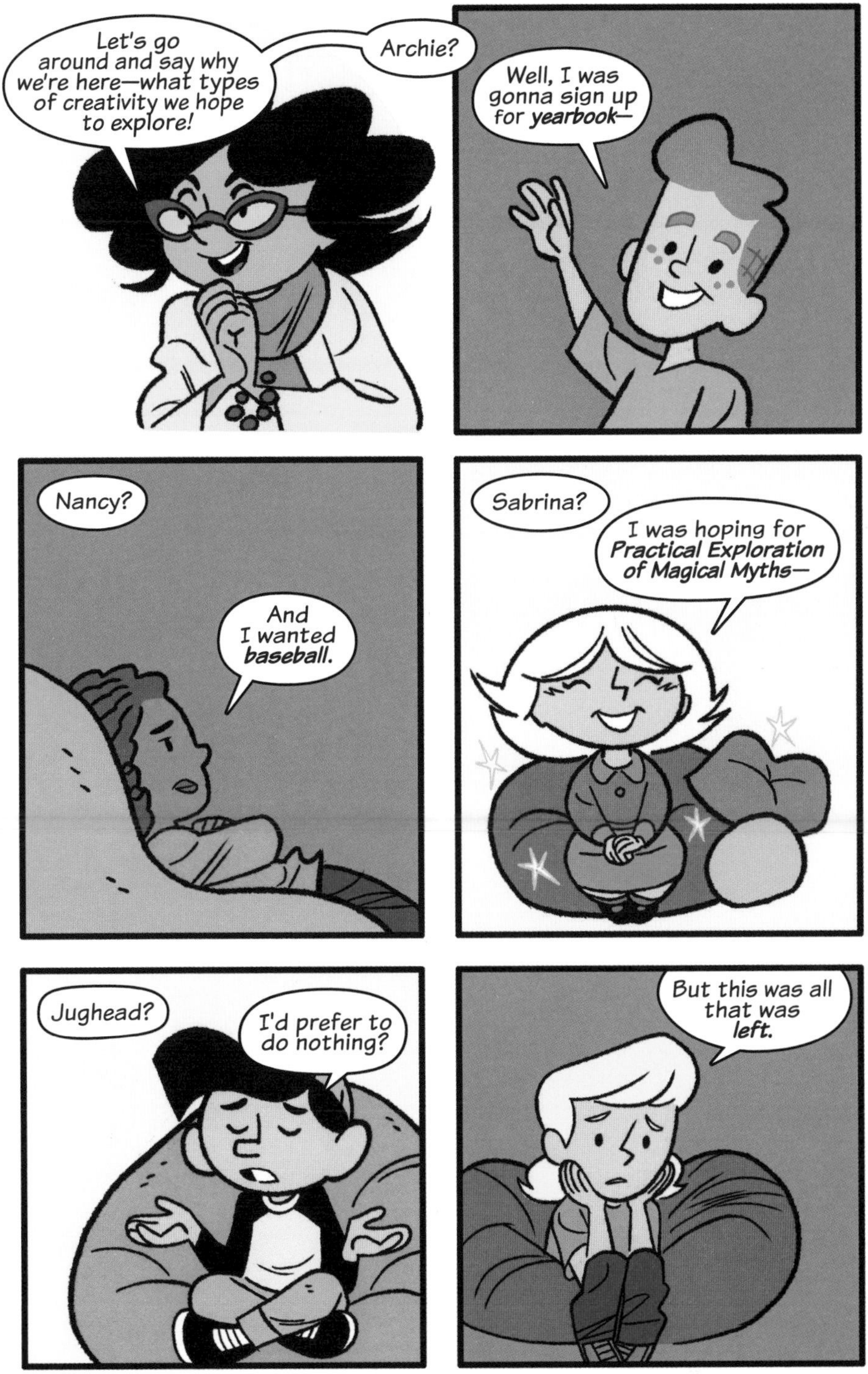
Let's go around and say why we're here—what types of creativity we hope to explore!
Archie?
Well, I was gonna sign up for *yearbook*—
Nancy?
And I wanted *baseball*.
Sabrina?
I was hoping for *Practical Exploration of Magical Myths*—
Jughead?
I'd prefer to do nothing?
But this was all that was *left*.

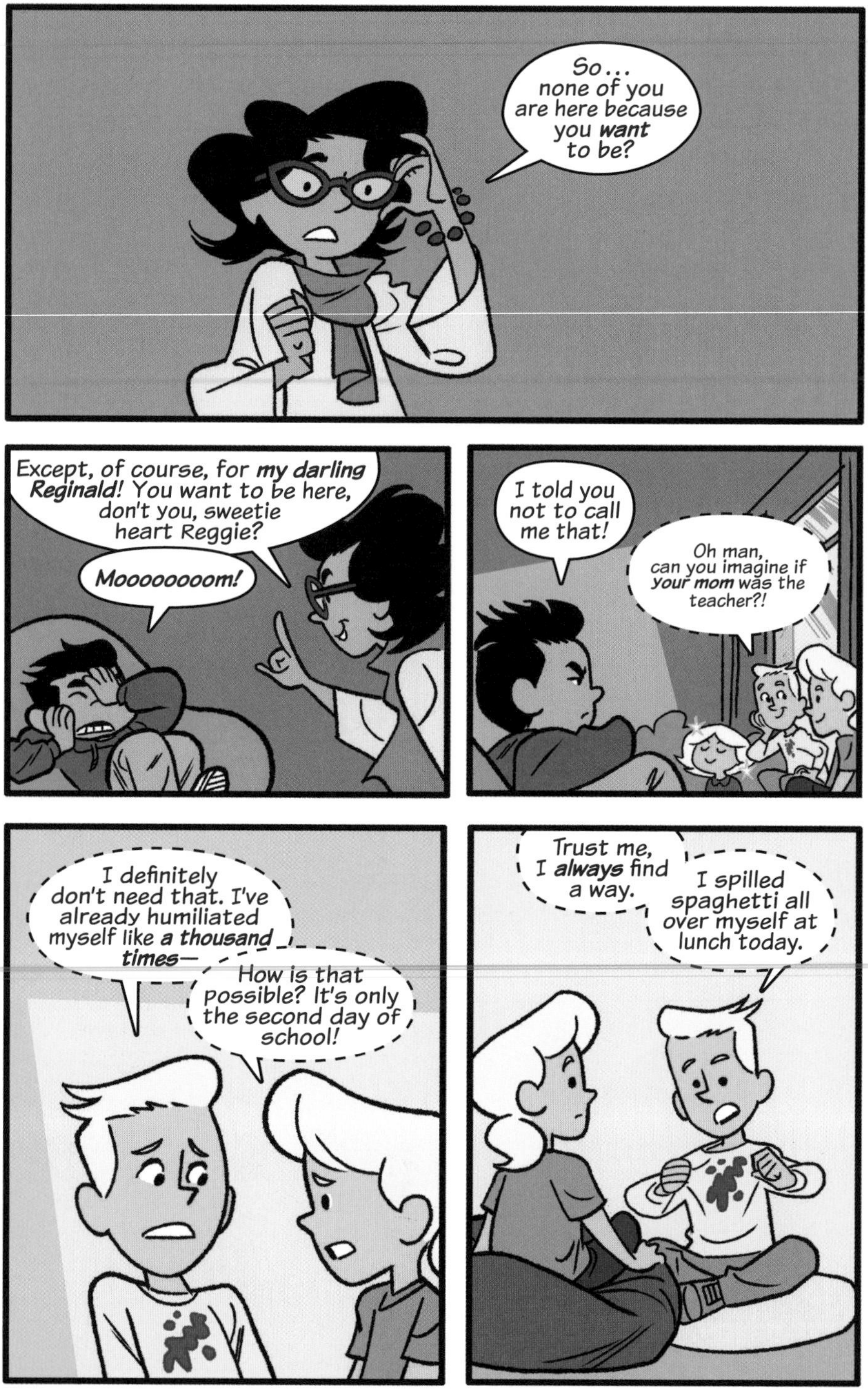
So... none of you are here because you **want** to be?
Except, of course, for **my darling Reginald**! You want to be here, don't you, sweetie heart Reggie?
Moooooooom!
I told you not to call me that!
Oh man, can you imagine if **your mom** was the teacher?!
I definitely don't need that. I've already humiliated myself like **a thousand times**—
How is that possible? It's only the second day of school!
Trust me, I **always** find a way.
I spilled spaghetti all over myself at lunch today.

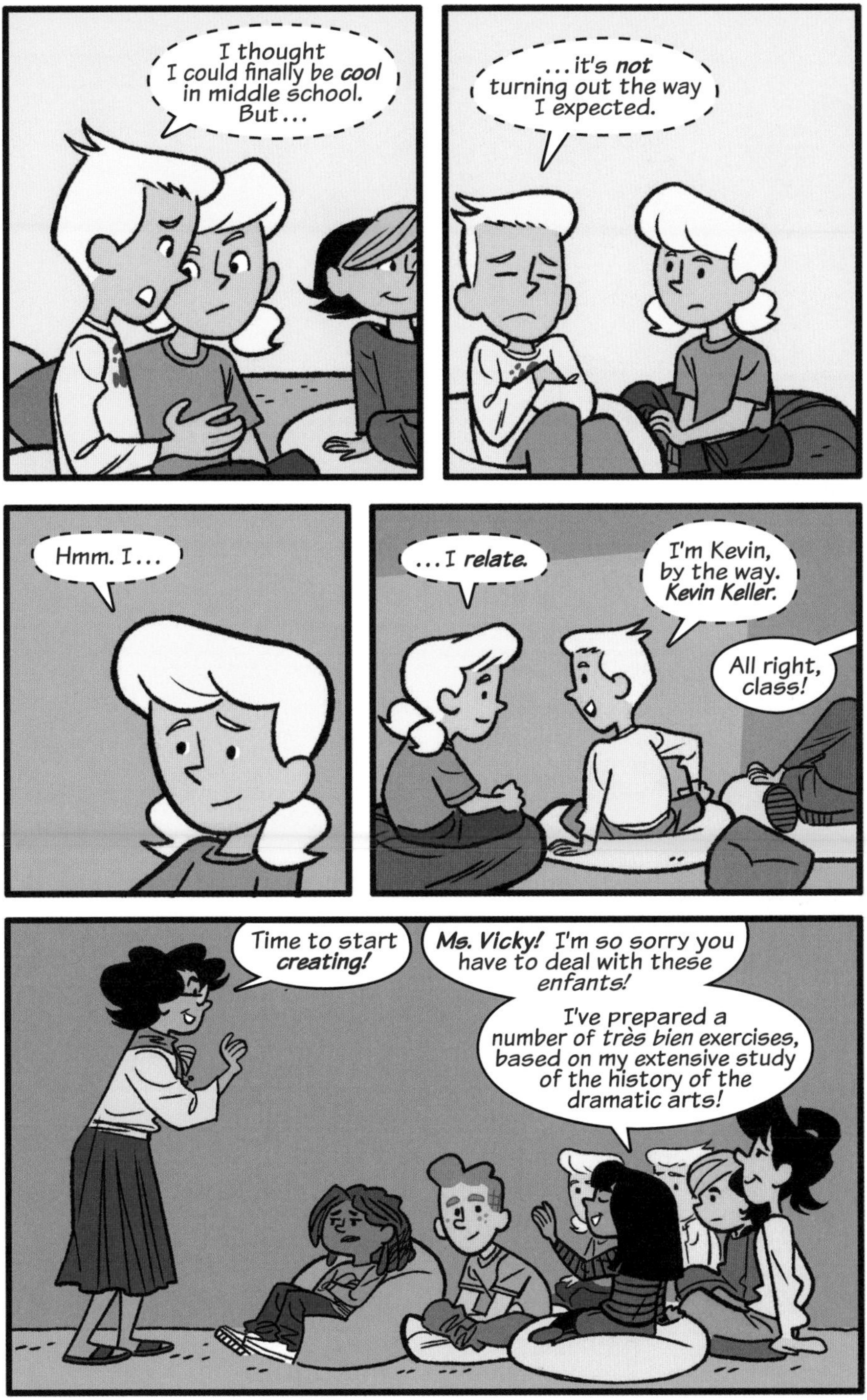
I thought I could finally be *cool* in middle school. But...
...it's *not* turning out the way I expected.
Hmm. I...
...I *relate.*
I'm Kevin, by the way. ***Kevin Keller.***
All right, class!
Time to start ***creating!***
Ms. Vicky! I'm so sorry you have to deal with these *enfants!*
I've prepared a number of *très bien* exercises, based on my extensive study of the history of the dramatic arts!

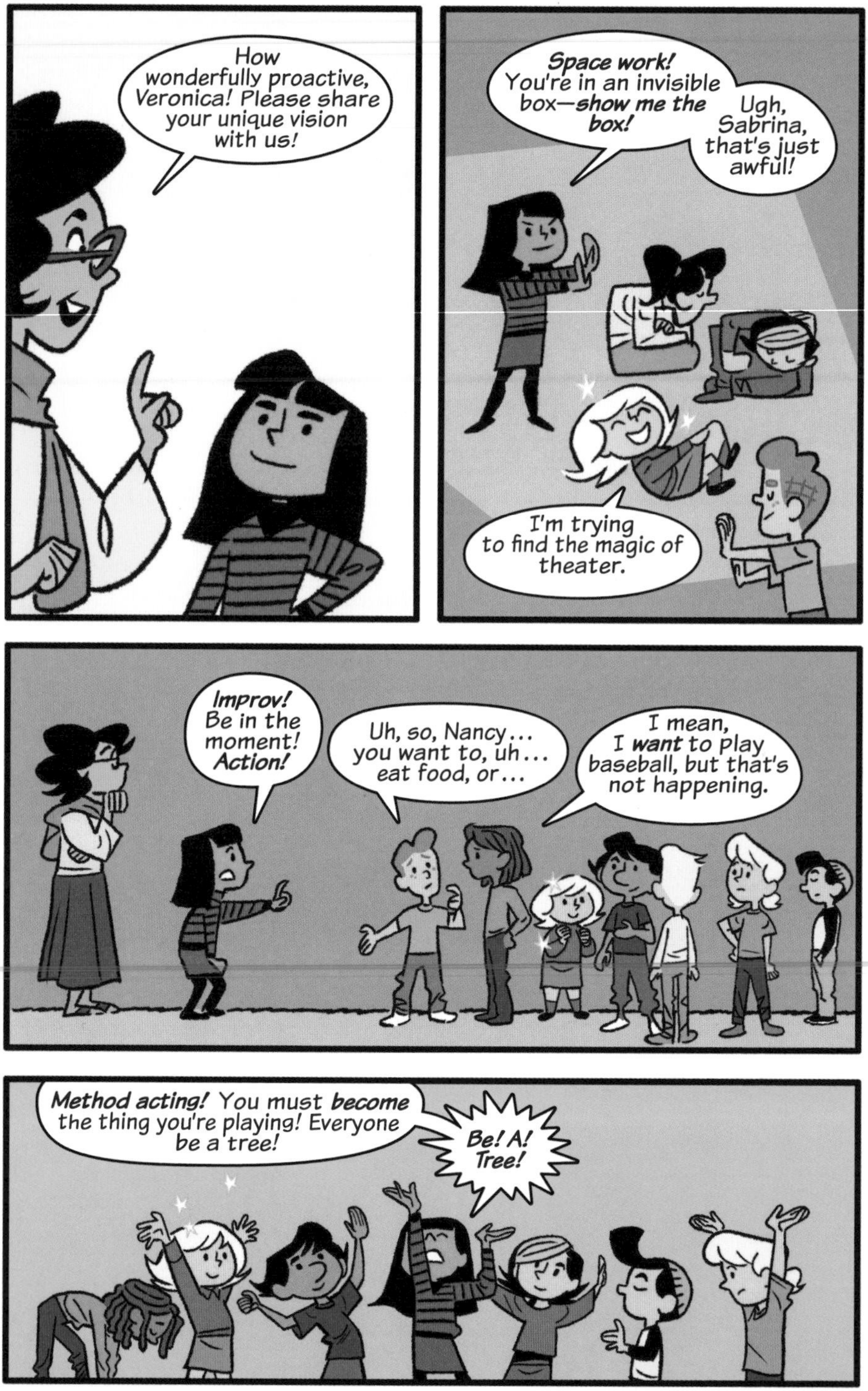
How wonderfully proactive, Veronica! Please share your unique vision with us!
Space work! You're in an invisible box—**show me the box!**
Ugh, Sabrina, that's just awful!
I'm trying to find the magic of theater.
Improv! Be in the moment! **Action!**
Uh, so, Nancy... you want to, uh... eat food, or...
I mean, I **want** to play baseball, but that's not happening.
Method acting! You must **become** the thing you're playing! Everyone be a tree!
Be! A! Tree!

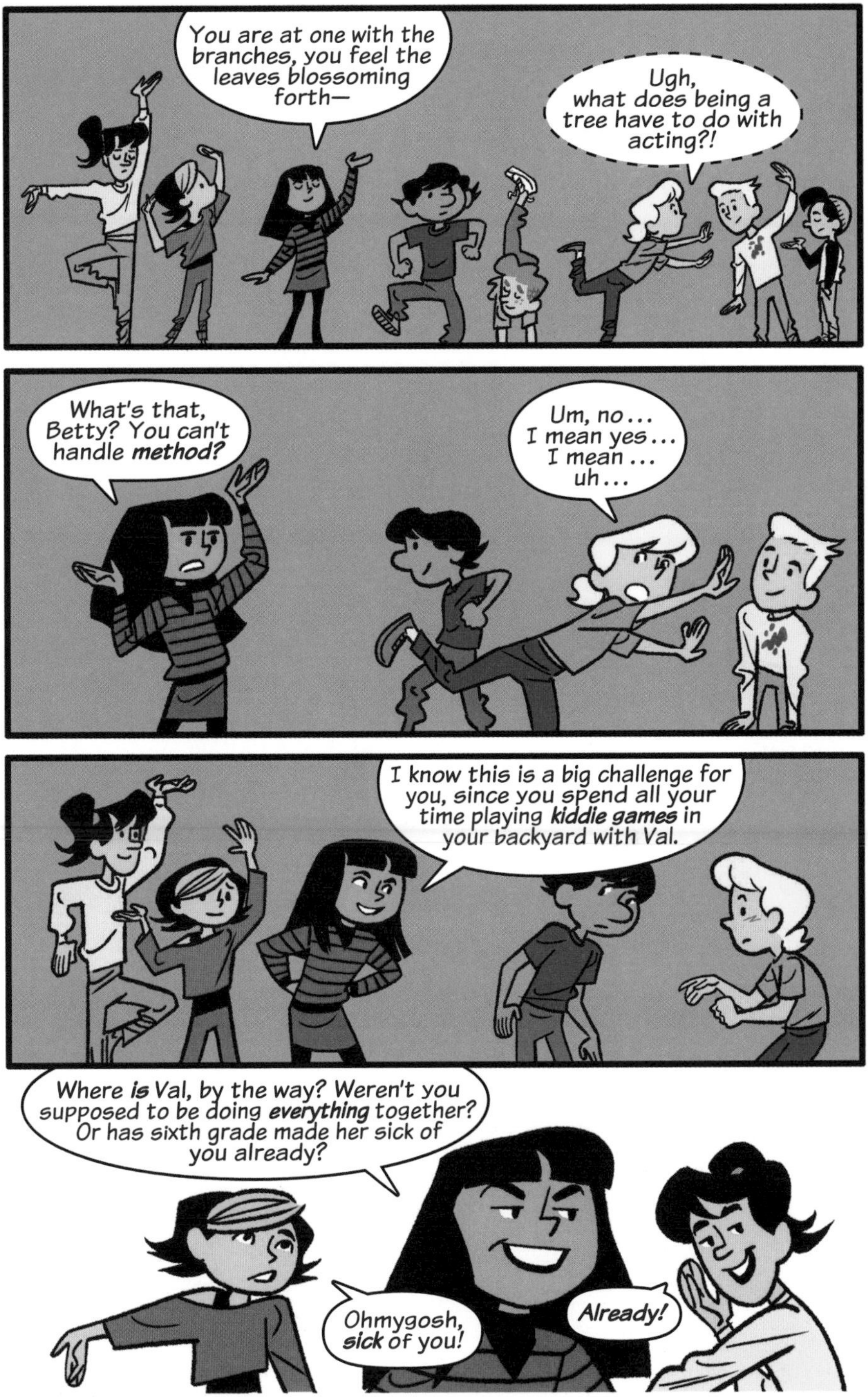
You are at one with the branches, you feel the leaves blossoming forth—
Ugh, what does being a tree have to do with acting?!
What's that, Betty? You can't handle *method?*
Um, no... I mean yes... I mean... uh...
I know this is a big challenge for you, since you spend all your time playing *kiddie games* in your backyard with Val.
Where *is* Val, by the way? Weren't you supposed to be doing *everything* together? Or has sixth grade made her sick of you already?
Ohmygosh, *sick* of you!
Already!

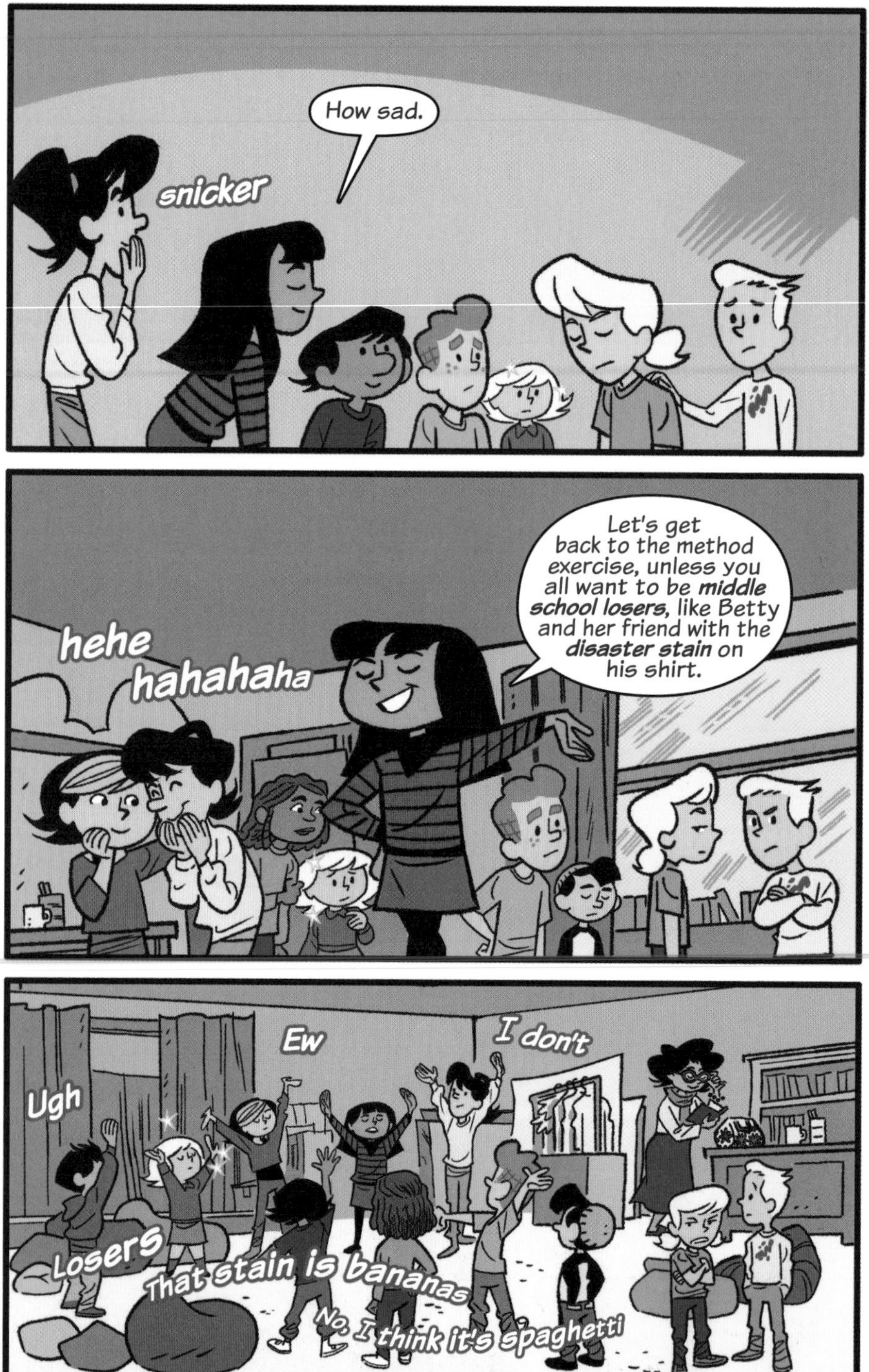
How sad.
snicker
Let's get back to the method exercise, unless you all want to be **middle school losers,** like Betty and her friend with the **disaster stain** on his shirt.
hehe
hahahaha
Ugh
Ew
I don't
Losers
That stain is bananas
No, I think it's spaghetti

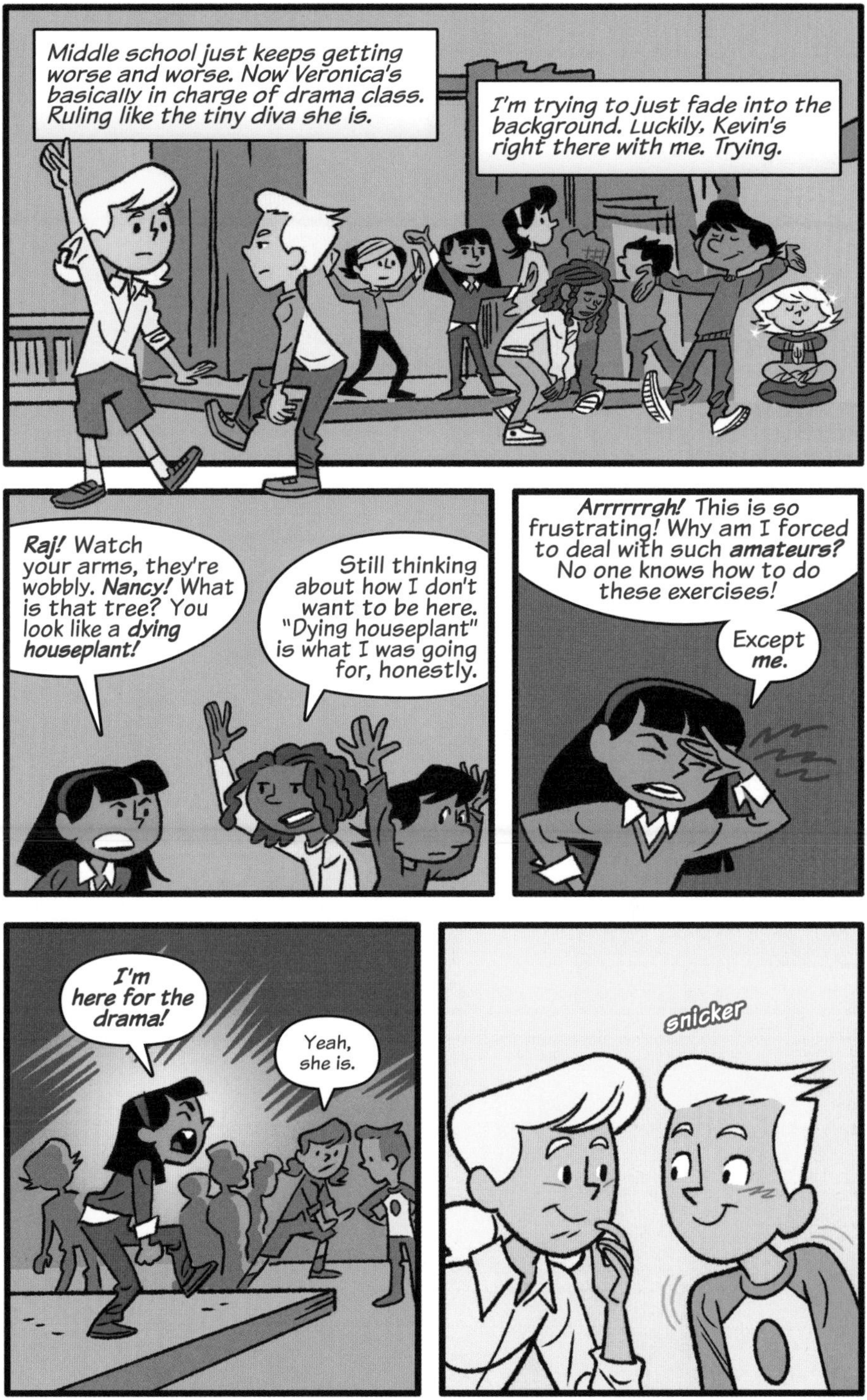

Middle school just keeps getting worse and worse. Now Veronica's basically in charge of drama class. Ruling like the tiny diva she is.
I'm trying to just fade into the background. Luckily, Kevin's right there with me. Trying.
Raj! Watch your arms, they're wobbly. Nancy! What is that tree? You look like a dying houseplant!
Still thinking about how I don't want to be here. "Dying houseplant" is what I was going for, honestly.
Arrrrrrgh! This is so frustrating! Why am I forced to deal with such amateurs? No one knows how to do these exercises!
Except me.
I'm here for the drama!
Yeah, she is.
snicker

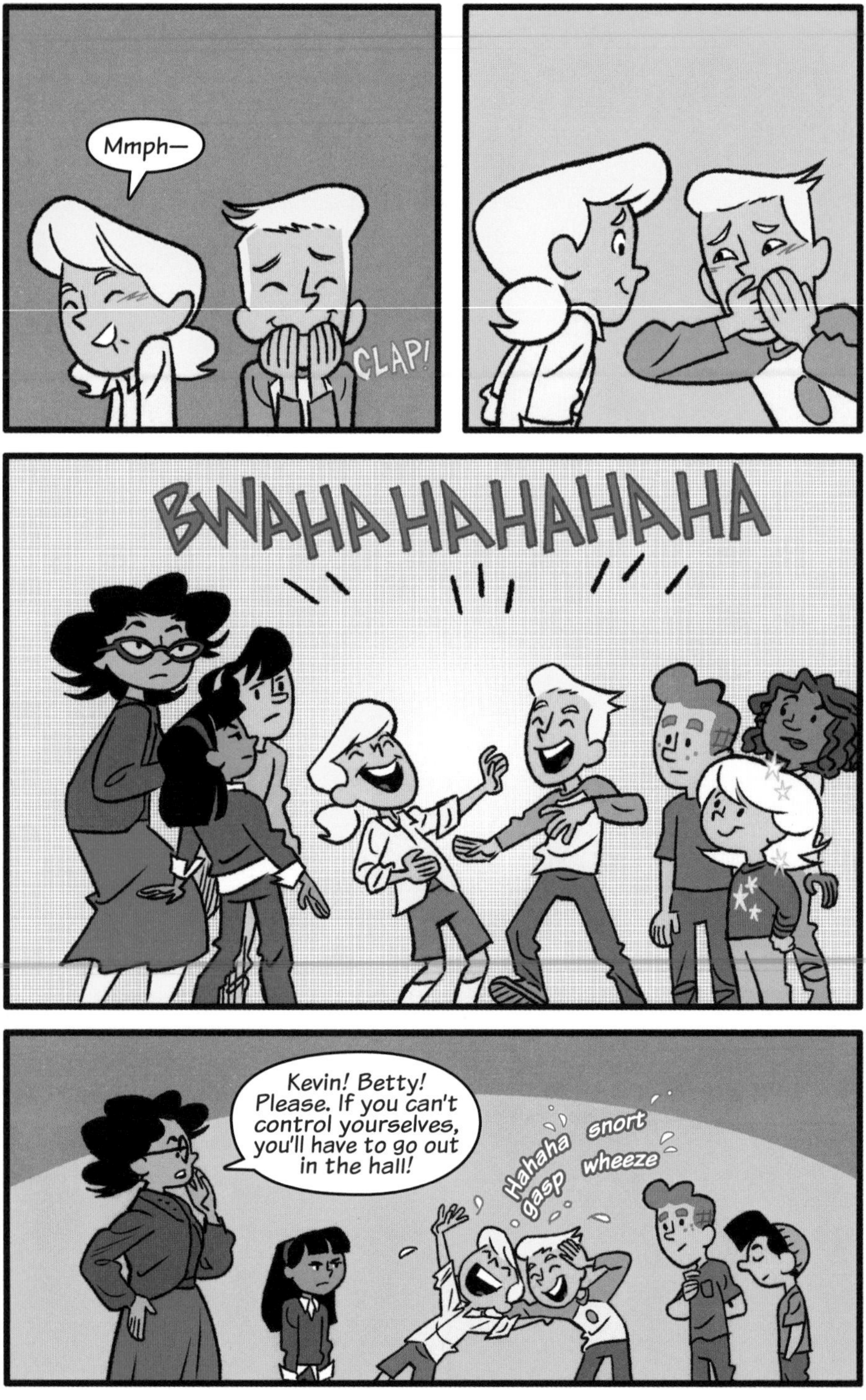
Mmph—
CLAP!
BWAHA HAHAHAHA
Kevin! Betty! Please. If you can't control yourselves, you'll have to go out in the hall!
Hahaha snort
gasp wheeze

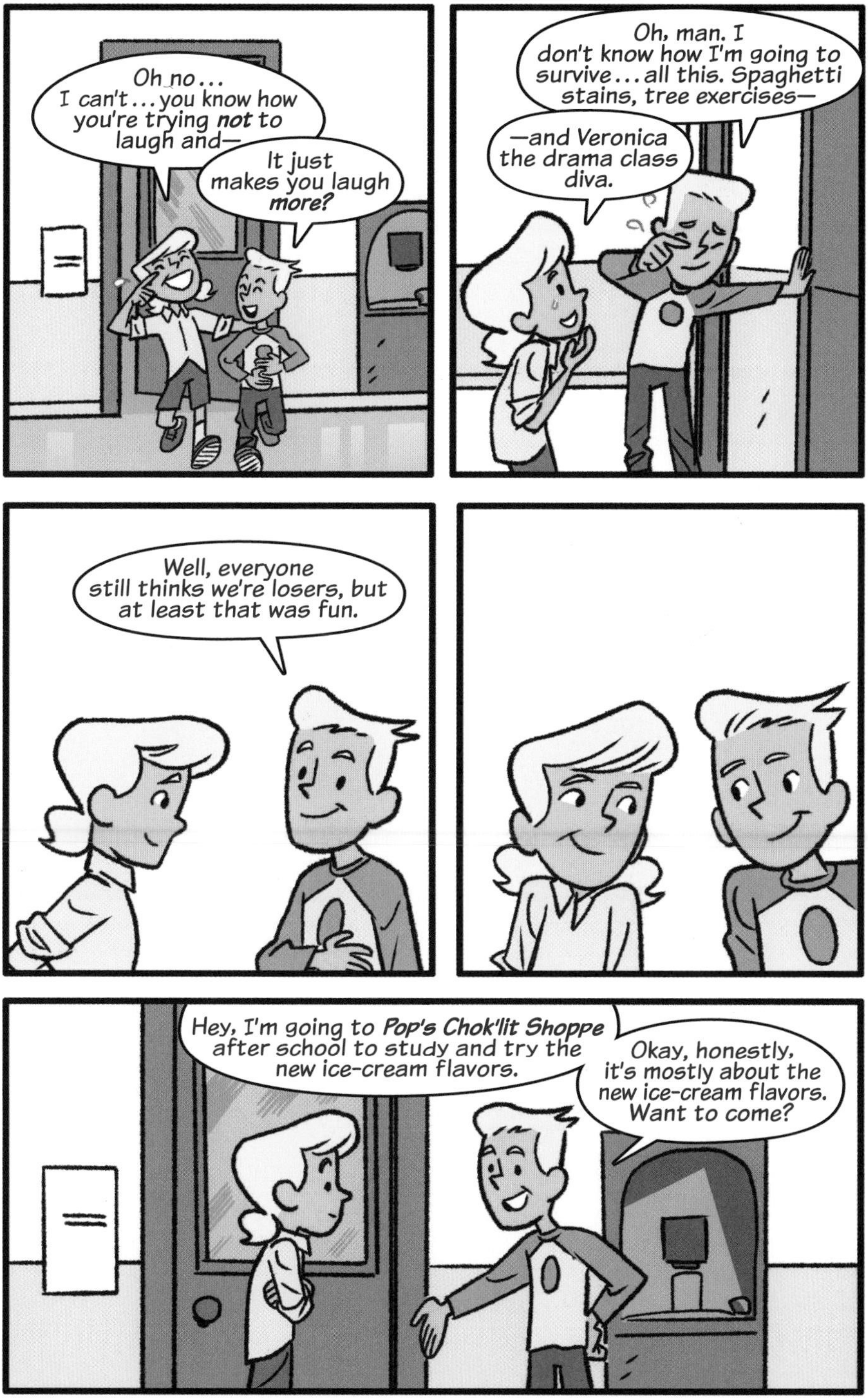
Oh no... I can't... you know how you're trying *not* to laugh and—
It just makes you laugh *more?*
Oh, man. I don't know how I'm going to survive... all this. Spaghetti stains, tree exercises—
—and Veronica the drama class diva.
Well, everyone still thinks we're losers, but at least that was fun.
Hey, I'm going to *Pop's Chok'lit Shoppe* after school to study and try the new ice-cream flavors.
Okay, honestly, it's mostly about the new ice-cream flavors. Want to come?

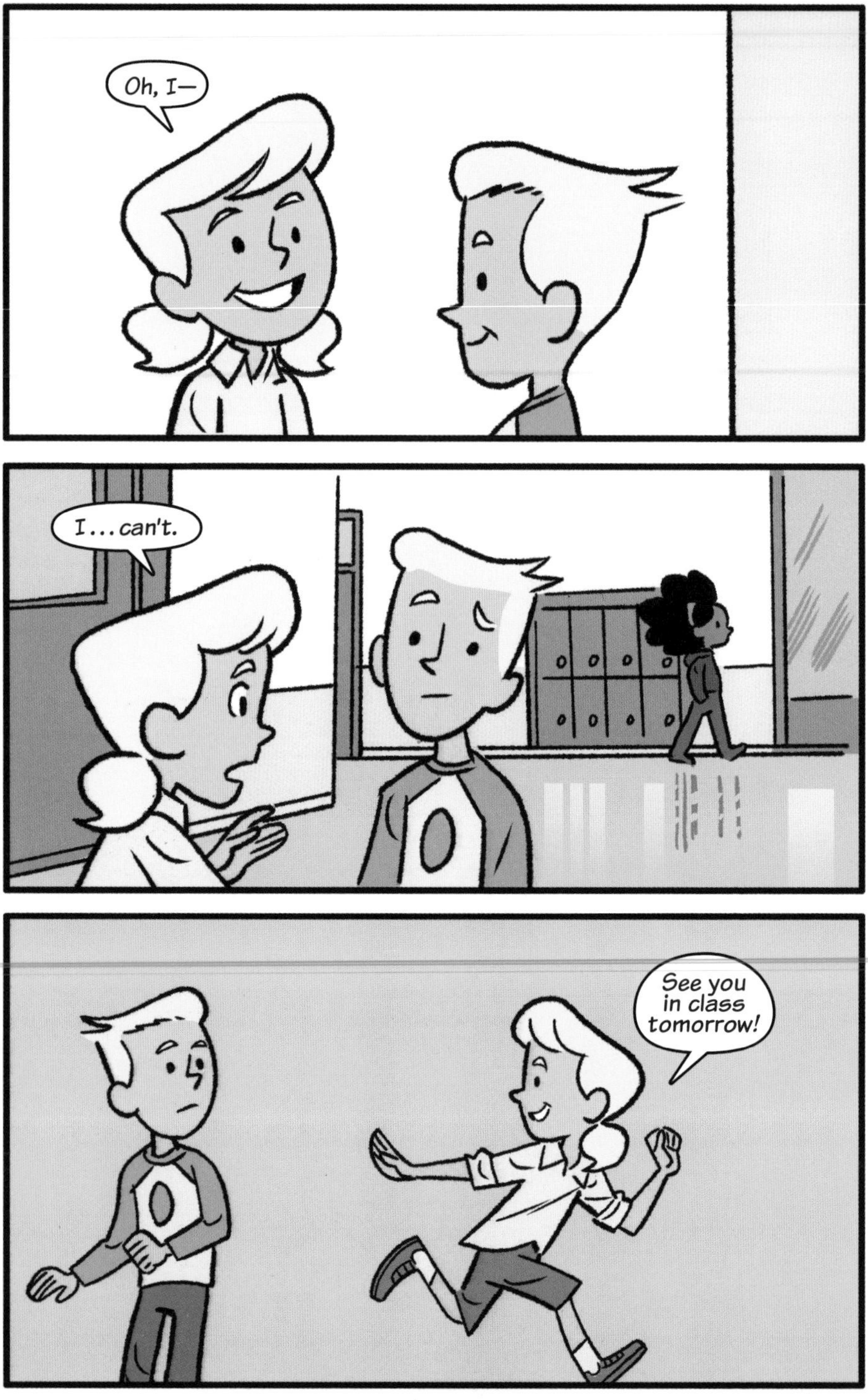
Oh, I—
I...can't.
See you in class tomorrow!

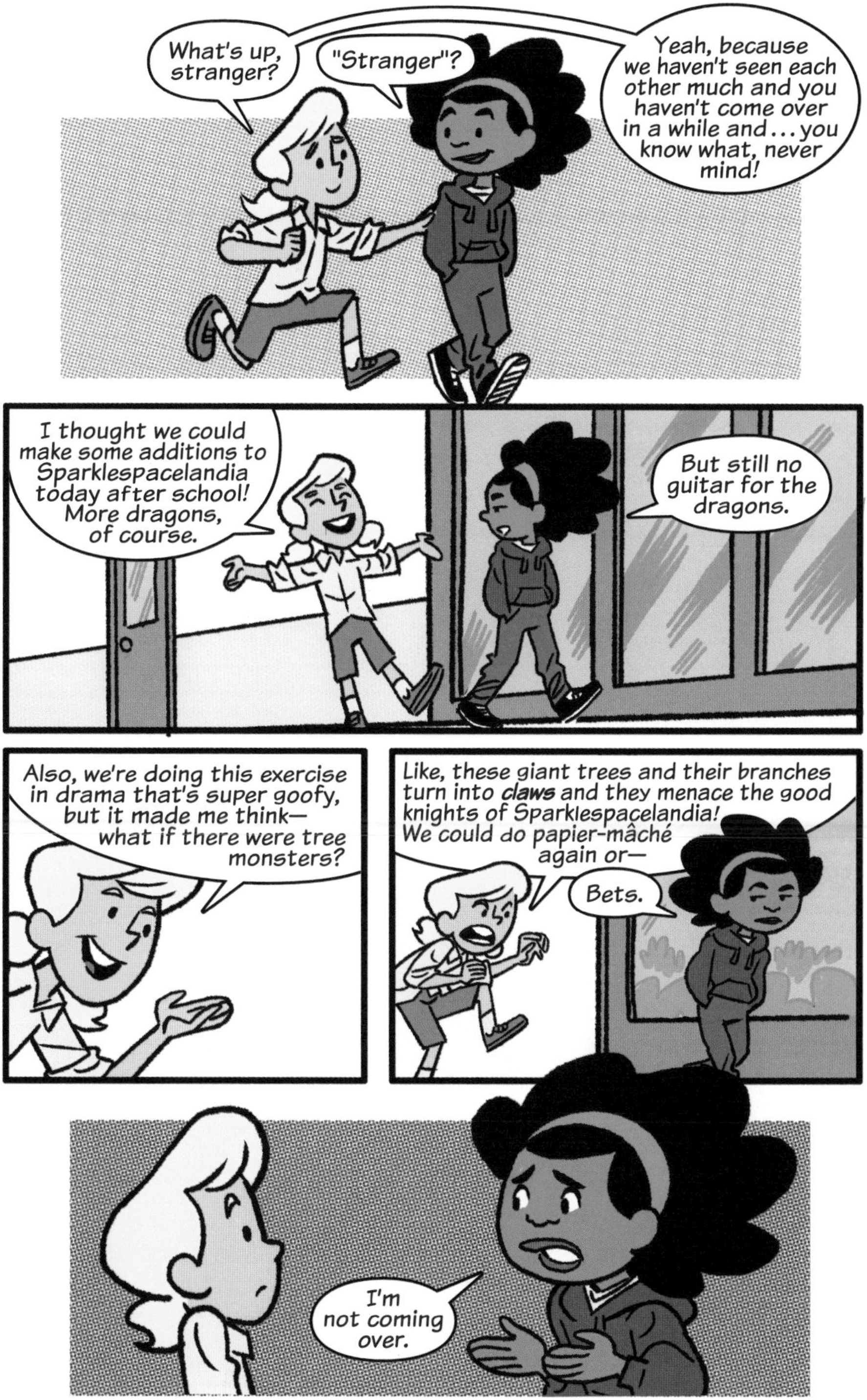
What's up, stranger?
"Stranger"?
Yeah, because we haven't seen each other much and you haven't come over in a while and . . . you know what, never mind!
I thought we could make some additions to Sparklespacelandia today after school! More dragons, of course.
But still no guitar for the dragons.
Also, we're doing this exercise in drama that's super goofy, but it made me think— what if there were tree monsters?
Like, these giant trees and their branches turn into *claws* and they menace the good knights of Sparklespacelandia! We could do papier-mâché again or—
Bets.
I'm not coming over.

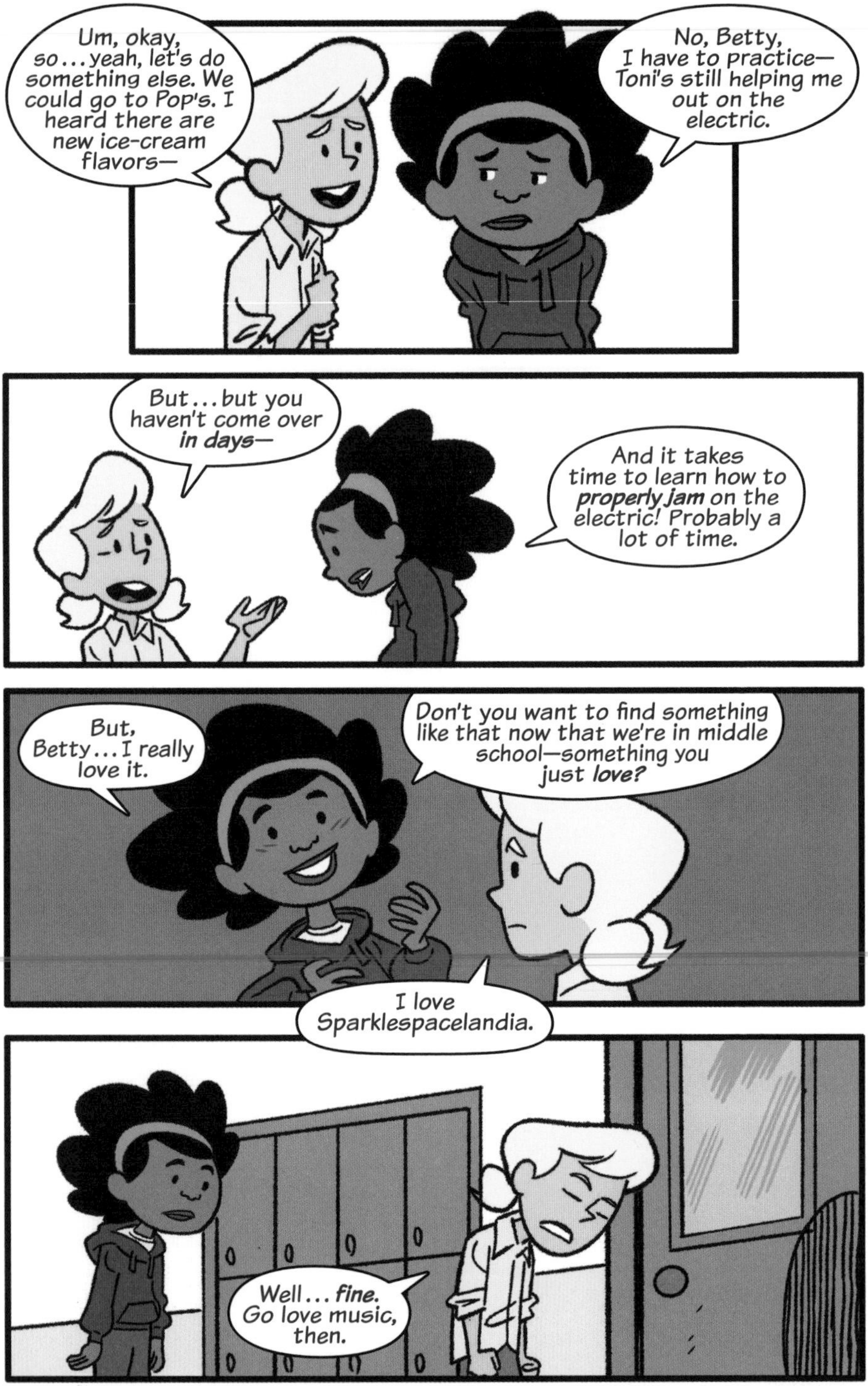

Um, okay, so...yeah, let's do something else. We could go to Pop's. I heard there are new ice-cream flavors—
No, Betty, I have to practice— Toni's still helping me out on the electric.
But...but you haven't come over *in days*—
And it takes time to learn how to ***properly jam*** on the electric! Probably a lot of time.
But, Betty...I really love it.
Don't you want to find something like that now that we're in middle school—something you just ***love?***
I love Sparklespacelandia.
Well... ***fine.*** Go love music, then.

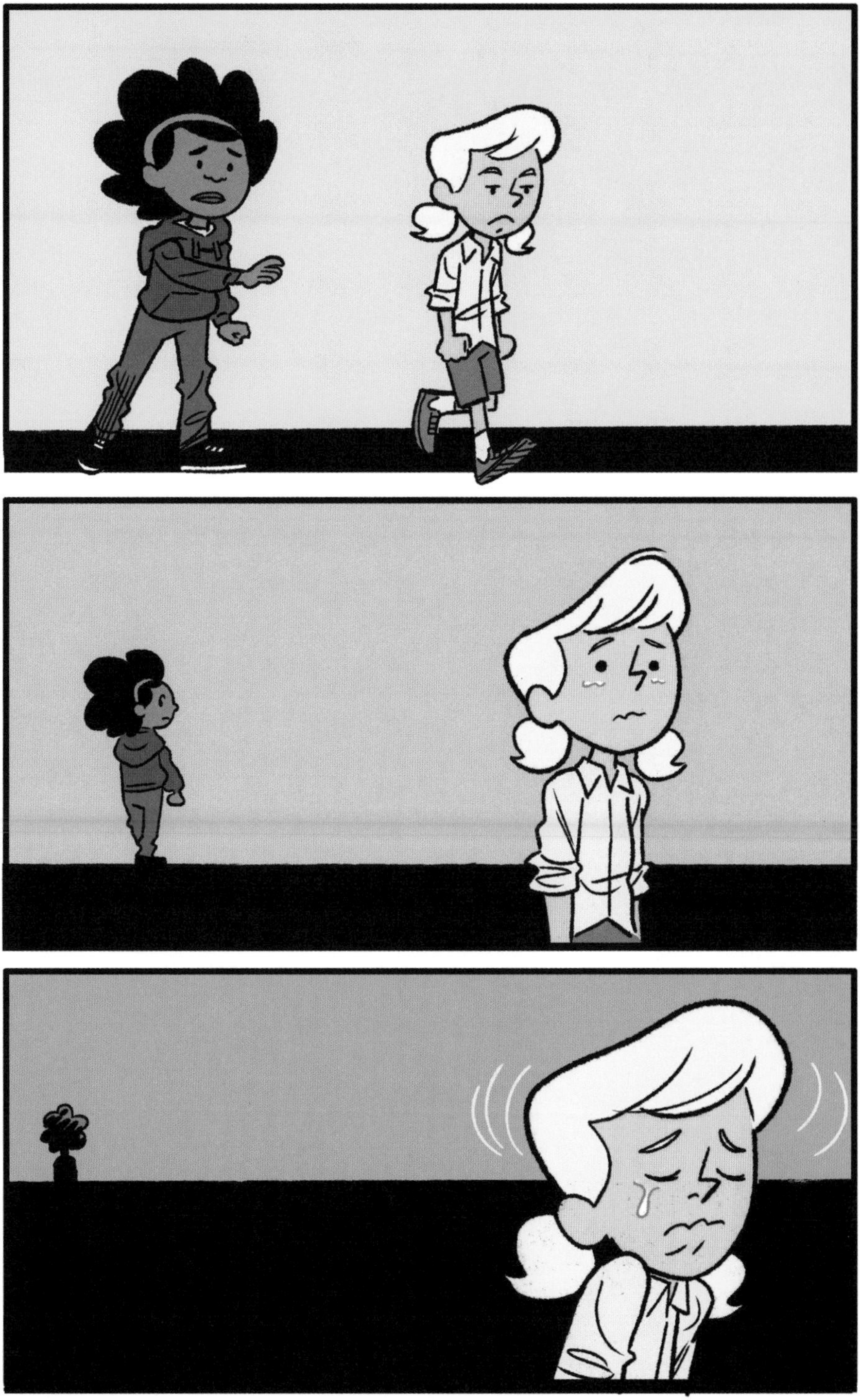

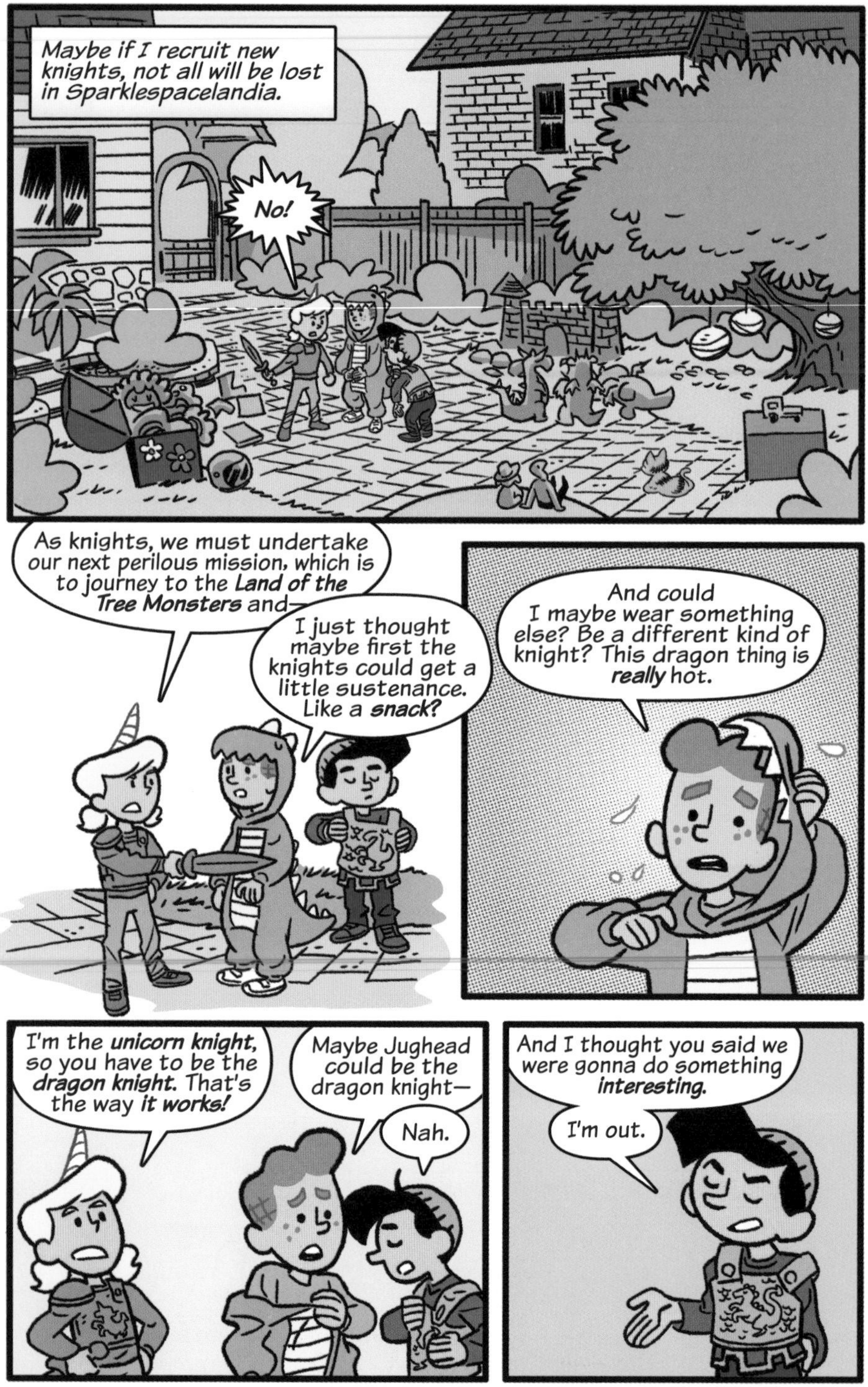
Maybe if I recruit new knights, not all will be lost in Sparklespacelandia.
No!
As knights, we must undertake our next perilous mission, which is to journey to the *Land of the Tree Monsters* and—
I just thought maybe first the knights could get a little sustenance. Like a *snack?*
And could I maybe wear something else? Be a different kind of knight? This dragon thing is *really* hot.
I'm the *unicorn knight*, so you have to be the *dragon knight*. That's the way *it works!*
Maybe Jughead could be the dragon knight—
Nah.
And I thought you said we were gonna do something *interesting*.
I'm out.

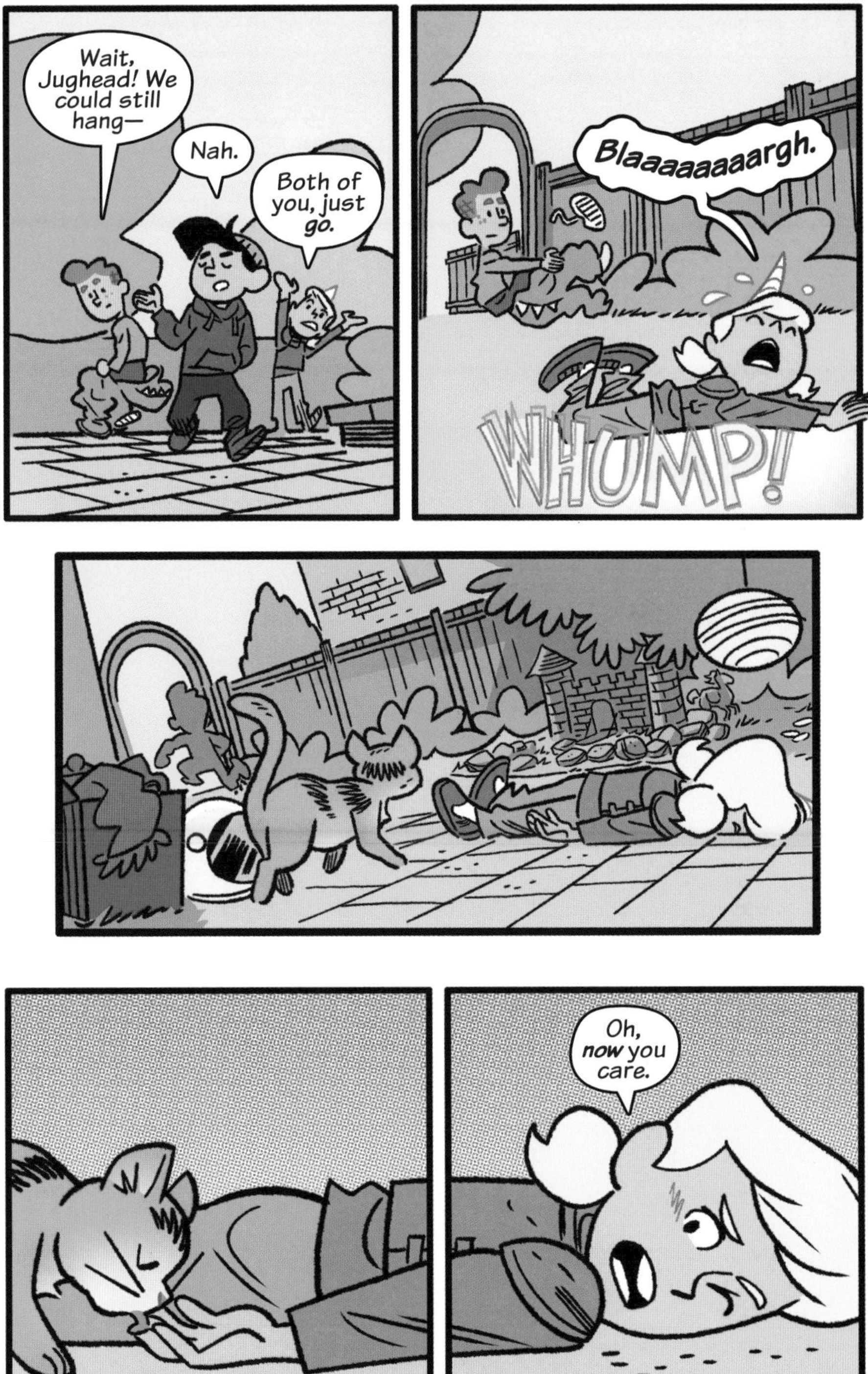

Wait, Jughead! We could still hang—
Nah.
Both of you, just *go.*
Blaaaaaaaaargh.
WHOMP!
Oh, *now* you care.

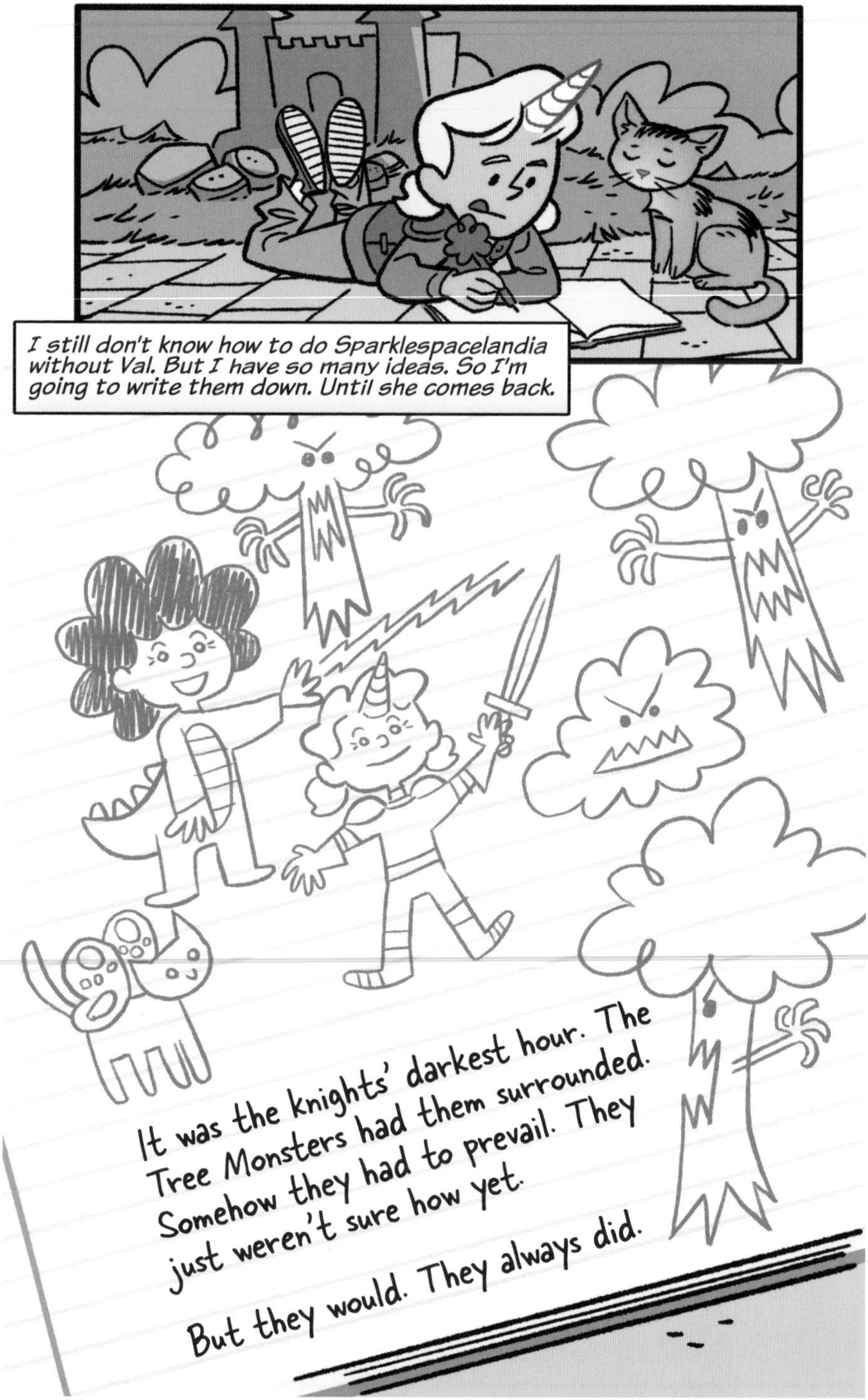
I still don't know how to do Sparklespacelandia without Val. But I have so many ideas. So I'm going to write them down. Until she comes back.
It was the knights' darkest hour. The Tree Monsters had them surrounded. Somehow they had to prevail. They just weren't sure how yet.
But they would. They always did.

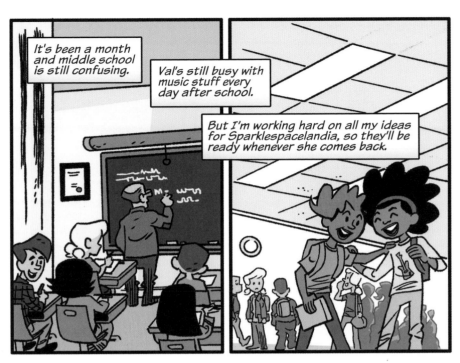

It's been a month and middle school is still confusing.

Val's still busy with music stuff every day after school.

But I'm working hard on all my ideas for Sparklespacelandia, so they'll be ready whenever she comes back.

Little thespians, we are still perfecting the tree exercise. Today's outdoor classroom is meant to make you feel truly at one with the trees! Take it all in!

Ugh, drama losers.

Come on, my sweetie heart Reggie! *Be the tree!* Find that creative spark I know exists within—

53

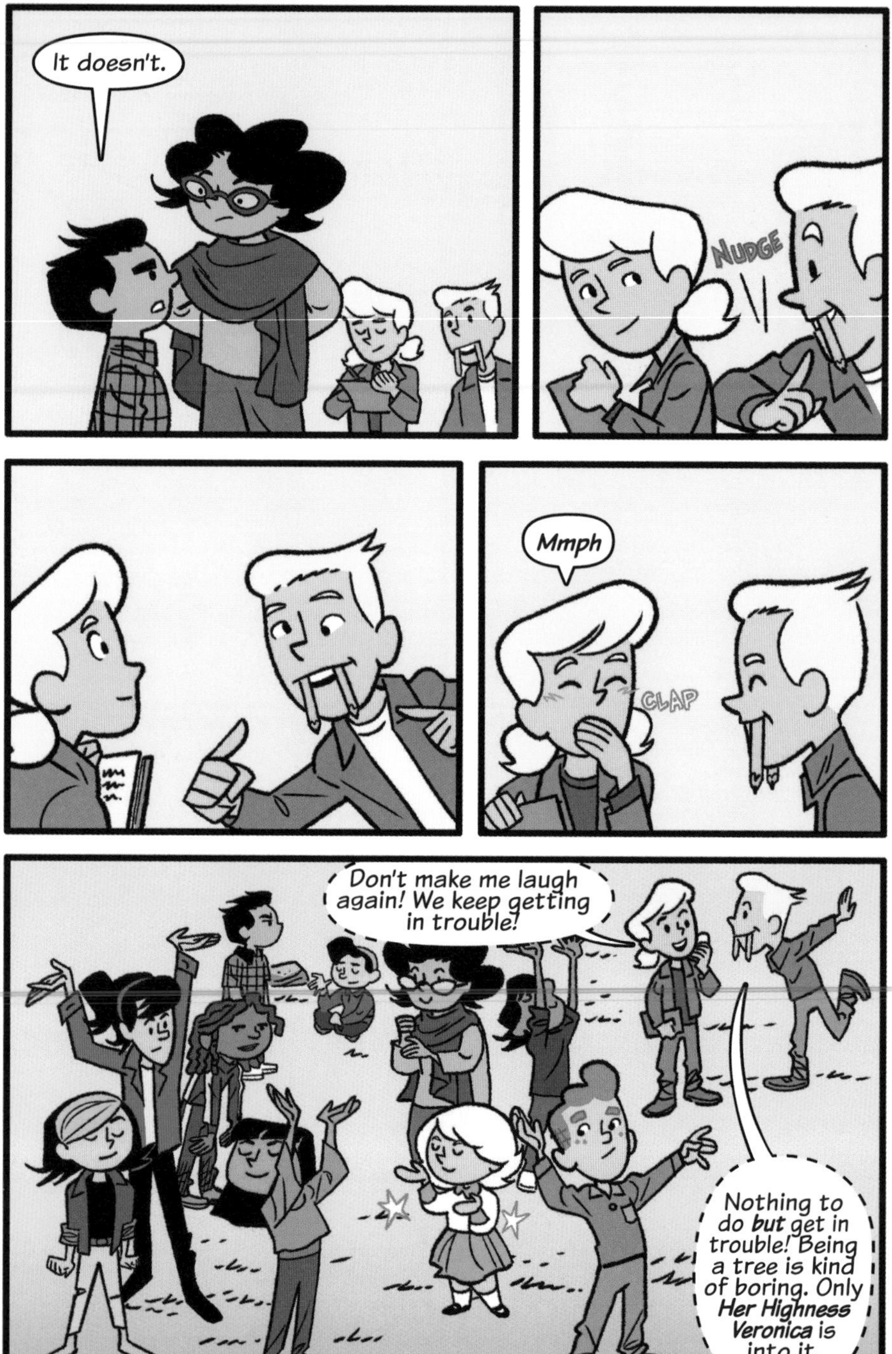
It doesn't.
NUDGE
Mmph
CLAP
Don't make me laugh again! We keep getting in trouble!
Nothing to do **but** get in trouble! Being a tree is kind of boring. Only ***Her Highness Veronica*** is into it.

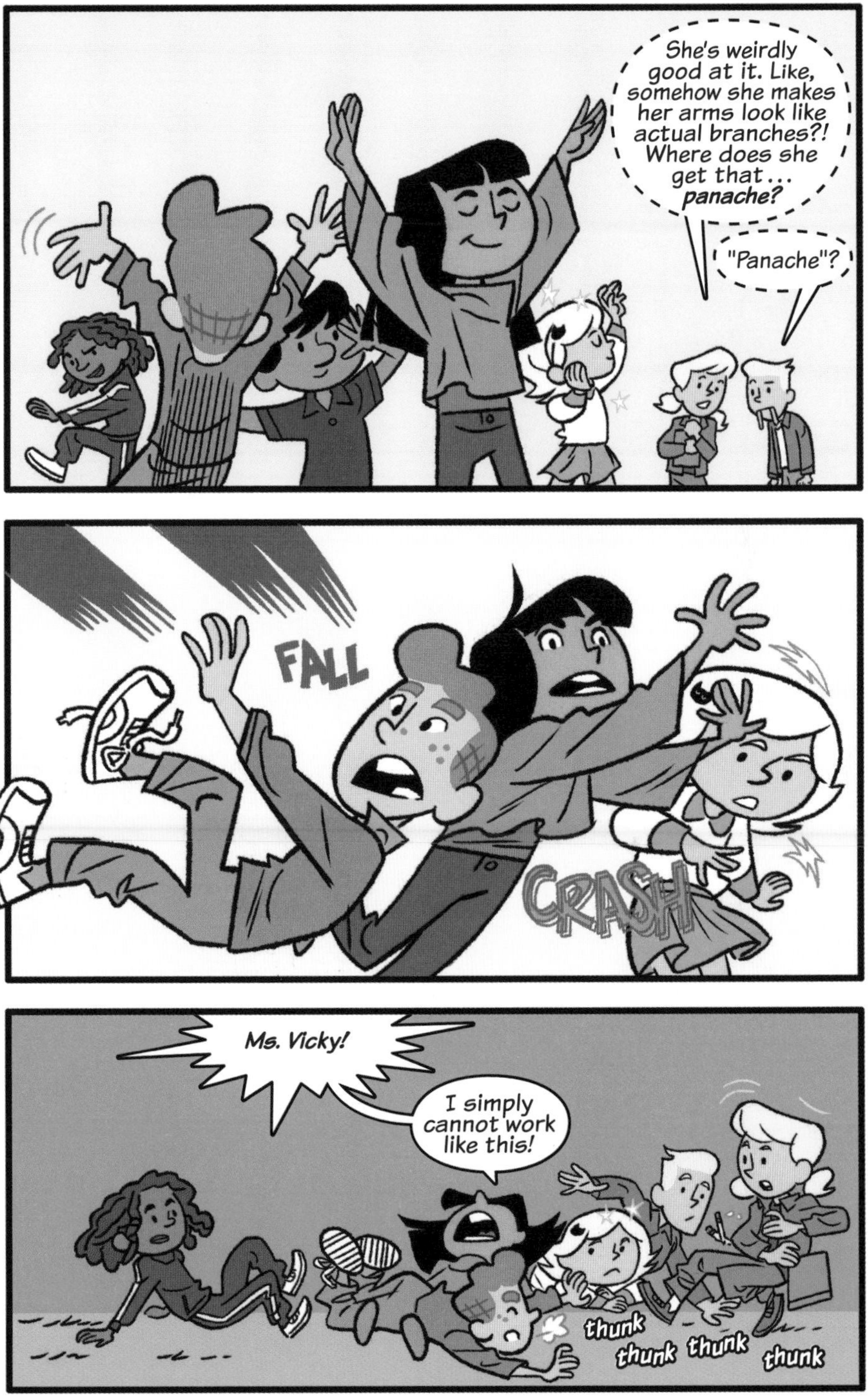
She's weirdly good at it. Like, somehow she makes her arms look like actual branches?! Where does she get that... *panache?*
"Panache"?
FALL
CRASH
Ms. Vicky!
I simply cannot work like this!
thunk
thunk
thunk
thunk

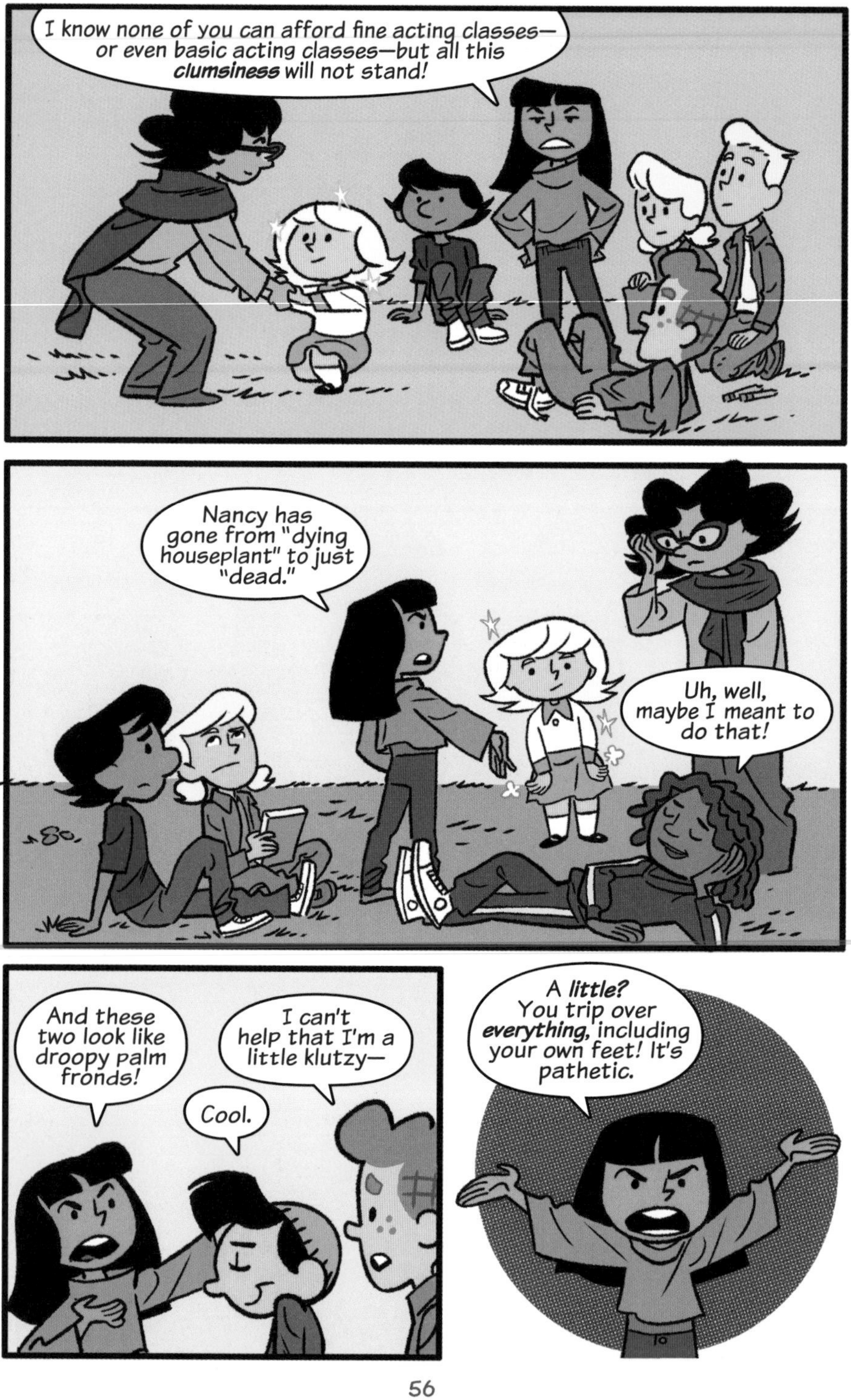

I know none of you can afford fine acting classes—or even basic acting classes—but all this ***clumsiness*** will not stand!
Nancy has gone from "dying houseplant" to just "dead."
Uh, well, maybe I meant to do that!
And these two look like droopy palm fronds!
I can't help that I'm a little klutzy—
Cool.
A ***little?*** You trip over ***everything,*** including your own feet! It's pathetic.

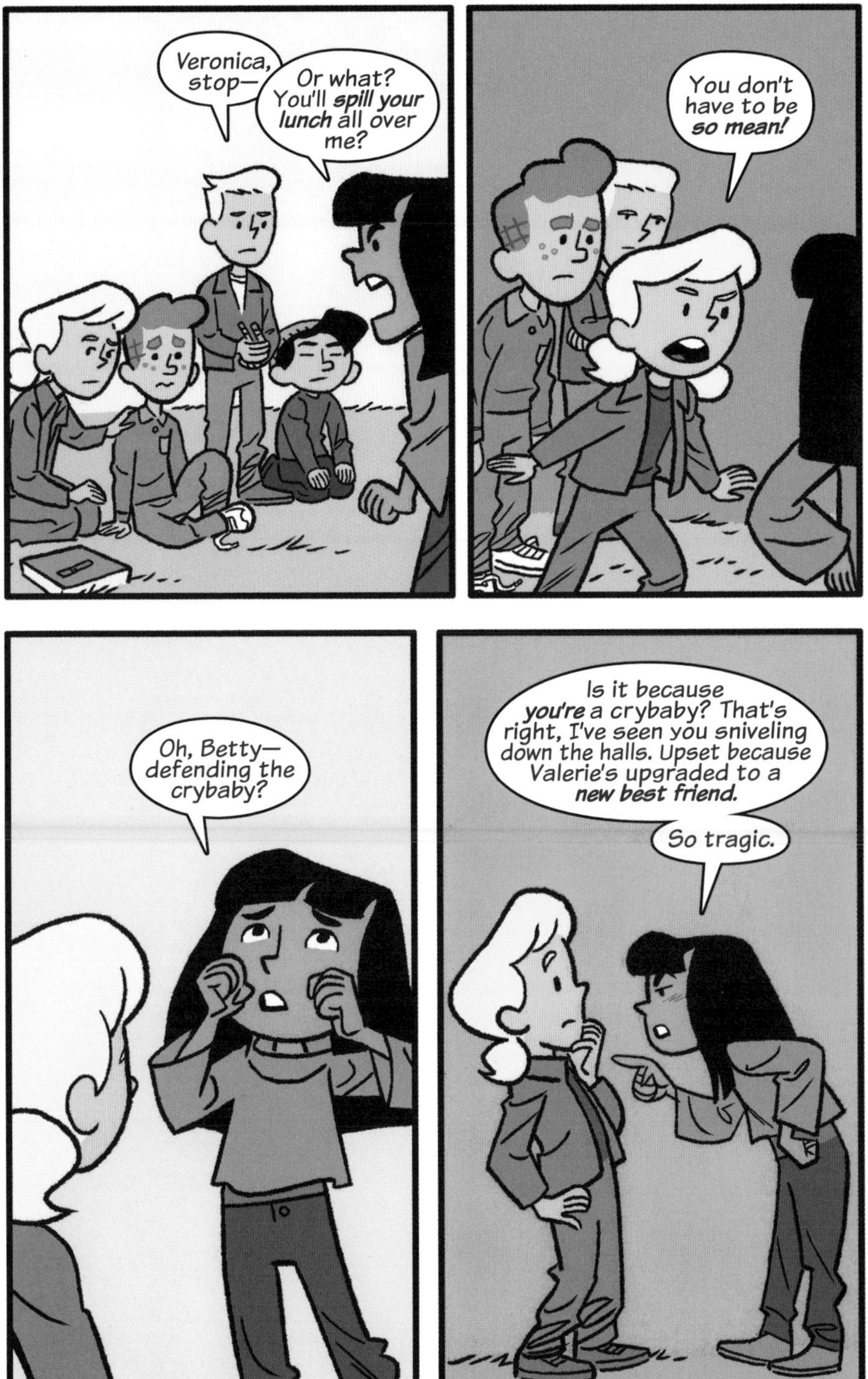
Veronica, stop—
Or what? You'll **spill your lunch** all over me?
You don't have to be **so mean!**
Oh, Betty— defending the crybaby?
Is it because **you're** a crybaby? That's right, I've seen you sniveling down the halls. Upset because Valerie's upgraded to a **new best friend.**
So tragic.

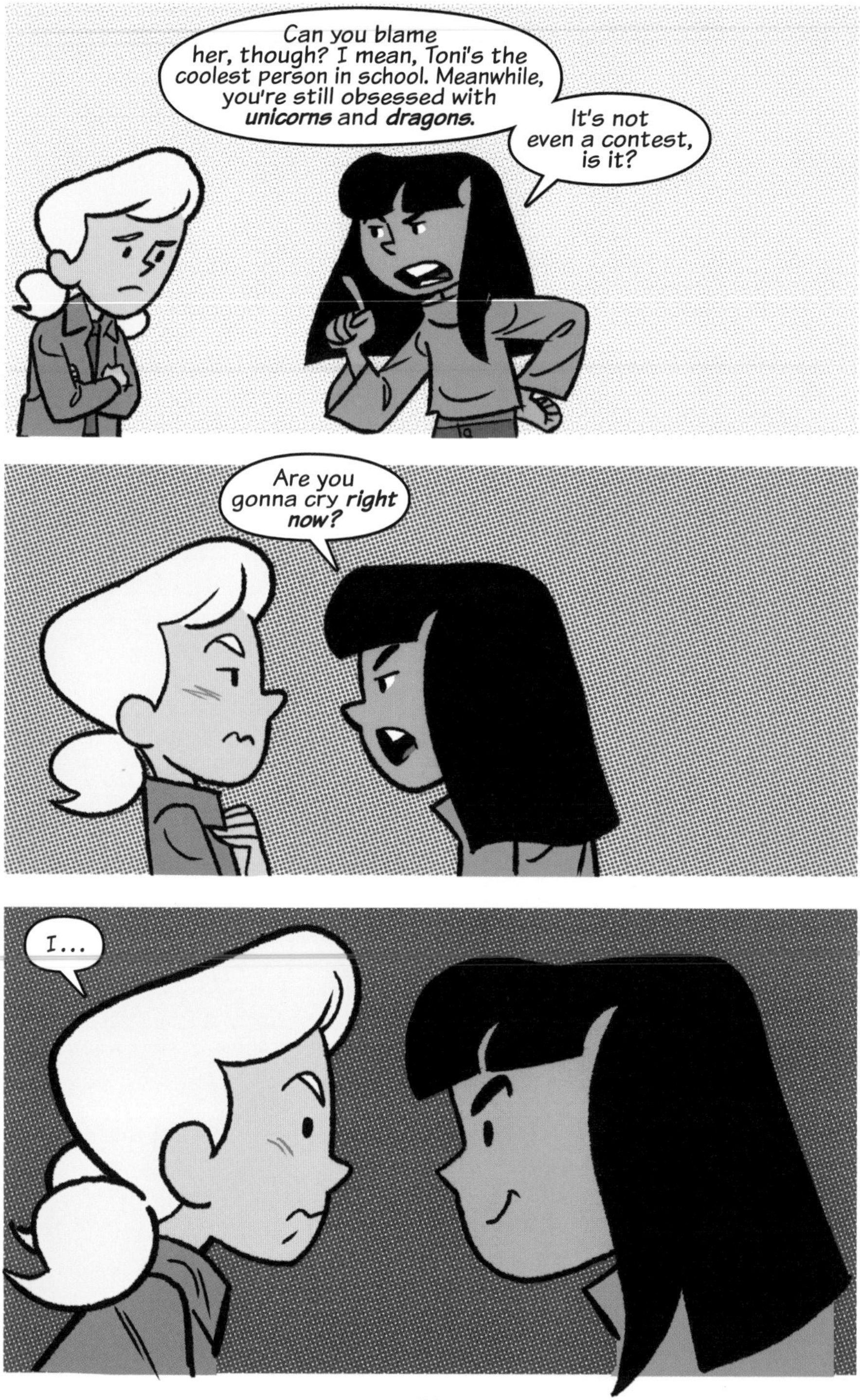
Can you blame her, though? I mean, Toni's the coolest person in school. Meanwhile, you're still obsessed with **unicorns** and **dragons.**
It's not even a contest, is it?
Are you gonna cry **right now?**
I...

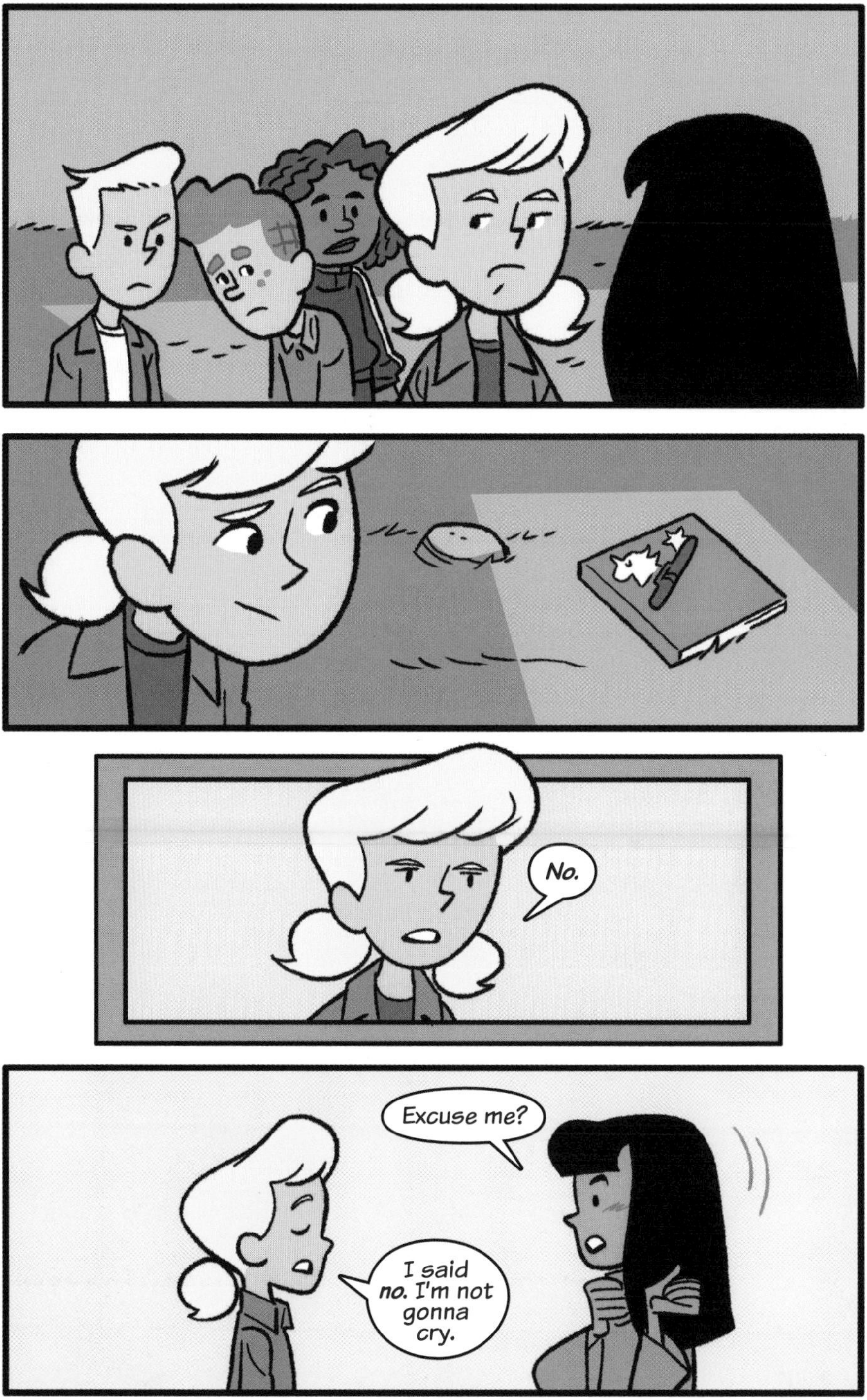
No.
Excuse me?
I said *no.* I'm not gonna cry.

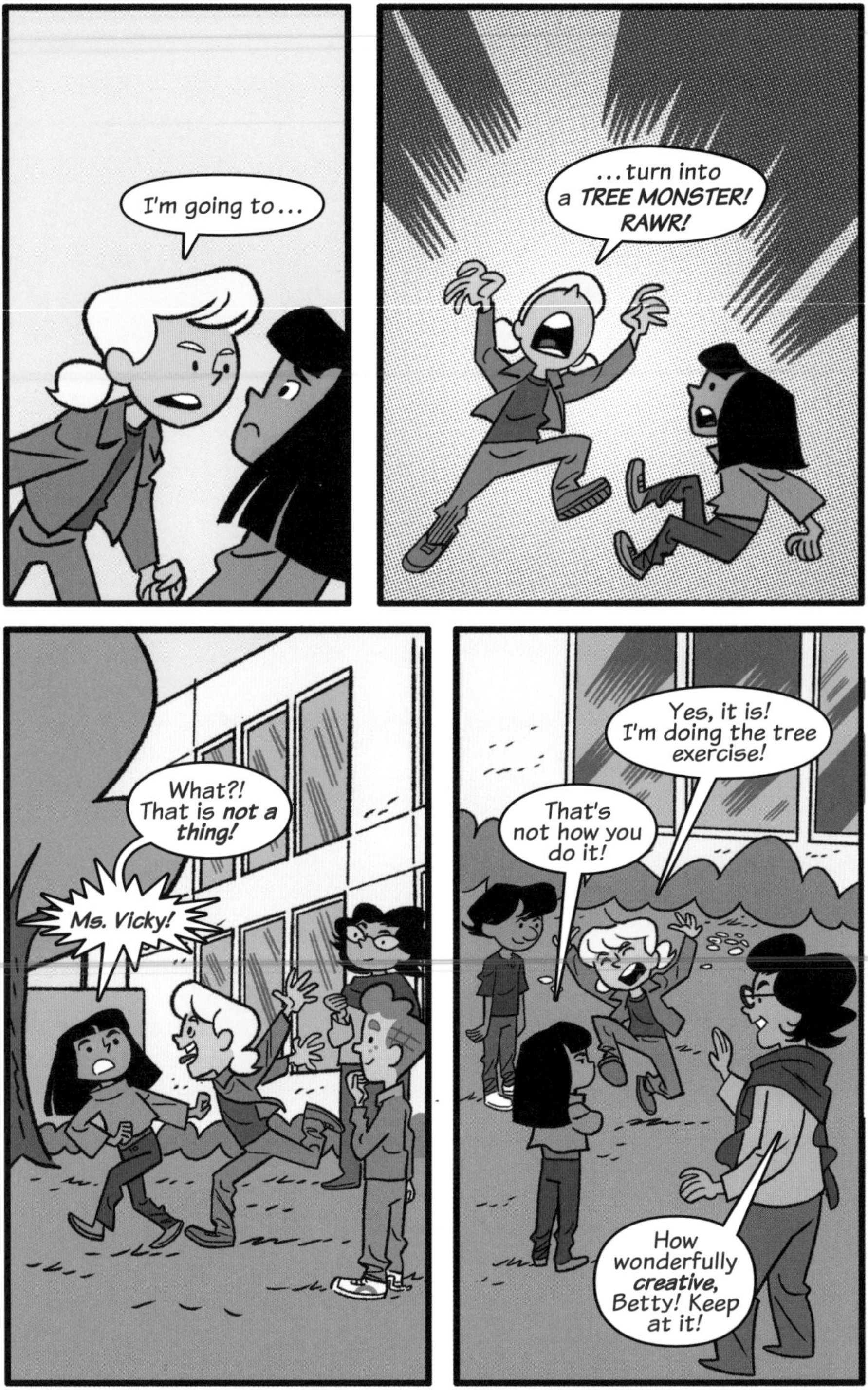
I'm going to...
...turn into a TREE MONSTER! RAWR!
Ms. Vicky!
What?! That is not a thing!
Yes, it is! I'm doing the tree exercise!
That's not how you do it!
How wonderfully creative, Betty! Keep at it!

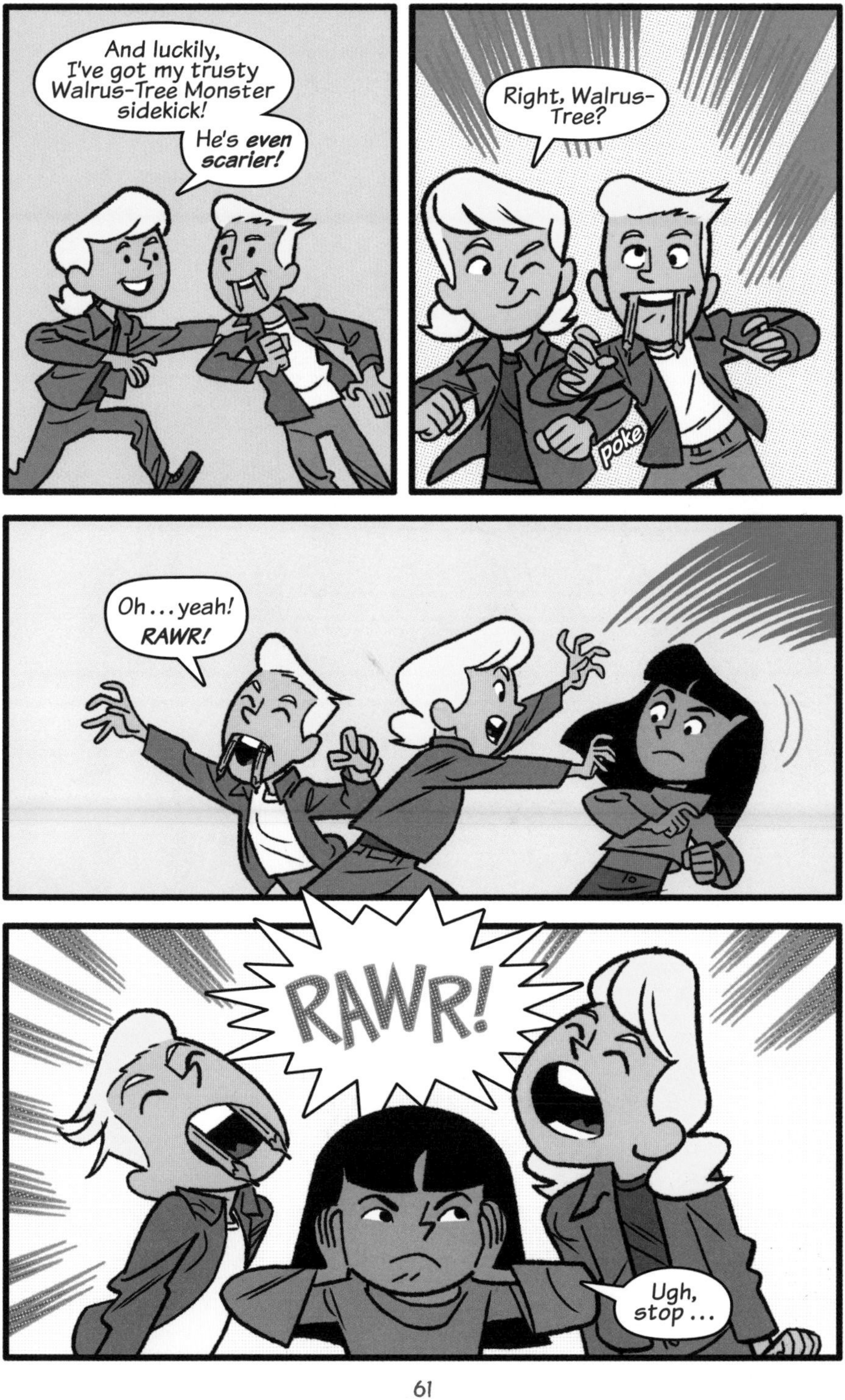
And luckily, I've got my trusty Walrus-Tree Monster sidekick!
He's *even* scarier!
Right, Walrus-Tree?
poke
Oh . . . yeah! **RAWR!**
RAWR!
Ugh, stop . . .

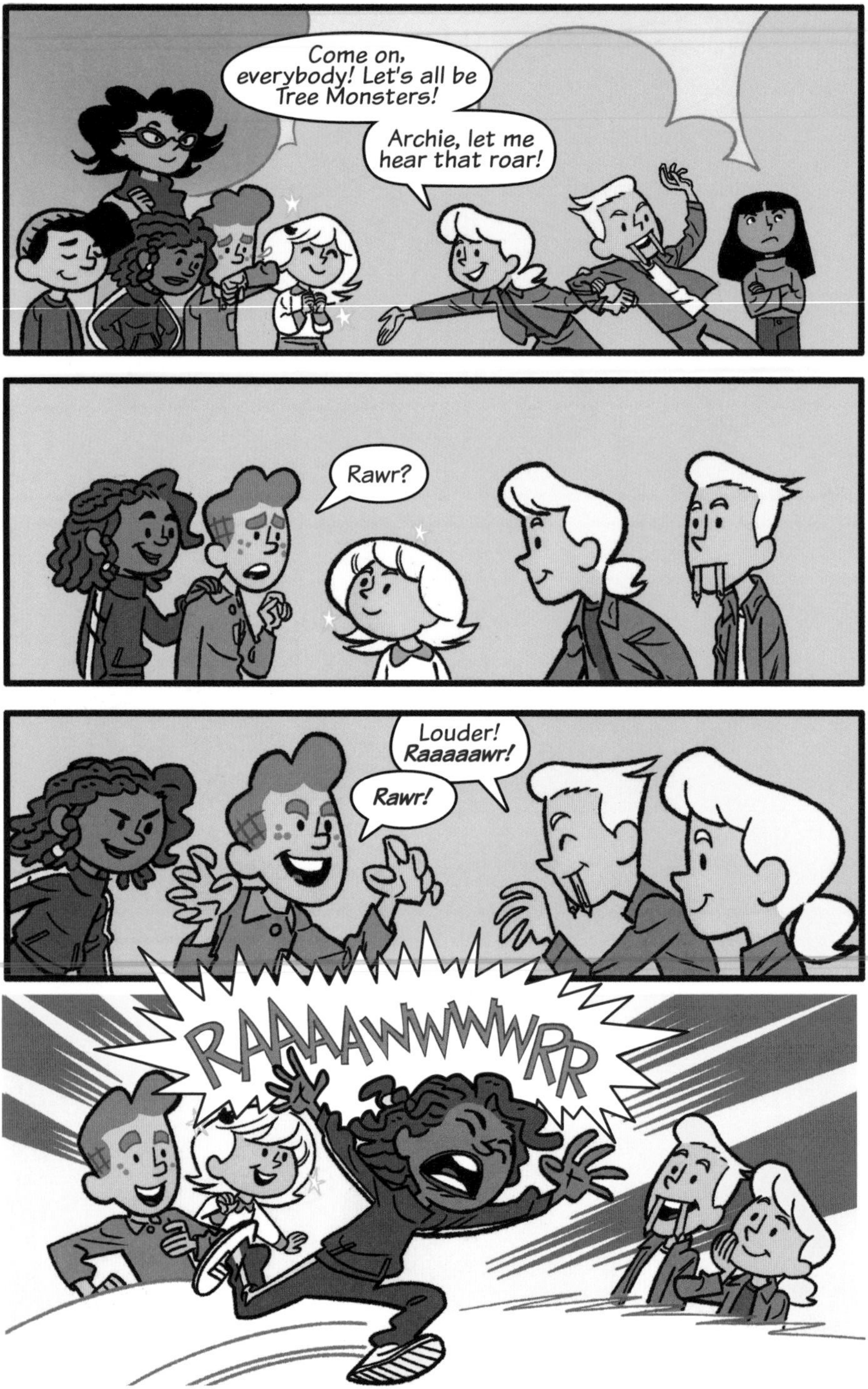
Come on, everybody! Let's all be Tree Monsters!
Archie, let me hear that roar!
Rawr?
Louder! Raaaaawr!
Rawr!
RAAAAWWWWRR

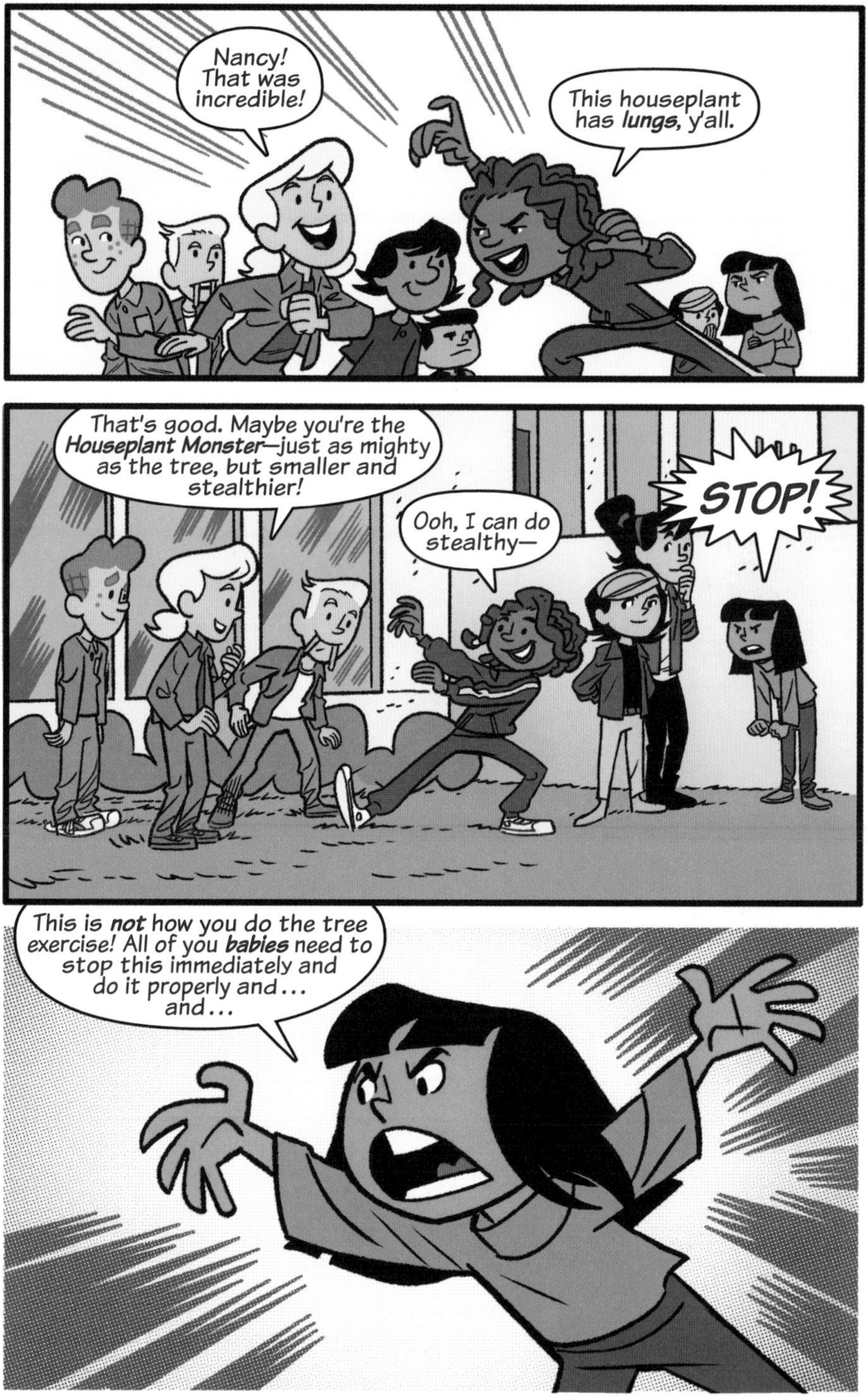
Nancy! That was incredible!
This houseplant has ***lungs***, y'all.
That's good. Maybe you're the ***Houseplant Monster***—just as mighty as the tree, but smaller and stealthier!
Ooh, I can do stealthy—
STOP!
This is ***not*** how you do the tree exercise! All of you ***babies*** need to stop this immediately and do it properly and... and...

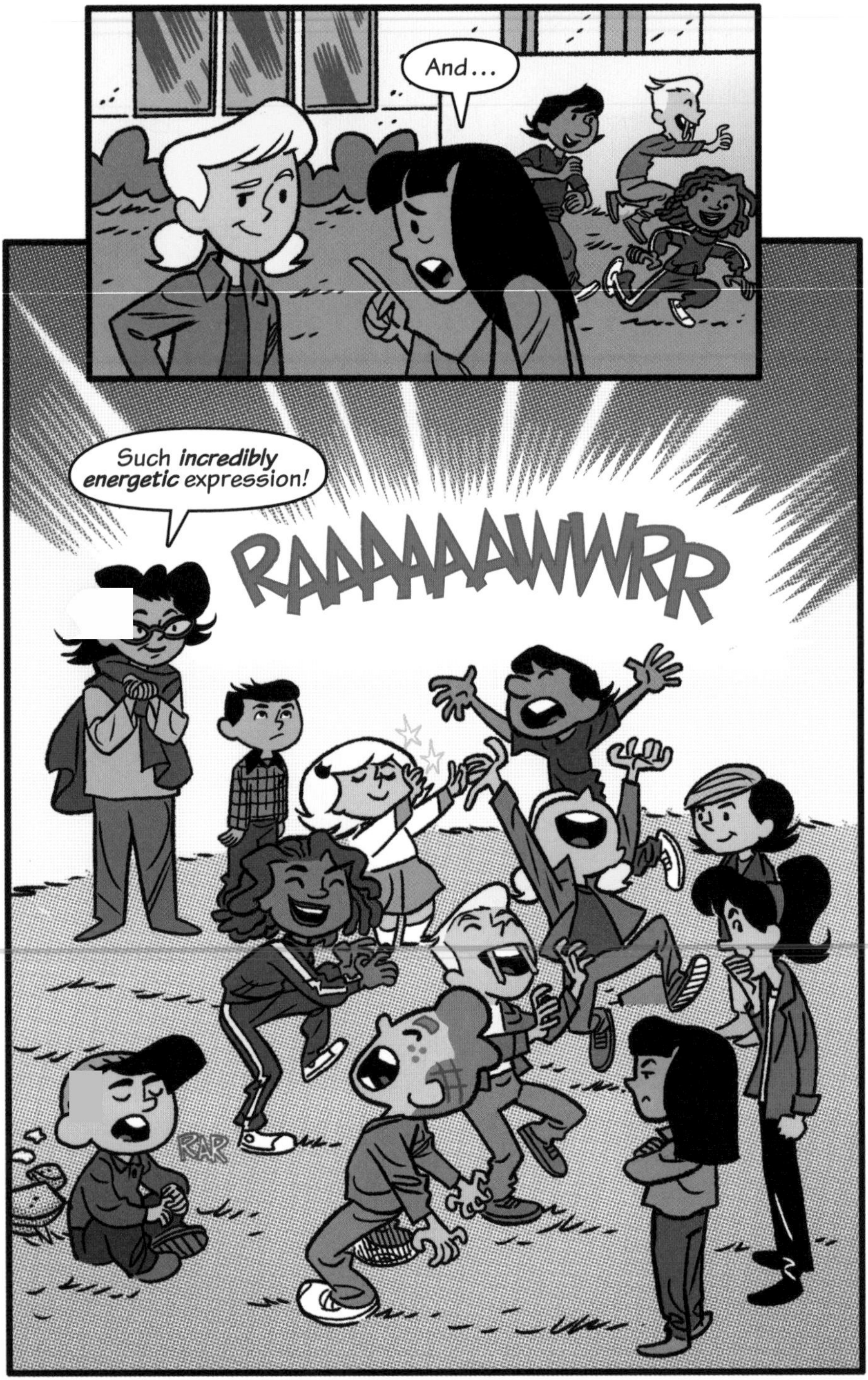

And...
Such *incredibly energetic* expression!
RAAAAAAWWRR
RAR

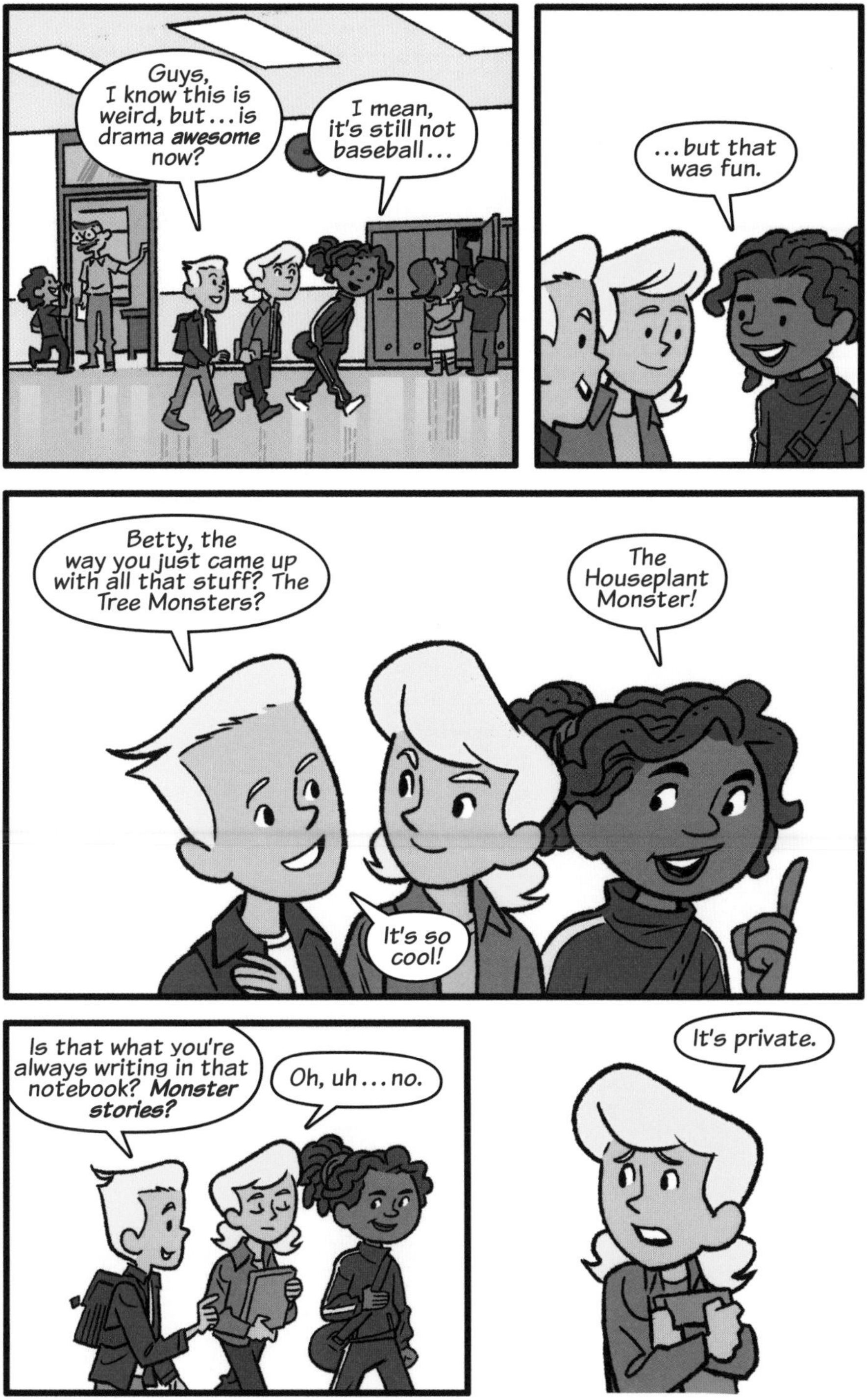

Guys, I know this is weird, but... is drama ***awesome*** now?
I mean, it's still not baseball...
...but that was fun.
Betty, the way you just came up with all that stuff? The Tree Monsters?
The Houseplant Monster!
It's so cool!
Is that what you're always writing in that notebook? ***Monster stories?***
Oh, uh... no.
It's private.

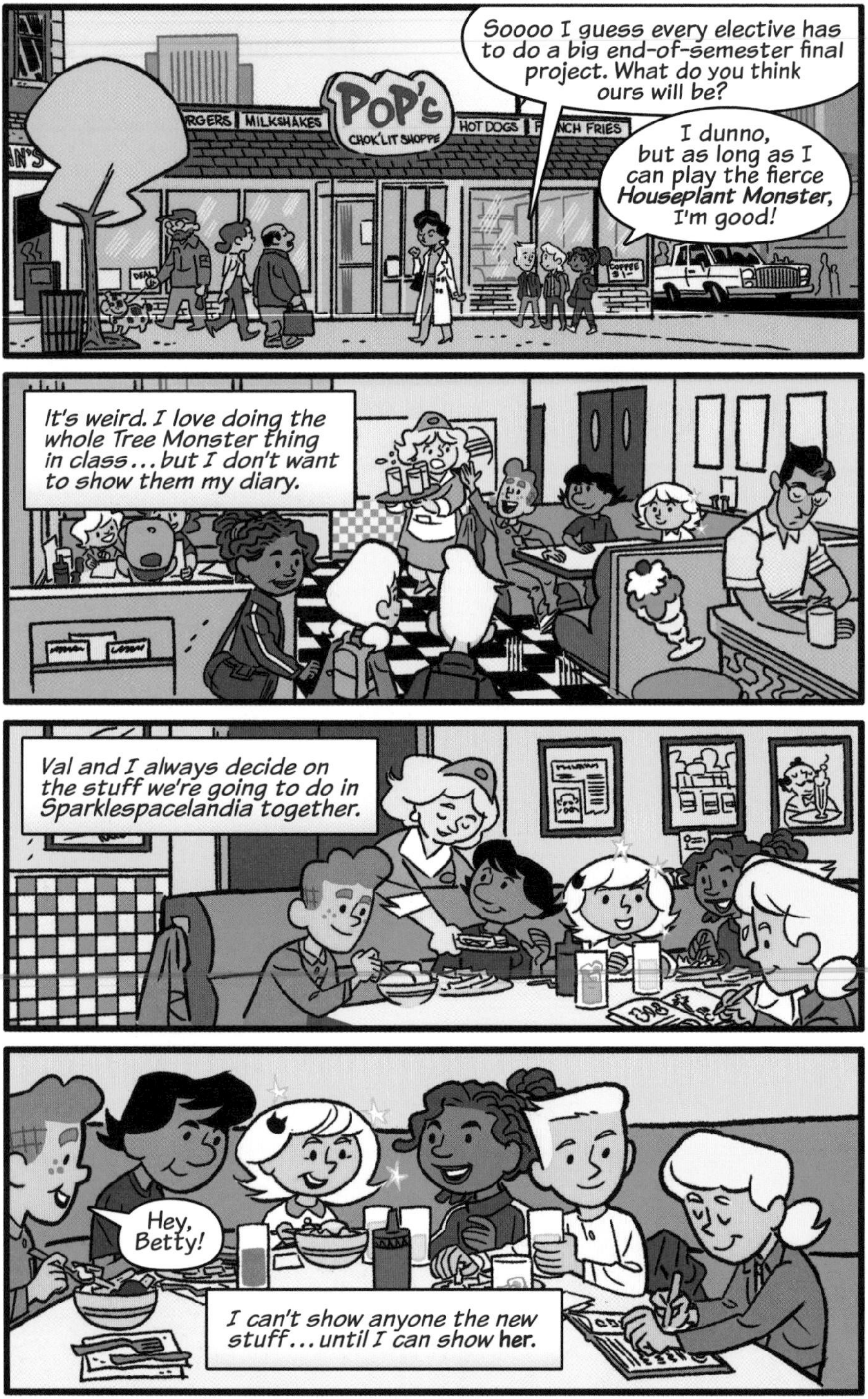
POP'S
CHOK'LIT SHOPPE
MILKSHAKES
HOT DOGS
Soooo I guess every elective has to do a big end-of-semester final project. What do you think ours will be?
I dunno, but as long as I can play the fierce Houseplant Monster, I'm good!
It's weird. I love doing the whole Tree Monster thing in class... but I don't want to show them my diary.
Val and I always decide on the stuff we're going to do in Sparklespacelandia together.
Hey, Betty!
I can't show anyone the new stuff... until I can show her.

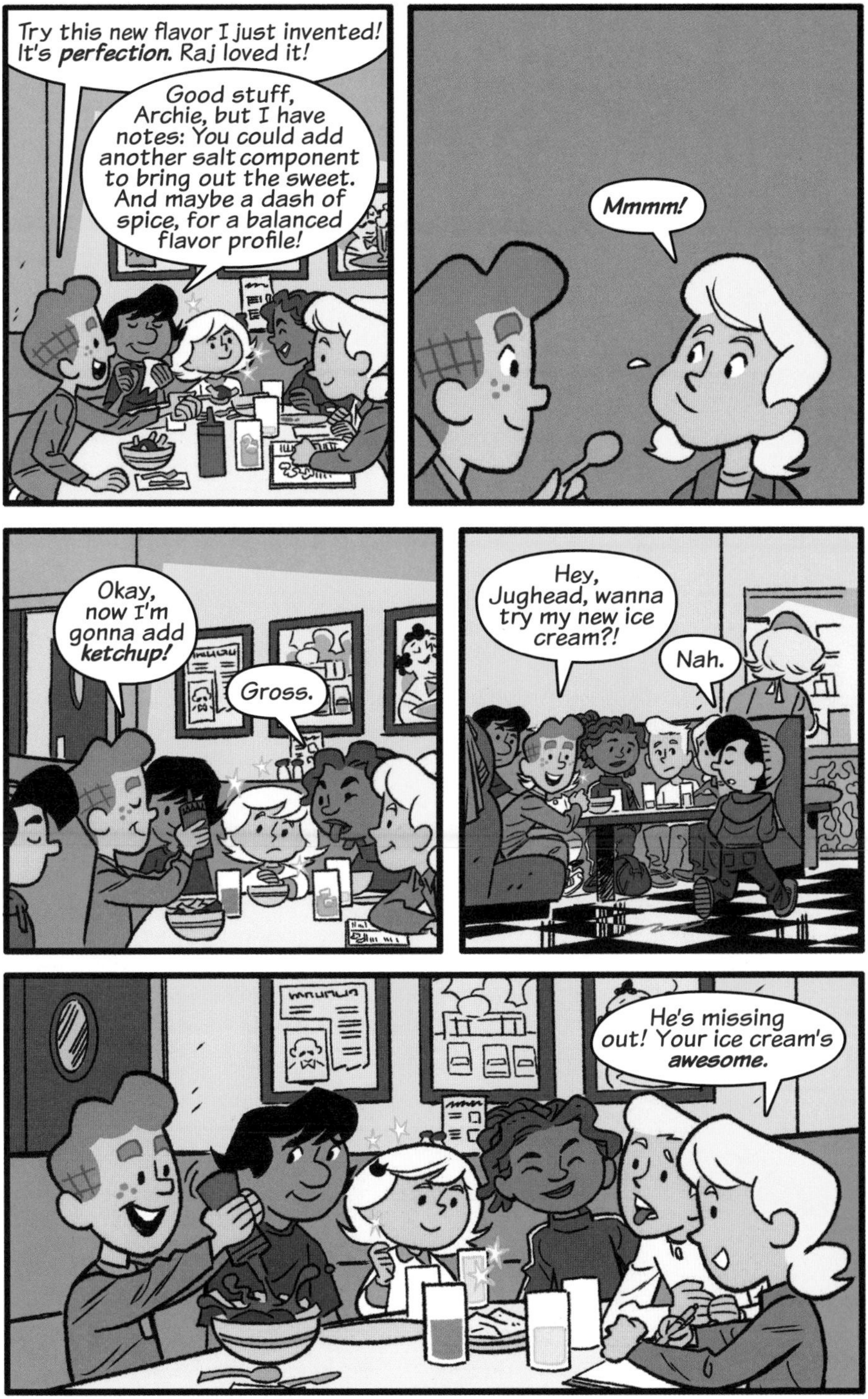
Try this new flavor I just invented! It's ***perfection.*** Raj loved it!
Good stuff, Archie, but I have notes: You could add another salt component to bring out the sweet. And maybe a dash of spice, for a balanced flavor profile!
Mmmm!
Okay, now I'm gonna add ***ketchup!***
Gross.
Hey, Jughead, wanna try my new ice cream?!
Nah.
He's missing out! Your ice cream's ***awesome.***

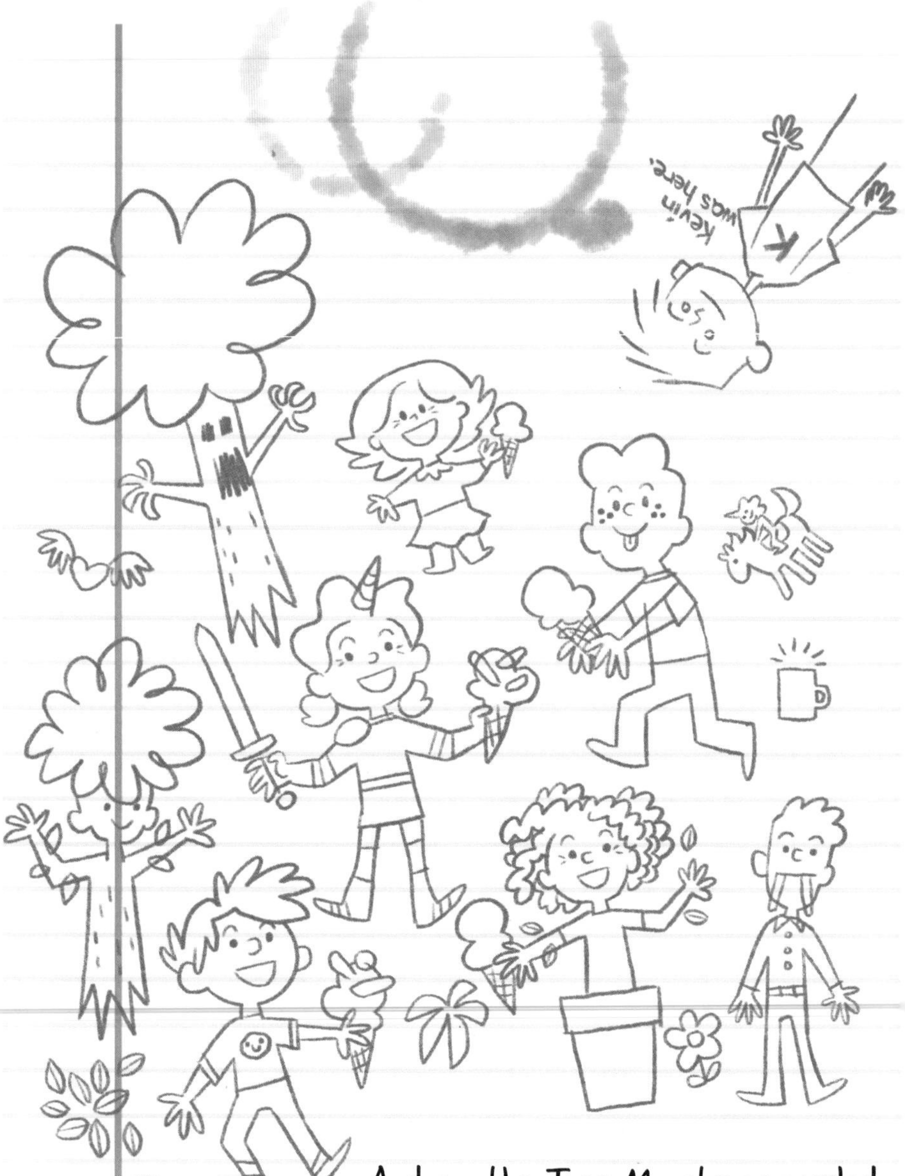
Kevin was here.

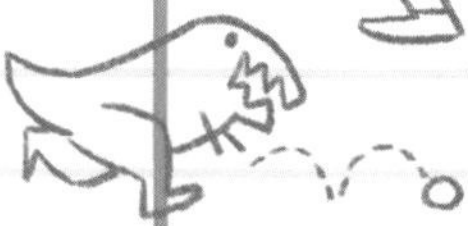

And so, the Tree Monsters revealed themselves to be friends rather than foes—they were not a mighty evil for the knights to defeat, but a force for good. And they made truly excellent ice cream.

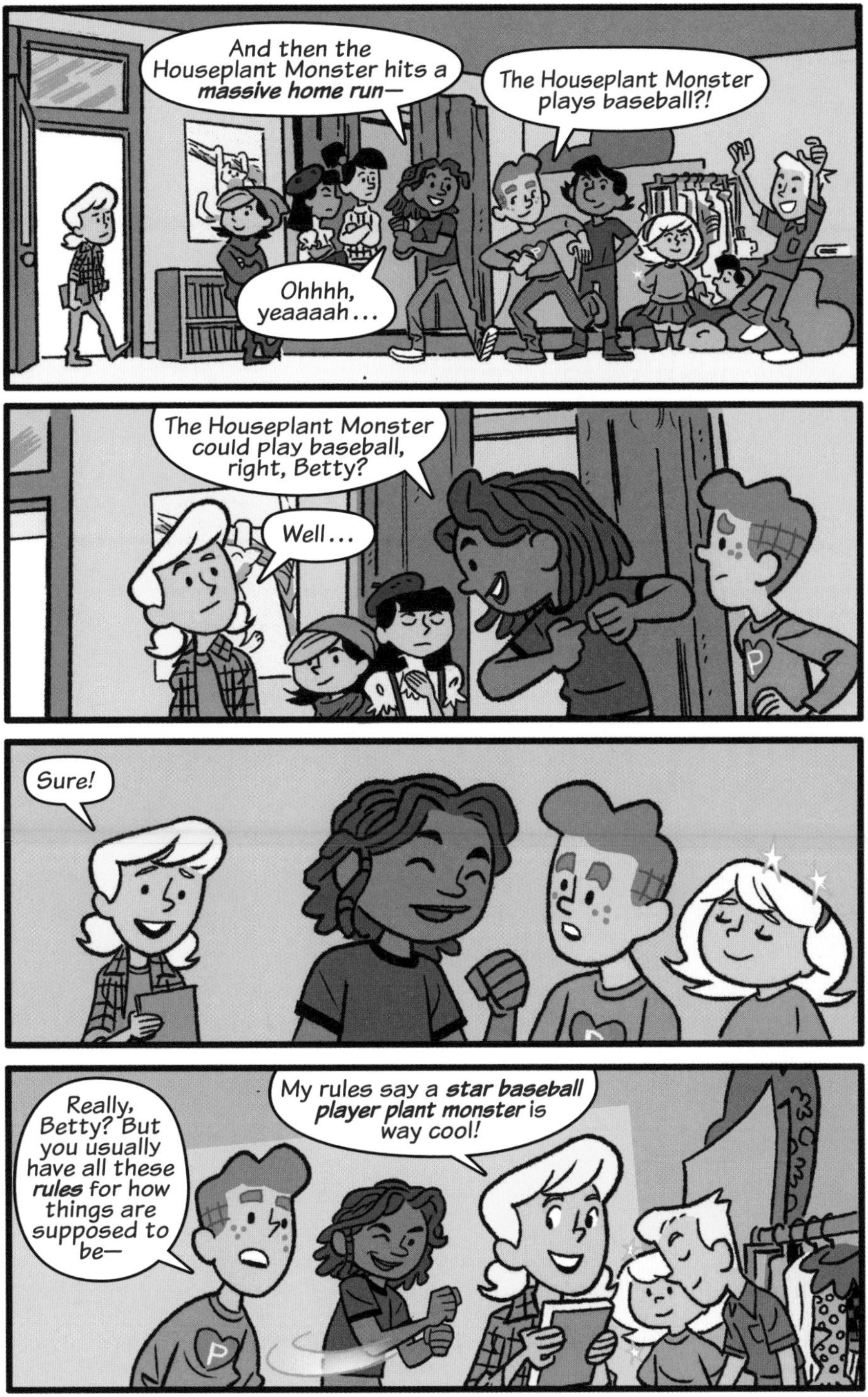
And then the Houseplant Monster hits a *massive home run*—
The Houseplant Monster plays baseball?!
Ohhhh, yeaaaah...
The Houseplant Monster could play baseball, right, Betty?
Well...
Sure!
Really, Betty? But you usually have all these *rules* for how things are supposed to be—
My rules say a *star baseball player plant monster* is way cool!

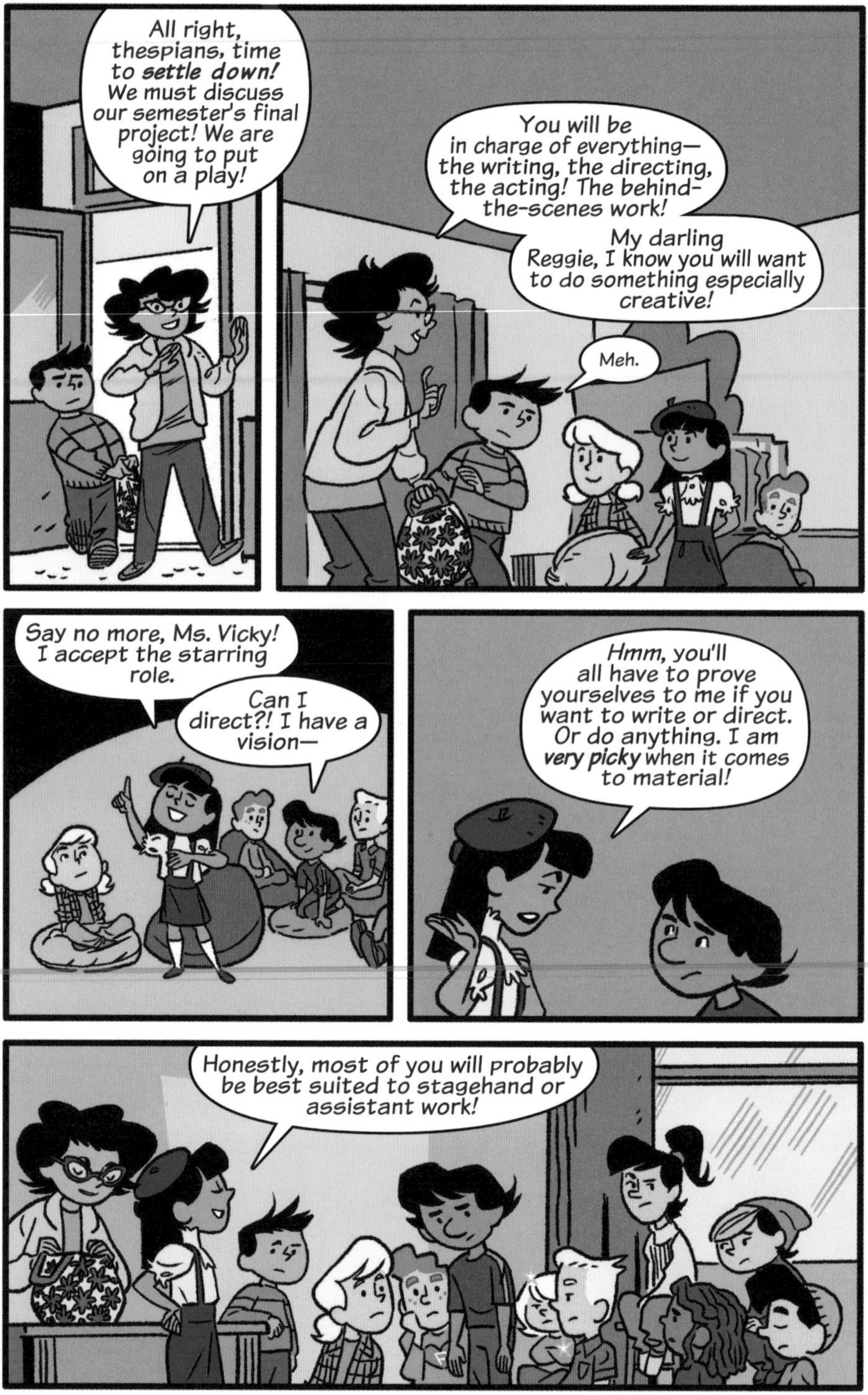
All right, thespians, time to **settle down!** We must discuss our semester's final project! We are going to put on a play!
You will be in charge of everything— the writing, the directing, the acting! The behind-the-scenes work!
My darling Reggie, I know you will want to do something especially creative!
Meh.
Say no more, Ms. Vicky! I accept the starring role.
Can I direct?! I have a vision—
Hmm, you'll all have to prove yourselves to me if you want to write or direct. Or do anything. I am ***very picky*** when it comes to material!
Honestly, most of you will probably be best suited to stagehand or assistant work!

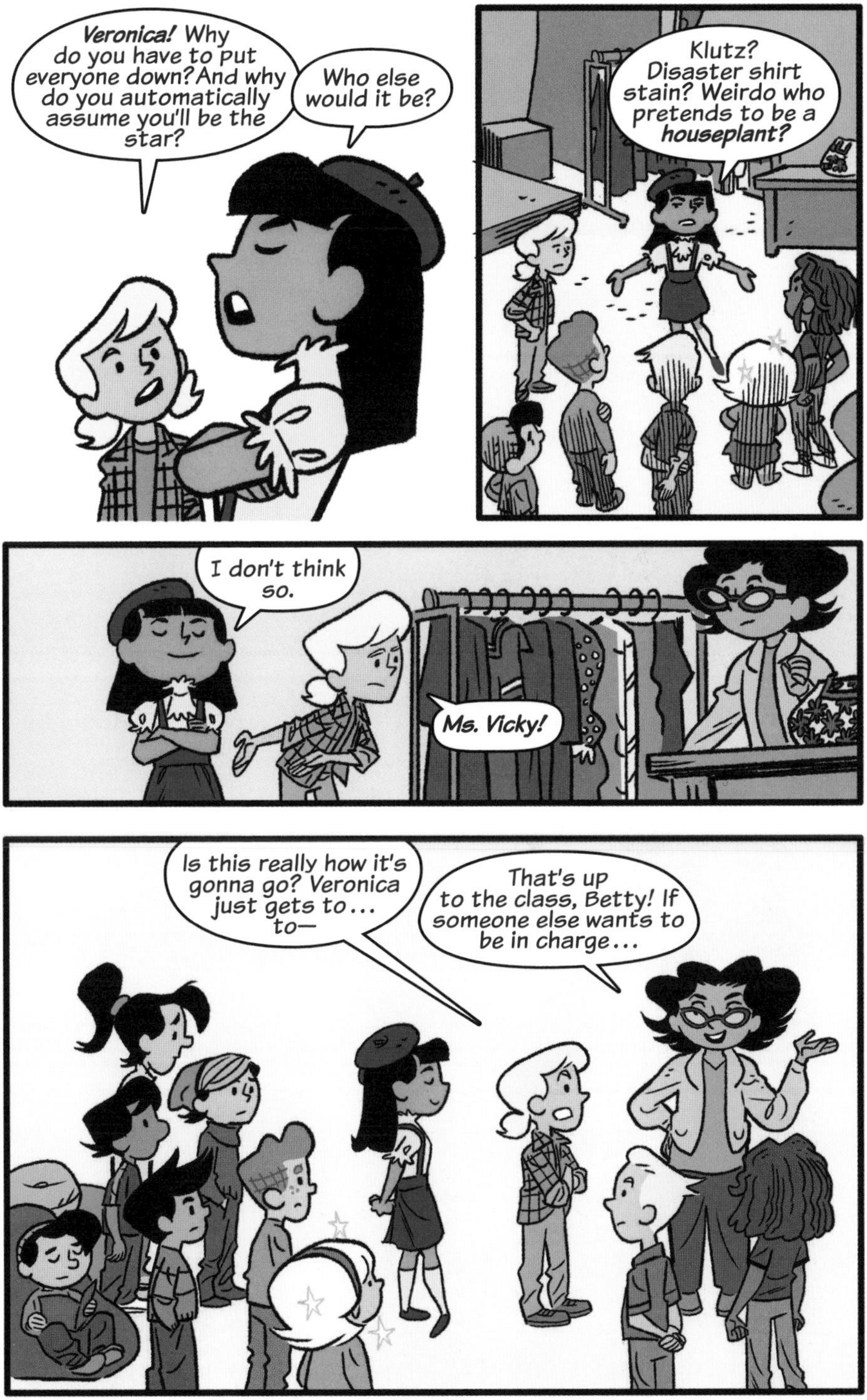
Veronica! Why do you have to put everyone down? And why do you automatically assume you'll be the star?
Who else would it be?
Klutz? Disaster shirt stain? Weirdo who pretends to be a *houseplant?*
I don't think so.
Ms. Vicky!
Is this really how it's gonna go? Veronica just gets to... to—
That's up to the class, Betty! If someone else wants to be in charge...

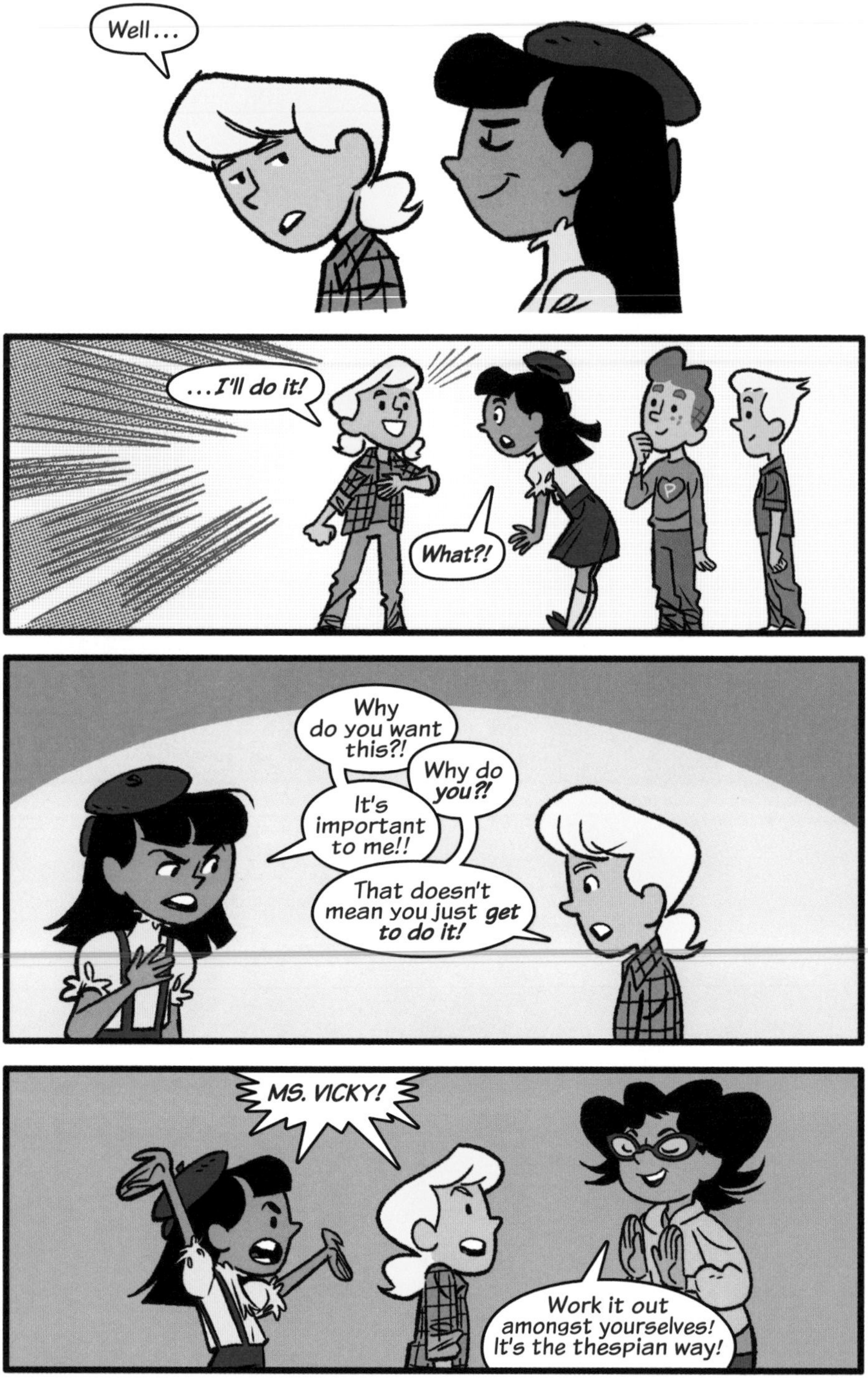
Well...
...I'll do it!
What?!
Why do you want this?!
It's important to me!!
Why do you?!
That doesn't mean you just get to do it!
MS. VICKY!
Work it out amongst yourselves! It's the thespian way!

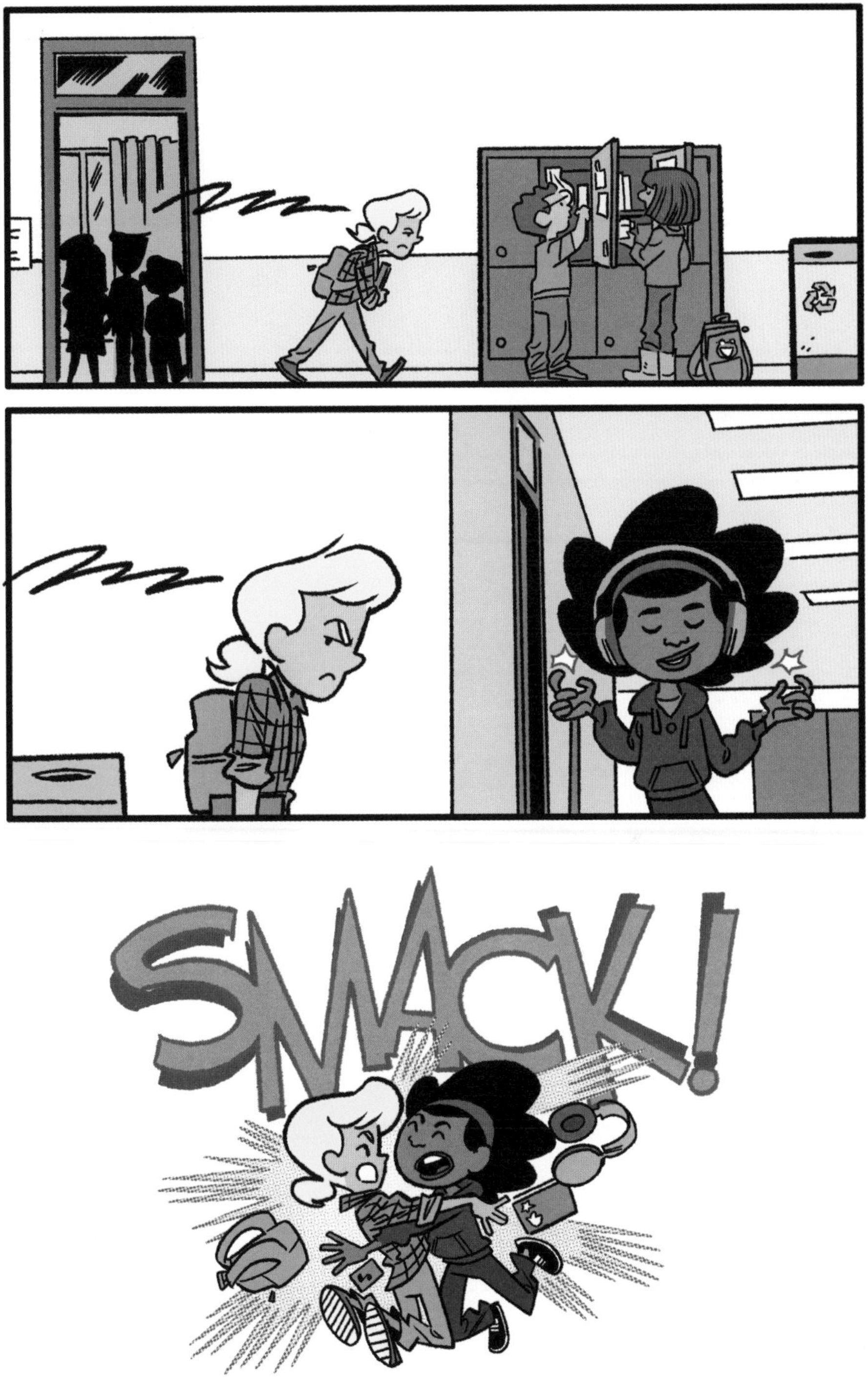
SMACK!

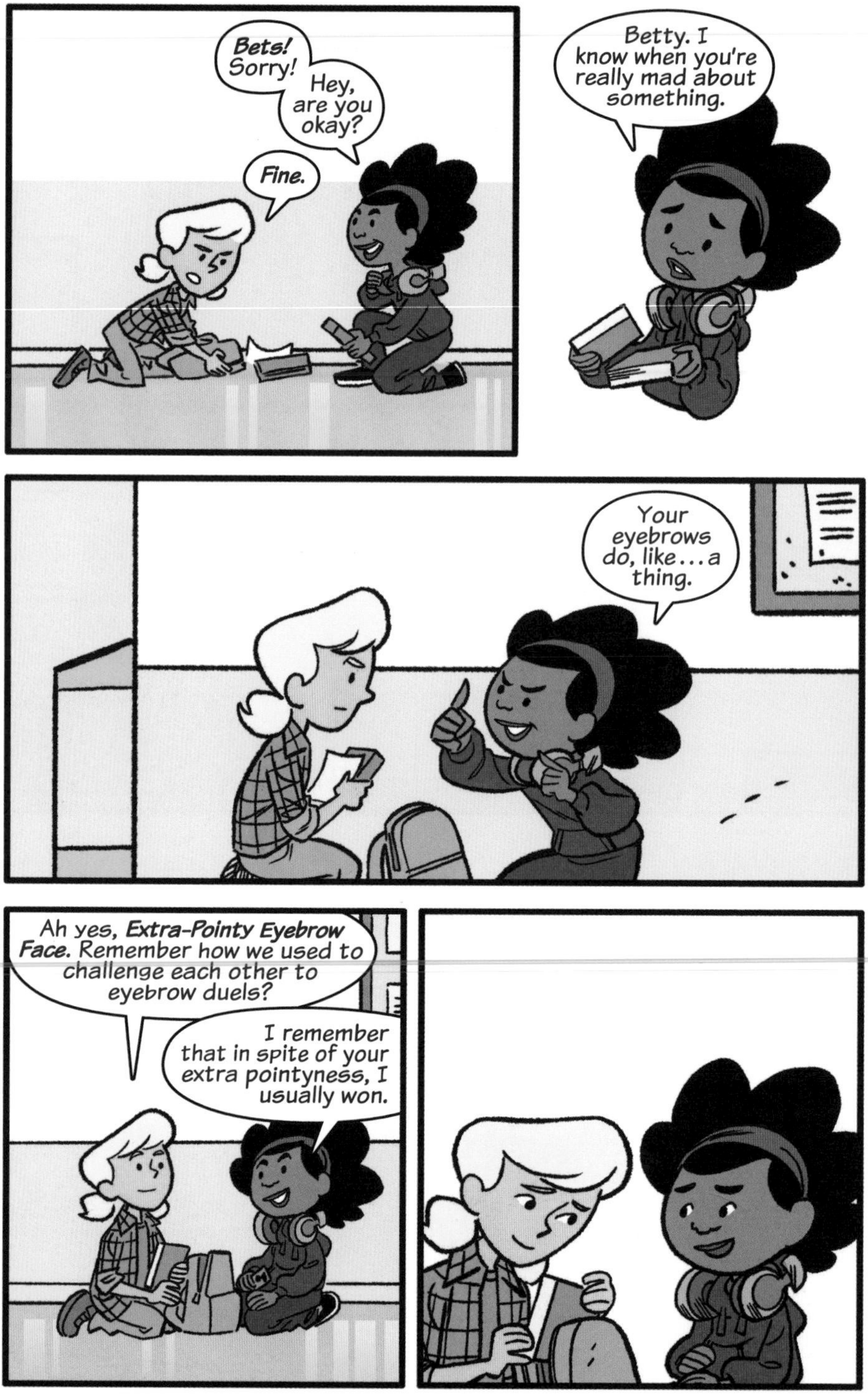
Bets! Sorry!
Hey, are you okay?
Fine.
Betty. I know when you're really mad about something.
Your eyebrows do, like... a thing.
Ah yes, ***Extra-Pointy Eyebrow Face.*** Remember how we used to challenge each other to eyebrow duels?
I remember that in spite of your extra pointyness, I usually won.

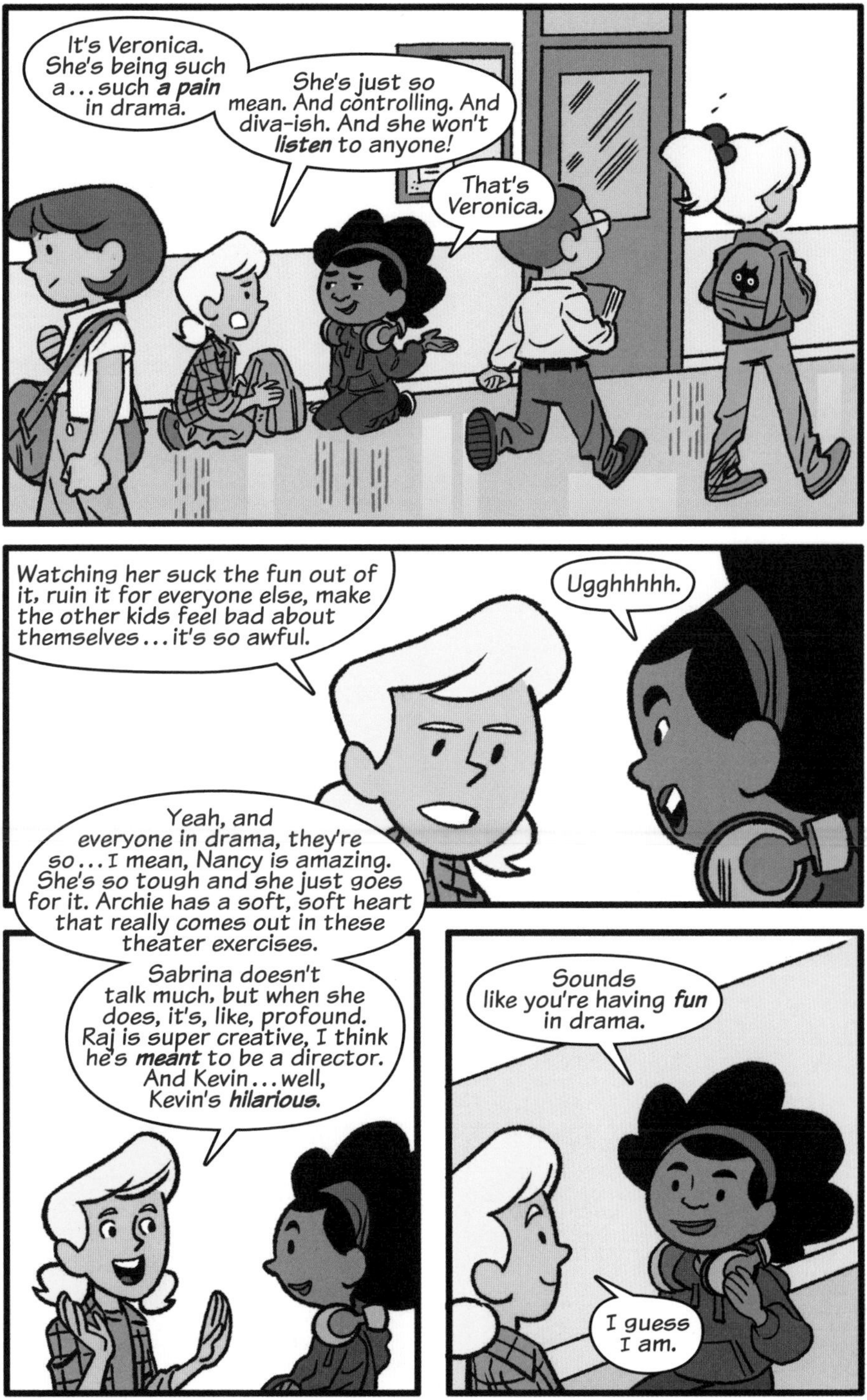
It's Veronica. She's being such a... such **a pain** in drama.
She's just so mean. And controlling. And diva-ish. And she won't ***listen*** to anyone!
That's Veronica.
Watching her suck the fun out of it, ruin it for everyone else, make the other kids feel bad about themselves... it's so awful.
Ugghhhhh.
Yeah, and everyone in drama, they're so... I mean, Nancy is amazing. She's so tough and she just goes for it. Archie has a soft, soft heart that really comes out in these theater exercises.
Sabrina doesn't talk much, but when she does, it's, like, profound. Raj is super creative, I think he's ***meant*** to be a director. And Kevin... well, Kevin's ***hilarious***.
Sounds like you're having ***fun*** in drama.
I guess I am.

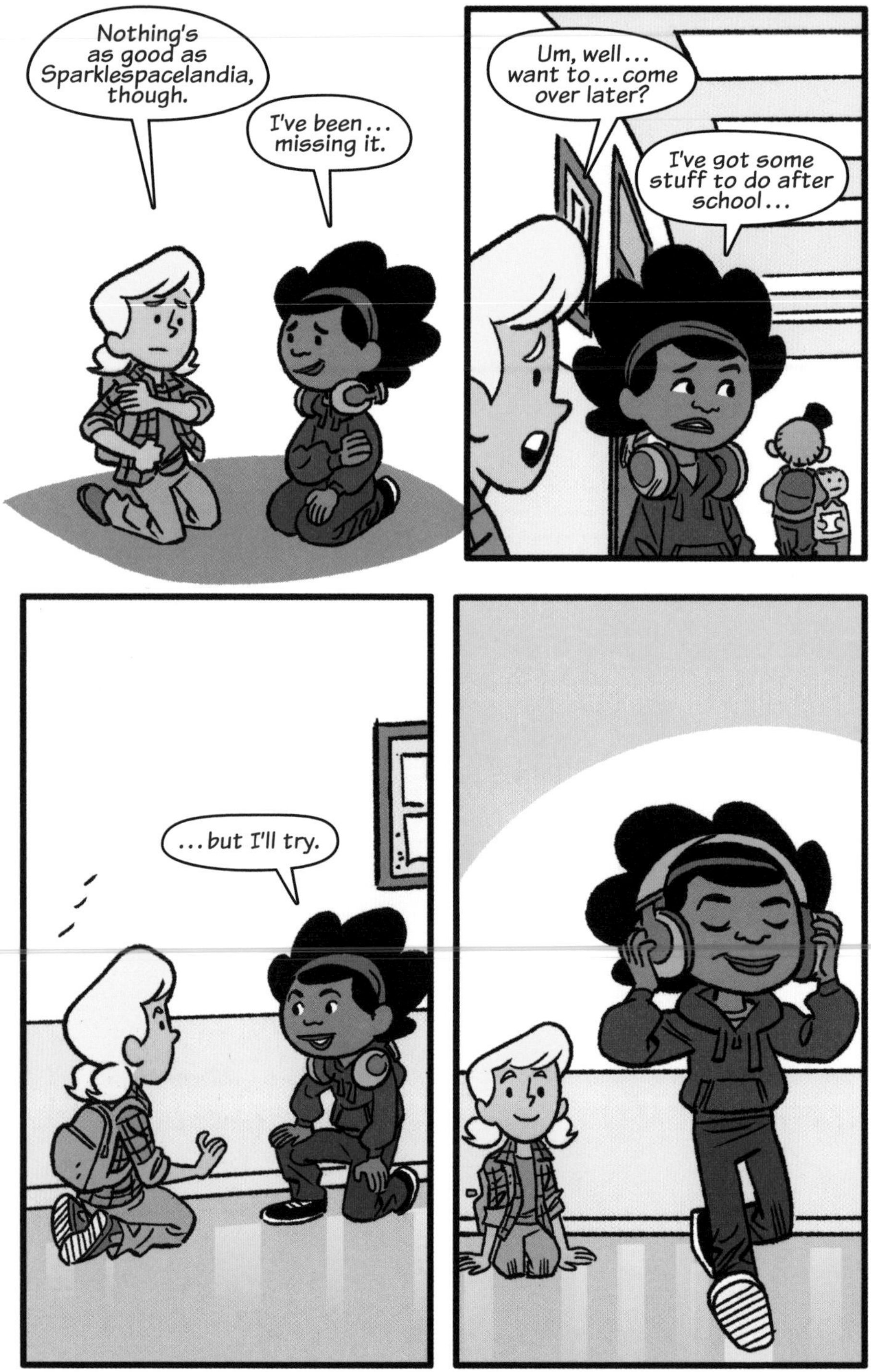
Nothing's as good as Sparklespacelandia, though.
I've been... missing it.
Um, well... want to... come over later?
I've got some stuff to do after school...
...but I'll try.

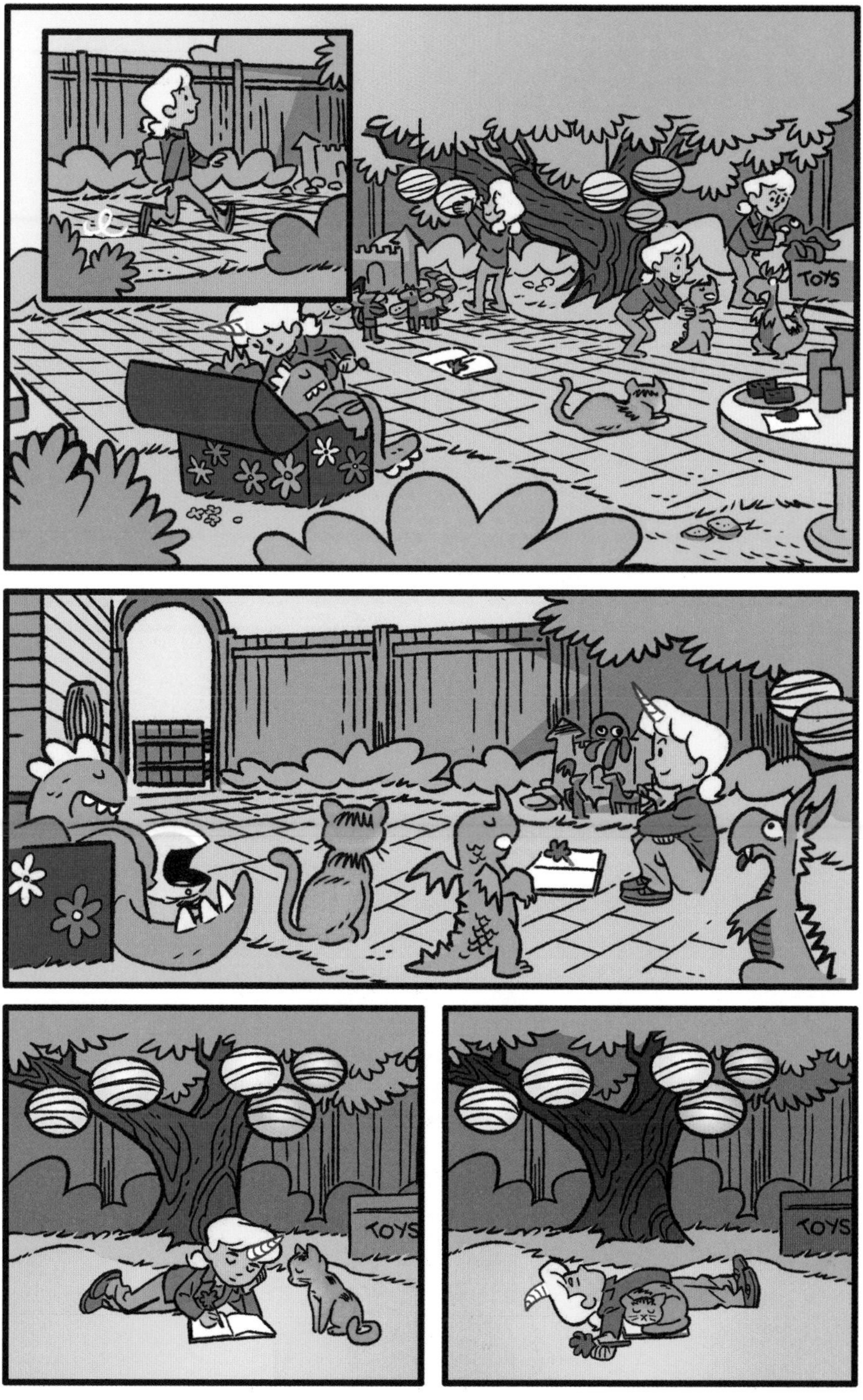
TOYS
TOYS
TOYS

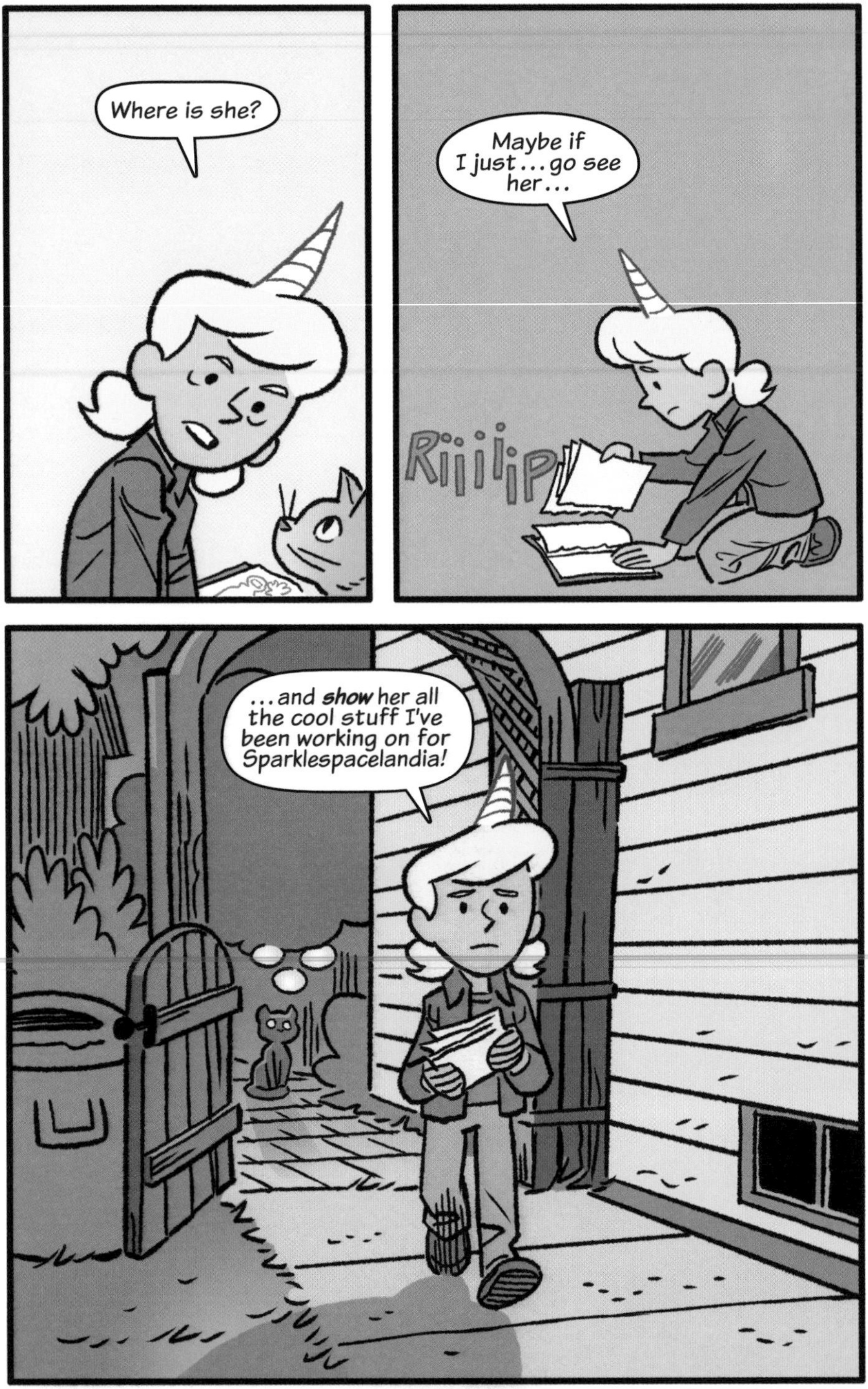
Where is she?
Maybe if I just . . . go see her . . .
Riiiiip
. . . and **show** her all the cool stuff I've been working on for Sparklespacelandia!

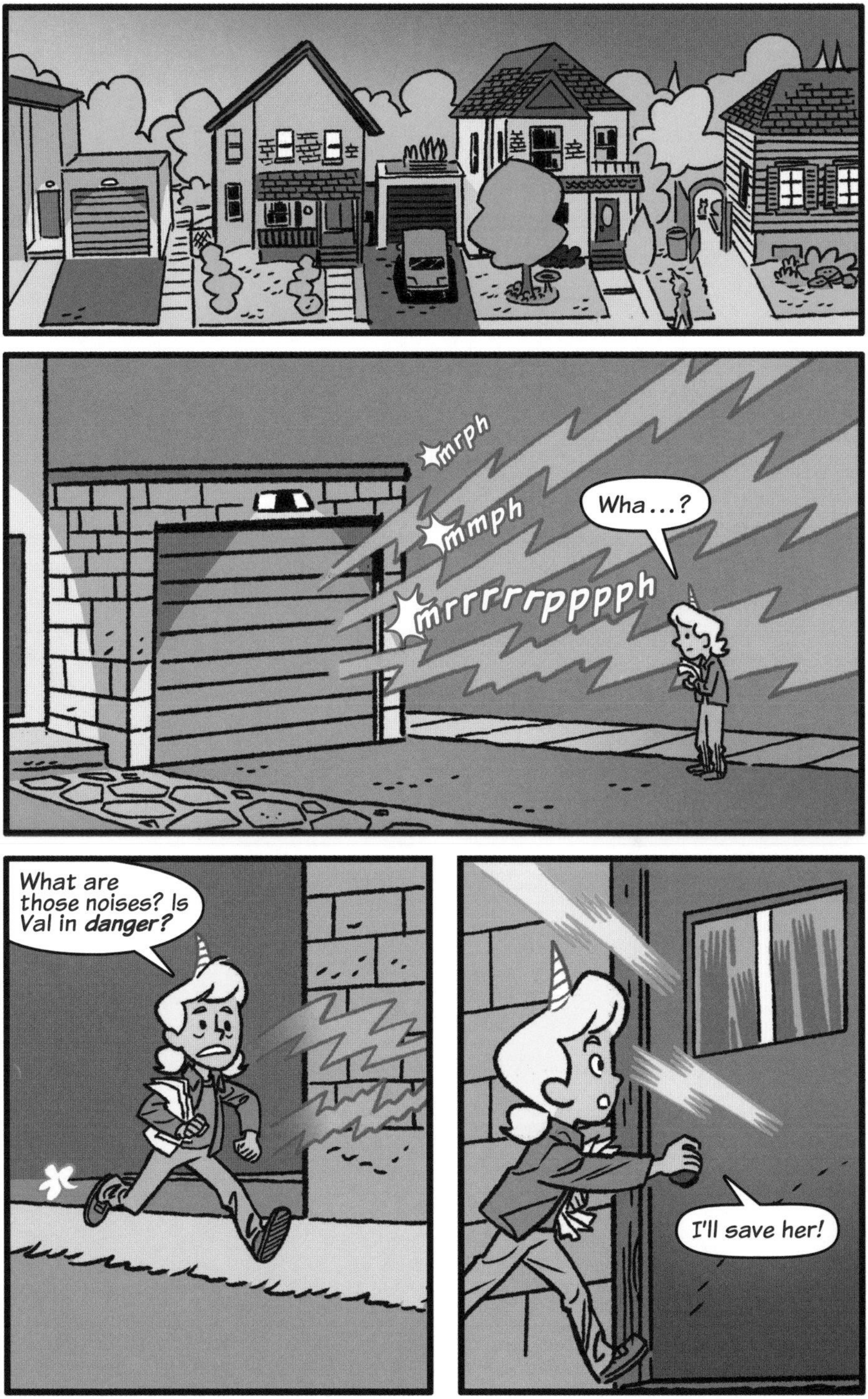
mrph
mmph
mrrrrrpppph
Wha...?
What are those noises? Is Val in *danger?*
I'll save her!

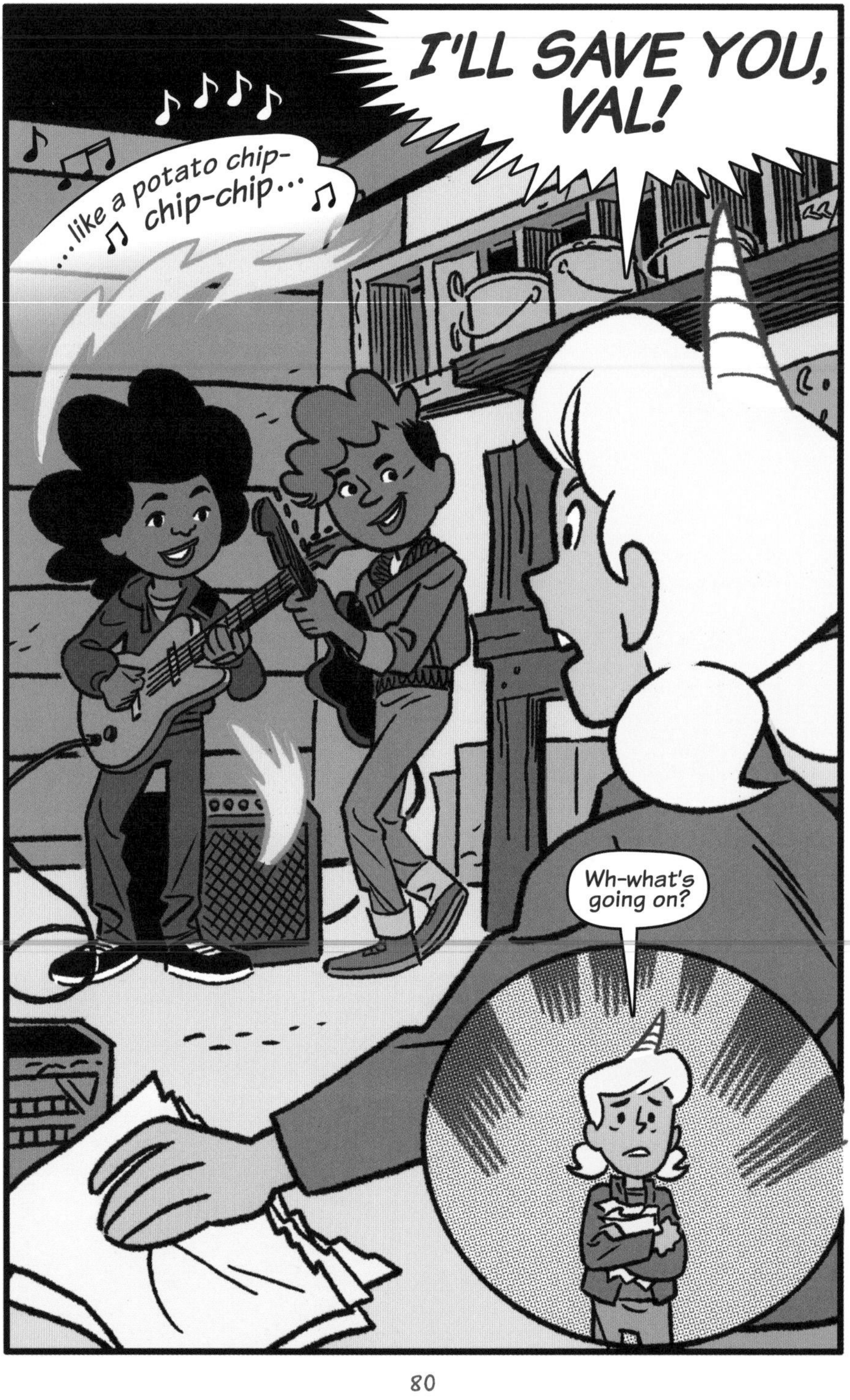
I'LL SAVE YOU, VAL!
...like a potato chip- chip-chip...
Wh-what's going on?

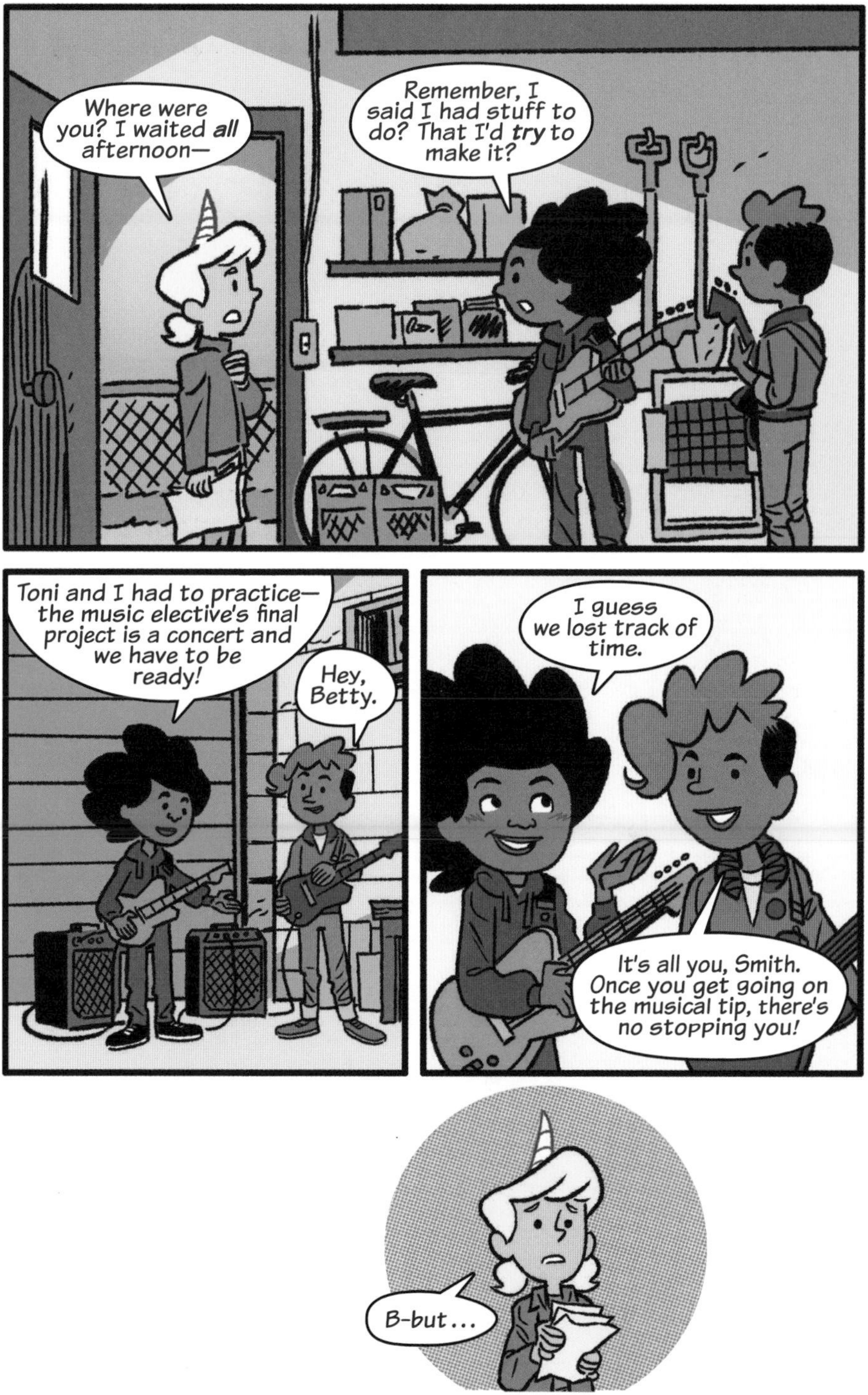
Where were you? I waited *all* afternoon—
Remember, I said I had stuff to do? That I'd *try* to make it?
Toni and I had to practice—the music elective's final project is a concert and we have to be ready!
Hey, Betty.
I guess we lost track of time.
It's all you, Smith. Once you get going on the musical tip, there's no stopping you!
B-but...

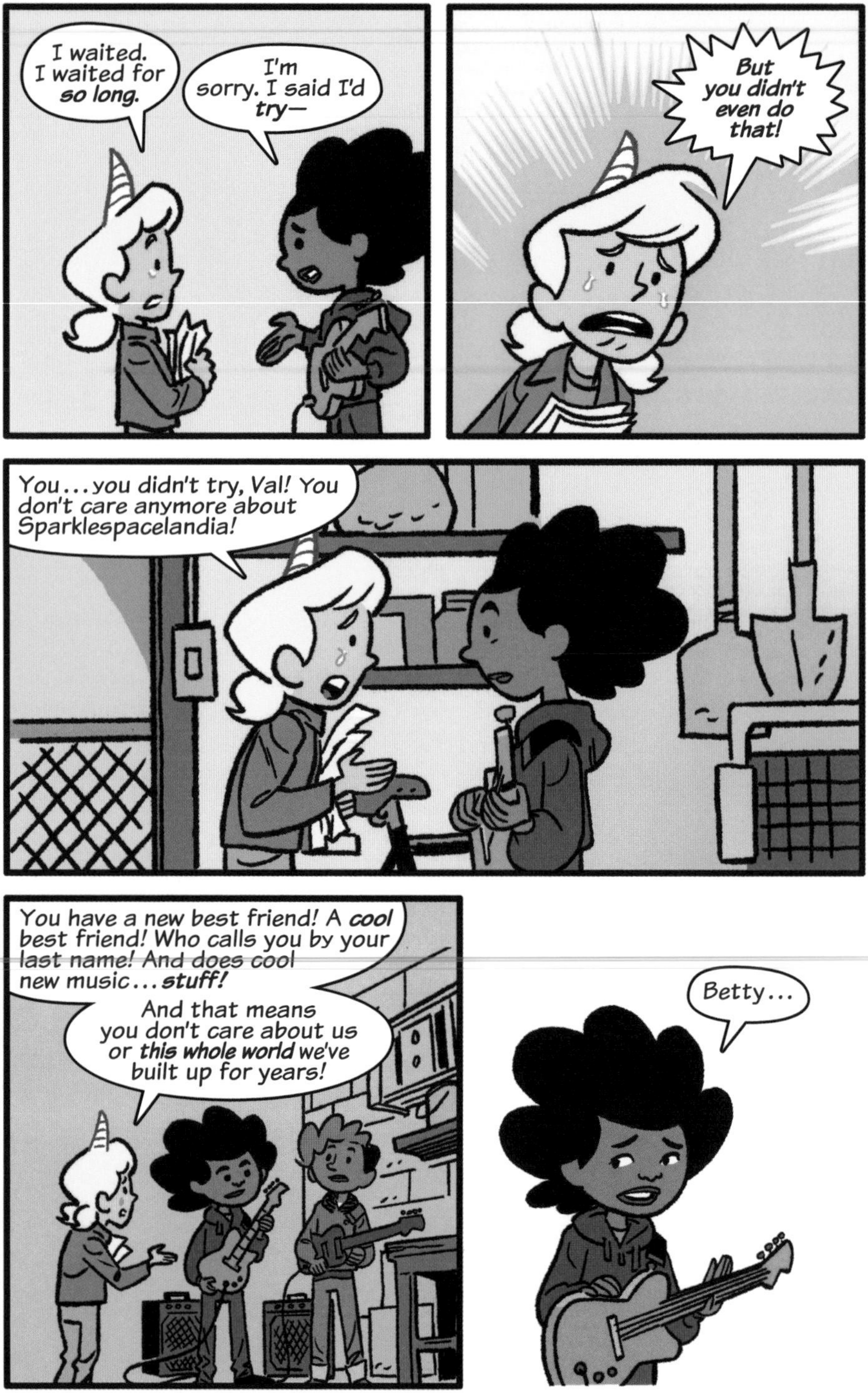
I waited. I waited for *so long.*
I'm sorry. I said I'd *try—*
But you didn't even do that!
You...you didn't try, Val! You don't care anymore about Sparklespacelandia!
You have a new best friend! A *cool* best friend! Who calls you by your last name! And does cool new music...*stuff!*
And that means you don't care about us or *this whole world* we've built up for years!
Betty...

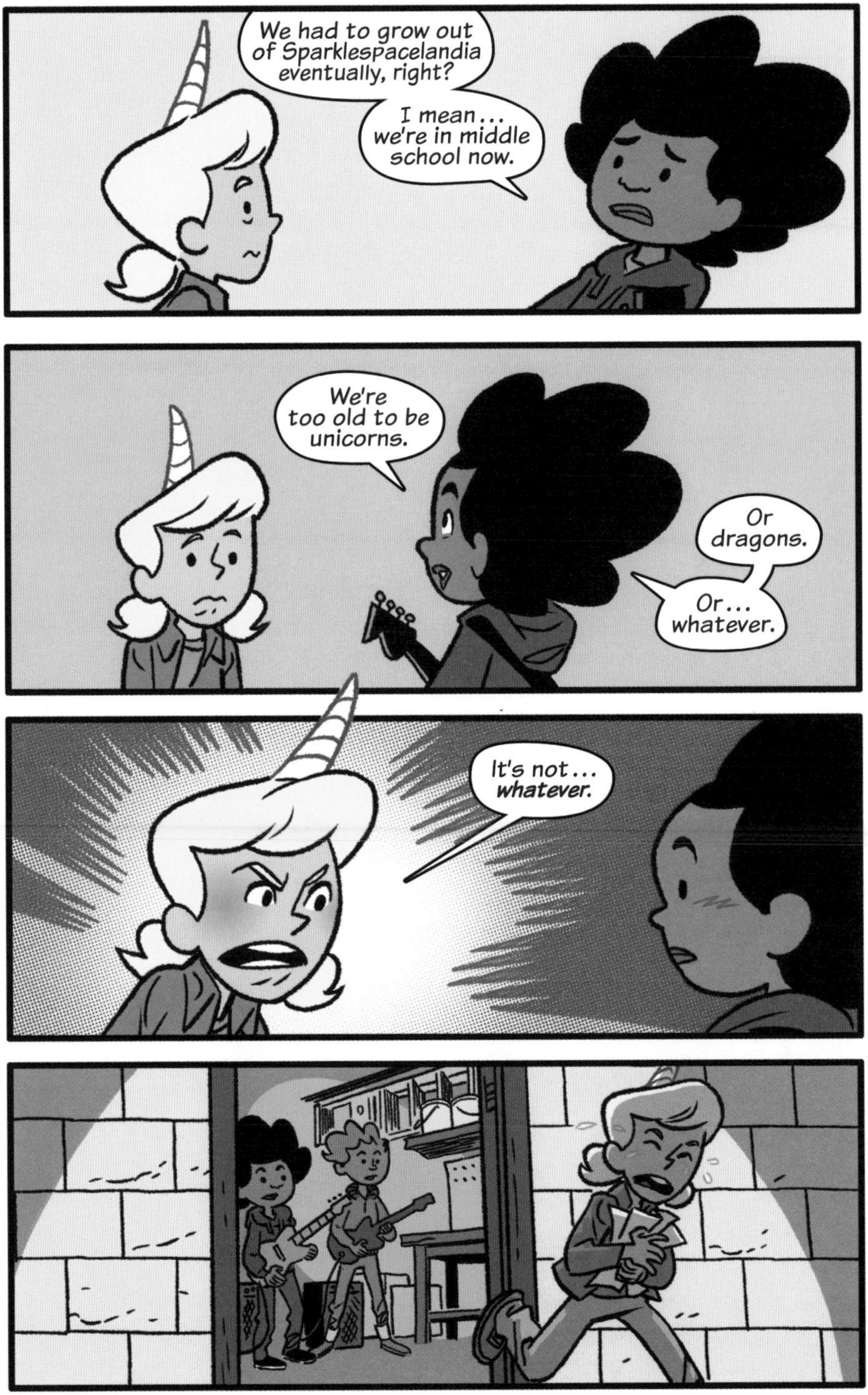
We had to grow out of Sparklespacelandia eventually, right?
I mean... we're in middle school now.
We're too old to be unicorns.
Or dragons.
Or... whatever.
It's not... *whatever*.

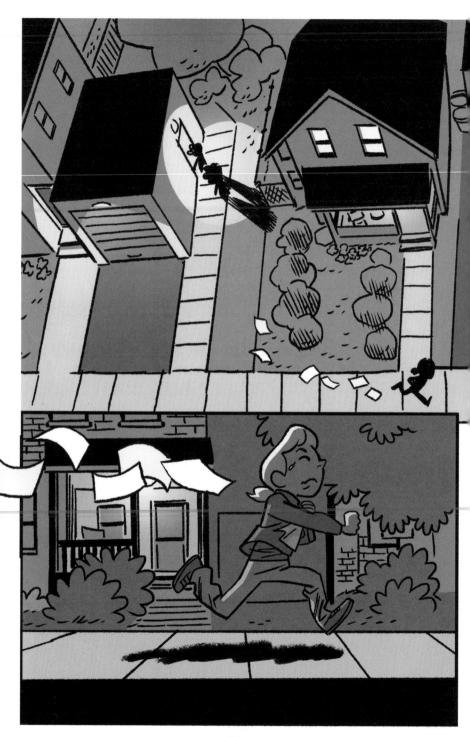

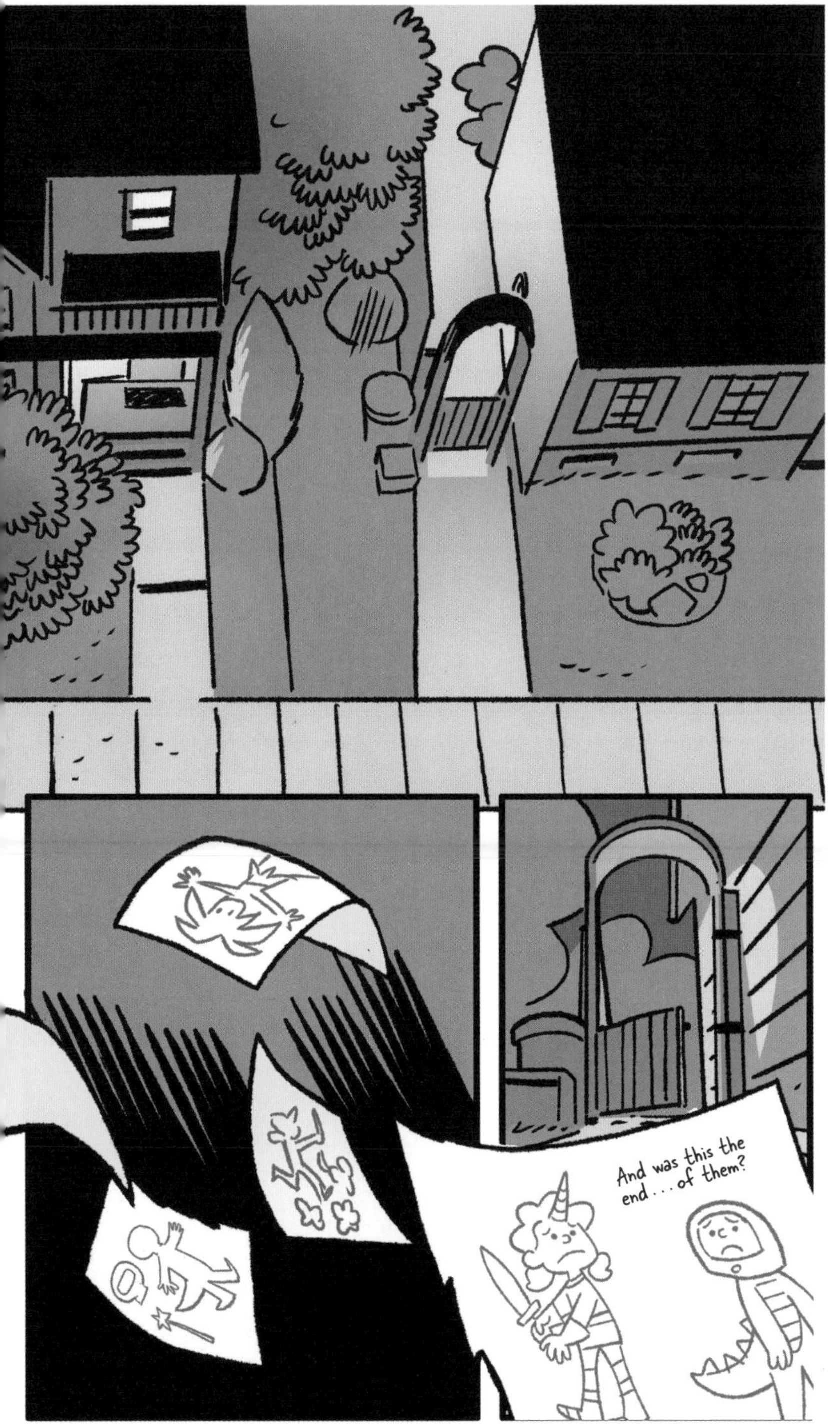
And was this the
end . . . of them?

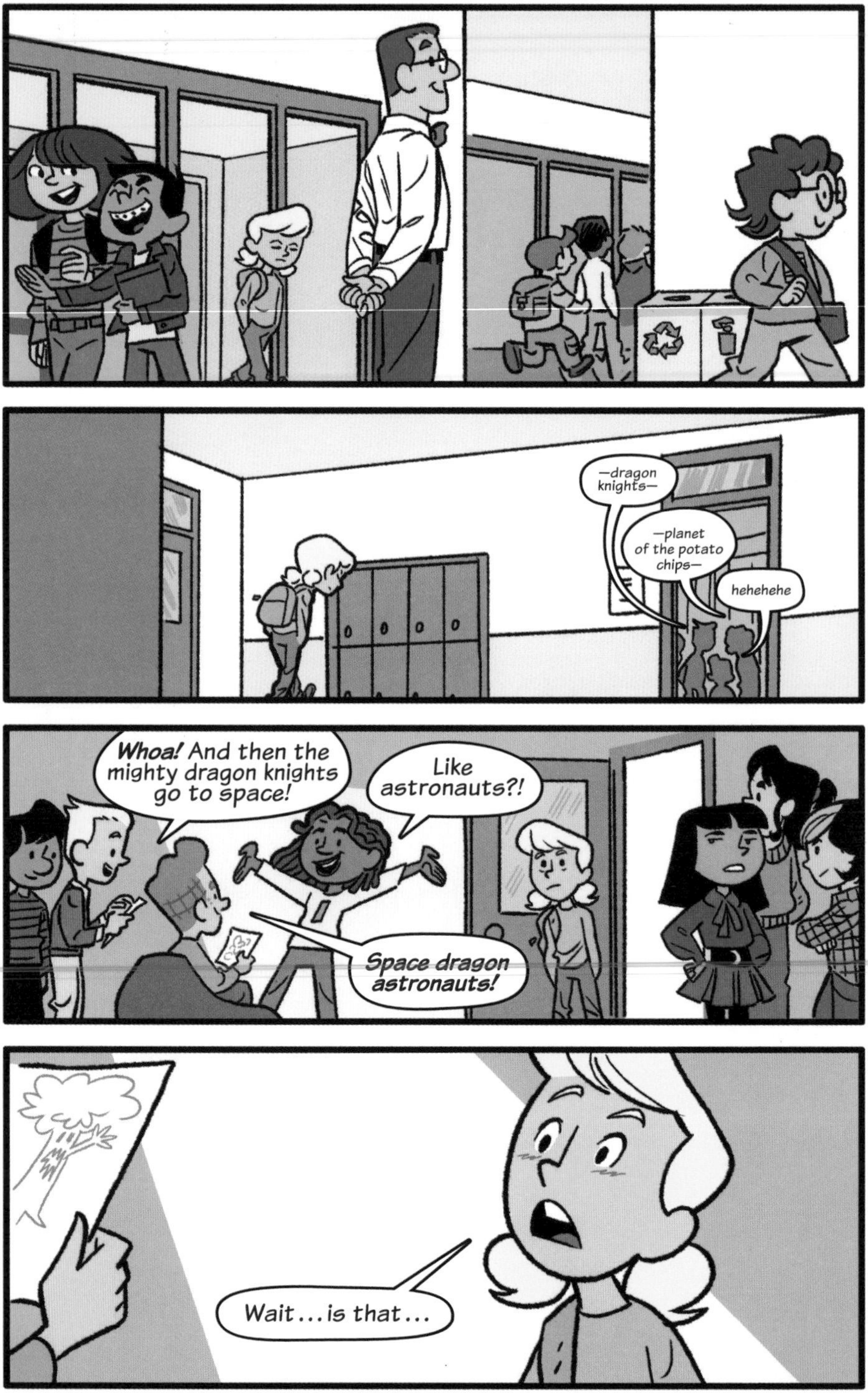

—dragon knights—
—planet of the potato chips—
hehehehe
Whoa! And then the mighty dragon knights go to space!
Like astronauts?!
Space dragon astronauts!
Wait... is that...

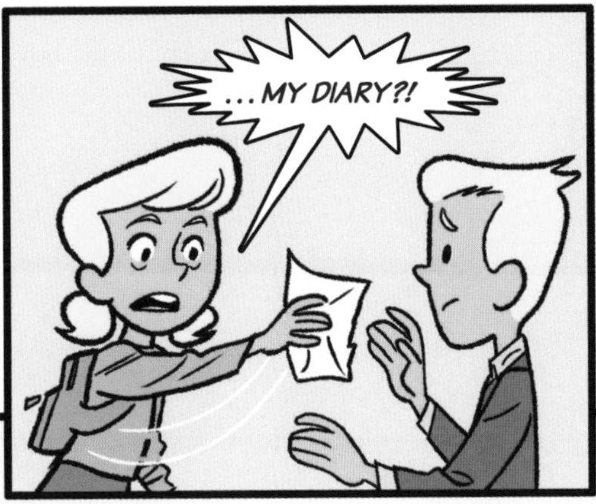
...MY DIARY?!

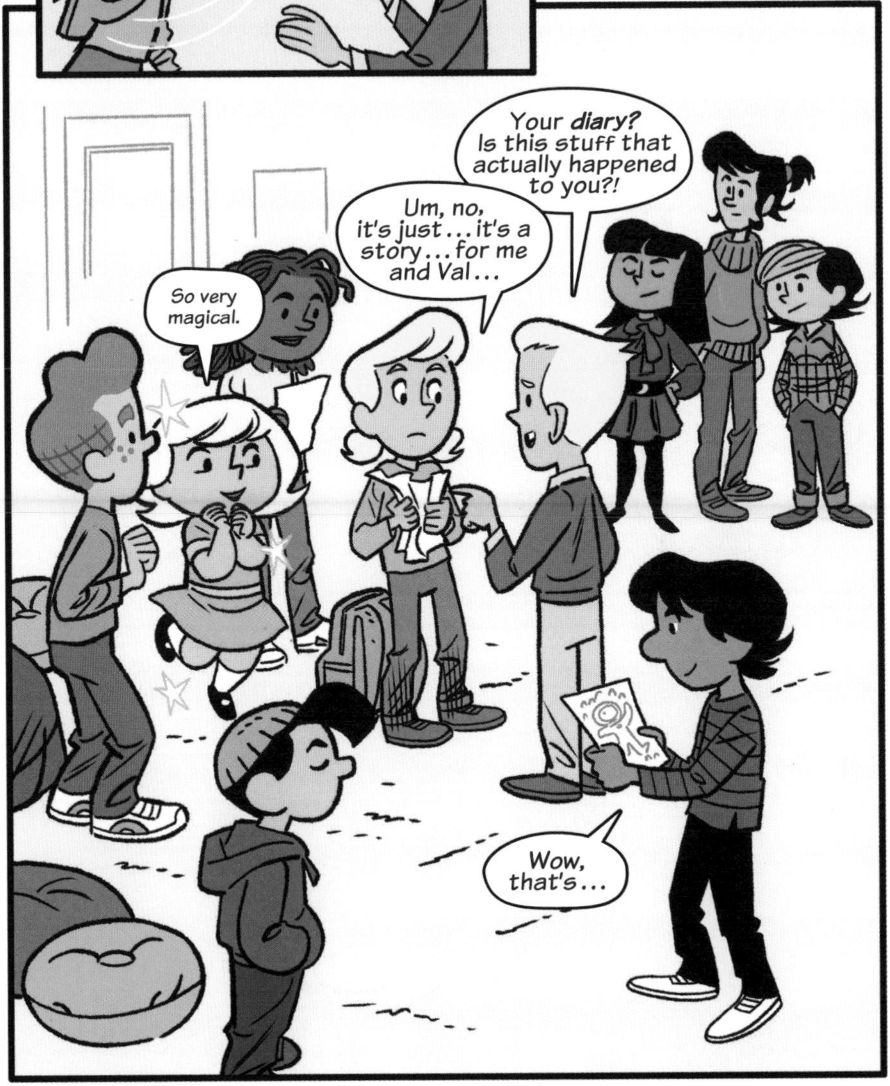
So very magical.
Um, no, it's just... it's a story... for me and Val...
Your *diary?* Is this stuff that actually happened to you?!
Wow, that's...

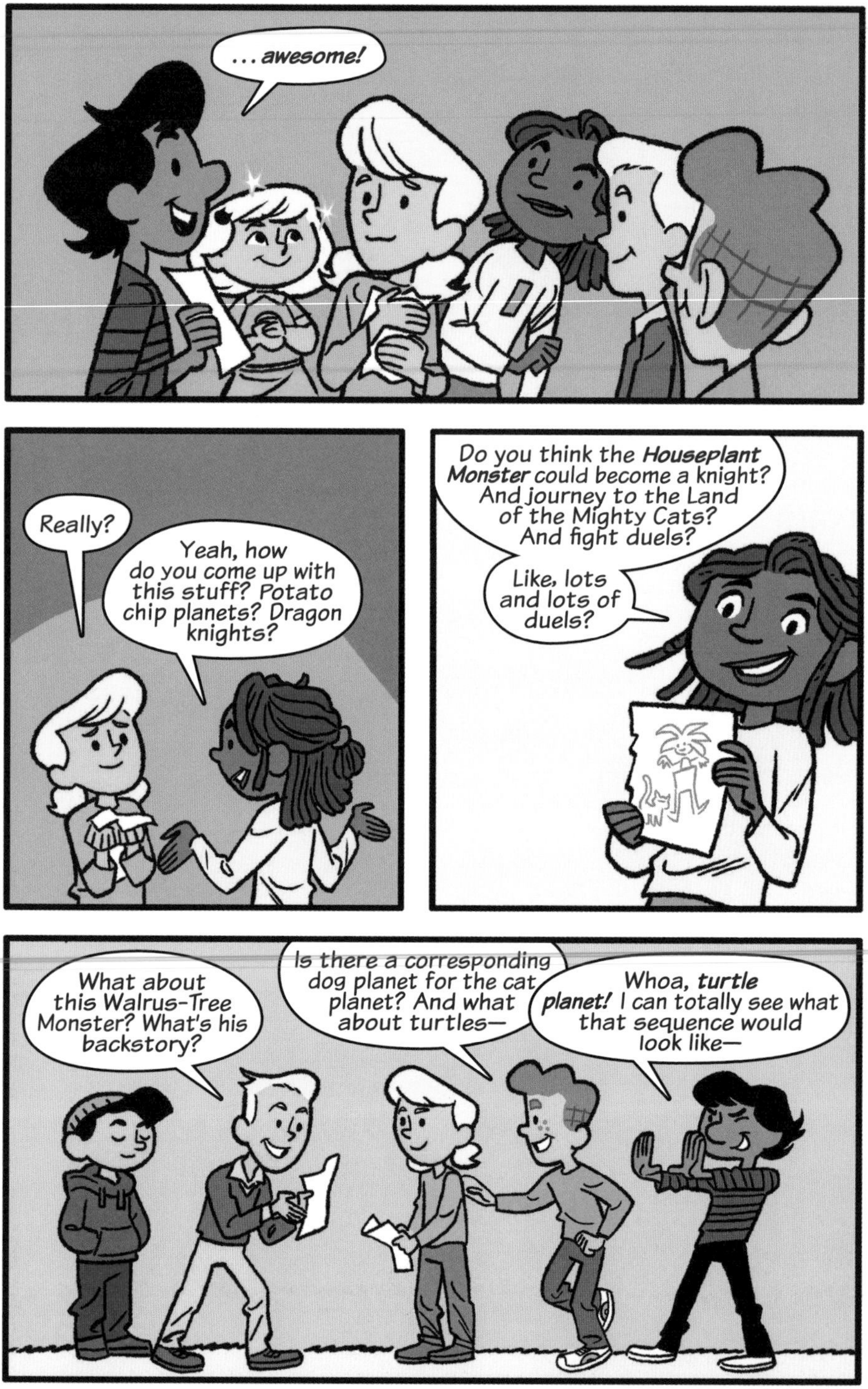
...awesome!
Really?
Yeah, how do you come up with this stuff? Potato chip planets? Dragon knights?
Do you think the *Houseplant Monster* could become a knight? And journey to the Land of the Mighty Cats? And fight duels?
Like, lots and lots of duels?
What about this Walrus-Tree Monster? What's his backstory?
Is there a corresponding dog planet for the cat planet? And what about turtles—
Whoa, *turtle planet!* I can totally see what that sequence would look like—

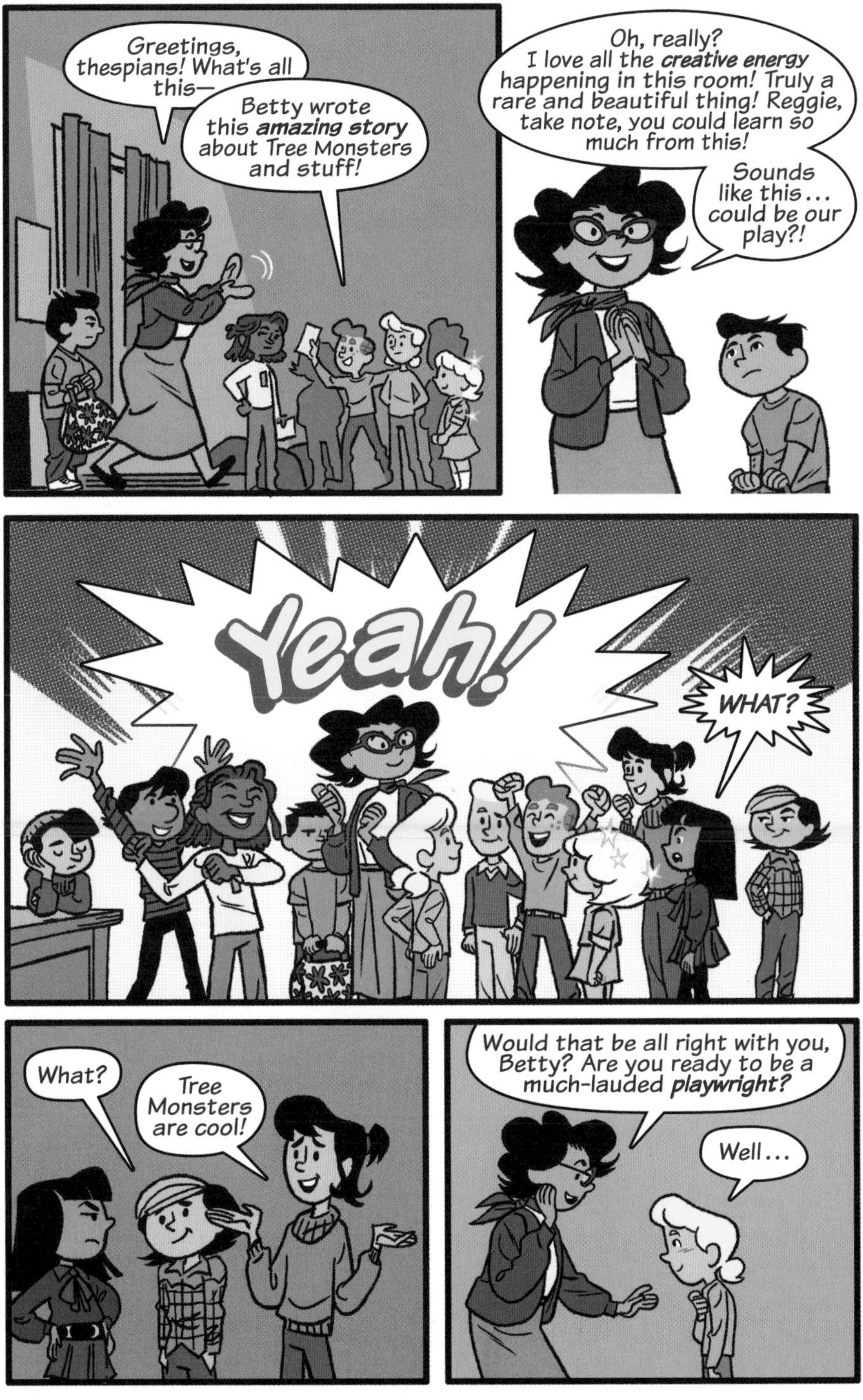
Greetings, thespians! What's all this—
Betty wrote this **amazing story** about Tree Monsters and stuff!
Oh, really? I love all the **creative energy** happening in this room! Truly a rare and beautiful thing! Reggie, take note, you could learn so much from this!
Sounds like this... could be our play?!
Yeah!
WHAT?
What?
Tree Monsters are cool!
Would that be all right with you, Betty? Are you ready to be a much-lauded **playwright?**
Well...

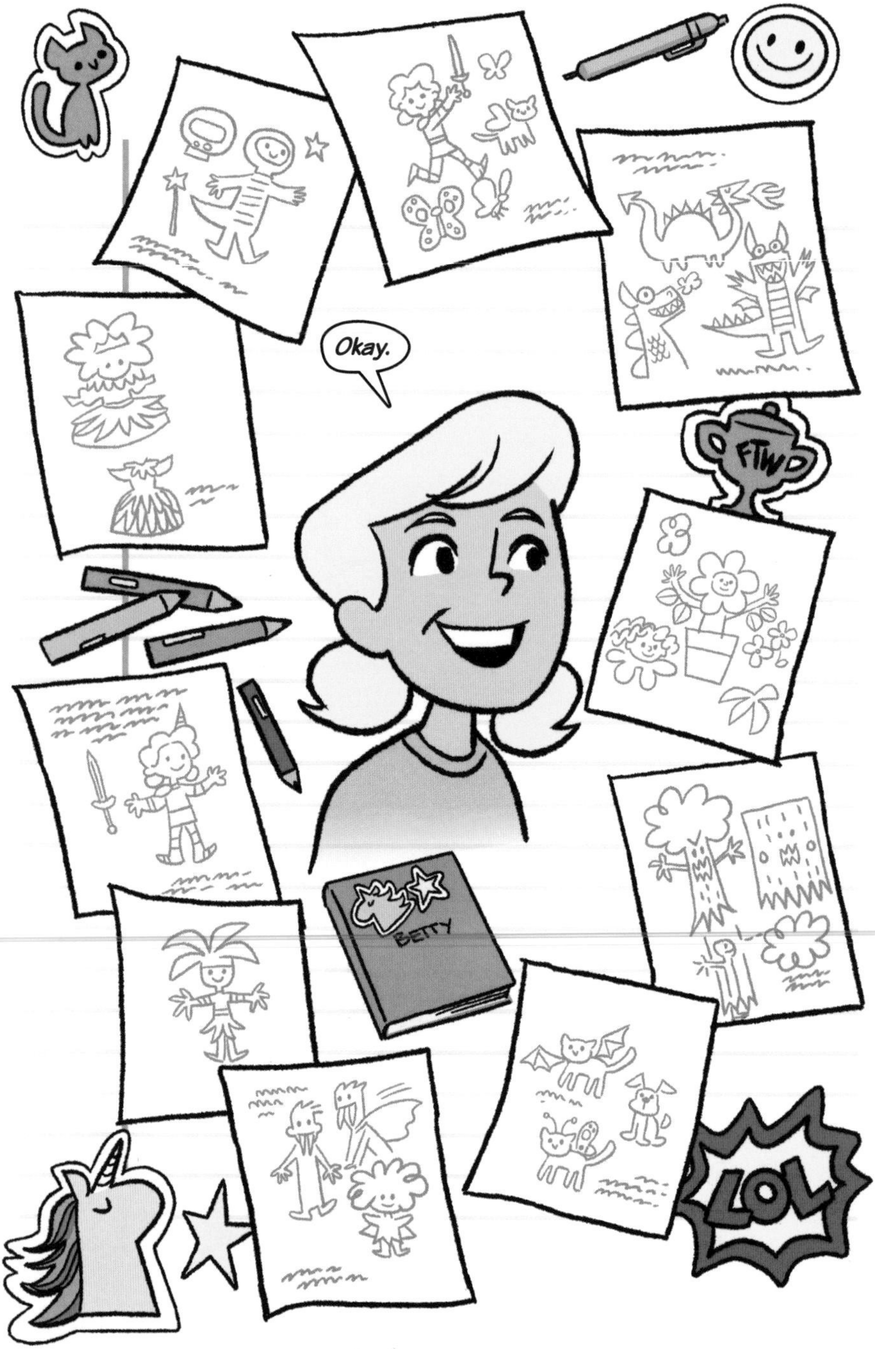
Okay.
FTW
BETTY
LOL

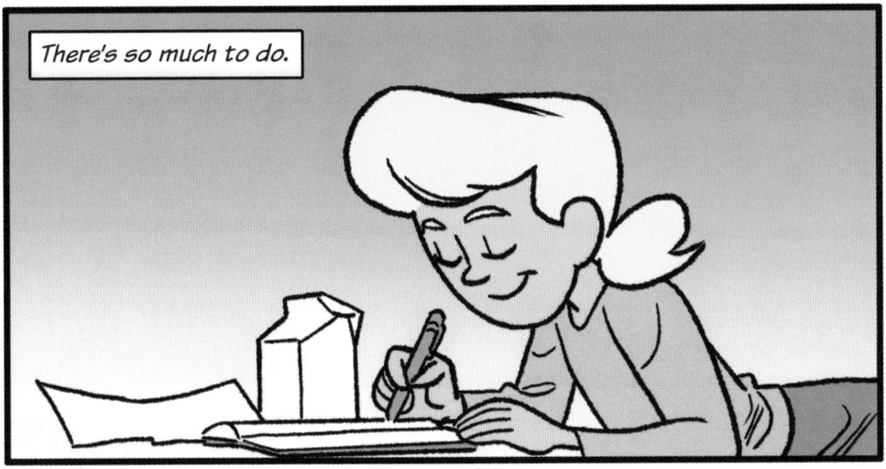
There's so much to do.

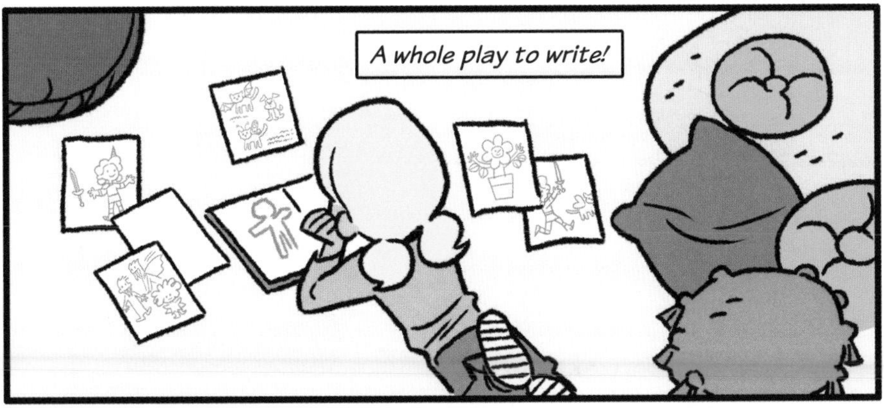
A whole play to write!

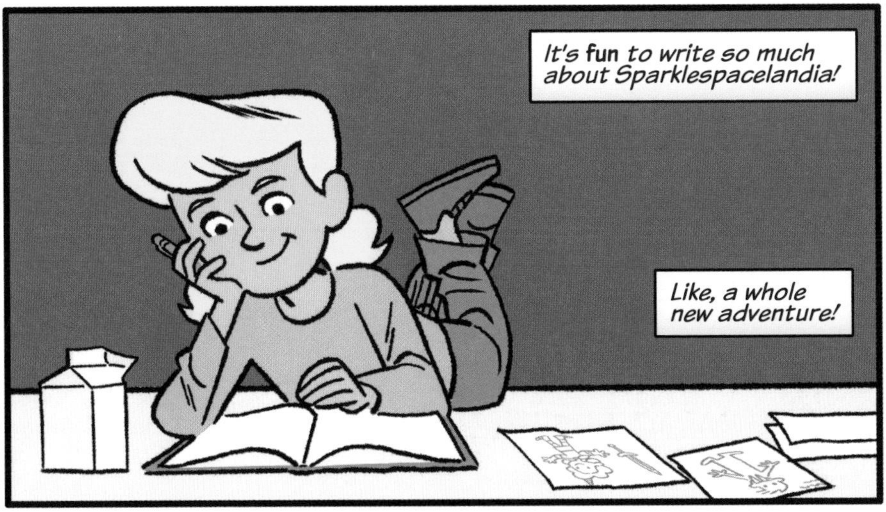
It's **fun** to write so much about Sparklespacelandia!
Like, a whole new adventure!

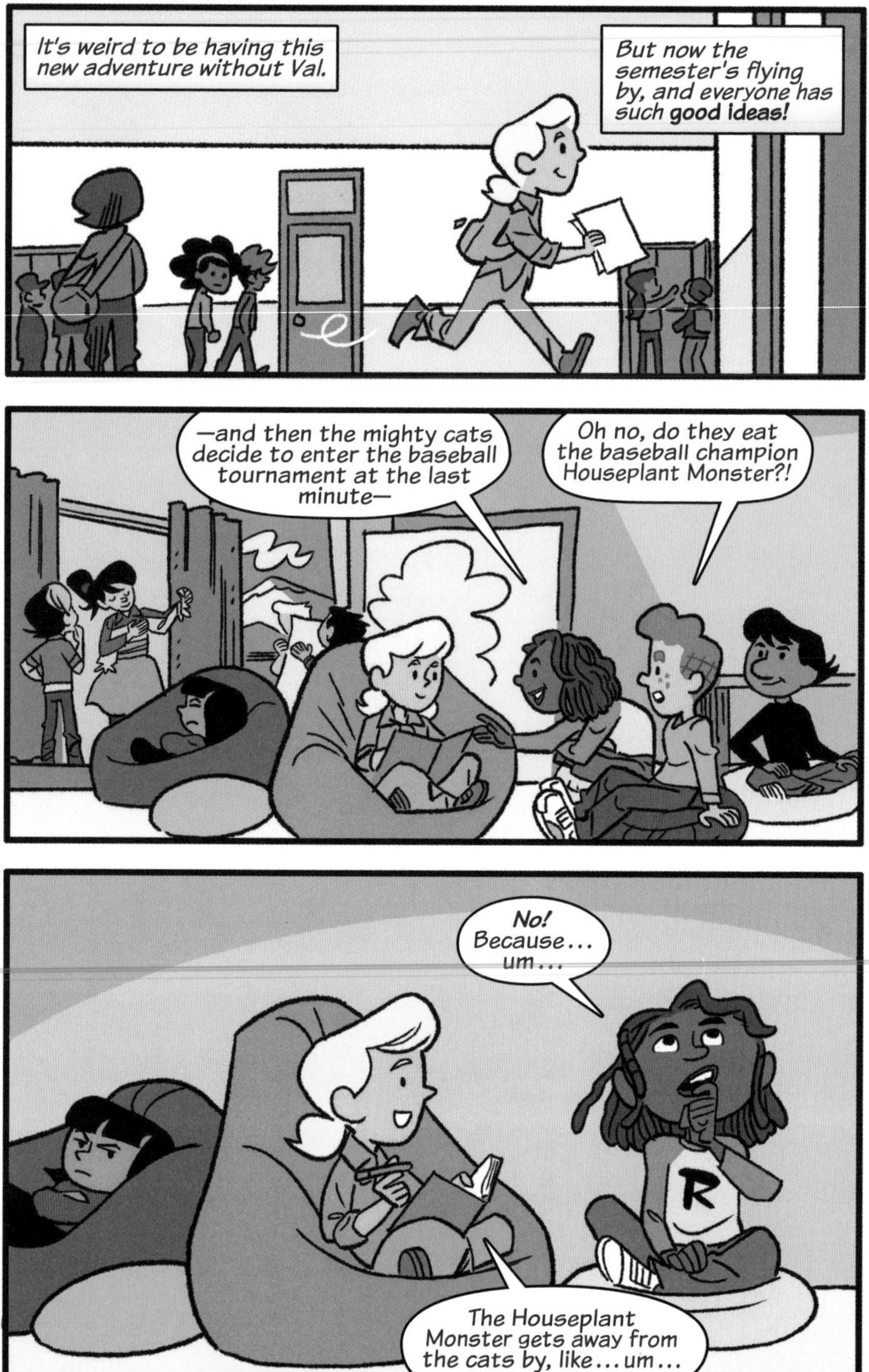
It's weird to be having this new adventure without Val.
But now the semester's flying by, and everyone has such **good ideas!**
—and then the mighty cats decide to enter the baseball tournament at the last minute—
Oh no, do they eat the baseball champion Houseplant Monster?!
No! Because... um...
R
The Houseplant Monster gets away from the cats by, like... um...

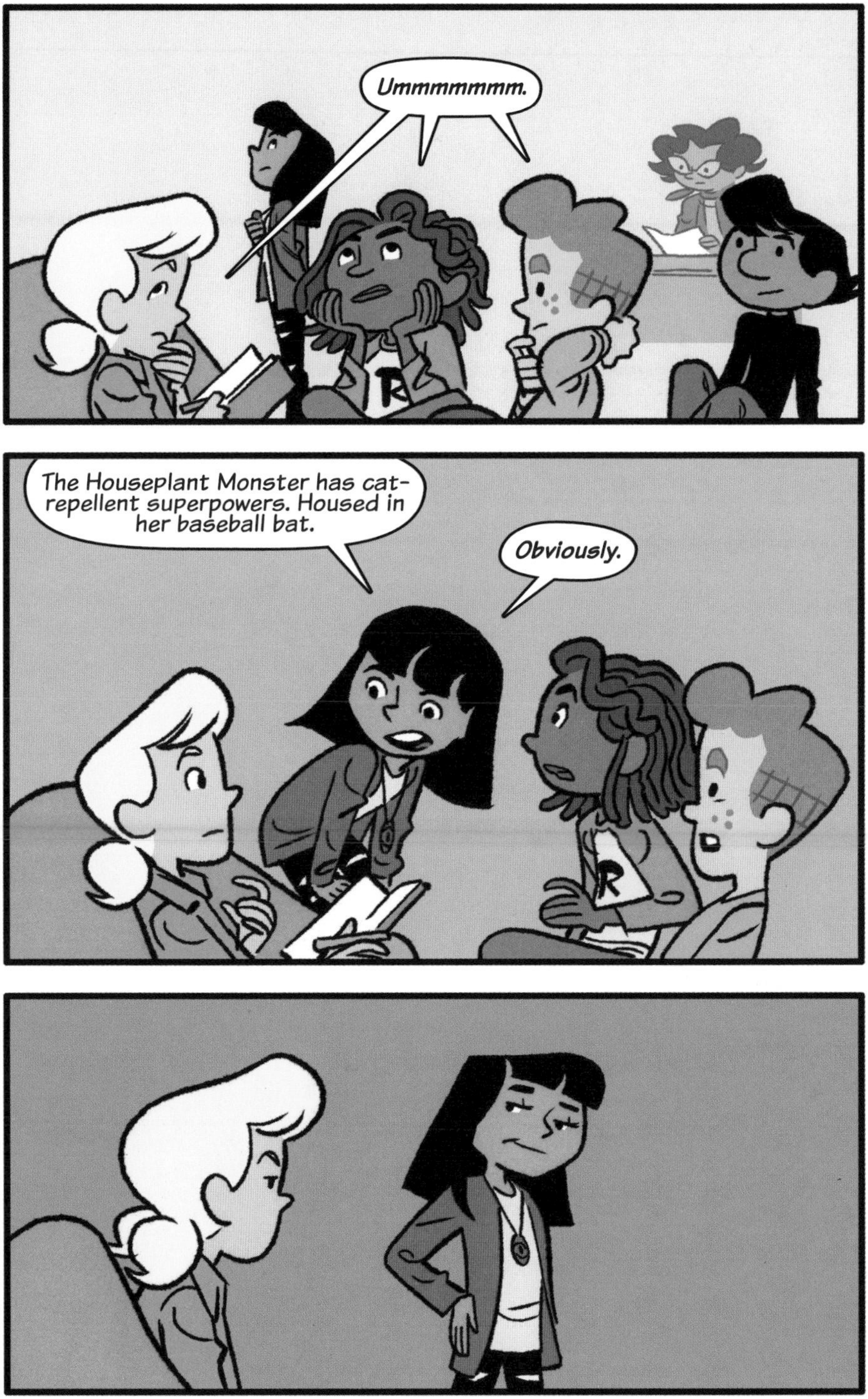
Ummmmmmm.
The Houseplant Monster has cat-repellent superpowers. Housed in her baseball bat.
Obviously.

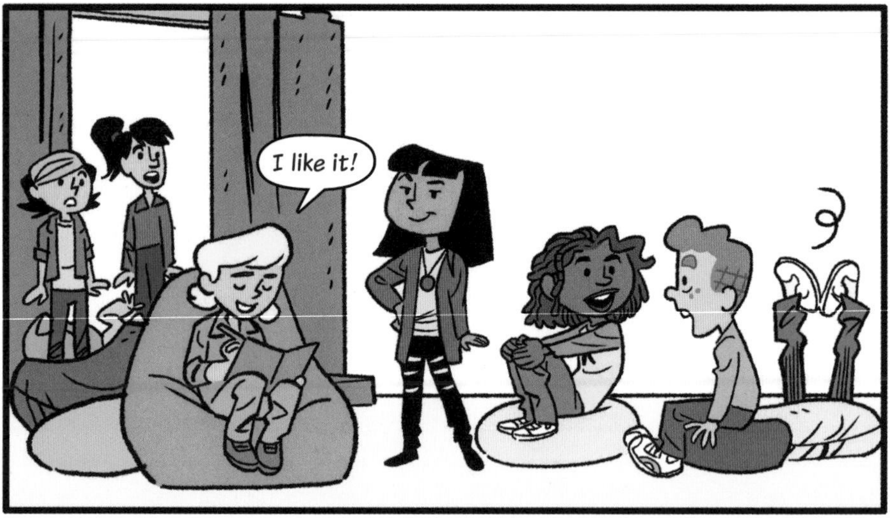
I like it!

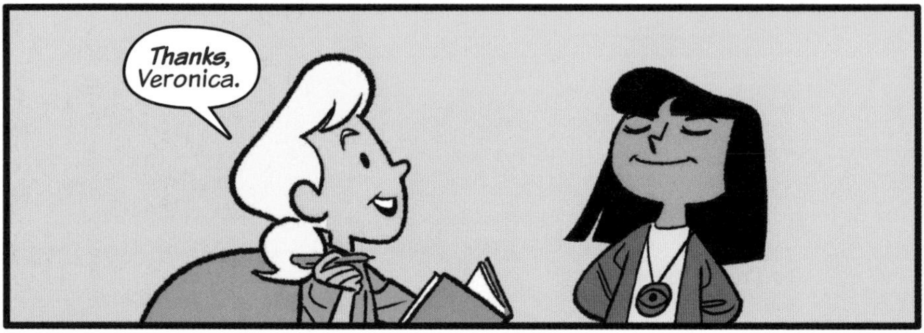
Thanks, Veronica.

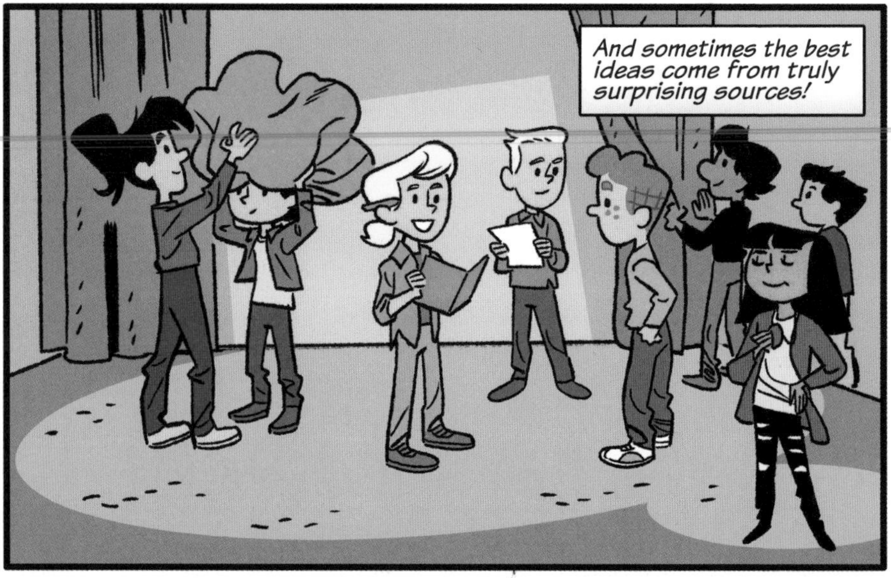
And sometimes the best ideas come from truly surprising sources!

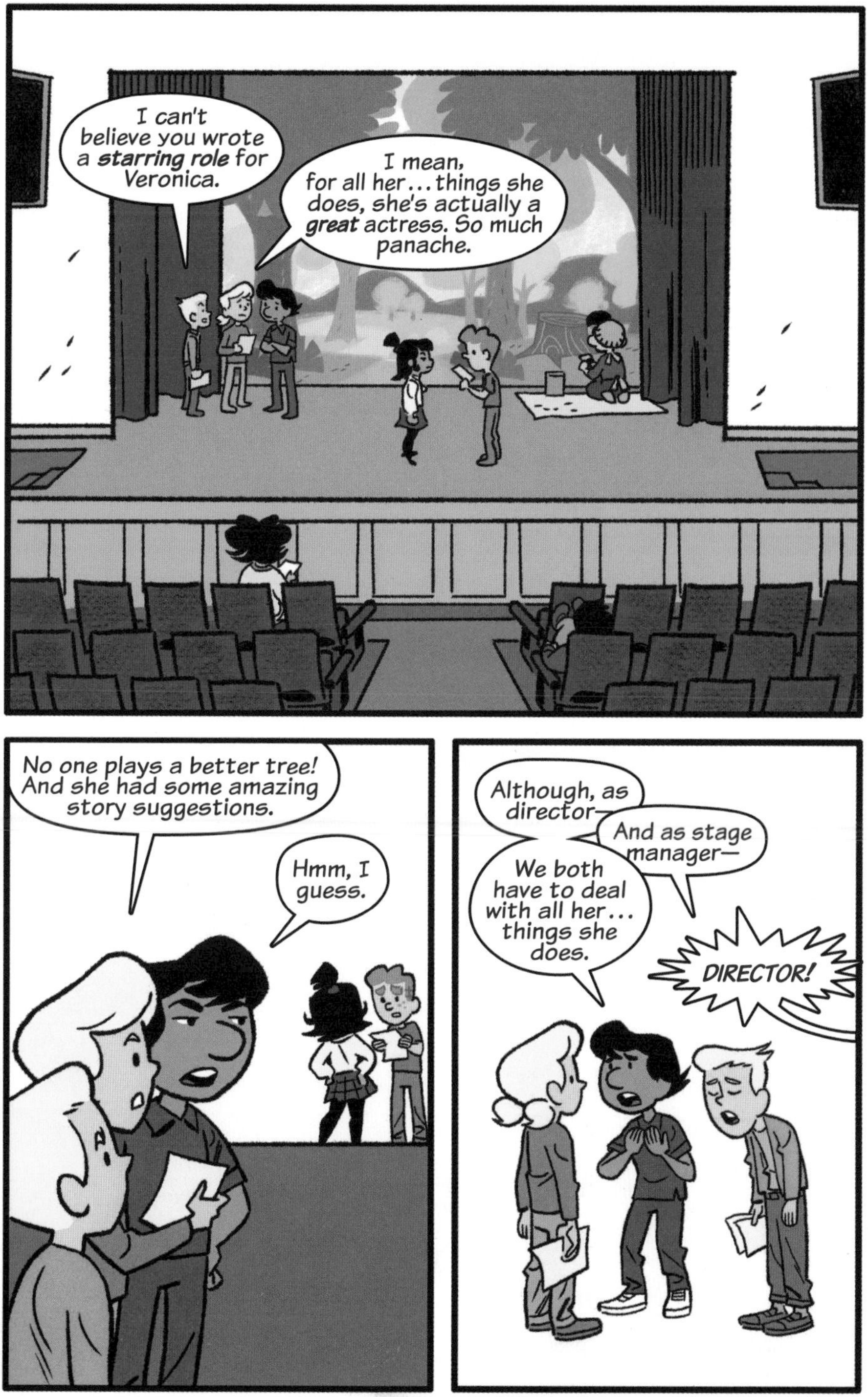
I can't believe you wrote a **starring role** for Veronica.
I mean, for all her... things she does, she's actually a **great** actress. So much panache.
No one plays a better tree! And she had some amazing story suggestions.
Hmm, I guess.
Although, as director—
And as stage manager—
We both have to deal with all her... things she does.
DIRECTOR!

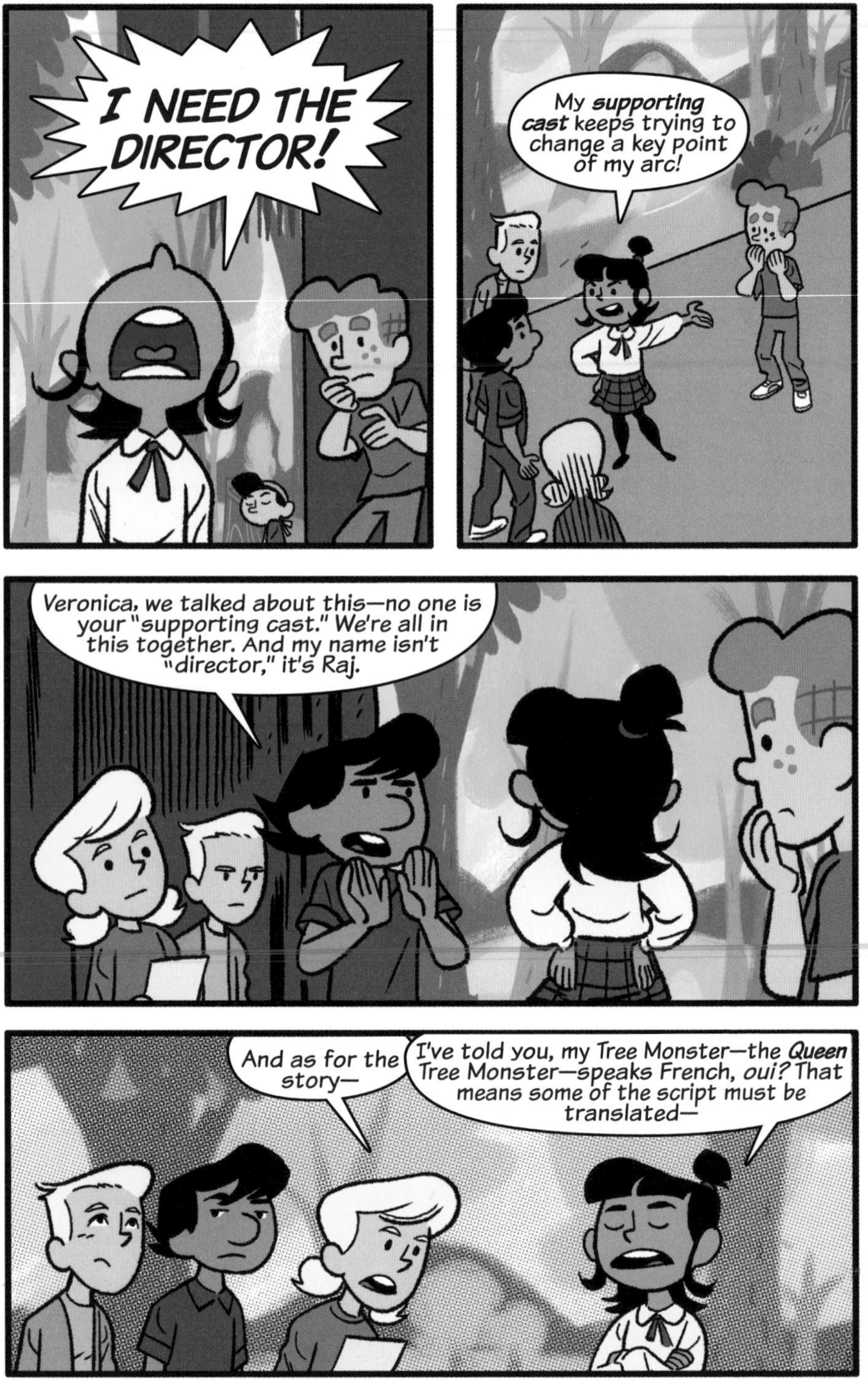
I NEED THE DIRECTOR!
My *supporting cast* keeps trying to change a key point of my arc!
Veronica, we talked about this—no one is your "supporting cast." We're all in this together. And my name isn't "director," it's Raj.
And as for the story—
I've told you, my Tree Monster—the *Queen* Tree Monster—speaks French, *oui?* That means some of the script must be translated—

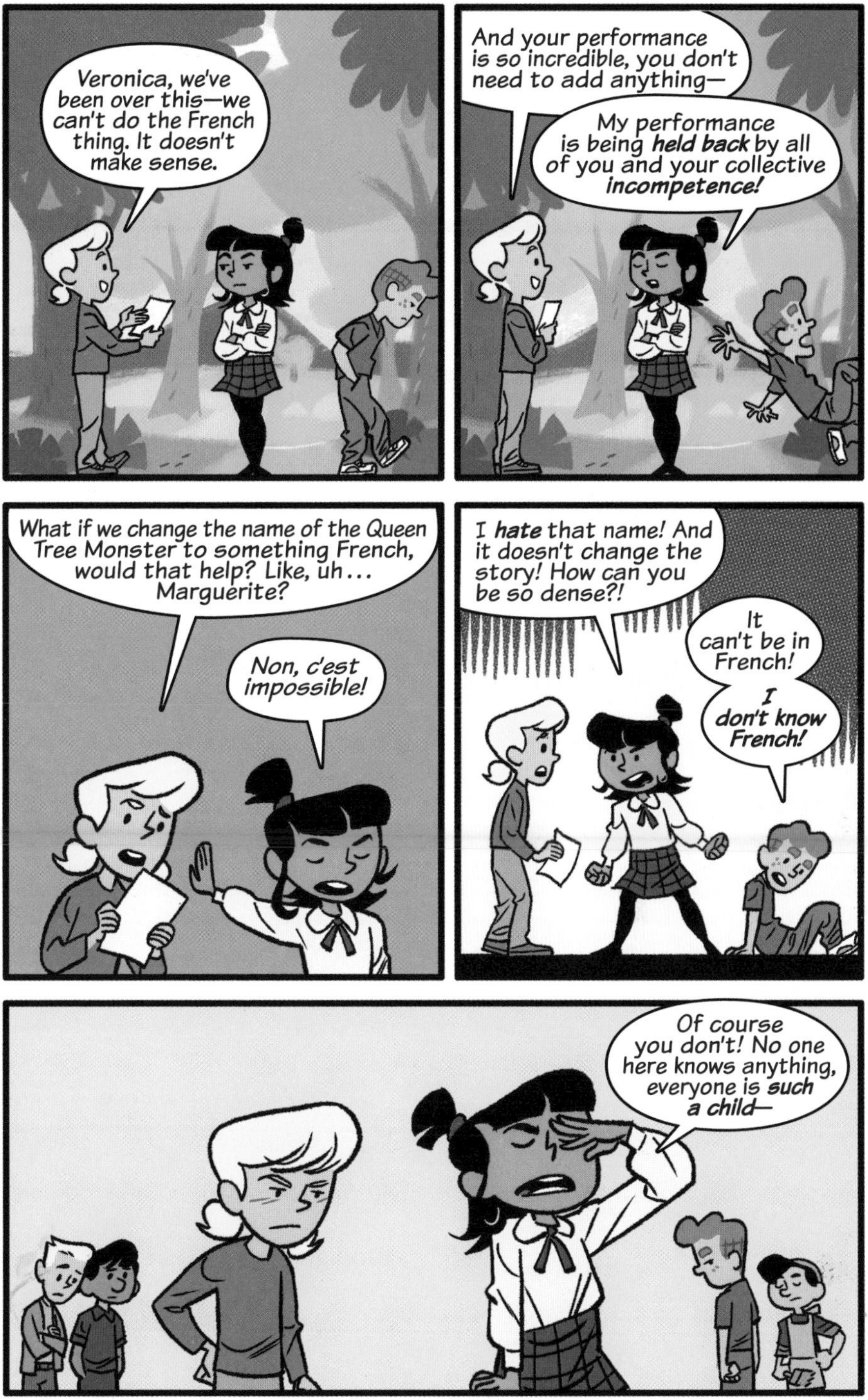

Veronica, we've been over this—we can't do the French thing. It doesn't make sense.
And your performance is so incredible, you don't need to add anything—
My performance is being **held back** by all of you and your collective ***incompetence!***
What if we change the name of the Queen Tree Monster to something French, would that help? Like, uh... Marguerite?
Non, c'est impossible!
I **hate** that name! And it doesn't change the story! How can you be so dense?!
It can't be in French!
I don't know French!
Of course you don't! No one here knows anything, everyone is **such a child**—

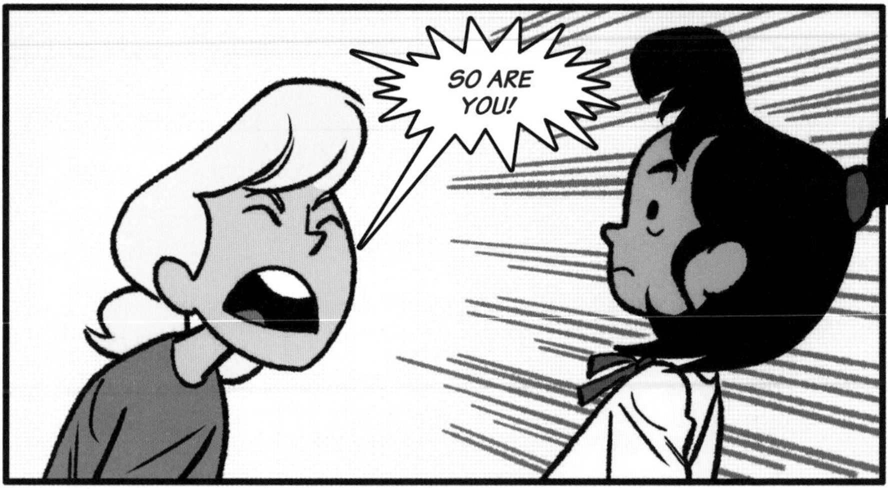
SO ARE YOU!

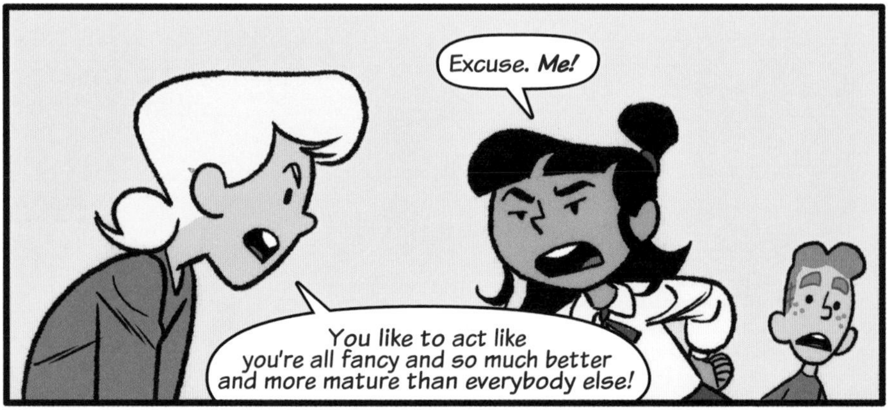
Excuse. *Me!*
You like to act like you're all fancy and so much better and more mature than everybody else!

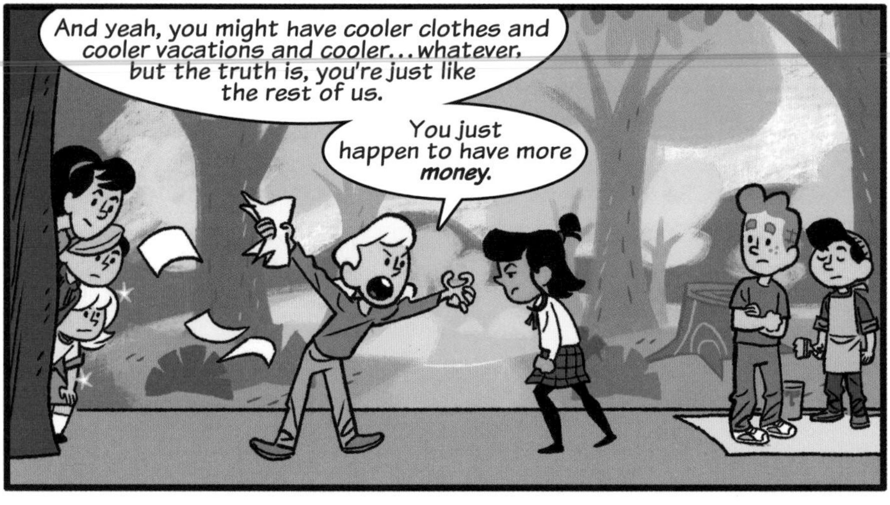
And yeah, you might have cooler clothes and cooler vacations and cooler... whatever, but the truth is, you're just like the rest of us.
You just happen to have more *money.*

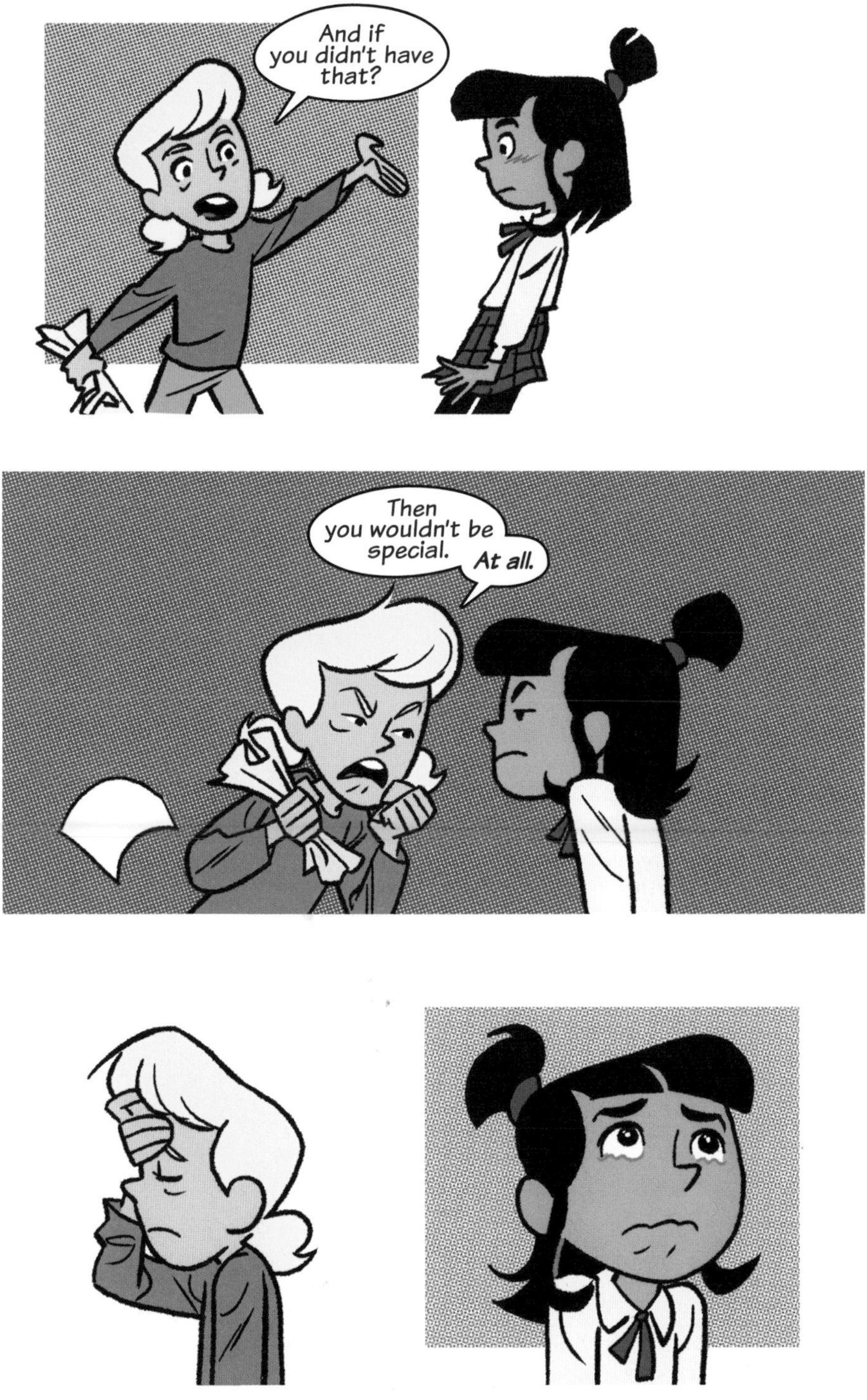
And if you didn't have that?
Then you wouldn't be special.
At all.

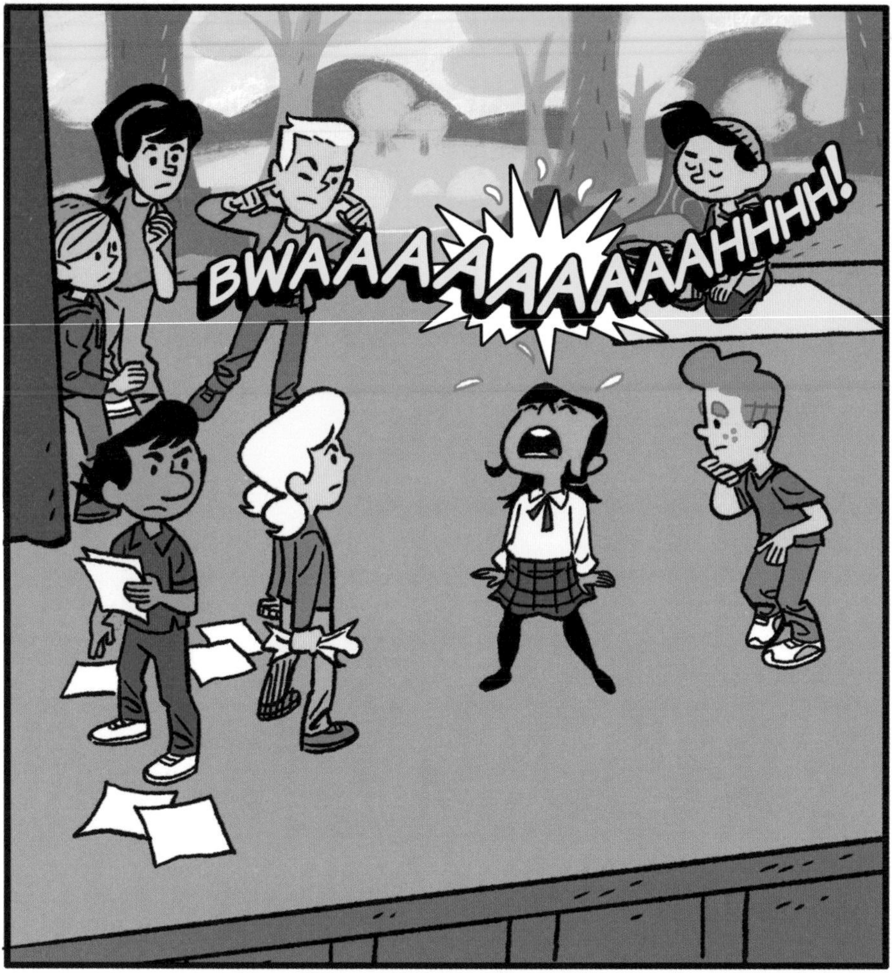
BWAAAAAAAAAAAHHHH!

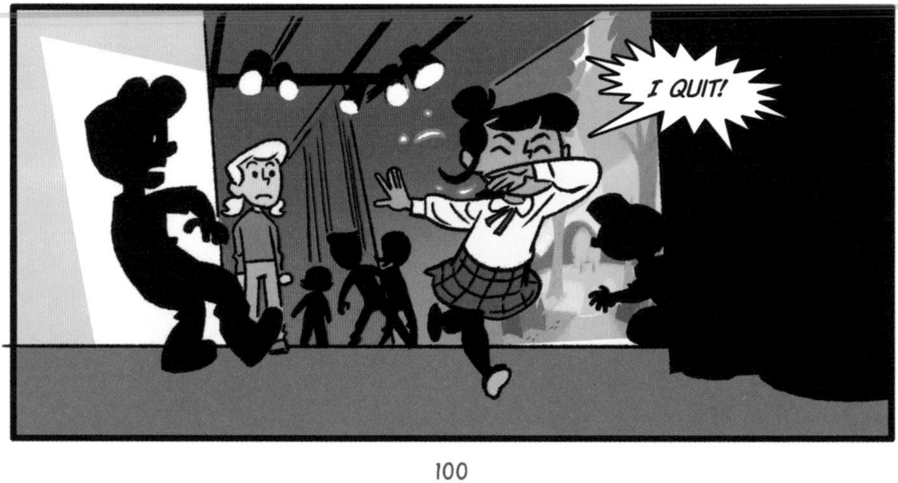
I QUIT!

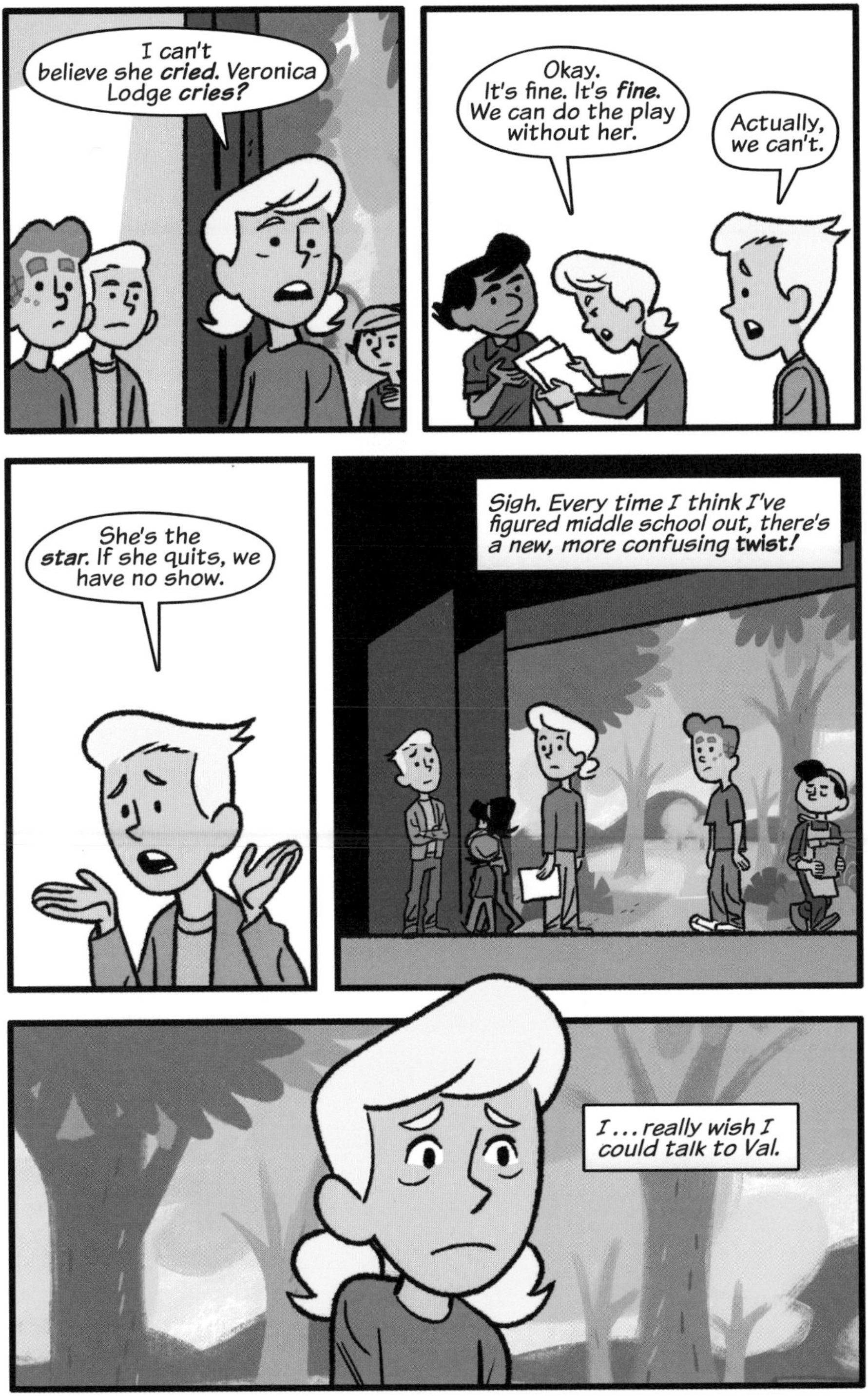
I can't believe she **cried**. Veronica Lodge **cries?**
Okay. It's fine. It's **fine**. We can do the play without her.
Actually, we can't.
She's the **star**. If she quits, we have no show.
Sigh. Every time I think I've figured middle school out, there's a new, more confusing **twist!**
I... really wish I could talk to Val.

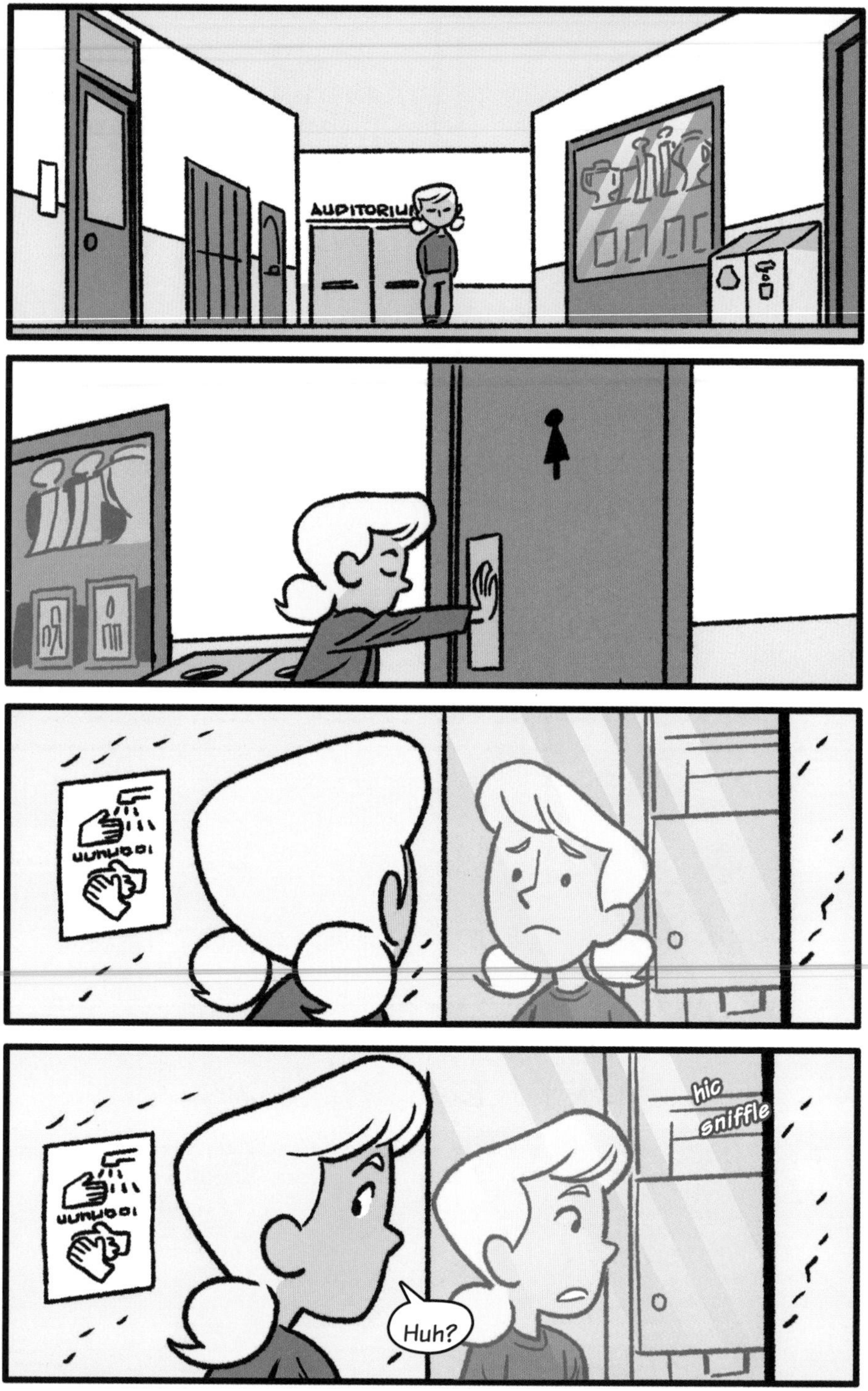
AUDITORIU
hic
sniffle
Huh?

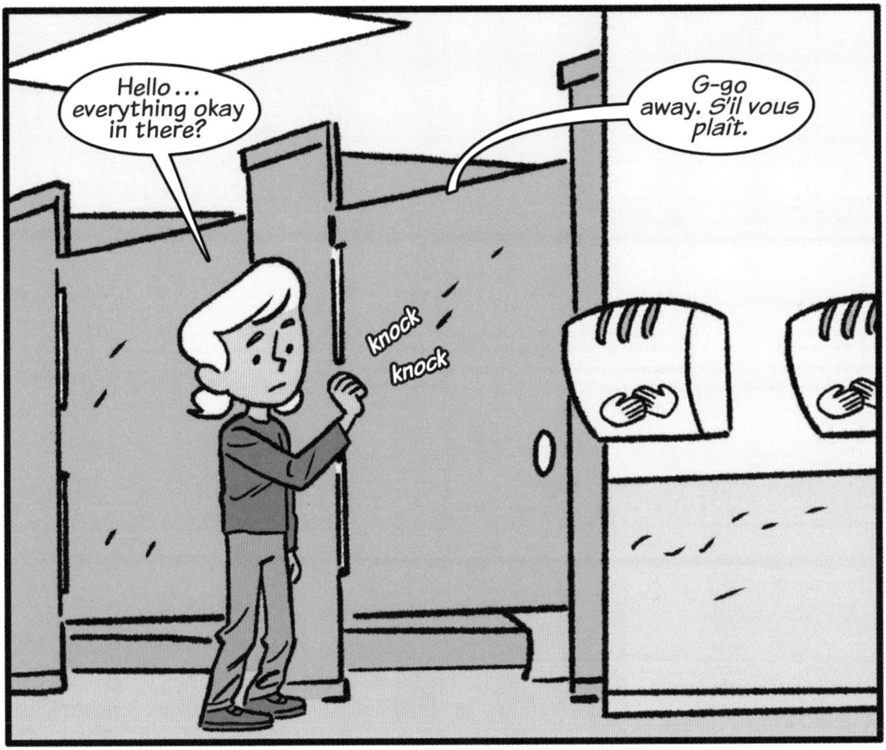
Hello... everything okay in there?
G-go away. S'il vous plaît.
knock
knock

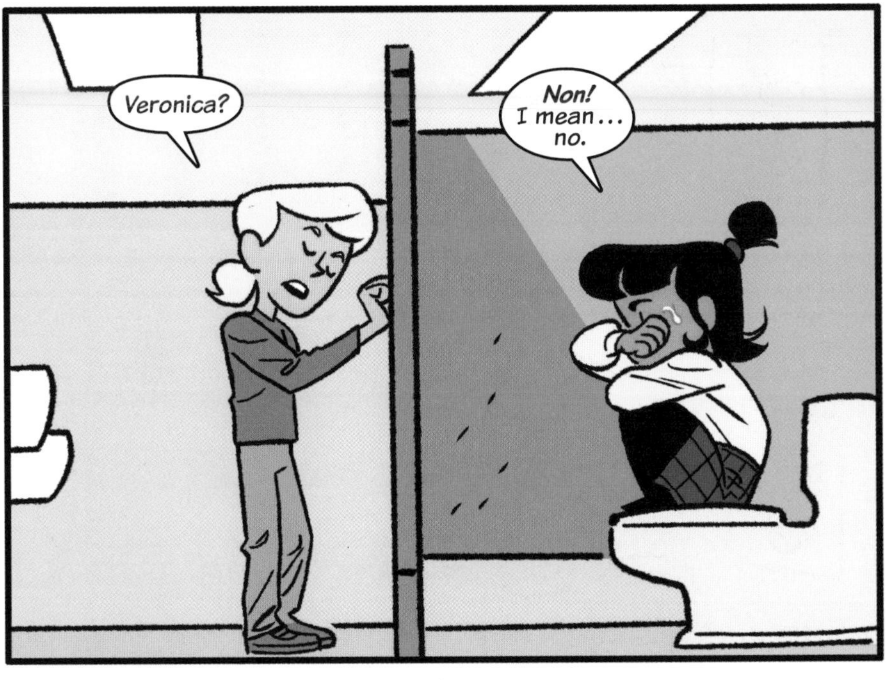
Veronica?
Non! I mean... no.

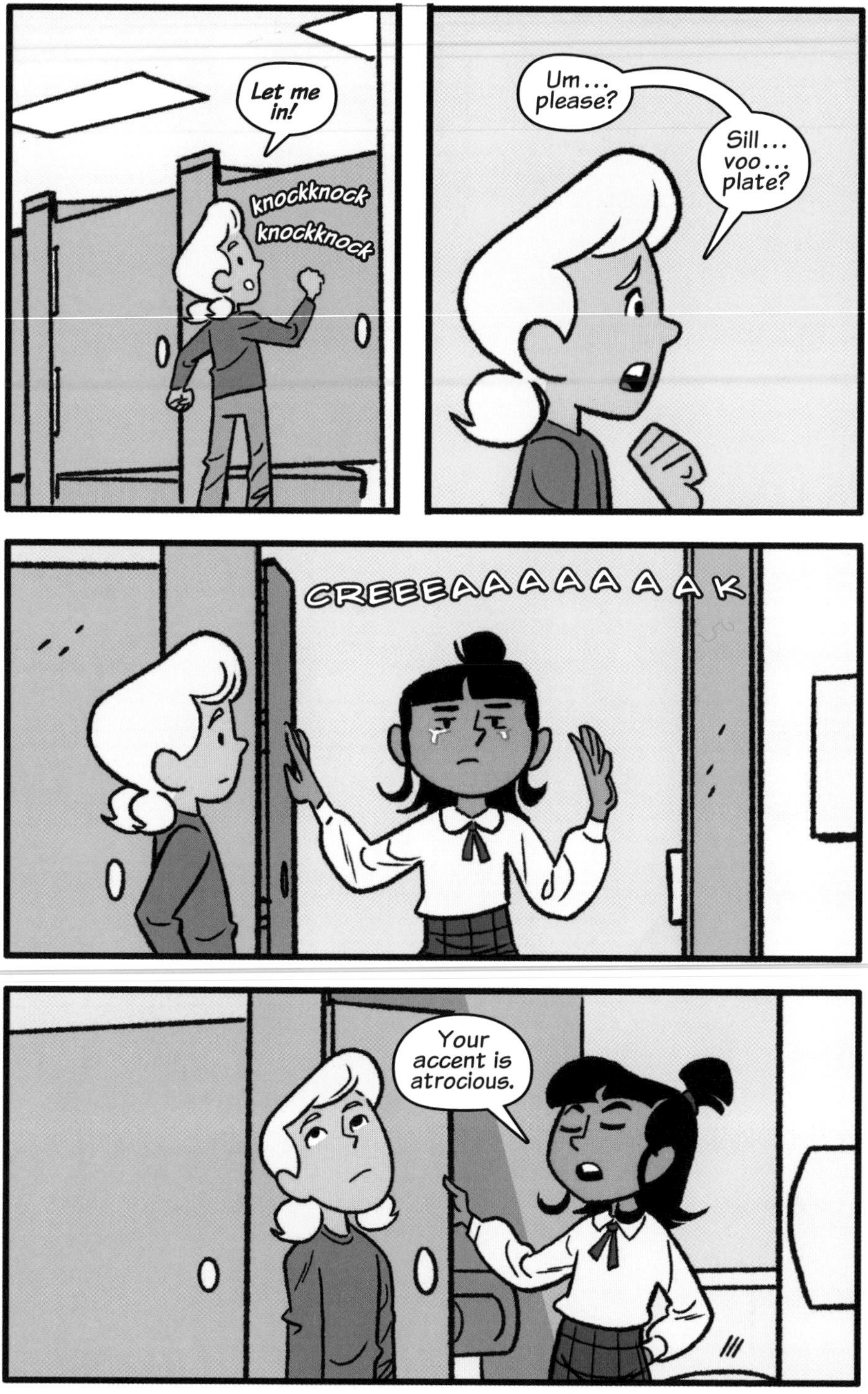
Let me in!
knockknock
knockknock
Um... please?
Sill... voo... plate?
CREEEAAAAAAAK
Your accent is atrocious.

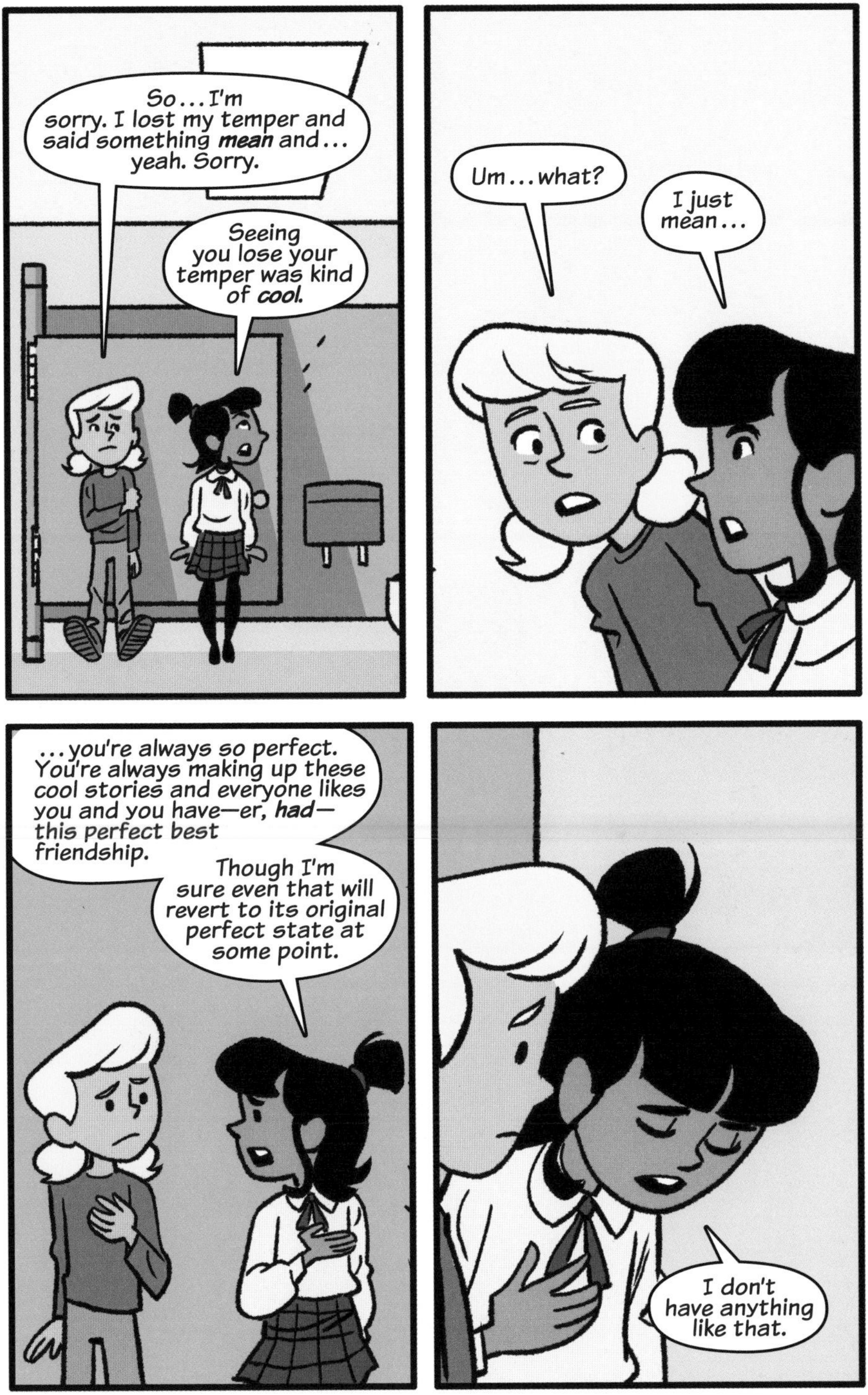

So... I'm sorry. I lost my temper and said something mean and... yeah. Sorry.
Seeing you lose your temper was kind of cool.
Um... what?
I just mean...
...you're always so perfect. You're always making up these cool stories and everyone likes you and you have—er, had—this perfect best friendship.
Though I'm sure even that will revert to its original perfect state at some point.
I don't have anything like that.

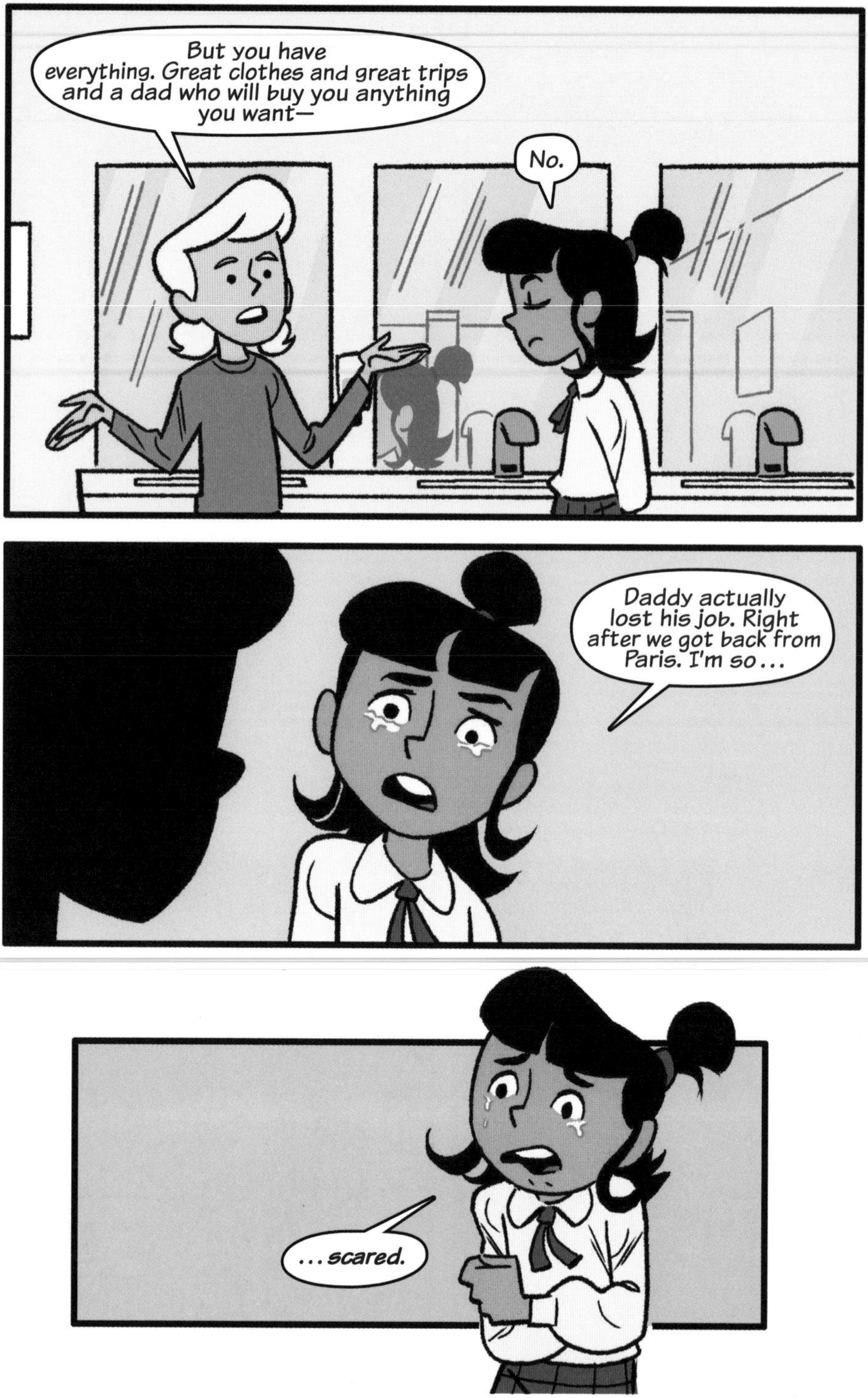
But you have everything. Great clothes and great trips and a dad who will buy you anything you want—
No.
Daddy actually lost his job. Right after we got back from Paris. I'm so...
...scared.

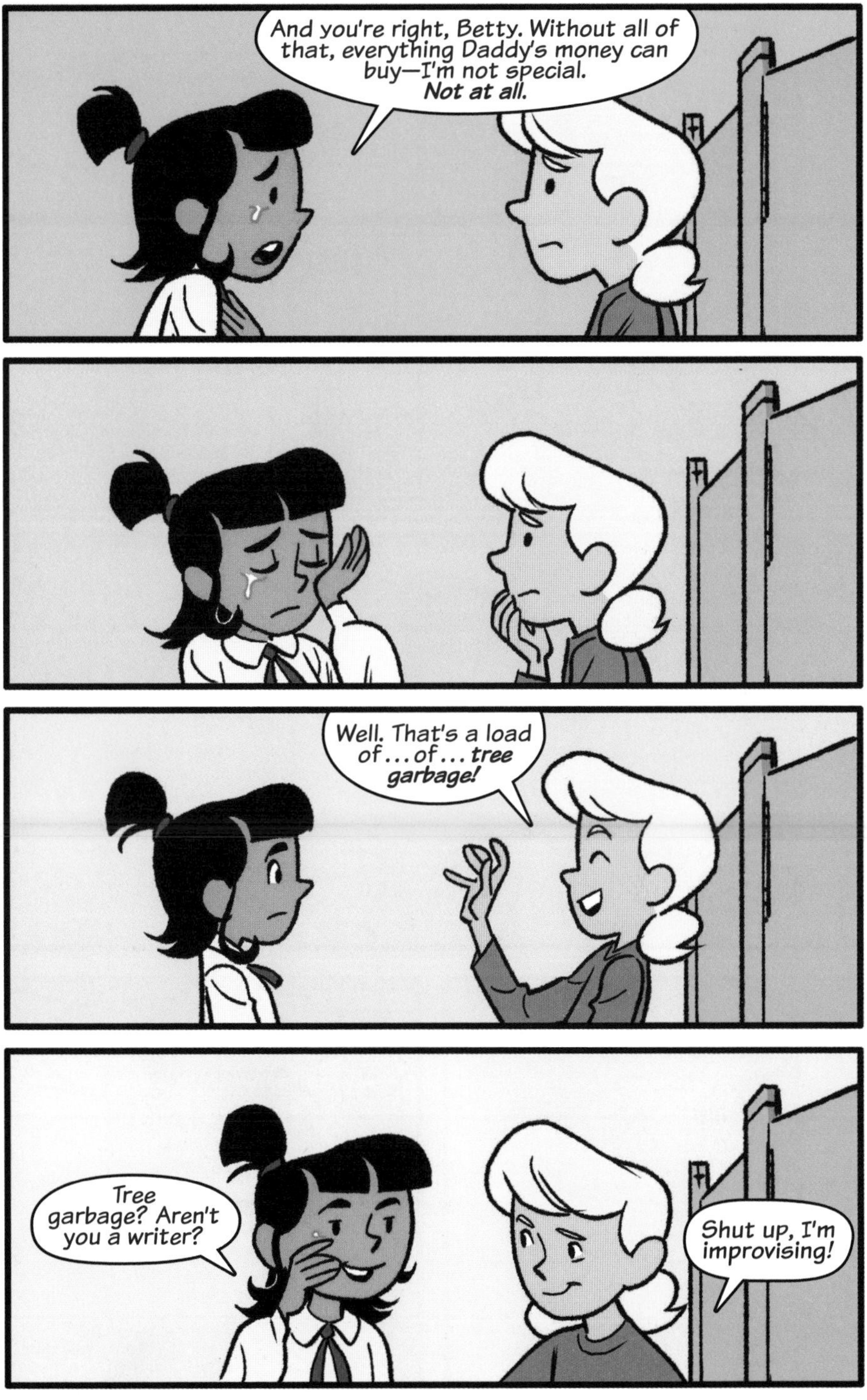
And you're right, Betty. Without all of that, everything Daddy's money can buy—I'm not special. ***Not at all.***
Well. That's a load of... of... ***tree garbage!***
Tree garbage? Aren't you a writer?
Shut up, I'm improvising!

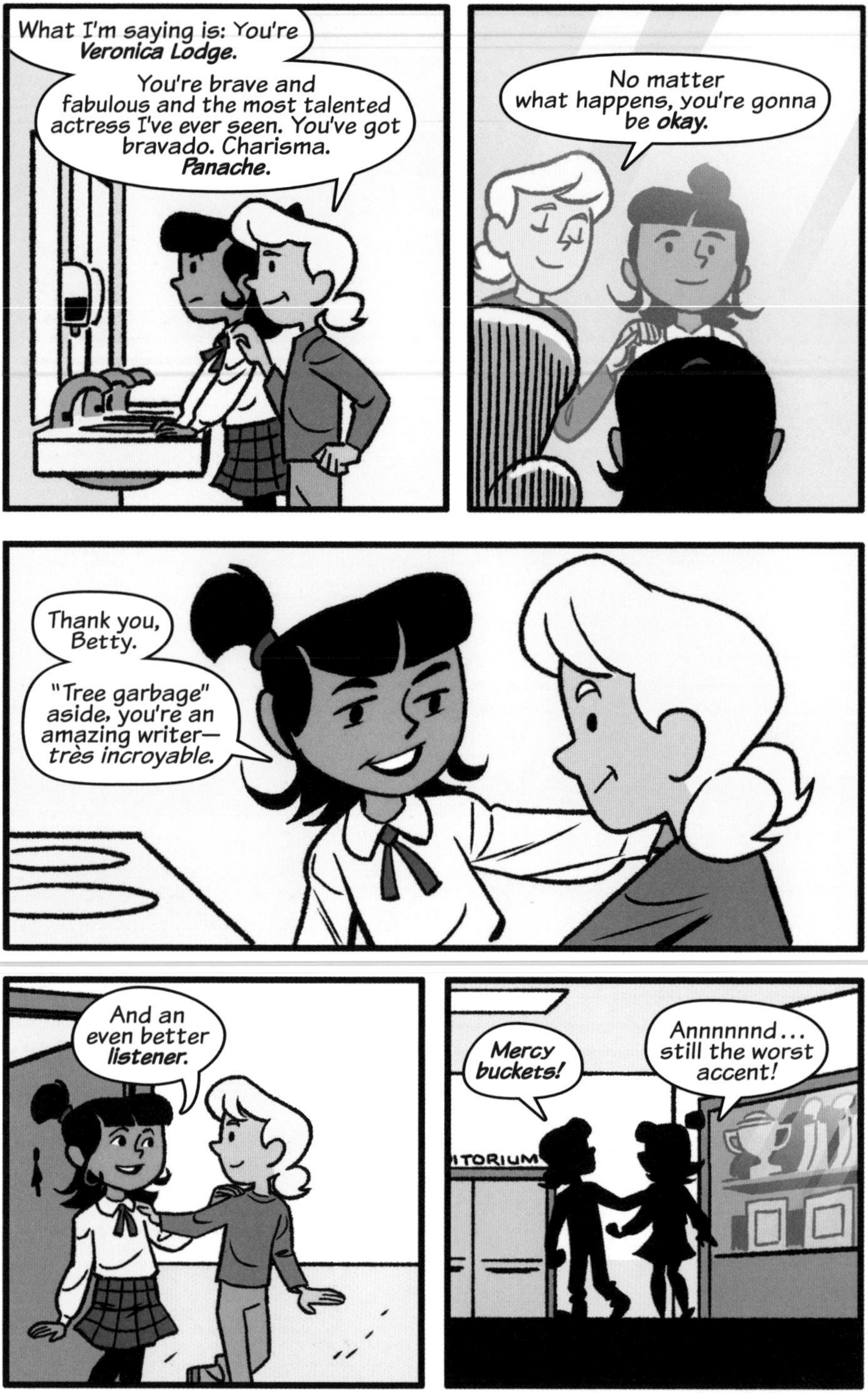
What I'm saying is: You're **Veronica Lodge.**
You're brave and fabulous and the most talented actress I've ever seen. You've got bravado. Charisma. **Panache.**
No matter what happens, you're gonna be **okay.**
Thank you, Betty.
"Tree garbage" aside, you're an amazing writer— *très incroyable.*
And an even better **listener.**
ITORIUM
Mercy buckets!
Annnnnnd... still the worst accent!

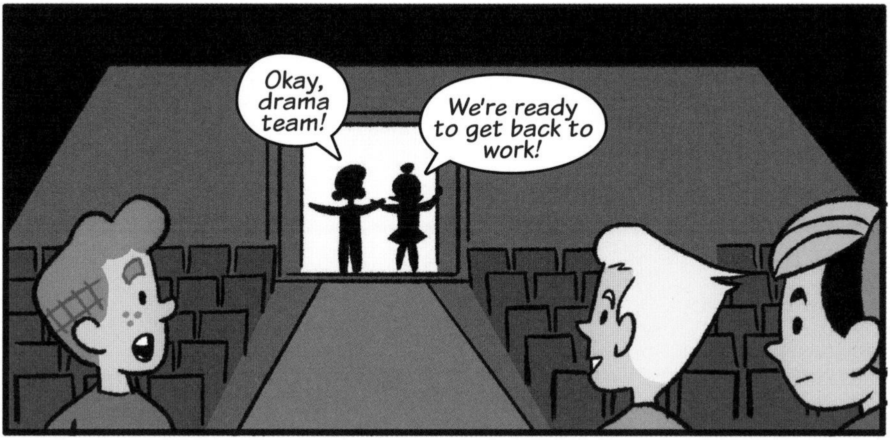
Okay, drama team!
We're ready to get back to work!

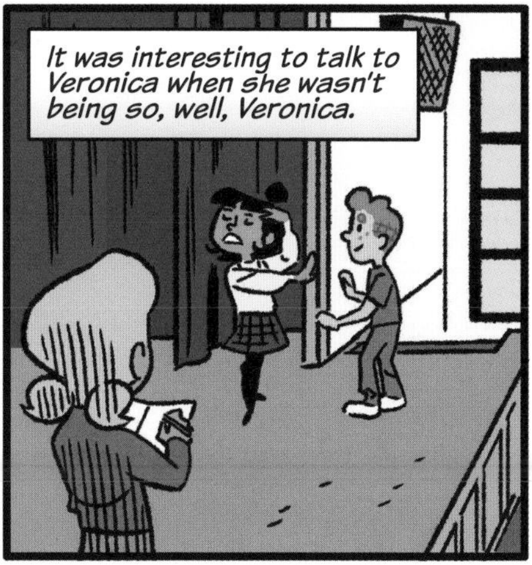
It was interesting to talk to Veronica when she wasn't being so, well, Veronica.

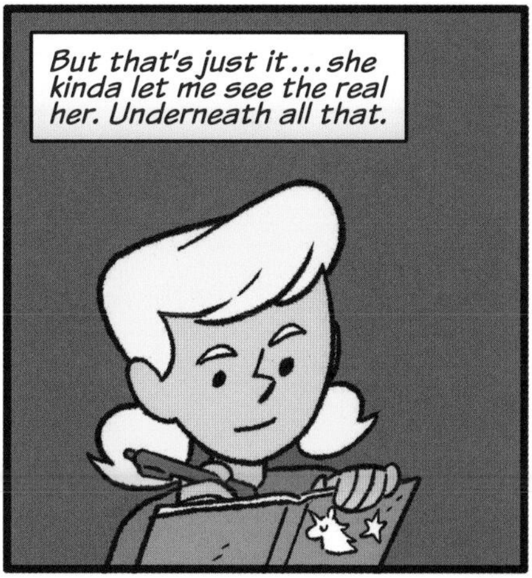
But that's just it... she kinda let me see the real her. Underneath all that.

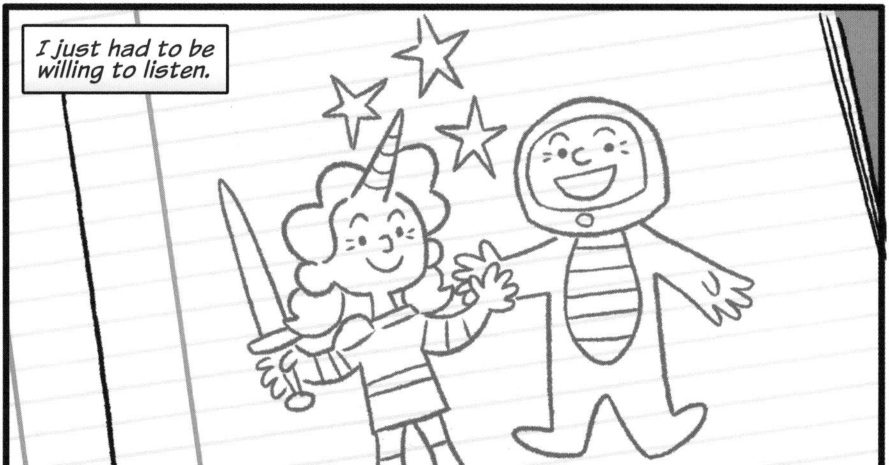
I just had to be willing to listen.

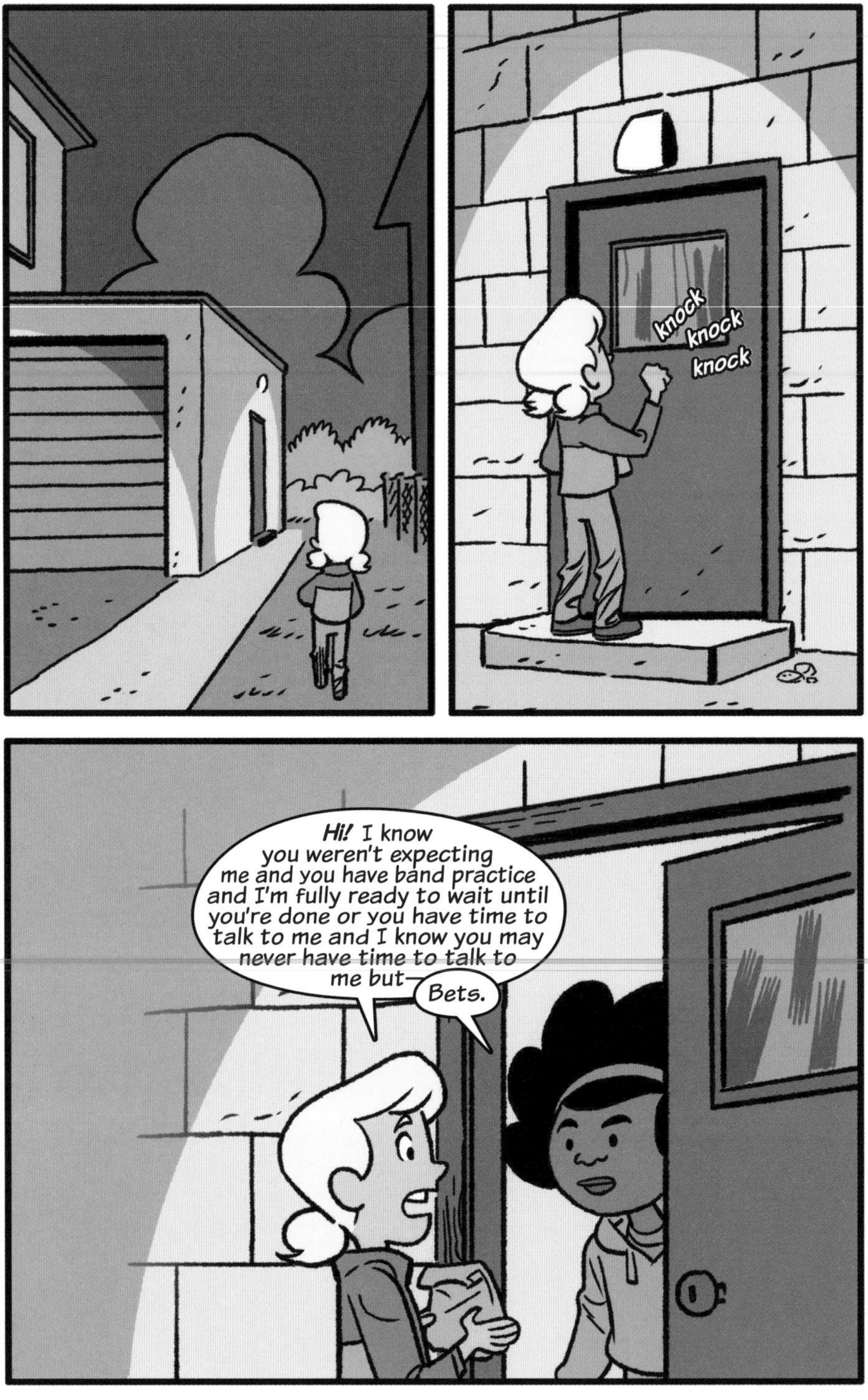
knock
knock
knock
Hi! I know you weren't expecting me and you have band practice and I'm fully ready to wait until you're done or you have time to talk to me and I know you may never have time to talk to me but—
Bets.

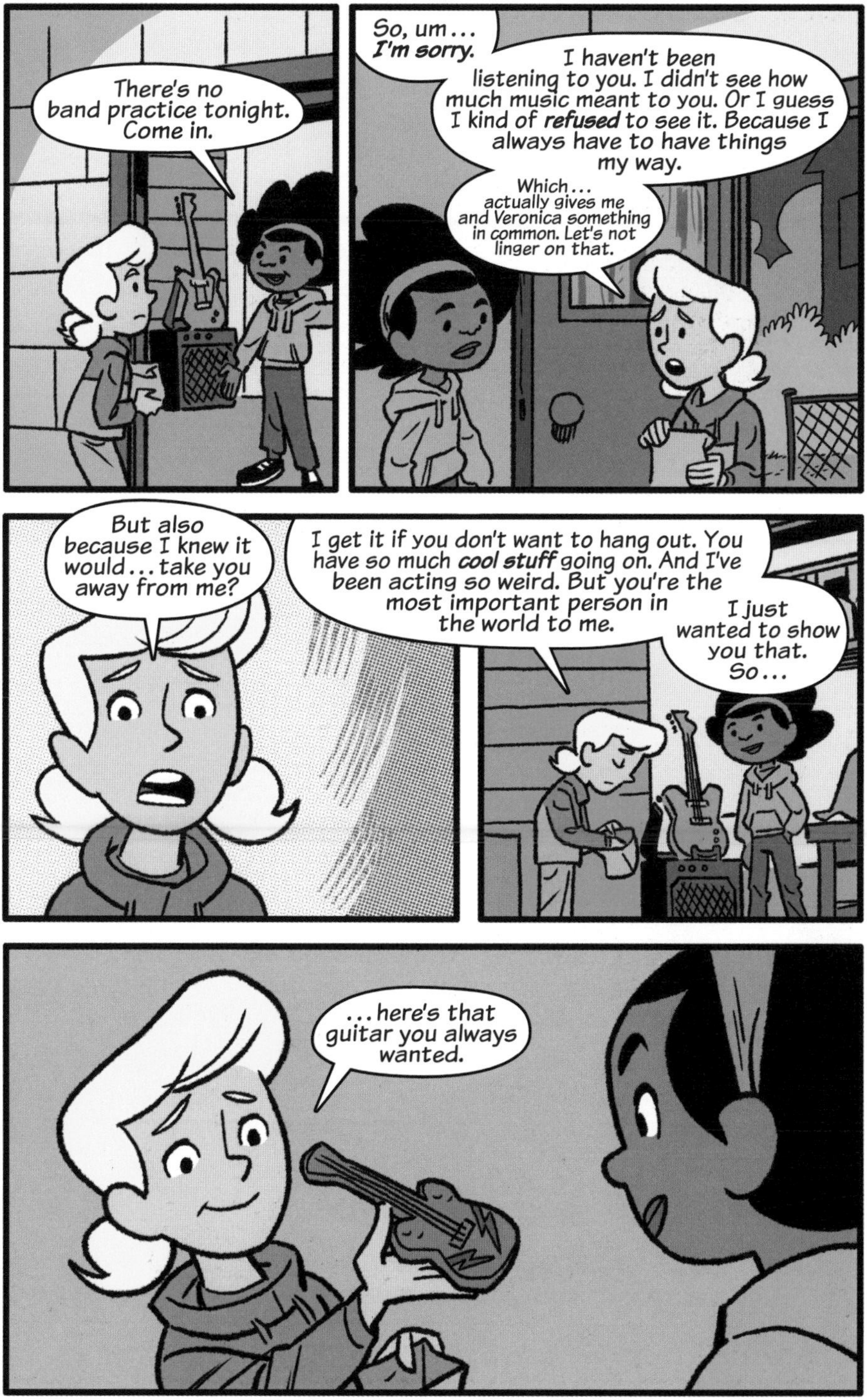
There's no band practice tonight. Come in.
So, um... I'm sorry.
I haven't been listening to you. I didn't see how much music meant to you. Or I guess I kind of refused to see it. Because I always have to have things my way.
Which... actually gives me and Veronica something in common. Let's not linger on that.
But also because I knew it would... take you away from me?
I get it if you don't want to hang out. You have so much cool stuff going on. And I've been acting so weird. But you're the most important person in the world to me.
I just wanted to show you that. So...
...here's that guitar you always wanted.

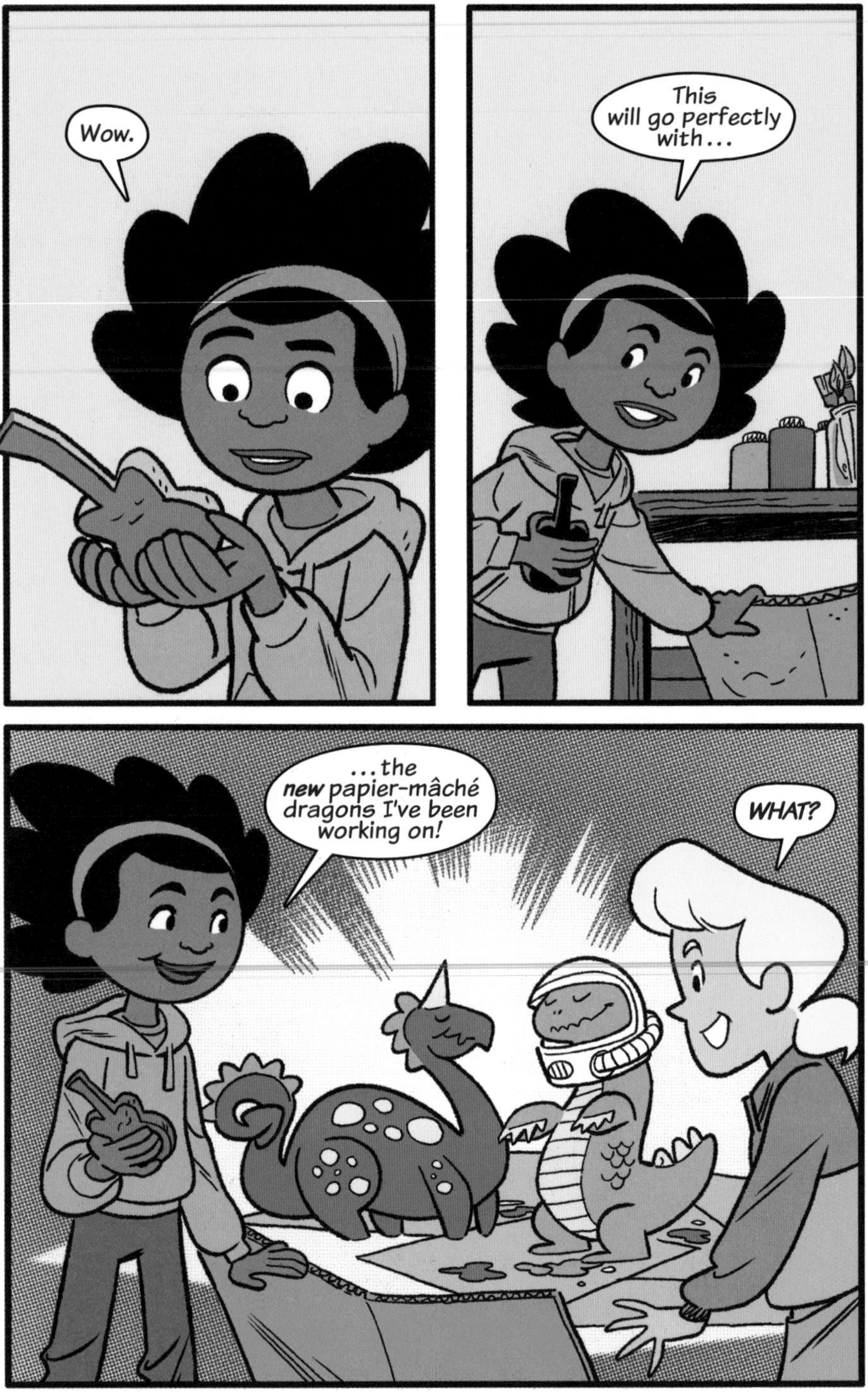
Wow.
This will go perfectly with...
...the *new* papier-mâché dragons I've been working on!
WHAT?

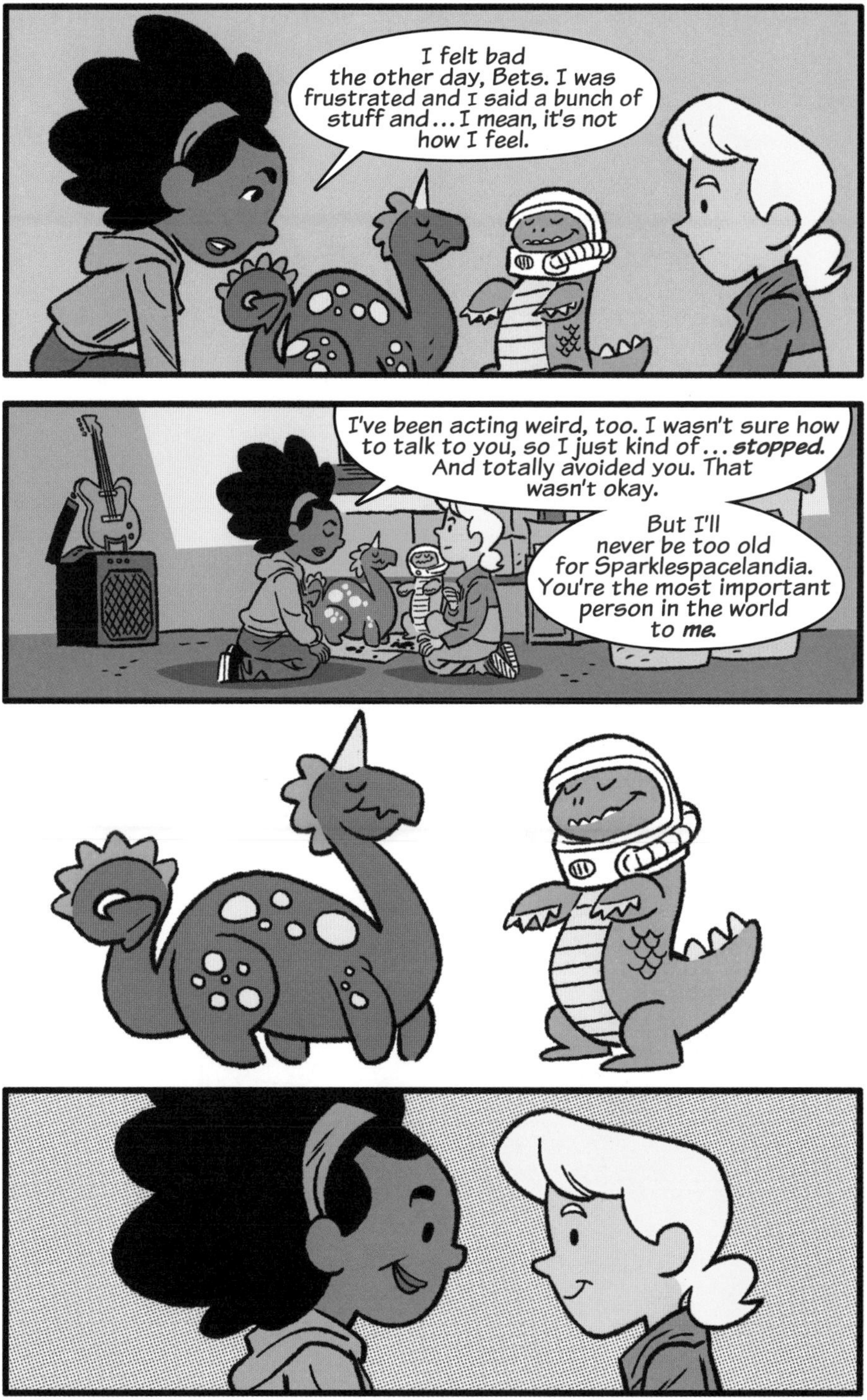
I felt bad the other day, Bets. I was frustrated and I said a bunch of stuff and... I mean, it's not how I feel.
I've been acting weird, too. I wasn't sure how to talk to you, so I just kind of... ***stopped.*** And totally avoided you. That wasn't okay.
But I'll never be too old for Sparklespacelandia. You're the most important person in the world to ***me.***

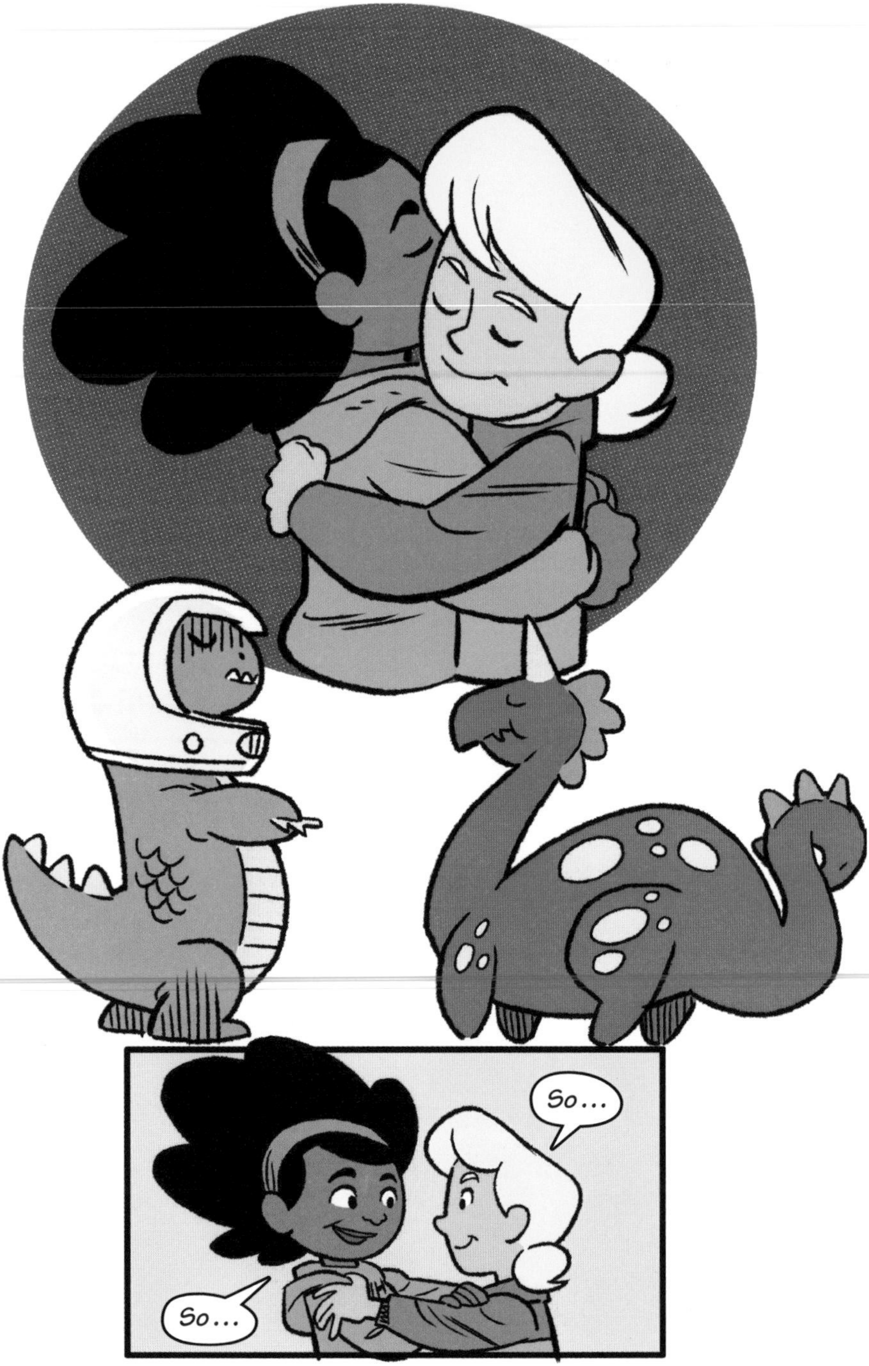
So...
So...

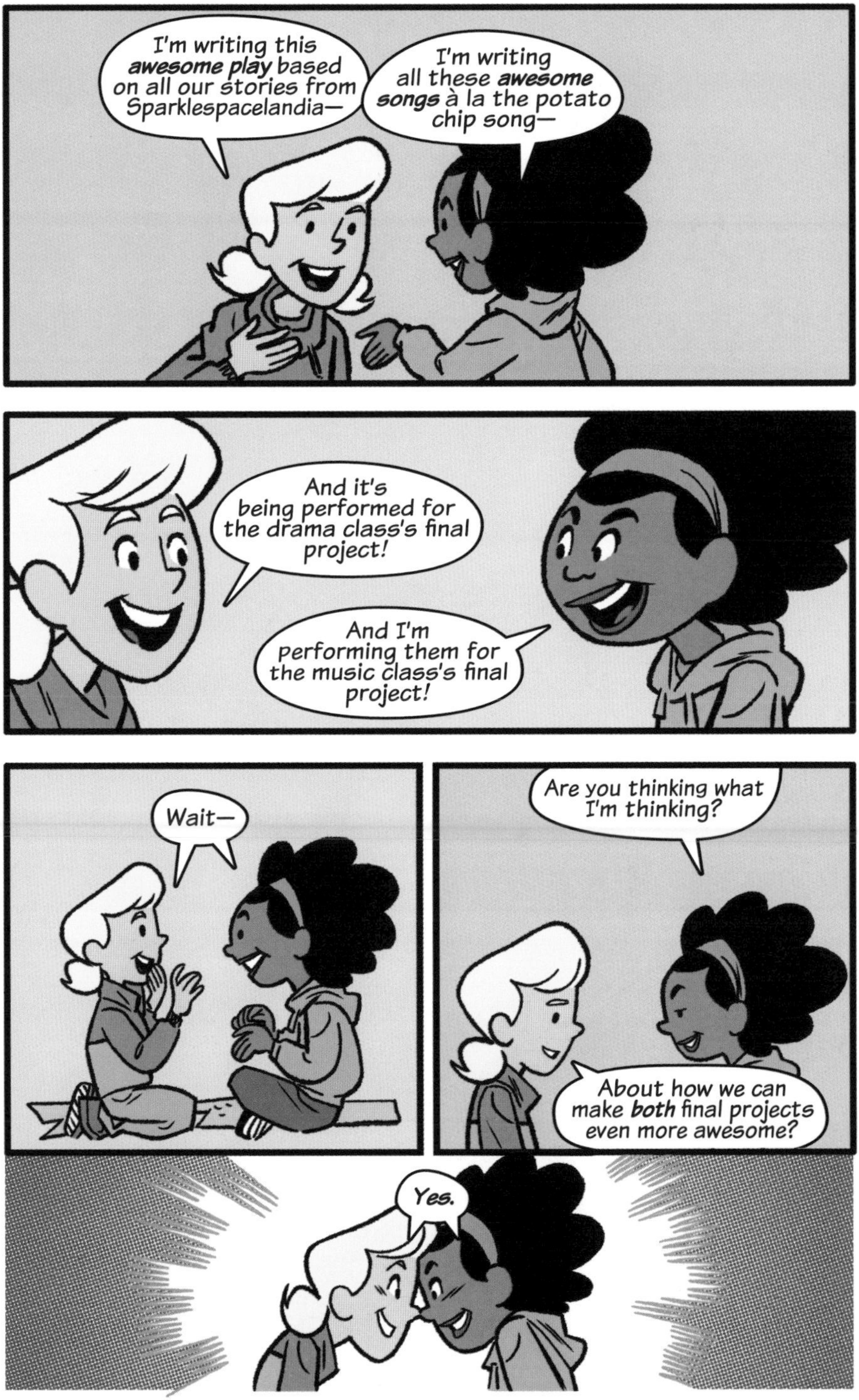
I'm writing this **awesome play** based on all our stories from Sparklespacelandia—
I'm writing all these **awesome songs** à la the potato chip song—
And it's being performed for the drama class's final project!
And I'm performing them for the music class's final project!
Wait—
Are you thinking what I'm thinking?
About how we can make **both** final projects even more awesome?
Yes.

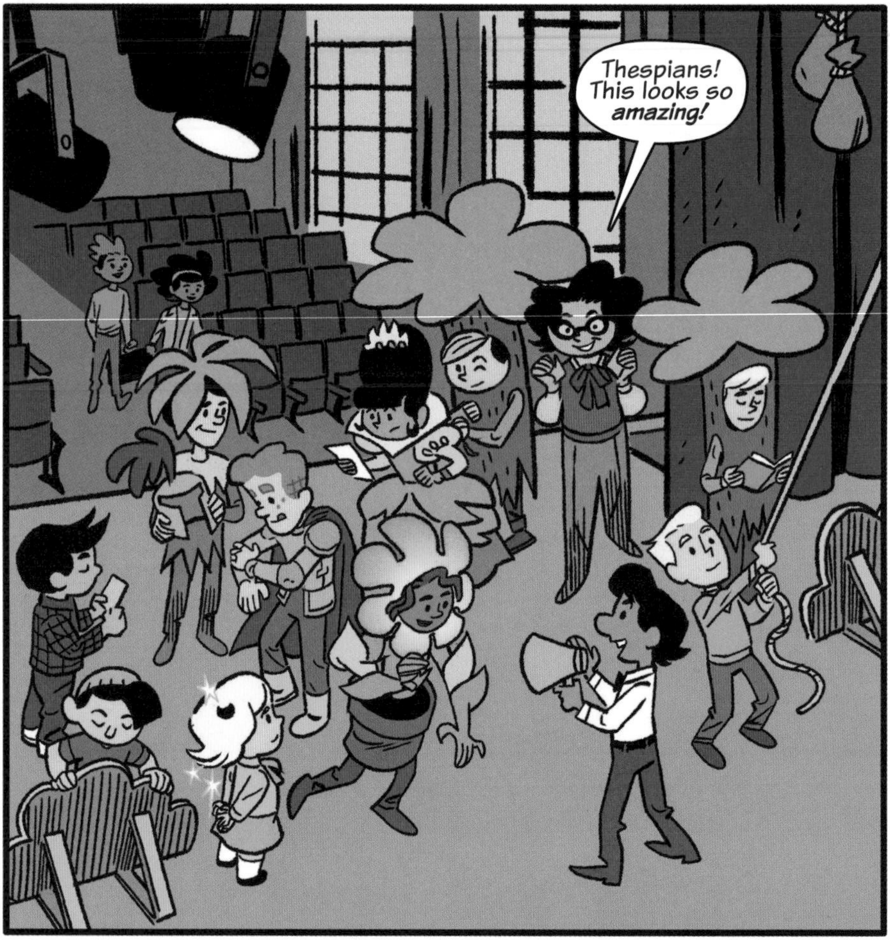
Thespians! This looks so *amazing!*

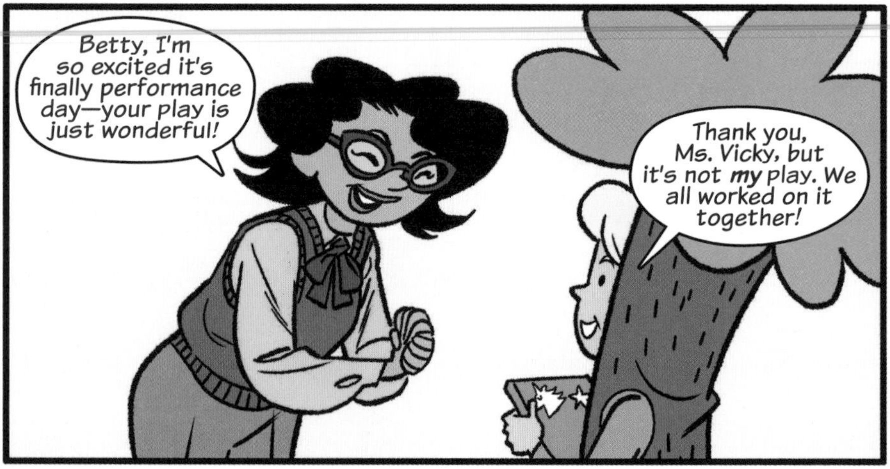
Betty, I'm so excited it's finally performance day—your play is just wonderful!
Thank you, Ms. Vicky, but it's not *my* play. We all worked on it together!

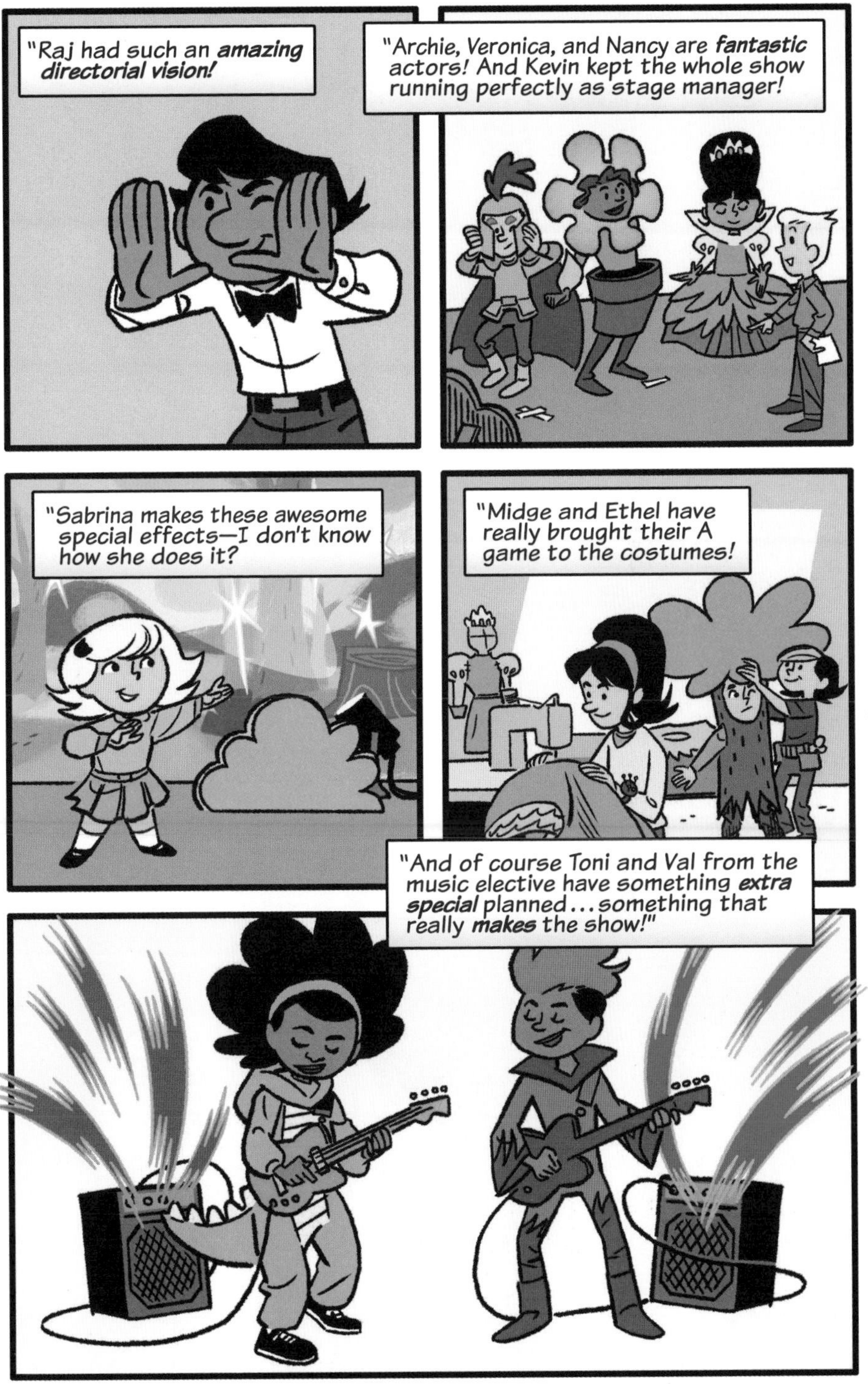
"Raj had such an ***amazing directorial vision!***
"Archie, Veronica, and Nancy are ***fantastic*** actors! And Kevin kept the whole show running perfectly as stage manager!
"Sabrina makes these awesome special effects—I don't know how she does it?
"Midge and Ethel have really brought their A game to the costumes!
"And of course Toni and Val from the music elective have something ***extra special*** planned... something that really ***makes*** the show!"

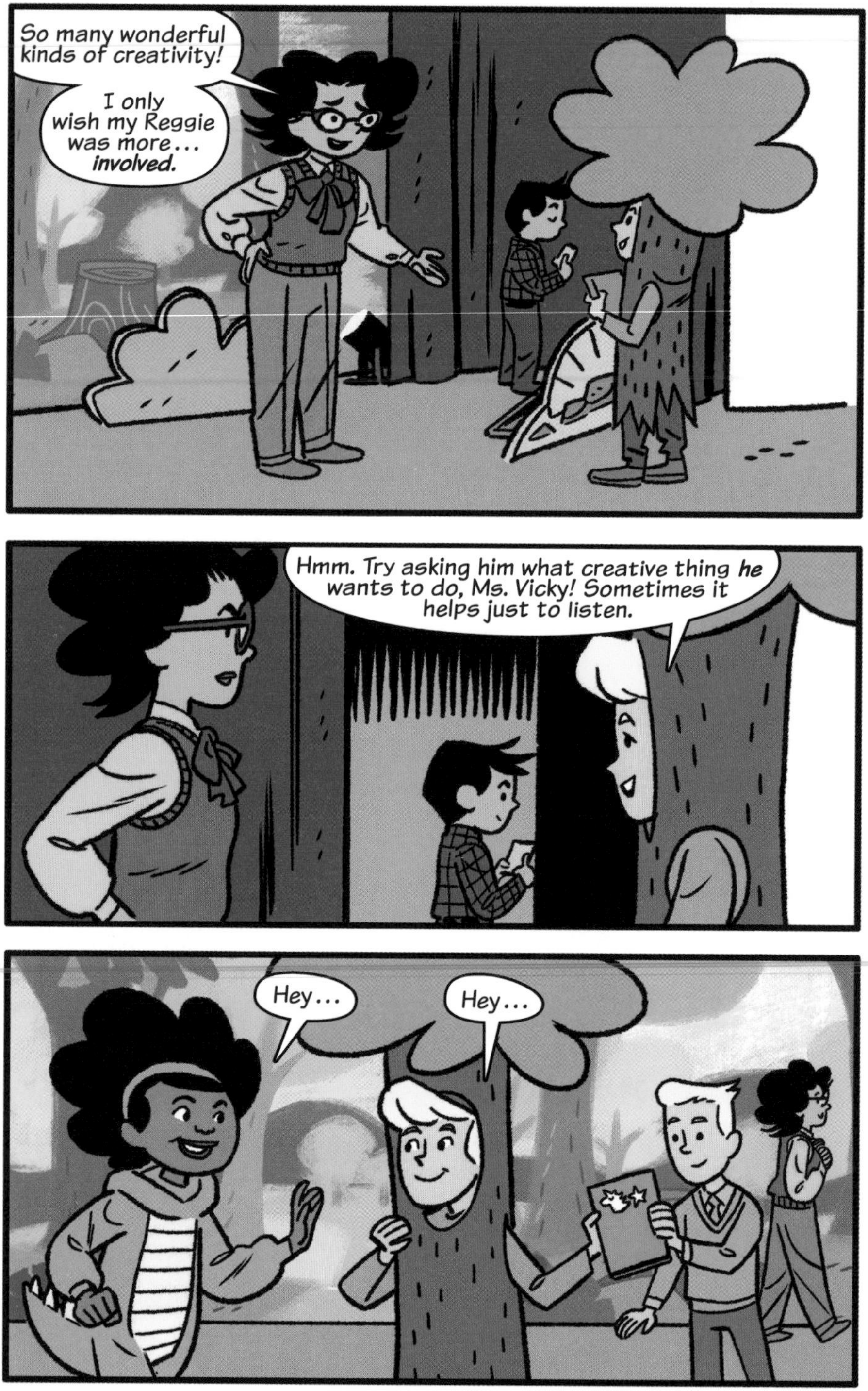
So many wonderful kinds of creativity!
I only wish my Reggie was more... *involved.*
Hmm. Try asking him what creative thing *he* wants to do, Ms. Vicky! Sometimes it helps just to listen.
Hey...
Hey...

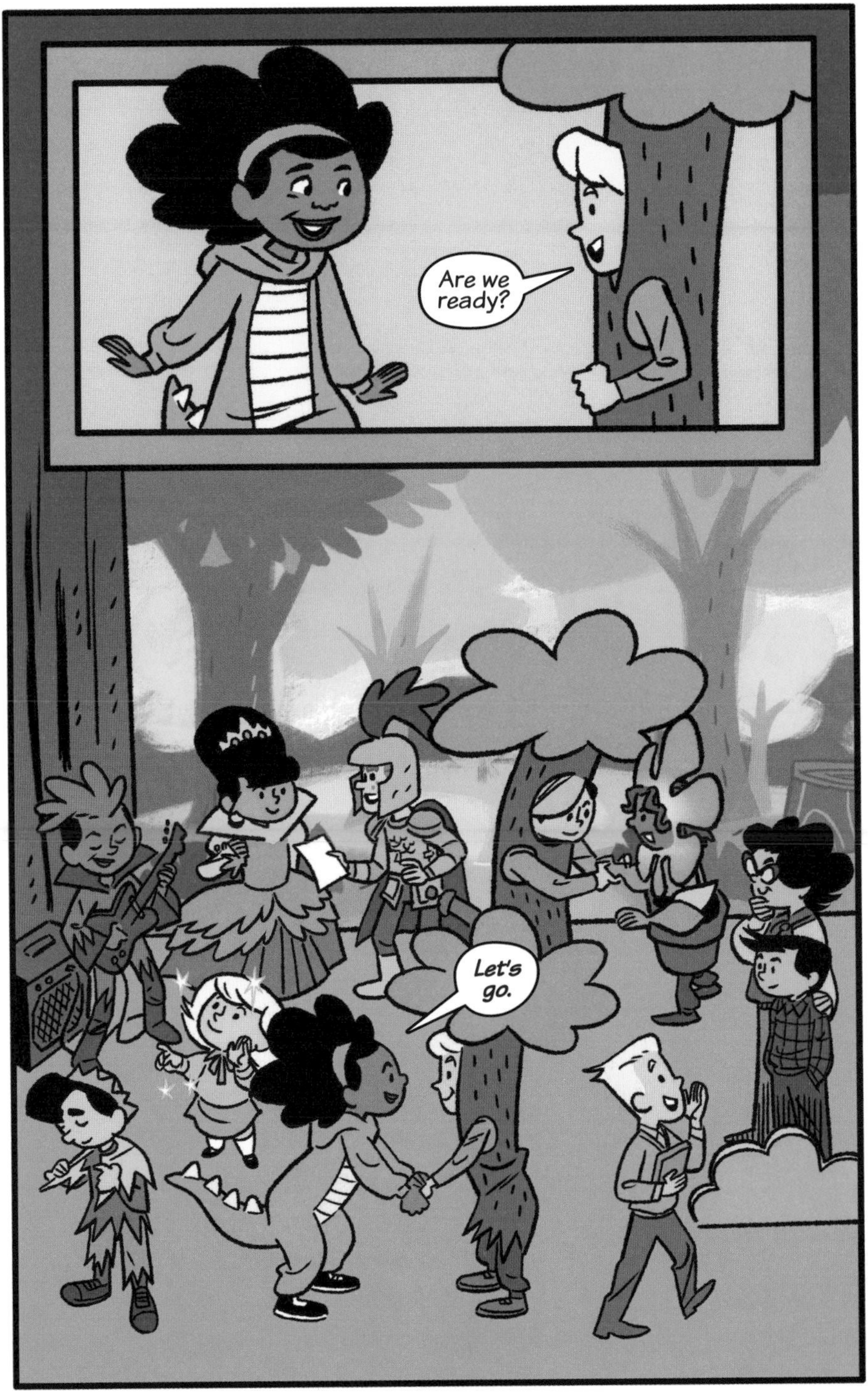
Are we ready?
Let's go.

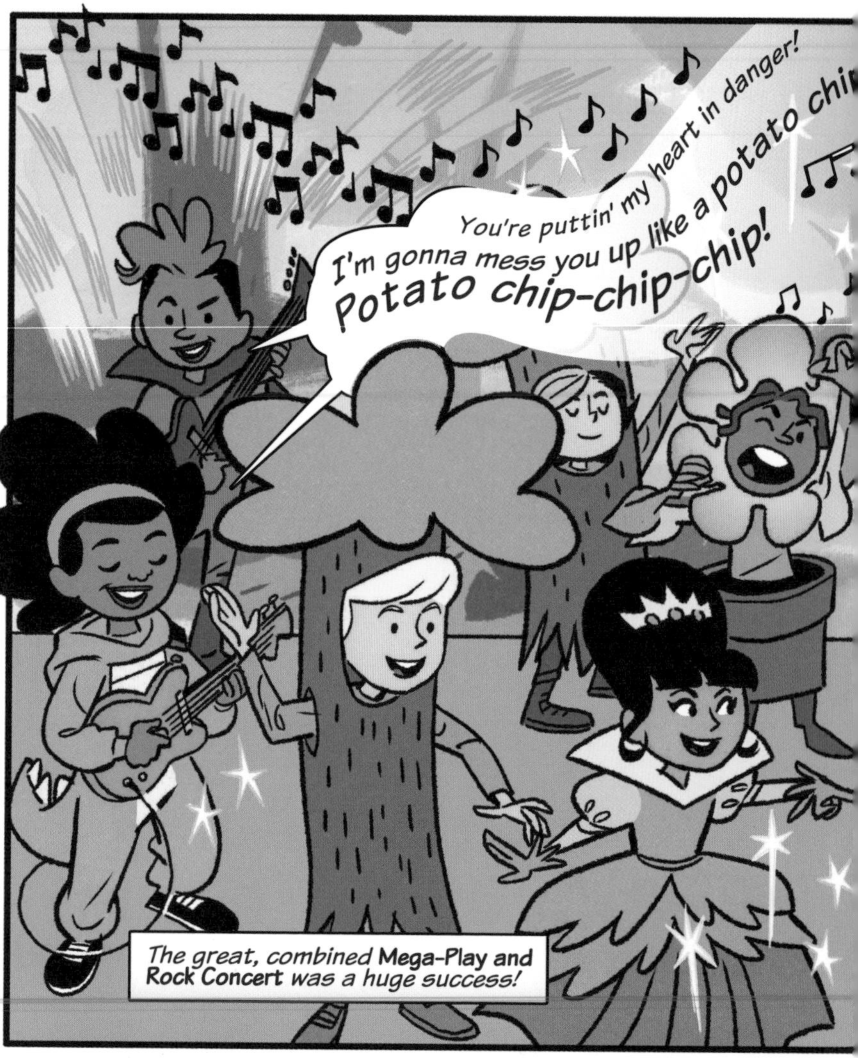
You're puttin' my heart in danger!
I'm gonna mess you up like a potato chi
Potato chip-chip-chip!
The great, combined Mega-Play and Rock Concert was a huge success!

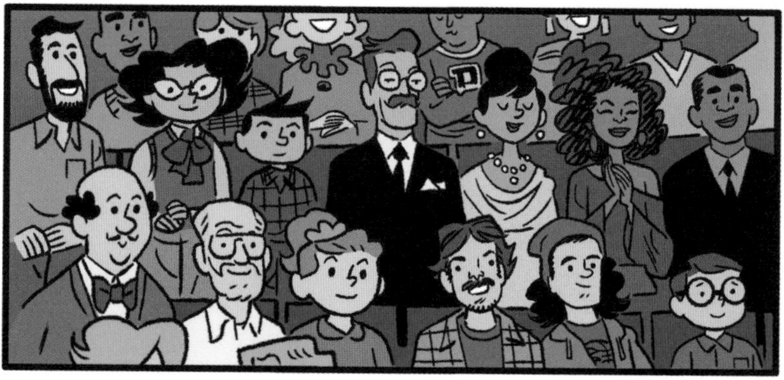

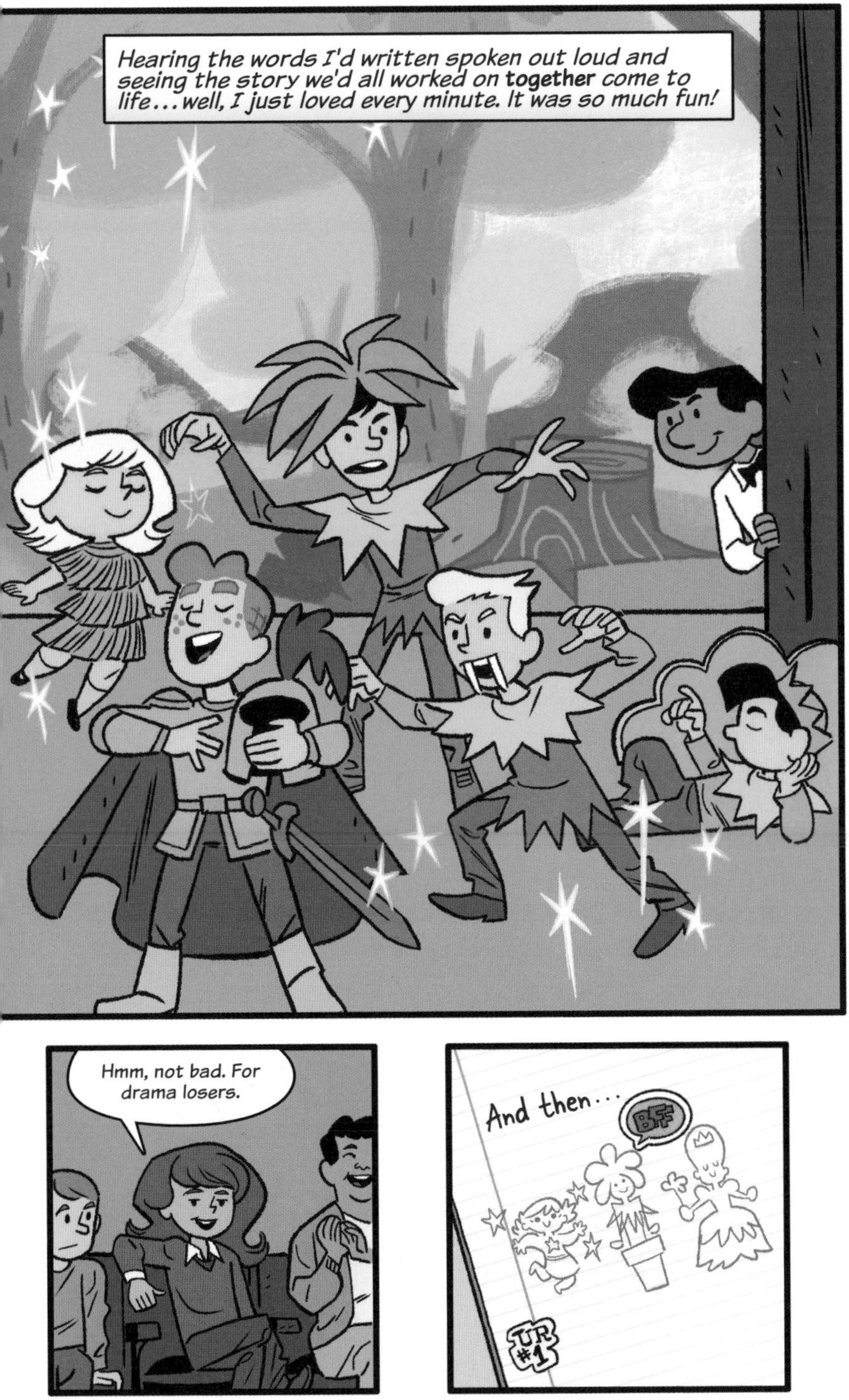
Hearing the words I'd written spoken out loud and seeing the story we'd all worked on **together** come to life... well, I just loved every minute. It was so much fun!
Hmm, not bad. For drama losers.
And then...
BFF
UR #1

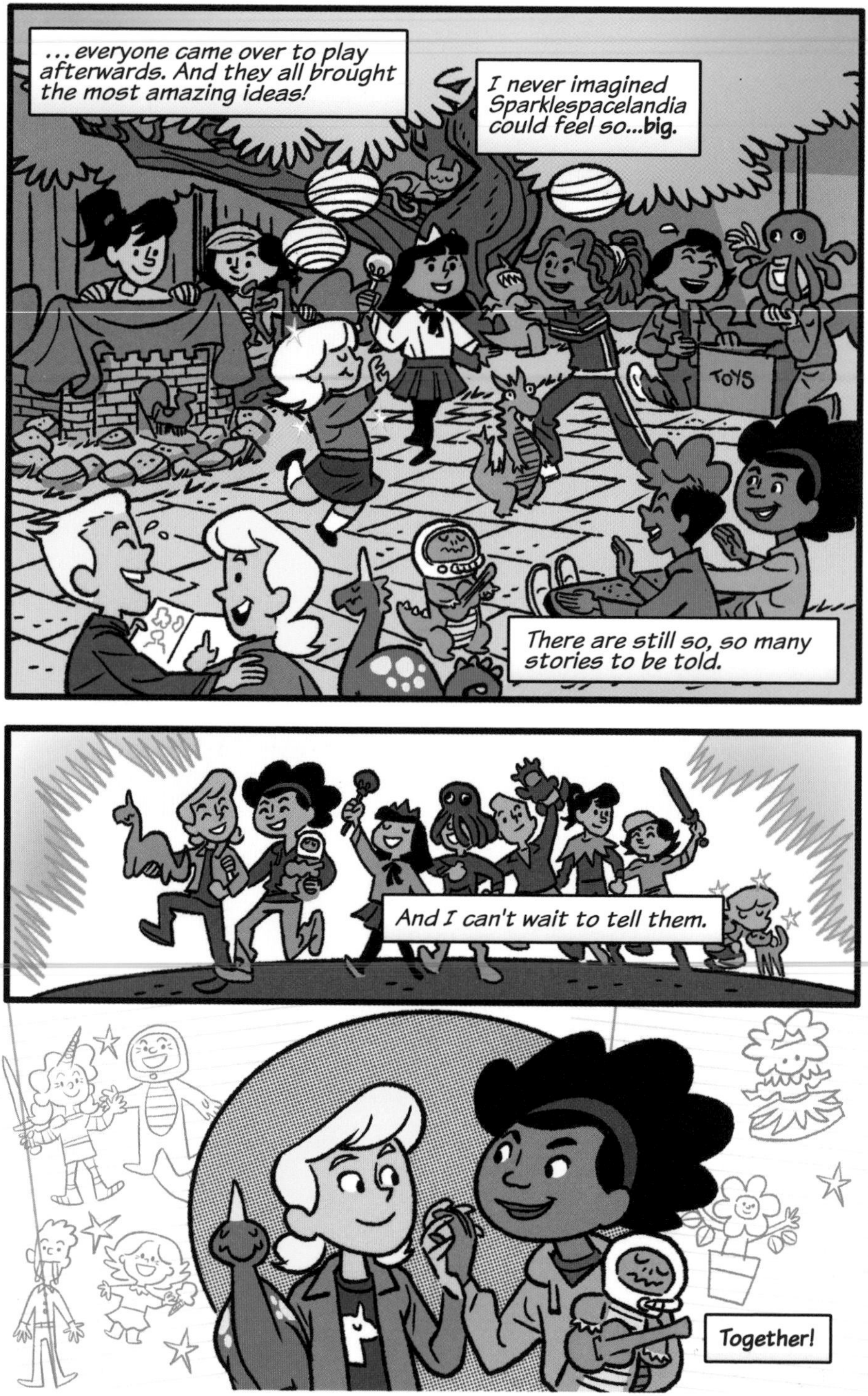
...everyone came over to play afterwards. And they all brought the most amazing ideas!
I never imagined Sparklespacelandia could feel so...big.
TOYS
There are still so, so many stories to be told.
And I can't wait to tell them.
Together!

ACKNOWLEDGMENTS

As a lifelong fan of Betty, Valerie, Veronica, and the whole Archie Comics gang, it was a thrill to get to write these kids. Thank you to my awesome collaborator, J. Bone, and to our fabulous editor, Rachel Gluckstern, for playing with me in this world and bringing it to life so beautifully. Thank you to my agent, Diana Fox, for working your usual magic, and to Bethany Bryan for knowing that we girls can do anything. Thank you to everyone at Little Bee Books and Archie Comics for all the work and love you put into this book. My communities make me who I am, so thank you to all the denizens of my personal Sparklespacelandia: the Girl Gang(s), the Shamers, TRB crew, Heroine Club, the Kuhn-Yoneyama-Chen-Coffeys, and the incredible Asian American arts community of LA. And a special shout-out to Team Batgirl, Sara Miller and Nicole Goux: You made me a better comics writer, and I can't thank you enough. And thank you to Jeff Chen, my most favorite Dragon Scientist Knight of all. I love you. —*Sarah Kuhn*

First of all, I want to thank Rachel Gluckstern for inviting me into this project, and to Sarah Kuhn for writing a fun story with so much drahhh-maaahh. My thanks to Jaime Gelman and Rob Wall for catching my early mistakes and making sure the book looks so good. Penciling and inking 122 pages was a massive undertaking and I would have gone crazy by the time I got to the colors if not for the help of Riely McFarlane, who flatted a gajillion layers for me. Thank you to Danny B., who helped keep me going with weekly tea and comic breaks. Thank you also to Cliff for regular video chats that had nothing to do with comic books. I shared many stressed-out deadline chats with my equally under pressure writer friend Rachelle. I'm grateful for our friendship and shared love of WS. I want to thank Dan Parent, who pulled me into the working world of Archie Comics when we teamed up to draw Kevin Keller however many years ago. And my thanks to Darwyn Cooke, who I talk to every day even though he's not here to listen anymore. —*J. Bone*

ABOUT THE WRITER

Sarah Kuhn is the writer of the critically acclaimed teen graphic novel *Shadow of the Batgirl* for DC Comics. Her teen novel debut, the Japan-set romantic comedy *I Love You So Mochi*, was a Junior Library Guild selection and a nominee for YALSA's Best Fiction for Young Adults. She has also penned a variety of short fiction and comics, including a series of Barbie comics. A third-generation Japanese American, she lives in Los Angeles with her husband and a closet overflowing with vintage treasures.

ABOUT THE ARTIST

J. Bone is an Eisner-nominated comics veteran. He's perhaps best known for his work on *The Spirit* and *The New Frontier*, both from DC Comics, and *Spider-Man's Tangled Web* from Marvel Comics. Most recently, J. Bone has been inking a number of Archie projects, including a Kevin Keller miniseries and *Archie Meets Batman '66*.